© Karen Brown

Minnie Darke is grateful for gifts of all kinds, including words, 2B pencils, sunflowers, libraries, interchangeable circular knitting needles, music, Russian Caravan tea and the friendship of extraordinary people. The best gift she was ever given was a grey-and-tan kelpie pup, and the most useful was a spirit measure to prevent her bloody marys from blowing other people's socks off. She is the author of two previous novels, *Star-crossed* and *The Lost Love Song*, and lives on the island of lutruwita/Tasmania with her family. *With Love from Wish & Co* is her gift to you.

ALSO BY MINNIE DARKE

Star-crossed
The Lost Love Song

WITH LOVE FROM
Wish & Co

MINNIE DARKE

MICHAEL JOSEPH
an imprint of
PENGUIN BOOKS

MICHAEL JOSEPH

UK | USA | Canada | Ireland | Australia
India | New Zealand | South Africa | China

Michael Joseph is part of the Penguin Random House group of companies whose addresses can be found at global.penguinrandomhouse.com

First published by Michael Joseph in 2022

Copyright © Minnie Darke 2022

The moral right of the author has been asserted.

All rights reserved. No part of this publication may be reproduced, published, performed in public or communicated to the public in any form or by any means without prior written permission from Penguin Random House Australia Pty Ltd or its authorised licensees.

Photograph on p. 397 used by permission of Penny Pearce

Cover photography © Ruth Black / Stocksy United
Cover design by Lisa White
Internal illustrations and design by Julian Mole, Post Pre-press, Australia
Typeset in 12/17 pt Adobe Garamond Pro by Post Pre-press, Australia

Printed and bound in Australia by Griffin Press, part of Ovato, an accredited ISO AS/NZS 14001 Environmental Management Systems printer

 A catalogue record for this book is available from the National Library of Australia

ISBN 978 1 76089 779 6

penguin.com.au

We at Penguin Random House Australia acknowledge that Aboriginal and Torres Strait Islander peoples are the Traditional Custodians and the first storytellers of the lands on which we live and work. We honour Aboriginal and Torres Strait Islander peoples' continuous connection to Country, waters, skies and communities. We celebrate Aboriginal and Torres Strait Islander stories, traditions and living cultures; and we pay our respects to Elders past and present.

For my mother

I know what I have given you.
I do not know what you have received.

Antonio Porchia

— PART ONE —

Nine days before the implosion of the Charlesworth marriage

Alone in the quiet of Wish & Co after closing time, Marnie Fairchild decided to give it a try. With the shop's front door locked and the blinds drawn to shut out Rathbone Street's evening rush, she reached beneath the counter for a magazine of a kind she did not, officially, read. Marnie wasn't the type for crystal healing, moon-phase gardening or the study of tea leaves. But since she'd already done all the sensible, practical things she could think of to do, and none of them had worked, she was now prepared to try anything – even 'Manifestation for Beginners'.

First, the magazine instructed, *make sure you are in a pleasing space.*

Marnie frowned, feeling the urge to argue. The precise problem, she wanted to tell the magazine, was that her shop was not a pleasing space. It was what had brought her to something as airy-fairy as manifesting in the first place; the very reason she had blown her grocery budget by slipping into her basket a magazine with a title like *Celestial Being*.

There was not, and never had been, any beholder alive who would have said Wish & Co's rented premises were any kind of beautiful. Too old to be modern, and too young to be charmingly vintage, the shop had cheap fibreboard walls, flimsy aluminium windows, and nothing interesting waiting to be discovered under the linoleum flooring.

Marnie had done her best with paint, furnishings and taste. She'd had a wall fitted out in nicely battered recycled timber shelves, so that now, when the ladies of the eastern suburbs were hosting the kind of dinners where the candles matched the napkins, they found themselves standing at those shelves, trying to decide between the equally luscious colourways of Wish & Co's quality party supplies. Sea Glass or Rose Quartz? Moonstone or Onyx?

In the section of the shop that was set up as a wrapping studio, Marnie had covered the walls with racks of luxury gift wrap and installed a huge, rustic table to distract from the floor. But despite all her efforts, the shop continued to prove the old saying about sow ears and silk purses.

As a gesture towards making the space more pleasing, Marnie lit a pillar candle from the Rose Quartz range and switched off the fluorescent overheads. The edges of the store softened to a circle of candlelight, and she read on.

Focus your mind. Make sure you have a clear vision of what it is that you want.

Easy. For there it was, in the framed photograph she kept propped on the countertop, in all the glory of its heyday. She could see it only dimly in the candlelight, but Marnie didn't really need to look. She knew the old shop by heart. In her sleep she could have sketched the mullioned front window with its twenty-eight gridded panes of glass. She'd have been able, blindfolded, to draw the three neo-Gothic arches of the top-storey windows, as well as the ornamentations on the steeply pitched bargeboards that framed them.

Fairchild & Sons was still standing, also on Rathbone Street, seven blocks away in the direction of Alexandria Park. But just barely. To Marnie's uncle, who now owned it, the shop was nothing more than a heritage-listed irritation taking up space on a square of valuable real estate. If it hadn't been earmarked by the council for preservation, Lewis Fairchild would long ago have had it demolished.

The place was already in a serious state of disrepair when, two winters ago, it had almost burned to the ground. The morning Marnie had woken to news of the fire, she'd flung a coat over her pyjamas and run up the street. Behind a hastily erected barricade, she'd joined local business owners and other bystanders, and watched as the brightly clad firefighters rolled away their hoses and the last twists of smoke drifted out of the broken front windows. Arson was the verdict of the investigations that followed, though nobody was ever convicted.

The shop had been saved, but every time Marnie walked past she grieved the charring on the beautiful bargeboards and the graffiti on the hoardings that now covered the main window. Her uncle seemed content to leave the old building in its dilapidated state, perhaps hoping that it would fall down of its own accord, or that a second arsonist would come along and do a better job than the first.

Marnie pulled her sleeve down over the heel of her hand and wiped a fine layer of dust from the glass of the framed picture. In her great-grandfather's day, the store had sold groceries. When her grandfather took over the business, he'd transformed it into a high-end shoe shop, with stock both imported from Europe and handmade on the premises. This photo had been taken on the day of the shoe shop's official opening, and the grandfather she had known less than half as well as she should have done stood proudly in his cobbler's apron, arms crossed, in the doorway.

Archie Fairchild hadn't lived long enough to see the opening of Wish & Co, but Marnie felt sure he'd have been proud of her, for taking the risk of starting her own business in the first place, and also for the way she'd grown it from a simple retail outlet into a diversified enterprise that included custom gift-wrapping, gift-wrapping workshops, and – most profitably – a boutique and highly personalised gift-buying service. All of which now needed a better, more substantial, more beautiful home.

Marnie breathed in the rose scent of the candle and brought her vision into focus. When the old shop was hers, the weather-boards would once again be painted in crisp, fresh white; her gift-wrapping papers on their racks would be backgrounded by traditional lathe and plaster walls; the wrapping table would stand on the kind of rustic floorboards it deserved. She would no longer have to go out the back at the end of a workday and climb metal stairs to a tiny flat with a cupboard-sized bathroom and a foldaway bed. Rather, she would ascend a circular timber staircase at the back of the shop to find herself at home in a tastefully renovated retreat, with sloping ceilings and pine floors that glowed in light softened and shaped by a triple-arched window.

Now, the magazine article instructed, *picture what needs to happen for your vision to become a reality. Be very specific.*

Marnie closed her eyes. She would be standing at the wrapping table, wearing her gingham apron, sleeves rolled. Her mobile phone would ring and the sight of her uncle's name on the screen would give her a little jump of excitement.

'Lewis!' she'd say. And he'd say, 'Marnie, how are you?' But they wouldn't chat, Marnie decided. Mostly because she could not imagine anything she and her uncle would have to chat about. Instead, he'd cut right to the chase.

'I'm ringing about Fairchild and Sons,' he'd say. 'It's past time I did something with the place, and I reckon your grandfather would have wanted you to take it on.'

But was that exactly what he'd say? She was supposed to be very specific, and Marnie wasn't sure her uncle would use a matey word like 'reckon'. It was hard to know. She'd been in Lewis's company four or five times in her entire life. One of those was at her father's memorial service, which she had been too young to remember, and another was at her grandfather's funeral, where Marnie and her mother had stood at the back and slipped out before the coffee and Scotch Fingers.

The last two times she'd seen her uncle were when she'd made appointments, through his personal assistant, to visit him at the top-notch financial advice firm Fairchild & Rooke. Both times, he'd leaned back in his big leather armchair, bow-tie askew, and failed – if he was even trying – to hide his expression of bemusement. That the daughter of his black-sheep younger brother seriously thought she was in the market to buy, outright, a property at the Alexandria Park end of Rathbone Street clearly struck him as smirk-worthy.

Both times, he'd told her he wasn't selling. However, she had managed to extract from him a promise that he would contact her if ever he changed his mind. To keep herself in his thoughts she sent an email every month – each one slightly different, but always respectful and brief. By the time he made the phone call she was now manifesting, he would have realised that she was serious. Her persistent emails would have impressed upon him that even if borrowing the kind of money the shop would fetch would be a stretch for her, it was not an impossibility.

So, once he'd told her he was thinking of selling, she'd say, 'You want to sell me the shop? Are you serious?'

'Absolutely,' he'd reply. 'I know how hard you've worked to build your business while most people your age were off travelling or out partying.'

And Marnie would feel herself swell ever so slightly, knowing that it had all been worth it. The long, long hours she'd sunk into her first business: a popular coffee van, called Geraldine, that she'd started up on little more than a wing, a prayer, and a third-hand coffee machine. The years she had stuck to a regime of generic brand groceries, homemade lunches, darned socks and public transport, all so she could save or reinvest the lion's share of her profits. The years when she'd put every spare cent into real estate; the nail-biting months when business had slowed and she'd wondered if she had overextended by buying a new property; the relief when trade picked up again and she was rewarded for holding her nerve. The courage it had taken to sell all her properties and invest, instead, in financial products, and all so that she'd be able to readily get her hands on real money if Fairchild & Sons came onto the market.

'That means a lot to me,' she visualised herself saying.

But would she actually say that? Not on your life. Her uncle didn't need to know – nobody needed to know – how much she hungered for the approval of her father's family. So, on second thoughts, she'd simply say, with cool sincerity, 'This is wonderful news. Thank you for contacting me.'

After which he'd go on to say, 'Look, that stuff with your father . . . it had nothing to do with you. You were barely more than a baby. And, you know, out of all the grandkids, you're really the only one with a head for business. You're a true Fairchild, Marnie.'

Okay, so now she was in fantasy land. Her uncle was about as likely to say any of that as he was to donate half his net worth to Greenpeace, so she pulled herself back into the realm of possibility and imagined him saying, soberly, 'You know I can't let the place go too cheaply.'

To which she would reply, 'Of course not. But I wouldn't be a Fairchild if I paid too much, now would I?'

At this point, her uncle would give an indulgent laugh. And name a figure. She'd counter, and he'd counter-counter, and she'd make a fresh offer, and he'd respond, and this would go on for quite some swashbuckling time, until – at last – they would agree on the perfect price, low enough that even though Marnie would have to borrow a significant sum, she'd not only be able to afford the shop, but to renovate it too.

And Marnie would smile, and sigh with satisfaction, just the way she did right now.

She opened her eyes.

Finally, the magazine told her, *believe that the Universe will provide.*

Believe?

Marnie blinked.

She read the sentence again. She was supposed to just *believe*? Was believing even a thing you could do on command? Marnie didn't know, but if she was serious about this manifesting business, then she supposed she was going to have to give it a try.

And so, as the homeward-bound traffic dwindled to a slow stream along Rathbone Street beyond Wish & Co's closed blinds, and a new moon ascended into the ink-dark sky over the city, Marnie leaned on the countertop and did her best to believe that her arrogant, entitled, wealthy arsehole of an uncle would one day, quite out of the blue, ring her up and offer to sell her the old shop for a price she could afford.

But what did Marnie's manifesting have to do with the Charlesworth marriage and its implosion, which was by now just nine days away?

Perhaps nothing at all.

Or else, everything.

It's impossible to know.

What is certain is that on the late August evening that Marnie manifested her perfect future, two identical cardboard boxes sat – quite harmlessly – on the undershelf of her table, waiting to be wrapped.

Six days before the implosion of the Charlesworth marriage

Suzanne Charlesworth didn't want to do beef. Beef was obvious and, therefore, boring. Lamb was also boring. Pork was too fatty for Brian, and when it came to Suzanne's crackling, he didn't have it in him to be moderate. Chicken wasn't special enough. Not for their fortieth wedding anniversary lunch. Salmon? Out of the question. Fish that came from farms were like cheap sausages – best not to know what went into them.

In the after-dinner hush of her Alexandria Park kitchen, Suzanne sat on a high stool with her elbows on the marble benchtop, the wide expanse of which was covered with recipe books stacked in low piles or splayed open to glossy spreads.

There would be two starters. Toffee truss tomatoes on basil leaves, paired with a nice rosé, and freshly shucked oysters that she'd serve with chilled sake. For dessert, she couldn't go past a towering croquembouche, which she would match with a gorgeous dessert semillon. And, to finish, homemade panforte for the adults, with a scrumptious chardonnay to keep drinking into the afternoon. And for the grandchildren, pink lemonade and the gingerbread house she'd already made and stored out of sight on the top shelf of the pantry. But in the middle of her planning page, where the perfect main course ought to be, was a blank space.

Aware that Brian had come into the room behind her, Suzanne said, 'What about quail?'

But her question was drowned out by the hum of their colourful, Smeg-meets-Dolce-&-Gabbana coffee machine. Which matched the toaster. Which in turn matched the juicer. Which in turn almost matched Suzanne's oldest but most favourite apron – hand-embroidered with wild, bright flowers – which she'd bought in Mexico on their honeymoon.

'Sorry, what was that?' Brian said, coming to stand beside her. She frowned at the steaming mug he set down on the bench. It was 8 pm, and far too late for coffee. He'd be up half the night complaining that he couldn't sleep. But she let it slide. 'What about quail?'

'For what?'

'For *what*?' She elbowed him in the ribs. 'For lunch. On Sunday.'

'Sunday?' Brian deadpanned. 'Do we have something on?'

Realising she'd been taken in, she smiled. 'Bastard.'

Aged sixty-seven, her husband of thirty-nine years and fifty-one weeks was in disgustingly good physical shape. His middle was only a little thicker than it had been when she'd stood beside him at the altar, and although his sandy hair had changed colour, his grey had been kind enough to emerge as a shimmering silver. Brian was not a tall person, but he had good, strong features. Glasses suited him, and his olive skin had withstood the years remarkably well. Like all the men in his family, he had kissable Cupid's-bow lips and shapely calves – both of which had remained virtually untouched by the ravages of time.

Catching the subtext of the look Suzanne was giving him, Brian smiled.

'My lovely wife,' he said, and dropped a kiss onto the top of her head.

She was aware of the stripe of regrowth – a shade of grey she found murky and lifeless – at the parting of her bright blonde bob. Still, her hair – unlike her girth, which had increased considerably since she was a bride – could be rectified before Sunday. The same was true of her eyebrows, eyelashes and nails, which was why the Friday page of her diary was sprinkled with appointments. On Saturday, though, she'd be at home. Cooking.

'Well? What do you think?' she asked, and pointed to a recipe for baked quail.

'Looks fiddly.'

'Looks rather fun, actually,' she said, imagining the almond meal, pine nut, herb and butter combination of the stuffing. 'And I could do a sparkling Shiraz and chilli jelly to go on the side. It would melt down with the heat of the quail. Or . . . oh, I know! A pomegranate jus.'

Brian rolled his eyes, and Suzanne knew what was coming next.

'I will never understand why you don't just get caterers in. I mean, by all means, decide what you want on the menu, but then get somebody else to do the grunt work. Delegate, love. De-le-gate.'

But Suzanne didn't want to delegate her position as the queen of her kitchen any more than Brian was ready to retire from his position as CEO of the Charlesworth Group. He was proud of his career, of the way he'd taken a starting position as an architectural draftsman and worked his way up to being one of the city's most prominent property developers. In much the same way, Suzanne had found a professional satisfaction in hosting the dinner parties that had smoothed his progress, keeping the flower arrangements in the house fresh, having the children washed and pyjama-clad and calm when Brian got home late at night, and being sure that his favourite gin – citrus-infused, and available only from a boutique distillery two states away – was always in good supply in the liquor cabinet.

'We're a long way from Kelsey Street now, love,' Brian said, for perhaps the thousandth time in their lives. 'It's not like we can't afford it. We've got the money, Suze. I wish you'd just spend it.'

Suzanne allowed herself a tiny eye-roll but didn't reply. It was an old debate. If she were to open her mouth, all that would come out would be a well-rehearsed protest that the years they'd spent living in a draughty weatherboard cottage in Kelsey Street had been among the best of her life. She'd been just out of art school, but unlike her peers, she'd had no serious fire in her belly for making it as a painter. Always it had been Brian with the big dreams, his head full of plans for the buildings he'd bring into reality, the affluent life he'd build for his family. Suzanne hadn't cared that she'd needed to kit out that tiny little kitchen from thrift stores. It hadn't worried her in the least that most of Caroline's first clothes were hand-me-downs from the children of cousins and neighbours and friends. She and Brian had been young, in love and full of optimism. The theme song to that era of their marriage could easily have been a Carpenters song.

Both Suzanne and Brian had grown up in families where there hadn't been a lot of money to go around, but while Brian had embarked on adult life wanting to cast off every last vestige of austerity as quickly as possible, Suzanne had been a little different. As Brian's income grew, she'd adjusted only too easily to splurging on good food and excellent wine, and on making their home a beautiful space, but she'd never graduated to spending a lot on herself. Had she wanted to, she could have shopped for clothes in the most upmarket of boutiques, bedecked herself in expensive jewellery, gone to the hairdresser every week. But no matter how well Brian's business ventures went, somewhere inside she was still young Suzanne Wright, happy with one or two nice outfits in her wardrobe, content with a couple of simple pieces of jewellery, and always pleased with a bargain at the shops.

Neither had Suzanne ever become a big spender when it came to gifts, and this had been a source of amazement and frustration to Brian. Even when he was raking in the dollars, Suzanne kept the kids' Christmas and birthday presents decidedly modest, often giving them something they needed, like new bathers or a pair of sneakers. Brian, who'd always felt monumentally ripped off when his parents had put an inflated balloon in his Christmas stocking to make it appear fuller, and who considered clothing to be the ultimate dud gift for a child, didn't see why his children shouldn't have the best and latest of everything. He expressed this to Suzanne sufficiently often that when Caroline and Luke were approaching their teenage years, she announced her partial abdication. If Brian thought their kids ought to have trampolines and gaming consoles, new bicycles every other year, remote-control cars and fancy watches . . . then he could organise his own gifts for them. She'd give them what she thought they should have, and he could be as extravagant as he wanted.

Suzanne had very clear ideas about where money was well spent, and where it was not. Food, wine, art, fresh flowers, hairdressing and bed linen were in. Extravagant gifts, flash cars, electronic gadgets and restaurant meals were out. Caterers? They were so far out they may as well have been from Alpha Centauri. Suzanne, sitting there in her kitchen, surrounded by cookbooks, might have said all of this to Brian, but he already knew her position. She'd said it all before, and he'd heard it all before, so all she did was kiss him on the smooth space of his cheek. Not content with that, he took her chin in his fingers and kissed her on the lips. A sweet, rich kiss infused with the familiar and comfortable taste of coffee. She drank in the smell of him. Not a smell of soap or aftershave, but simply of Brian. Her Brian.

'Love you,' he said.

'Love you too.'

Through the open door to the television room, Suzanne heard an electronic chime. Different, though, from the usual tone that announced one of Brian's frequent text messages.

'Was that your phone?' Suzanne asked.

Brian picked up his coffee and made to leave the kitchen. 'Scrabble notification,' he said.

'Oh,' Suzanne said, only mildly surprised, and as she heard the door close behind her she thought how lucky they were. So many couples of their vintage had separated, and there were others who only stayed together out of financial necessity or convenience. She and Brian were blessed to be still in love.

Of course, it wasn't as if she and Brian had never had any troubles. Nobody lived a perfect life, except on Facebook. For Suzanne and Brian, there had been those years when Luke had gone wild, and she and Brian had reacted so differently – Brian tough, Suzanne soft – that it had nearly torn them apart. And, before that, there'd been the time when Brian had lost a significant amount of money on a failed venture right around the time one of his former girlfriends had been widowed.

It was no mystery to Suzanne how it had happened. The misadventure in business had left Brian feeling like a failure; Leona, meanwhile, had been grief-stricken and in need. Leona. Intellectual, elegant and accomplished. Not to mention whip-thin in the way that you'd expect of a woman who went to Pilates every other day and had never had children. Suzanne supposed that Brian's dalliance with Leona had made him feel successful, but it had shattered the trust in their marriage. Still, that was twenty years ago. With time and work, Suzanne and Brian had managed to put the pieces back together.

Now they'd made it to forty years of marriage, enjoying the better, having weathered the worse. It was quite an achievement, really. Definitely something to celebrate with their oldest and dearest friends, and closest family. She was fortunate; unlike a lot of her friends, she had her son and daughter living close by. So, Caroline would be there on Sunday, along with her husband and children. And Luke, too, although he'd be on his own now that it was all off with the German girlfriend, something Suzanne was quietly pleased about. There might, after all, be more grandchildren one day, and she hated the idea of them getting to know her only as a pixelated image on a screen.

She should remind Luke to pick up his grandmother for Sunday lunch. She looked at the time. Probably, he'd still be in his workshop – sandy hair mussed, big plastic earmuffs slung around his neck, a shallow sea of wood shavings scattered at his boot soles. On his worktable, a sleek native timber sideboard, chair or cabinet would be taking shape. The things he made fetched good prices, but they took so long to make! Brian had never been able to understand why Luke didn't change his business model – focus on the designs, outsource the manufacturing. Suzanne marvelled that two men could look so much alike and yet have so little else in common.

She thumbed a message into her phone. *Can you get Gran on the way to Sunday lunch? And take her home? Sorry, that's going to put the brakes on your* 🍷🍷🍷

Suzanne was never sure whether using those emojo things showed that she was keeping up with the times or only served to reveal her as a hopeless try-hard.

A reply pinged up on her screen. *Yep.*

Suzanne smiled. No words wasted there.

In the space at the centre of her page, she wrote *Quail, with pomegranate jus.* And, *charred young broad beans, honey-roasted carrots and kipfler potatoes.*

Perfect, she thought. She would create the perfect lunch, and Sunday would be a perfect day.

Two days before the implosion of the Charlesworth marriage

When the mid-morning lull of that September Friday descended upon Wish & Co, Marnie lifted the two gifts for the Charlesworth account from the undershelf to the surface of the wrapping table. They were the same size, the same shape, and the same cardboard brown colour. The only difference between them was that while one was heavy, the other was feather-light. Which could probably, Marnie mused, be read as a metaphor. Something about the relative weight of a four-decade marriage, and an affair.

She decided to wrap the wife's gift first.

'Suzanne,' she murmured, surveying her range of wrapping papers. 'Suzanne, Suzanne, Suzanne.'

Marnie had never met Mrs Charlesworth, of course, but for five years she'd been buying gifts for her birthdays, anniversaries, Easters and Christmases, as well as purchasing the sorry-I-was-an-arsehole gifts that her husband too regularly required. After all the time she had spent stalking Suzanne on social media channels, agonising over which colour of possum-merino wrap would please her most, ringing around florists in search of out-of-season frangipanis, Marnie had come to think of her as something like a friend.

The paper should be a soft shade, Marnie thought. Feminine.

Her gaze drifted over florals, paisleys, polka-dots, plaids and stripes, past tissue-thin papers marbled in bright colours, novelty papers for children, and thick handmade papers scattered with petals and leaves. It landed, at last, on a rainbow of plain colours. Paper colours were a little like colouring-in pencils – the favourites got used up much more quickly than the rest. Marnie's assistant, Alice, wouldn't be in again until next week, but when she was, Marnie would get her to order in some more of the mid-blues and emerald greens.

'I think . . . *you*.' Sheeny without being glossy, the paper was the perfect shade of dusky pink: not too candy, not too brown. Gently, Marnie coaxed a huge sheet from the rack and laid it on the wrapping table.

One of the things Marnie told the participants in her gift-wrapping workshops was that there was nothing so useful as a plain cardboard box. This was why she always had a vast range of them in stock, from small enough to hold a necklace, to wide and flat enough to accommodate a framed painting, to large enough for a matching pair of suitcases. For one thing, boxes eliminated the wrapping problems created by items of a difficult or irregular shape and allowed for an entirely smooth, professional look. But there was more to it than that. Even when gift items came ready-boxed, the packaging was often covered with the brand name and pictures of the contents. And where was the pleasure, the suspense, in that? Part of the Wish & Co experience was that when the wrapping paper came off, there was still another layer of concealment beneath.

It took some effort to tip Suzanne's gift upside down and centre it on the dusky-pink paper. She had just finished taping the first fold when she heard the jangle of the bell above the front door. Upon seeing who had entered the shop, she felt a jolt of delighted surprise. But kept it, carefully, in check.

It was Owen Kingston, wearing a denim jacket over a Nirvana T-shirt she could have sworn he'd been wearing since they were both teenagers. His dark hair was longer than she'd seen it in years.

'Kiddo,' he greeted her. An old nickname, derived from the 'child' part of 'Fairchild'.

'Kingo,' she returned, and he switched on that smile. That mind-melting smile.

Broadly speaking, the men in Marnie's romantic history had fallen into two categories. There had been the entitled ones, born with silver spoons shoved into every available orifice, who had expected her – and the demands of her business – to fit conveniently around their own ambitions. And then there had been the slackers, men with McJobs or never-ending university studies, who saw Marnie as the key to the lifestyle to which they would happily become accustomed. And then there was Owen Kingston, who managed to effortlessly, seductively, bring together aspects from both camps.

Although Marnie allowed herself to glow, just a little, with pleasure at seeing him, she didn't pause in her work. Not even if it had been, what . . . six months? Longer? Long enough, anyway, that she had begun to wonder if some woman or other had finally secured the fidelity of her old . . . her old *what*? Schoolmate? Friend? No, more than that. Lover? No, less than that. Playmate?

'I was in the neighbourhood,' he said, as if in reply to a question.

Marnie gave a casual shrug and invisibly fixed one of the side joins of Suzanne's parcel with several short lengths of double-sided tape. Tape did not show. Not ever. Not on a Wish & Co gift.

'So, how's business?' Owen enquired, resting a hip against the far side of the wrapping table.

'Never better.' She'd have told him this regardless, but as it happened, it was true – largely thanks to the recommendations that increasingly flowed from Brian Charlesworth. Five years back, when the property developer had approached her to manage his gift-buying needs, it had taken every bit of her courage to look him steadily in the eye and demand a fee for her services that even she had thought staggering. But he hadn't so much as blinked, and – as a bonus – he had turned out to be generous in sending his friends and colleagues her way, all of them expecting to pay top dollar.

Owen hoisted himself up to sit on the far edge of the table. 'And your mum? How's Chrissie doing?'

Marnie smiled but did not look up. They both knew how this would go. She would make her expert folds, scoring the diagonals with a deft, practised thumbnail. She would tuck and stick, cut ribbon to length with her big, sharp shears. When the time came to tie a bow, she would perform each bight and flick with a modicum of extra flourish. Not that she would show off, exactly. And all the while, they would chat.

Eventually Owen would ask her, 'And what about you? How are *you*?' A coded way, as they both well knew, of his asking, 'So, anyone special in your life right now?' If there wasn't – as had been the case for Marnie for quite a long time now – the BACK IN 15 MINUTES sign would appear on the plate glass of the front door, and Marnie and Owen would climb the narrow stairs to her tiny apartment, where they would hinge down her foldaway bed and proceed to rumple her sheets.

Somehow, despite the fact that they loved each other, Marnie and Owen had managed never to fall in love. Instead, they had established a friendship (with benefits) that had now lasted half their lives. They had been each other's date for their high school leavers' dinner; Owen had been Marnie's handbag at the ceremony when the success of Geraldine, her coffee van, had led to Marnie being nominated for a Young Businesswoman of the Year Award. Later, he'd comforted her when she hadn't won. Each of them had been known to appear on the other's doorstep late at night after relationships with lovers had gone pear-shaped, turning for consolation to tried-and-true sex with the person with whom they'd each lost their virginity.

Was he nursing a broken heart? Was that why he was here? Or was it every bit as simple as he'd said? That he'd just happened to find himself in her neighbourhood?

'Mum? She's fine,' Marnie said, and tugged a length of cream velvet ribbon from its reel. 'And yes, still living in deepest, darkest Casterbrook, reading her tarot cards, buying her Lotto tickets, waiting for her ship to come in while complaining that the world's against her and nothing's fair. What about your dad? How is the old devil?'

Marnie owed a debt of gratitude to Gerry Kingston, a retired surgeon who had almost as many ex-wives as he had luxury cars. Back when she'd been a penniless teenager, he'd found odd jobs he could pay her for, like detailing his cars and wrapping his Christmas presents. Later, when she started her coffee van business, he'd helped her apply – successfully – for permission to park Geraldine in a prime position on the edge of Alexandria Park. When she'd made enough money from the van to consider moving on to a bigger venture, it was Gerry who'd reminded her that she had a special talent for wrapping gifts. He'd been half in jest when he'd told Marnie there was a business to be built around buying gifts on behalf of wealthy men with complicated lives, but the idea had stuck in her head.

'Men don't want to remember dates,' he'd told her. 'We don't want to go shopping. We don't want every gift to be a test of whether or not we've been paying attention, or of whether we really know someone, through to their very soul. We just want the present to turn up on the right day and keep everybody happy.'

'He's getting married,' Owen said, the look on his face half admiring, half despairing.

'How old's this one?'

'Thirty-two,' Owen said.

'Ouch,' said Marnie. It was Owen's age. Hers, too.

'It was my fault. She's a singer. Came into the studio to sing backup on a Cryptics track.'

'Uh-oh. You didn't . . .?'

'I was hoping to. But I only got as far as taking her around to Dad's to borrow the Porsche. So, she saw the house, the pool, the tennis court . . . you get the picture.'

'When's the wedding?'

'November. I don't suppose you'd . . .?'

Ah, handbag duty. Perhaps that was the reason he'd come now – so the phone call to ask her to the wedding didn't seem entirely out of the blue.

'Your wish. My command,' she said.

As she turned back to her work, Marnie caught sight of a persistent and annoying thought slinking towards the centre of her mind: the one about how, if she was actually a sensible thirty-two-year-old, she'd be making at least some sort of progress, herself, towards finding a partner. But she silently sent the thought packing and refocused her attention on the complex bow she was tying. Twist, knot, twist again, knot again, pull tight, cut the loose ends into perfect diagonals, plump and primp, and . . . hey presto!

'Impressive,' Owen said.

Marnie drew a filing box out from beneath the counter. It was divided up into sections – one for each portfolio – and contained greeting cards ready-filled by her clients in their own handwriting. Generic or mass-produced greeting cards, with impersonal notes, were not tolerated. Not on Wish & Co gifts. Not ever. The aim of Marnie's service, after all, was to obscure her own involvement in the process – to allow her clients to maintain the fiction that every gift selection was all their own, careful work.

From the Charlesworth section, the largest in the filing box, Marnie plucked a thick, creamy envelope. *Suzanne*, it read, in Brian's firm, confident hand. Marnie selected the cards herself, of course. A detail so important was not one she would leave to chance. Or worse, to her clients. Since most of her customers filled their cards in batches, she always double-checked that the right card had gone into each envelope. And so, she tugged the card from Suzanne's envelope, just to be on the safe side. It showed a reproduction of a Georgia O'Keeffe painting of a pink-tinged rose, and inside Brian had written: *To my darling Suzanne, with thanks for four decades of love, B.* Satisfied, Marnie slipped the card back into the envelope, which she sealed. Not wanting Owen to catch sight of Suzanne's name, she turned the envelope face down on the counter. Discretion was key, and even a first name might be enough to identify one of her clients. She knew only too well how fast gossip travelled the tangled networks of the eastern suburbs.

'Well, make yourself useful.' She nodded in the direction of the wrapped box.

'Where do you want it?' Owen asked.

'Shelf by the door, please,' she said. The courier was due in just three-quarters of an hour. Which meant she was going to have to get a move on with wrapping the other Charlesworth gift if there was going to be time to put up that BACK IN 15 MINUTES sign.

'Far out,' Owen complained, taking the weight of Suzanne's parcel. 'What the hell have you got in here?'

'Same as always,' Marnie said, with her customary discretion. 'The perfect thing.'

Marnie tugged the second box, the light one, towards her on the table. Now she thought of it, Brian Charlesworth wasn't unlike Owen's father. Gerry's motto in life could easily have been: why have a Porsche or a Ferrari, when you can just have both?

Of course, Brian was a long way from being the only one of Marnie's clients whose portfolio demanded absolute confidentiality. But he was her most valuable. Eighteen months ago, he'd called her to his office for an in-person catch-up. 'To add a couple of things to the list,' he'd said.

Elbows on desk, fingers steepled, he'd looked Marnie up and down as if assessing her trustworthiness, and then said, 'There's a woman.'

Notebook in hand, and with her face totally organised, Marnie had simply asked, 'Her name?'

'Leona Quick.'

Leona *Quick*? The high court judge? *LQ*, as she was known in the local press? Wasn't she a bit fierce, a bit . . . *feminist*, for Brian Charlesworth? Talk about divergent tastes, Marnie had thought. From what she knew of the outspoken judge, she resembled Suzanne Charlesworth about as much as a black patent leather stiletto did a feather bed.

Marnie had simply continued on with her standard questions. Age? Birthday? Likes? Dislikes? Hobbies? Allergies (could be important in the case of flowers or chocolates)? She'd left out, however, her usual question about the nature of the relationship. When a man said 'there's a woman', it was safe to assume.

'Did you say her birthday was the eighth of September?' Marnie had asked.

'I did,' Brian confirmed, and Marnie had studiously kept her eyebrows in check. She had also worked hard to stop her gaze from sliding to the cluster of family photos on Brian's desk. He and Suzanne, smiling; their children, Caroline and Luke, growing, frame by frame, into adults.

Had Brian realised, Marnie wondered, that his lover's birthday was the same day as his wedding anniversary? And, if so, what did he think about that? Had the coincidence given him a pang of guilt? Or had it seemed like a convenience? An efficiency that would make it easier for him to remember both occasions?

She hadn't asked, of course. These were not the kind of questions a gift-buyer asked of a client, let alone a client with such deep pockets as Brian Charlesworth's. And anyway, the answers were none of her business. Her business was to choose gifts, wrap them exquisitely, add the right gift card, and make sure they were delivered on time.

With Leona on her mind, Marnie returned to the paper racks. She tapped her finger on her lips, considering.

'What kind of vibe are we after for this one?' Owen asked. Standing close behind her, he rested his chin on her shoulder. The way he might have done when they were sixteen and she was standing at the open door of her locker in the C-block hallway at Meltonside Grammar.

'We're going for stylish,' Marnie said. There was something pleasurable about keeping her mind on the job, even while her body was starting to get distracted by the warmth of Owen's proximity and the leather-and-petrol smell of his aftershave. 'Definitely not pink.'

Not lemon, pistachio or lilac, either. Actually, the entire pastel section was out. Since Leona didn't do social media, she was more of a challenge to stalk than Suzanne, but she turned up in the social pages of the newspapers enough for Marnie to know that she was all angles and statement glasses, Issey Miyake frocks and opening nights at the opera. Brian had instructed that Marnie should not hold back on the expense. As if she ever did.

'White?' Owen suggested.

'Too bridal. And not bold enough.'

'Red?'

'Nope.' There could be no echo of 'scarlet woman'.

'What about this one?' Owen said, gesturing to a black handmade paper that was studded here and there with the faintest wisps of grey and white fibres.

'By George, I think you've got it.'

The black came in sheets half the size of the pink that Marnie had used for Suzanne's parcel, so she extracted two, mentally calculating the cost. She joined the sheets invisibly and this time she positioned the box horizontally, and on the diagonal.

She did not cut or trim the black paper; instead, she folded back its corners to create three-dimensional features. Then she wrapped a length of black satin ribbon around the box, tugging on one end until she was sure the bow would land at the perfect spot.

'Here,' she demanded, indicating that she wanted Owen to put his finger on the first cross of the bow, 'if you please.'

'Like this?'

'Why, thank you, sir.'

After she had pulled the ribbon into a tight bow above his finger, he did not step away.

'So, how have you been?' Owen asked.

Marnie smiled. Paused. Then said, 'Nothing to report. Just working hard.'

'Too hard to take a little break?'

Should she? Marnie wondered. Or should she not? She had been here enough times to know that Owen Kingston was the human equivalent of a third margarita – a good idea at the time. He didn't leave her with a hangover, exactly. Just a touch of melancholy. A smidge of self-pity that the extent of her love life, if she wanted to make her way in the world, seemed to be retaining a friend with benefits who called by every now and then to take her to bed.

But it was sweet with Owen, was it not? He wasn't just *anybody*. And she would enjoy it, wouldn't she? And, really, what would it hurt? Even as Marnie recognised this 'third margarita' thinking, even as she watched it rolling through her mind on its well-worn tracks, she kissed him. The feeling reminded her of what it was like to jump into a pool for the first swim of the summertime – the cool, pleasurable shock of the water, a sensation unfamiliar and well remembered, all at once.

'Hang on,' she said, with the tingle of their kiss still on her lips.

Quickly, she took Leona's envelope out of the filing box and ran her customary double-check. Inside was a card with a black-and-white print by Japanese artist Yayoi Kusama. It might have been a drawing of a pumpkin. Or a tea cosy. It was hard to say, but the image was just nicely offbeat, which Marnie was sure Leona would appreciate. She flicked open the card and read: *LQ – so much to look forward to – Billy-Ray.* Billy-Ray? Where did *that* come from? For all the world, she would not have picked Brian as the type to call himself by a cutesy pet name.

Marnie returned the card to its envelope, which she put – again, face down – on the counter, beside Suzanne's.

'Come on, little worker ant,' Owen chided her.

'We can't all afford to live like grasshoppers,' Marnie responded, but it wasn't until the words were out of her mouth that she detected the hard edge of annoyance in her voice.

'Whoa,' he said, hands up to indicate he had meant no harm.

Then he dished out a smile. One of *those* smiles – capable of dissolving her irritation in a heartbeat.

She placed Leona's gift on the collection shelf by the door, right beside Suzanne's. Then she turned the lock, glanced at her watch – oh man, they were going to have to work fast – and stuck the BACK IN 15 MINUTES sign in place.

Beyond harbouring a vague awareness that he ought to buy an anniversary card and knowing that he should probably clean out his ute before collecting his grandmother on Sunday, Luke Charlesworth had dedicated very little brain-space to his parents' impending fortieth wedding anniversary. Today, although the celebration was only two days away, his mum and dad's special occasion wasn't even close to the forefront of Luke's mind. Standing in front of a cafe in an unfamiliar part of town, he was preoccupied with his hopes and fears for the meeting about to take place.

He'd found the cafe easily enough. A classic cheap and cheerful, it was exactly where she'd said it would be, on the stretch between the local high school and the train station. Luke was a little early. Maybe he could take a walk around the block. That would pass the time, burn off some nervous energy. Or he could just . . . do it. Pulse hammering in his throat, he pushed open the door. Smells of coffee grounds and burned toast met his nostrils. He looked around. For a girl, sitting alone, watching the door, waiting for a stranger.

But there was nobody at the tables who matched her profile. There was only the mid-morning crowd of parents with prams, and bike riders wearing Lycra, engrossed in their e-readers. Casually,

casually, Luke made his way to the back and slid into a booth seat to wait. When she arrived, he'd be the one sitting alone, watching the door, waiting for a stranger.

He picked up a ragged newspaper, a few days past its best, and leafed through its pages. But the pictures were just colours, and the headlines refused to organise themselves into anything other than squiggly black shapes. Each time he heard the door open, he glanced up. Not too quickly, he hoped. He didn't want to look over-eager. It wouldn't do to come across like he'd barely thought about anything else for five days. Like he'd been fretting about this meeting for just about every waking moment since her text message had flashed up onto the screen of his phone and effectively scrambled his reality.

Luke supposed it made sense that the revelation had occurred by SMS. It was the way so many things happened now. It was probably how the Annunciation itself would go down, were it to take place in this day and age.

If Luke had ever thought about being in this situation – which he hadn't – then he'd probably have expected her to turn up and declare herself in person on his doorstep. Or maybe that it would have happened in a more regulated fashion. He could have used some kind of warning. A letter from a third party. From someone responsible for this sort of thing. A government department, perhaps.

He knew that was just wishful thinking, though. It would be naive to believe there was any authority in charge of mopping up the messes you got yourself into half a lifetime ago, literally, when you were young and stupid and met a smart, pretty girl at a party you shouldn't have been at, driven to a distant suburb by friends who shouldn't have been driving, drinking vodka you shouldn't have stolen from your parents' liquor cabinet and smoking weed you shouldn't have bought, and that you'd paid too much for, because even in a ripped denim jacket you came off like exactly what you were – a rich private-school boy with too much of Daddy's money in his wallet.

The text had said: *My name is Ivy Yip. My mother is Gillian Yip. About sixteen and a half years ago you gave her money for an abortion. In case you've forgotten who she is, she went to Chester High. So, yes, apparently I'm your daughter. Would you like to meet for coffee? I can do after school on Tuesdays, or I have a double free period on Friday mornings.* She had signed off with an emoji of a smiling face that was flipped upside down.

It was no mystery how she'd got his number. All she'd have needed was his name. Once she had that, he was an open book, his contact details right there for the whole world to find on the website for Luke Charlesworth Timber Design.

In case you've forgotten who she is.

That had stung. Almost certainly, it had been meant to. Quite certainly, he had deserved for it to do so. He and Gillian had been an item for a couple of months, although he'd treated her in the casually hot-and-cold way that his sixteen-year-old self had copied from the few mates of his who had girlfriends. When she told him she was pregnant, he sold a brand-new laptop computer – let his father believe he'd left it on the train – for money to end Ivy Yip's life before it even began.

He'd thought himself so honourable. He'd been so utterly clueless.

In the years since Gillian, Luke had known women – friends, acquaintances – who'd ended pregnancies. He'd respected their right to do so, of course, but whenever the topic had come up in conversation, or on the news, he'd remembered that beautiful young woman whose hand he should have been there to hold, whose tears he should have been there to mop up. To share. Instead, all he'd done was send a wad of cash via a friend of a friend. And failed to find the courage to contact her ever again.

When Ivy's text message had arrived, all the images in his mind had reconfigured themselves in an instant. Doubtless there had still been tears, and yes, he should still have been there to hold Gillian's hand. But instead of a loss, a void, there had been a baby, a toddler, a girl. Now a young woman. He had a *daughter*. He was a father. This fact alone seemed somehow to increase his sense of his own specific gravity – as if he had become more substantial by no other mechanism than becoming aware that on this planet, there was a girl called Ivy Yip, and half her genetic code was his.

Luke had known immediately that he would reply to Ivy's text, but it took two restless nights of half-sleep for him to decide how, exactly. Her words were not difficult to decode, but what on earth did an upside-down-smiling-face emoji mean? He couldn't help but feel that it meant smiling, but possibly not smiling, also. An ironic smile? A provisional smile?

He knew he had to be gentle, the way you might be if you were approaching a skittish animal, and he knew that while he needed to be remorseful, a text message was the wrong way to deliver the huge apology he owed. He had drafted and redrafted his message, but everything he tried sounded hollow and pathetic. Or else it risked being over the top. At last, he'd settled on neutral: *Dear Ivy, hello. I would very much like to have coffee. I can do any Tuesday afternoon or Friday morning you like.* He attached a photograph of himself but would not have admitted to anybody how long it took him to choose the right one.

It had taken some time for her to reply, but when she did, naming the time and place, she also attached a picture of herself.

Another thing Luke would not have shared with a single soul was just how many times in the last few days he had opened it and studied her face. His daughter's face.

Luke looked up at the sound of the door, and there she was. Walking towards him, her school bag slung over her shoulder, the pleats of her plaid school dress hanging loosely on her slender frame. She had Gillian Yip's jet-black hair, but cut into an edgy, jagged bob. Her skin was a little lighter than Gillian's, her eyes slightly rounder, and her lips came straight from the Charlesworth gene pool. She radiated intelligence. He was willing to bet she was so smart she could fillet out his heart and soul with a few graceful strokes.

And now that she had arrived at the booth, was slinging her bag under the table in a practised motion, he could see something he hadn't seen in the photograph. On her chin and forehead were some spots that she had covered with make-up. With a twinge of shame and regret, he remembered his own troublesome teenage skin.

But now, Luke realised, there was a problem. His mind had emptied. He had thought about this meeting. Had thought about little else for days. He had mapped out the way it would go, considering several different pathways. Which one he took would depend on how things started, on how she seemed. But now he couldn't even remember if he should stand or remain seated. Should he get to his feet and hold out his arms to offer her an embrace? Or was that way too much? It turned out to be a moot point, because now that she was standing there, he couldn't move at all.

He had thought about his opening gambits. He had planned out things to say to her that were warm, but also cool. Now, he couldn't remember a single one of them. She stood looking at him, sitting there like a stunned mullet. She seemed to wait for him to do something, and when he didn't, a look came into her dark eyes that he suspected was somewhere at the disdain end of the spectrum. He half stood.

'Don't get up,' she said, sliding smoothly into the seat opposite him.

He sat back down. Which, at least, resolved the hugging issue. But maybe things would still go well enough that he could hug her when they said goodbye. Luke opened his mouth, but his tongue failed to operate. All he seemed to be able to do was worry that in years to come, when they told the story of how they met, they would both know that the first words they exchanged in real life were not perfect, or profound, or even funny. Just awkward. Maybe even a little scathing. *Don't get up.* Mercifully, a waiter materialised beside the booth.

'What will you have?' Luke asked.

Ivy tilted her head, considering.

'Have whatever you want,' Luke blurted, then wished he had not. Far out, he had made himself sound like the rich, benevolent father descended from on high. She looked at him as if he really was a moron.

'I have money,' she told him, and her choice of words felt meaningful. She turned to the waiter. 'A short black, please.'

'And, I'll have, uh . . .'

Even the knowledge of what kind of thing one ordered at a cafe had disappeared out of Luke's head. He was so busy having his mind blown by the self-possessed young woman sitting opposite him that, even when he remembered about coffee, he couldn't think what type he liked best.

'Cappuccino,' he managed. 'Thanks.'

When the waiter was gone, Luke attempted to reset.

'Hello, Ivy,' he said, remembering at least something of what he'd rehearsed. 'I'm really pleased to meet you. I'm glad, and grateful, that you reached out to me.'

She eyed him carefully, clearly reserving judgement.

'Mum said you were a charming little snake,' she said, testing.

From the back pocket of his jeans, he drew out the letter he'd written to Gillian – short but remorseful, offering his support, letting her know he welcomed communication.

'I thought you might deliver this to her,' he said, sliding it across the table.

She took it. A little too quickly for comprehensive coolness.

'I didn't seal it,' Luke said, risking a small smile. 'So, you won't have to steam it open if you want to read it. I figure it concerns you most of all.'

That seemed to meet with her approval. She settled herself into the seat a little more, as if preparing to begin an interview. 'So, you're my father.'

'It seems that way,' Luke said.

She crossed her arms on the table edge in a way that caused him to imagine she'd be formidable in a debating team. 'Tell me about you.'

'Where do you want me to start?'

'Do you have a wife? Other children?'

Luke shook his head. 'Neither.'

'Or at least not that you know of,' she said. It was a stab.

'Touché.'

'So, is there a significant other?'

'Nope.'

'Why not?'

Luke reeled slightly.

'I'm direct,' Ivy said.

'I noticed.'

The coffees landed on the table, the short black in front of Luke, the cappuccino in front of Ivy.

'They always do that. Like it's only men who drink serious coffee,' Ivy complained, switching the drinks to their rightful places. In her petulant tone, Luke got a sense of whatever childishness was left in this poised young woman, and felt a pang of loss. Almost all of her childhood had passed. Irretrievably.

'What about you?' Luke asked. 'I want to hear about you.'

'Uh-uh,' Ivy said. 'I'm not done. And you didn't answer my last question.'

'Ah. The why not question. Well, I did have a girlfriend, until a few months ago. She decided to go back to Germany to live.'

'Why?' She fired the word at him like a bullet.

Luke breathed. Chose honesty. 'She's in her thirties, like me. The clock was ticking. She wanted more than I was ready to give, I guess.'

'Is that a pattern for you?'

Luke swallowed. Chose deflection. 'I wouldn't say that, necessarily.'

'Hm,' Ivy said, in a somewhat diagnostic way. She stirred a spoon of sugar into her coffee, took a tiny sip.

'You have cousins,' Luke offered, hoping to bargain a way out of this particular cul-de-sac of the conversation. 'Benji is six. Loves gemstones. And Leila. She's four. Loves, um, chaos, I think it's fair to say. Their mother is my sister. My big sister, Caroline. So, you have an aunt. And grandparents – Suzanne and Brian. They're about to have their fortieth wedding anniversary, actually. On Sunday.'

Ivy nodded, taking it all in. 'Have you told them? About me?'

'Not yet.'

'Will you?'

'I'd . . . like to,' Luke said.

'But?'

'Mum will be fine.'

'Your father, though?'

'I wouldn't describe us as exactly close.'

'Because?'

'Doctor, lawyer, banker, dentist . . . he'd have liked something straightforwardly brag-worthy.'

'He doesn't like bespoke specialty-timber pieces?'

He smiled. She was quoting from his website. 'Oh, he likes them well enough. Even has a couple in his office. He'd just prefer that someone else's son had made them.'

'And you don't want to give him another reason. To be disappointed.'

He looked at her. At his daughter. She was smart. Smart enough to land a guess that was very, very close to correct. The complete truth was that what hurt Luke more than his father being disappointed in him was Brian Charlesworth's air of resignation when it happened. Like he'd expected nothing more.

Luke spooned the froth off the top of his cappuccino, wishing he'd ordered a flat white. 'Is it my turn to ask questions yet?'

'All right then.'

He had promised himself he wasn't going to ask any of *those* questions. The how's school/what grade are you in/what subjects do you like/what do you want to do when you leave school questions. He remembered hating them when he was a teenager.

'What makes you happy?'

Ivy's eyes narrowed suspiciously, as if the question might be a trick. 'What makes me happy?'

'Yep.'

'I am happy when . . . I'm playing music, when I'm listening to music, and when I feel like I'm making a difference.'

That was plenty, Luke thought, to be going on with, and for a time they just talked. Not like a father and a daughter. More like strangers sitting side by side on a long-haul flight. She told him she played the clarinet, showed him pictures of the sculptures she was making in her ceramics class, described the merchandise she'd designed for a climate action group. He asked what kind of music she liked to listen to, and although he didn't believe her when she told him he wouldn't be familiar with any of it, it turned out – when she rattled off an avalanche of names – that she was right. He told her about his furniture design business and about the music he liked, which she classified – factually, without venom – as 'old, white-guy music'.

Was it going well? Luke asked himself. Were they doing okay? On the scale of father-meets-hitherto-unknown-teenage-daughter-for-the-first-time encounters, where did theirs fit? He didn't know. Although she answered all of his questions, he would not have described her as warm. But he figured that her reserve, her terseness, were reasonable. He had done nothing to warrant her instant affection, though it surprised him how much he found himself wishing for it. He decided to take a step closer to the questions he really wanted to ask. *Are we going to get to know each other better? Are you going to be part of my life, or did you just want to check me out? Satisfy your curiosity? Is there room in your life for me to be some kind of actual father to you?*

'I know you've got to be turning sixteen fairly soon. Your birthday . . . is it in October?'

'Nice maths,' she said, with an edge to her voice. She downed the last of her coffee. He had barely touched his. 'It's the twentieth.'

He took a deep breath, readying himself to take another step. 'Ivy, when your mum told me she was pregnant . . . I was just a kid, you know. I was so young, and totally clueless —'

Ivy interrupted him with a loud sigh. 'Seriously?'

'What?'

She got to her feet. 'You know, I should really be getting back to school.'

'Did I say . . .?' he began.

'Something wrong?' she finished. 'I promised myself that if you started with any of that "I was so young and clueless" crap, I'd just walk away. You were sixteen. I'm nearly sixteen and, unless you're a sociopath, if you're my age then you know that you don't just get somebody pregnant and then walk away like nothing ever happened. You don't just assume that someone wants an abortion. You ask them what they want. You support them, whatever they choose.'

She reached for her bag under the table. Luke felt panicked. All the things he'd imagined he might say? He'd said none of them. All the pathways he'd scoped out? Not one of them had materialised. And now she was leaving. 'Ivy, I haven't said —'

'*You* haven't said?' Her eyes flashed.

'I wanted to say —'

'Well, here's what *I* want to say. *I* want to say that my mother wasn't just some stray cat to be dealt with. And I wasn't just some foetus.' She spat the word. 'We weren't just something that could be taken care of. We were worth more than your fucking money.'

She clattered ten dollars' worth of coins onto the table. This was something he'd done to his own father, too. More than once, he'd underscored his independence by tossing onto a table a quantity of money that, actually, he could ill-afford to part with. She really was his daughter.

'Let me get the coffee,' he said. 'Please.'

'How about no?'

'You're angry with me,' Luke said, as calmly as he could manage.

'You have no idea.'

'Ivy, I've handled this badly. Can we just . . . do you really have to go right now?'

She didn't move, seemed caught in the moment. He fancied he could see the rival thoughts flickering in her eyes. But then she shook back her hair with an air of defiance, adjusted the shoulder strap of her bag. 'Goodbye, Luke.'

Her strides were long as she made for the door. She didn't look back. Soon she was out on the street, passing in front of the cafe window, her face unreadable. Luke had an image of himself sitting there against the red vinyl of the booth seat, neatly sliced down the middle, like a gutted fish.

Goodbye, Luke.

What had he expected? For her to call him 'Dad'?

Upstairs, Marnie and Owen did not take the time to undress. Only kicked off their shoes. Unbuckled. Unzipped. Marnie hinged down her foldaway bed and she and Owen fell together onto its neatly tucked surface, not bothering to pull back the covers.

Straddling Owen, Marnie was no longer thinking about whether or not this was a good idea. She wasn't thinking at all. She was only feeling what it was like to be touched in all of the warm, pulsing parts of her that had almost forgotten what it was like to be wanted.

The skirts of her linen dress were rucked up over Owen's chest and spread out to either side of his body, and although the strings of her apron were untied at the back, the garment still hung loosely from her neck. Her long dark-red hair, falling down across her shoulder in a loose ponytail, touched his face, which wore a gratifyingly blissed-out expression. She felt soft, and supple – so light-headed with pleasure that her tiny apartment seemed almost to spin around her.

She moved against him, making him sigh, and he took her hips in his hands as if he could pull her even closer to him. She felt her body collecting up sensation, gathering it all together like an outdrawn tide before a wave. But just as it was all about to come flooding back in again, her mobile phone began to chime.

Owen said, 'Let it ring,' but Marnie was already feeling for the pocket of her apron. She pulled out her phone, intending to silence it, but then – without exactly meaning to – she glanced at the screen.

Fairchild & Rooke.

Her uncle's firm.

Her *uncle's* firm.

And, with that realisation, every sexual feeling left her body on a rapid, outgoing tide. 'Holy shit,' she said.

She became quite still.

'What is it?' Owen asked, brow furrowed.

'I did it,' she said, staring fixedly at the phone as it trilled again.

'Did what?'

She fancied she caught a whiff of the Rose Quartz candle. 'I actually *did* it.'

'What did you do? Hello? Marnie?'

'Holy shit,' she said again. She disentangled herself from Owen and clambered off the bed. 'Sorry. I have to take this. Sorry.'

Crumpled skirts falling back into place, she moved towards

the window. As she swiped with clumsy fingers at the screen, she tried to compose herself, to breathe normally.

'Hello,' she said, in the breeziest tone she could manage, 'this is Wish and Co.'

'Is that Marnie Fairchild?' It was a woman's voice. Smooth and plumped.

'Yes, it is.'

Marnie, hearing the creaking of bedsprings, turned to see Owen sitting up, flushed in the cheeks as he looked at her in disbelief, one of her pillows pulled over his lap.

'Sorry,' she mouthed to him.

'This is Tillie Grimes, Lewis Fairchild's personal assistant. This is just a courtesy call. In relation to the Fairchild and Sons property on Rathbone Street.'

'Yes?' Marnie said. She could feel her heartbeat in her throat.

'Mr Fairchild wanted you to know that he's planning to divest himself of that property.'

Marnie's heart thumped harder still. She really had done it. She had manifested this. She had asked the universe for what she wanted, and it had said *yes*. 'He is?'

'He asked me to let you know that he's begun discussions with a real estate agency.'

Real estate agency? No, that was wrong. That wasn't how it was supposed to go. He was supposed to call her himself. He was supposed to give her the first opportunity to buy.

'Real estate agency?' she repeated.

'That's correct.'

'Are you sure?'

'Quite sure,' Tillie said, as if fending off an insult.

Marnie processed. Lewis was putting the shop on the open

market. He wasn't even going to give her a chance to negotiate. Inside her brain, the vision of herself and her uncle engaged in a swaggering battle of financial wits evaporated – *poof!* – into the naive fantasy it always was.

'When's this happening? Is Mr Fairchild there? Can I talk to him?'

'Mr Fairchild asked me to let you know that you should contact the agent, directly, if you have an interest in the property.'

'I see,' Marnie said. Whatever trace of rose-coloured candle she thought she had smelled before was now entirely gone. What had she thought? That Lewis Fairchild, the patriarch of the Fairchild family proper, would suspend the cut-throat rules of business on behalf of a semi-Fairchild like herself? That he'd be sentimental about the child of his dead and disgraced brother? When large sums of money were involved?

'The agency is Parkside Realty . . .' Tillie said.

Of course it was Parkside, Marnie thought – the real estate agency of choice for the Alexandria Park establishment; synonymous with record-breaking prices and over-hyped auctions.

'. . . and the agent's name is Mark Wigston. His number . . . do you have a pen and paper?'

'Yes,' Marnie said. She grabbed a Sharpie pen and, across the back of her hand, scribbled down the phone number. Even if it were true that writing on your skin could poison you – which it probably wasn't, because that was almost certainly just an old wives' tale – in this moment Marnie wouldn't have cared.

'So, the shop is definitely going on the market through Parkside? That's a done deal?' Marnie demanded to know.

'I can't tell you anything more, I'm sorry. Mr Fairchild said you should contact the agent if you had any queries.'

'Is it going to auction?'

'As I already said' – Tillie's voice was aggressively calm – 'Mr Fairchild invites you to contact the agent. If you have any further queries.'

Further *queries*? Marnie had nothing but further queries. Still, she understood that there was little more to be gained from this phone call. Clearly the person she needed to talk to – right now – was Mark Wigston. Breathing in sharply through her nose, Marnie summoned the resolve to be polite.

'Thank you. I understand. And please thank Mr Fairchild for his courtesy.' As they said their goodbyes and have-a-nice-days, Marnie wondered if she had managed to keep the archness out of the word *courtesy*. Probably not.

Marnie's fingers itched to call the agent's number right away. But there was Owen, still sitting at the head of her bed, his back against the wall, although zipped up by now. Two sets of shoes were scattered together just inside the doorway. Her knickers were a scrap of pale blue cotton on the linoleum floor.

'So it was that good then, huh?' he said.

'Kingo, I'm sorry.'

'That call. It was about the old shop?' Owen asked.

Marnie nodded. Occasionally, back in the day, she'd taken him with her on one of her after-school visits to Fairchild & Sons. They'd show up in their Meltonside Grammar uniforms; Marnie's skirt too short, Owen's shirt untucked, and their brown leather Clarks so scuffed it hurt her grandfather in his cobbler's soul. The times she'd visited the shop – sometimes alone, sometimes with Owen – had given Marnie pretty much all the memories she had of her grandfather. Often, Archie would polish her shoes; always he would press upon her a mint chocolate truffle from the bowl on the counter; sometimes he would bestow the odd bit of advice. What would he have said to her today? *A fool and her money are soon parted, my girl.*

'Your uncle's finally going to let the place go?'

Marnie picked up her knickers and shoes. 'Looks like it.'

'Are you going to be able to afford it?'

'That's what I need to find out.'

Owen sat with his arms crossed over his chest, the cuffs of his denim jacket rolled two turns, allowing her a glimpse of his watch; it was almost noon.

'Shit, the courier!'

In the cramped bathroom, Marnie switched herself into reverse – putting on knickers that had been hurriedly yanked off, capturing sections of hair that had fallen loose, securing apron strings that had been untied, applying lipstick that had been kissed away. Stepping back into the main room, she found Owen now sitting on the side of her bed, putting on his own shoes. She kissed him on the top of his head.

'I really am sorry, but I still have the paperwork to do. Those gifts? They're for a client I cannot possibly disappoint. Make yourself a cup of tea or something, if you want. I think the milk's still okay. I'm sorry, Kingo. Sorry, sorry . . .' She was still saying it as she closed the door behind her.

As Marnie clattered down the metal steps, she dialled the phone number she'd written on the back of her hand. The phone rang. And rang. *Pick up, pick up.* But all she got was a recording.

'Ah!' she burst out, then recovered herself in time to leave a polite message after the beep.

She entered the shop through the back door. Questions, questions, questions. And no answers to any of them. Briskly, she crossed to the front door and unlocked it, and as she took down the BACK IN 15 MINUTES sign, she noticed that her hands were shaking.

The Charlesworth gifts – one black, one pink – waited on the collection shelf for the courier, but maybe once they were out the door, she could close up for the day and walk down to the offices of Parkside Realty to see Mark Wigston in person. But no. That would make her look too keen. That was not how a Fairchild did business.

Breathe, Marnie. Breathe. And get the parcels ready for collection.

At the counter, Marnie opened her laptop and clicked on the document in which she kept detailed notes of her delivery instructions. Brian had directed that Leona's parcel was to go to her riverside apartment, where it should be entrusted to the building's concierge, who would arrange for it to be left on her doorstep as a surprise. Suzanne's present, on the other hand, was to go to Brian's office at the Charlesworth Group, so that he could take it home and present it, in person.

Marnie tugged a pad of her courier service's consignment notes from under her cash register and carefully filled in the two addresses – Leona's apartment, Brian's office. When she was done, she tore the consignment notes from the pad and matched them, carefully, with the two envelopes she had set aside on the counter. Suzanne's card, Suzanne's address – check. Leona's card, Leona's address – check. Then she considered trying again to ring Mark Wigston. Perhaps, earlier, he'd just been on another call. Maybe he was free by now. *No, no, Marnie,* she told herself, *you can't look desperate. Even if you are. Especially if you are.* She was still arguing with herself when Owen appeared, struggling in through the back door with two mugs of tea.

'Black, one sugar,' he announced, setting one down on the counter for her. 'The milk was a science experiment.'

'Thanks, Kingo. And, you know, sorry. About . . .'

He shrugged. 'I get it. The shop is big stuff for you. Really, I get it.'

Marnie took a sip of her drink, but when the phone rang again, she all but dropped the mug. Tea slopped over the rim onto the counter. 'Hello?'

'Marnie? Mark Wigston. Parkside Realty. How can I help?'

Sound casual, sound casual, sound casual. 'It's about the Fairchild and Sons shop on Rathbone Street. I understand your firm might be listing it?'

'Indeed, indeed. But can I just ask? In your message . . . your name? Are you family?'

'I'm Archie's granddaughter,' Marnie said, guardedly.

'But you're not one of Lewis's girls.'

Marnie rolled her eyes. So, they were going to play a game of 'Which Fairchild Are You?'. Fairchild was an old Alexandria Park name. Like Clitheroe, Rooke and Wicks, it was synonymous with intergenerational wealth, established businesses and serious real estate. These were names that turned up on honour boards at private schools and cricket clubs, on the committee of the Dame Sutherland Club, and on tiny brass plaques on the best seats at the theatre. Fairchild was a surname that opened doors, but also one that came with questions. Too often, when Marnie presented her credit card in an Alexandria Park store or gave her name while making an appointment over the phone, she ended up being asked whether she was one of *those* Fairchilds, and, when she said 'yes', to explain where she fitted into the genealogy.

'Lewis is my uncle,' she told Mark.

'I see, I see. That must make you one of Marilyn's, then? Odd, though. You said your name was Fairchild and I was sure she became a Clitheroe?'

Marnie sighed. Sometimes the city seemed like a big place, but it rapidly shrunk to the gossipy dimensions of a village once you started bandying about the old names.

'Marilyn Clitheroe is my aunt,' she offered.

'Oh,' Mark said, and Marnie could hear the *tink* of a penny dropping. If she was Archie's granddaughter, and Lewis and Marilyn's niece . . . *Oh*, indeed.

'I'm Rory's daughter.'

A short silence.

'Rory? I see. I'm . . . sorry for your loss.'

'You're very kind. But it has been rather a long time.' Three decades' worth of a long time. 'Anyway, I wanted to enquire about the shop?'

Slightly too cheerfully, he said, 'Funny you should call. I'm right here at the shop at the moment.'

'If you're there . . . I don't suppose I could . . . I mean, if it's not any trouble to you . . .'

'You wish to come by? Now?'

'If that would suit?'

'How far away are you?'

She could close up the shop. Run there. *Not too eager, not too eager.* 'Not far,' Marnie said smoothly. 'I work on Rathbone Street. I could be there in' – she calculated. Seven blocks. An Uber, in that traffic? It would be quicker to walk – 'fifteen minutes?'

'Well, ah. I was actually on my way to another appointment, but I suppose I could wait. If you were sure you wouldn't be any longer?'

Cool, calm, collected. 'I'll leave right away.'

Marnie ended the call and held her phone to her chest, felt the adrenaline-fizz in her blood start to dissipate. She looked at Owen, who steadily met her eye over the rim of his mug.

'Was I okay? Did I keep my cool?'

He took a sip. 'I wouldn't have described you as relaxed, exactly.'

'But was I over-eager?'

'"I'll leave right away",' he mimicked.

'Oh, crap. I haven't blown it, have I?'

'You'd better get going if you're going to be there in fifteen minutes.'

Marnie untied her apron, shoved it under the counter, took her green woollen coat from a hook of the hatstand. She was halfway across the shop floor when it dawned on her that she couldn't simply close up.

'The courier. Shit, shit.' She looked at Owen plaintively.

'What?' he asked.

She didn't really want to leave him in charge of her shop, but she was desperate to see the inside of Fairchild & Sons. Right now. And yet, the Charlesworth parcels had to be delivered today. It was non-negotiable. 'Please?'

'You want me, what, to wait here? For how long?'

'Please? The courier can't be far away. They should have already been here.'

'Yes, but how long *might* they be?'

Marnie made an apologetic face. 'They're hardly ever more than an hour late.'

Owen looked at his watch. 'Go on, then. Get out of here.'

'I love you, Kingo. You're the best. Just put up the closed sign once they've been, yeah? And lock the door as you go?'

'Yes, yes, yes.'

Marnie kissed him then. On the lips, but not the way she had done before. This time it was pure gratitude.

'See you . . .' she began.

'. . . when I see you,' Owen finished. Which, Marnie knew, was another way of saying, *no promises*.

With fumbling fingers, Marnie snatched up the paired cards and consignment notes from the counter, and, as she hurtled out the door, placed the bundles – one each – on top of the two parcels that waited on the collection shelf.

Even though Marnie was rushing, she was careful. (Wasn't she?) She did take her customary extra-special care to match each gift with its corresponding paperwork. (Didn't she?) These questions occurred to Marnie, ever so briefly, as she passed by the shop window and caught a glimpse of herself shrugging on her coat.

Of course she had been careful. She was always careful. Careful was practically her middle name. There was nothing to worry about. So, she didn't. She just flicked her ponytail out from the collar of her coat and hurried down Rathbone Street in the direction of Fairchild & Sons.

One day before the implosion of the Charlesworth marriage

Leona Quick, on the eve of her sixty-fifth birthday, took the elevator in her apartment block down from the twelfth floor and struggled across the lobby of the tenth. In her arms was a fiendishly heavy parcel wrapped in dusky pink paper and tied with a cream velvet bow. With her elbow, she pressed the button for the doorbell that belonged to Cameron Fowler.

This, she knew, was not proper. One did not, on a Saturday night, make a social call to an apartment-block neighbour, when all one had done for the previous two years – since he'd moved in, after being widowed – was nod to him as they passed each other in the ground-floor lobby, and occasionally say 'evening', or 'morning' to him while riding the elevator. More pertinently, one did not, on a Saturday night, or at any other time of the week, make a social call to one's former psychologist.

Mind you, the fact that she and Cameron had once had a therapist–client association surely didn't ban them from having a more cordial relationship now. He was retired, after all. And it was five years or more since she'd last seen him in a professional context. Surely there had to be some kind of statute of limitation. But then, Leona admitted to herself, the statute of limitation probably didn't count if the reason one was going to visit one's former psychologist at his apartment on a Saturday night was to seek his professional opinion. About the parcel in her arms. Or, more precisely, about the problem of finding herself – at the age of sixty-four years and 364 days – back in the role of the 'other woman' to the man who had arranged for said parcel to arrive on her doorstep.

Buzzzzzzz went the doorbell and, following some miscellaneous shuffling noises, the door opened to reveal the bulky shape of Cameron Fowler. If Leona had not been struggling with the weight of the parcel in her arms, she would have been more amused than she was to see that, although he was not wearing the tweedy elbow-patched jacket that had always been his trademark, his slate-blue jumper had grey plaid patches on its elbows.

'Leona,' Cameron said, calmly surprised. 'Here, let me.'

'It's awfully heavy,' she said, gratefully bundling the parcel into his arms.

For a moment, they stood in his doorway. Cameron held the heavy parcel and blinked like a marsupial confronted by bright lights, and Leona realised that in her impetuous haste to come downstairs, she hadn't thought to change out of her slouchy cashmere jumper, Lululemon leggings and house slippers.

He gave her a quizzical look.

'Oh, that's my birthday present,' she explained.

'I see,' Cameron said.

'Tomorrow is my birthday.'

'Happy birthday for tomorrow.'

'Thank you.'

Cameron blinked again, and Leona realised she was going to have to be direct.

'Could I come in for a moment?' She gestured to the parcel. 'You see, I don't know what to do about it.'

Cameron nodded and moved back to allow Leona to step

inside. Since the floorplan of his apartment was exactly the same as that of her own, she easily found her way through to his living room, which was furnished in exactly the way you would expect of a man so devoted to elbow patches. Frozen on the screen of a large television was an image from the same Scandi-noir crime drama Leona herself had been binge-watching earlier in the evening. Cameron lowered the parcel to the coffee table, which held a bottle of very civilised single malt and a lone, substantial, tumbler. She must have allowed her eyes to linger on the bottle for just a little too long.

'Fancy a whisky? While we discuss your parcel problem?'

'Oh, I won't say no.'

'Ice? Water?'

'Heavens, no.'

'Excellent choice,' Cameron said.

He gestured for her to take a seat on the Chesterfield, and she perched on its arm as if she were only somewhat there. Cameron placed a substantial nip of whisky in front of her and sat back in the armchair she assumed was customarily his, bordered as it was by small tables piled high with books and newspapers.

'So, the parcel,' Leona began, getting right to the point.

'It's very nicely wrapped,' Cameron observed, and this was true. The colour palette wasn't particularly to Leona's taste, but she had to admit that whomever Brian had engaged to do the wrapping was quite the expert.

'Should I open it?'

'Why would you not?'

'Because it's from Brian.'

Cameron sat for a moment, quietly contemplating, and Leona reminded herself that she must not be taken in by him. She must not be fooled by his awkward silences, mumbling shyness, and reluctance to make eye contact. Because behind his metal-rimmed glasses, she knew, there lurked a brain the size of a planet, and a memory so good it was virtually a superpower.

'Brian. That would be . . . the university sweetheart,' Cameron recalled.

'That's him.'

'The cocky one. Whose heart you broke, over . . . oysters? At the Belvedere?'

She sipped her whisky, felt it set her tongue gently on fire. 'That's right.'

'You were arguing about politics, were you not?'

'Politics, power, privilege. All of the above. He'd just said something in the "let them eat cake" ballpark.'

'So, you told him . . . now, how did you put it? That you . . . would prefer to eat shit sandwiches at the beach . . . just so long as the person you were with had . . . a soul.'

'Your memory really is amazing.'

Cameron shrugged, pleased with the compliment. 'A dramatic way to end things. But then the relationship was rekindled, yes? Twenty or so years later?'

'After James died, yes.'

Cameron stroked his badly trimmed beard. 'Remind me how that came about?'

Leona gave him a *nice try* smile. A man who could remember an anecdote about how she had broken up with her lover when she was a strident final-year law student did not need a refresher on how that same lover had come back into her life when she was forty-five.

Quite simply, she'd been a mess. When Leona had married James, she'd known, of course, that it would almost certainly mean being widowed early, but as it had turned out, her mental preparations for that eventuality had done little to soften the blow.

'I was grieving. Vulnerable,' Leona said. And the flowers Brian arranged to arrive on her doorstep kept coming. Week after week after week.

Cameron leaned a patched elbow on the arm of his chair, set his chin on his fist. 'Is it grief again this time, do you think?'

Leona scoffed. When Toby had left, three years ago now, Leona had been the opposite of grief-stricken. In fact, she'd thrown a party to celebrate.

'Not grief this time, then,' Cameron confirmed. 'But nevertheless, Brian's *back*?'

'For the third time, yes.'

'And . . . how are things going?'

'Well, it's not as if we see each other every day. Unless you count the Scrabble. But that's just online. We meet for coffee once a week or so, and every couple of months we go away together, for a weekend. It's just such tremendous fun, as if we're back in our university days.'

There were few people remaining in her life who'd known Leona for as long as Brian had. It had been Brian who had coined the nickname that had stuck – LQ. He was one of just a handful of people who remembered the young woman she'd been before she was James Forde's wife, before she was admitted to the bar, before she developed the brittle public carapace of a high-profile lawyer, a judge. There was almost nobody else alive, and absolutely nobody in her social circle, who remembered her when she'd been able to drink most of her male classmates under the table. Or the time she'd won a karaoke contest with a smouldering rendition of 'Son of a Preacher Man'. But Brian had been there – on the floor, at her feet, at the karaoke bar. Leona caught herself smiling and suddenly felt stupid.

'Remind me . . .' Cameron began, ponderously, 'why didn't the relationship go anywhere twenty years ago?'

'He wouldn't leave his wife.'

'His wife. Who is very different to you, no?'

'I don't know a thing about her, really. I mean, I've met her. Vaguely. At charity dinners, that sort of thing.'

'That would be enough for you to have an impression of her. I think you once said she was . . . the sort of woman who dressed in curtain fabric?'

Leona burst out laughing. 'Did I really say something so bitchy?'

Cameron raised his prodigious eyebrows, but only good-naturedly. 'And why was it, that he wouldn't leave his wife?'

'Oh, you know. His children were young. He was on the make in his career. I don't suppose he had time for the kind of mess that divorce brings with it.'

'But now he *has* left her?'

'No,' she admitted.

'But that's what you want? For him to leave his wife? And be with you?'

'You don't think I like it, do you? It's hardly honourable, being the "other woman".'

'It doesn't seem to bother you terribly much, though,' Cameron observed.

Leona bristled. 'Brian's wife is one of those women. You know the sort.'

'I'm not sure I do.'

'They marry a wealthy man, quite deliberately, so they never have to take responsibility for themselves. They can just drive around in their big cars, dropping their children off at private schools, and sit around admiring their Royal Doulton dinner sets while somebody else does all the work. Brian's marriage . . . it's transactional.' She loaded the last word with all the disdain she could muster. 'I have always worked.'

Cameron fell silent for a moment, and Leona suspected he was allowing everything she'd just said to echo in her own ears. Admittedly, it had sounded a bit jaundiced.

Cameron adjusted his spectacles. 'Where is it that his wife thinks he is, during these weekends that you go away?'

'Fishing,' Leona said.

Cameron's eyebrows lifted again.

Leona said, 'It is true that we *go* to the Highlands. We just don't . . . catch trout.'

'So, is he planning to leave this transactional marriage of his?'

'I have no idea. It's not something we've talked about. We've just been, you know, having a good time.'

'So why are you here? Wondering whether or not to open this gift from him? If all is well?'

It was, Leona recognised, an excellent question. She folded her hands in her lap to stop herself from picking at the cracks in the leather arm of the Chesterfield. 'Well, it can't go on like this. We have to decide, one way or another. I can't be bothered with all this ridiculous sneaking around.'

'And how long have you two being seeing each other this time?' Cameron asked.

'A year and a half?'

'Now you want to build a future with Brian? Openly? Honourably, as you say?'

'I don't know what I want! But he just keeps coming back! Is it some kind of cosmic test of my character? Sometimes I think the universe is telling me that I'm just supposed to walk away from him. That I'm supposed to prove my honour by sending him packing. But then I think, perhaps the reason he's back, again, is because the universe is banging me over the head with the message that he and I are meant to be together. Cameron, I have to work out what I am supposed to do!'

Her former psychologist looked at her very directly. His eyes were an unthreatening brown, and his gaze too gentle to be piercing. And yet the way he looked at her made her feel utterly naked.

'This urgency of yours,' he said. 'What's that all about?'

Leona felt for her thick-rimmed, oversized glasses, checking they were still in place. She dipped her head so that the silvered curls of her bobbed hair fell down to cover just a little more of her forehead and cheekbones.

'Leona?'

Fuck it all. Tears were welling up in her eyes. Tears. *No, no, no, no.* She did not cry in front of other people.

'I'm going to be . . .' she began, but a sobbing sensation in her throat stopped her words.

Cameron leaned forward. 'You're going to be . . .?'

'Tomorrow,' Leona managed.

'Yes?'

Leona tried to breathe her way out of her distress, but she couldn't fight it down. Entirely without her consent, the welling tears escaped her eyelids and dripped down her cheeks.

'Sixty-five,' Leona said, giving up and letting the tears flow. 'Cameron, I'm going to be *sixty-five*.'

Cameron reached into his pocket and fished out a handkerchief. It was perfectly clean, still neatly folded. When her sobs had subsided, Leona took the greeting card from the top of the parcel and passed it over to Cameron. She had already taken it out of its envelope some hours earlier, as a halfway measure between opening the entire gift and leaving it untouched.

'Go on,' she urged. 'Read it.'

The card inside bore a black-and-white Yayoi Kusama print – one of her famous pumpkins. The image had given Leona a jolt of pleasure, reminding her of the day she'd spent at the Kusama retrospective at the National Art Center in Tokyo, strolling through room after room of artworks by the ludicrously prolific artist.

'*LQ,*' Cameron read aloud, '*so much to look forward to. Billy-Ray.*'

Leona laughed through her tears. Crazy man.

'Billy-Ray?' Cameron asked.

'Was a preacher's son.'

'Ah.' Cameron hummed a few bars of the Dusty Springfield song. Badly. 'So, how does it make you feel? What he's written here? Your *Billy-Ray?*'

Leona thought. Wondered. *Did* she want a future with Brian? Or was she just remembering the fun they'd had in the past? Did she love him, or only the way he made her feel like her karaoke days were not, after all, so very long ago?

'Leona?' Cameron prompted. 'How does it make you feel?'

She cringed, and then admitted it. 'Younger.'

Cameron nodded. Possibly even a little proudly. 'Maybe *that* was the gift. Leona? Maybe that *was* the gift? Maybe now you have that, you could send the parcel back, unopened?'

Leona regarded the pink bulk of the wrapped box. 'I can't deny that I'm curious. Brian has quite a way with gifts.'

'So, what are you going to do?'

So much to look forward to, Leona repeated to herself. What might that mean? Did the message relate, somehow, to what was inside the box? What *was* inside the box? What would Brian give her that was so big? So heavy? Leona grabbed one of the legs of the immaculately tied bow and tugged on it. It came undone with delightful ease. The dusky pink paper tore away with satisfying rips. But the gift did not reveal itself immediately, for beneath the wrapping paper was a plain brown cardboard box.

'It's still quite returnable,' Cameron pointed out. 'Only the wrapping paper is missing. You don't have to go on, you know.'

Leona knew he was right, but by now she was too far gone. She hurried to open the flaps of the cardboard box with inquisitive fingers. And inside the box was . . . another box. But upon that box was a picture of a stand mixer. A Smeg stand mixer, decorated in bright, primary colours by Dolce & Gabbana.

A kitchen appliance.

For her sixty-fifth birthday, Brian had bought her a stand mixer, with rosettes, daisies and curling flourishes rioting all over its red background in yellow, blue and aqua.

Who bought their lover a kitchen appliance? And, further, if one *was* to buy one's lover a kitchen appliance, why this dreadful thing? Her kitchen was elegantly fitted out in brushed stainless steel and various shades and textures of black. It wasn't as if Brian had never been there. He had to know the mixer would stand out like dog's balls. And, while Leona was obviously capable of preparing food, she doubted Brian had ever seen her put together anything beyond a platter with, say, a wedge of blue cheese, seedy crackers, slivers of prosciutto and a cluster of muscatels. Although this would have made her poor mother clutch at her pearls up in heaven, Leona hadn't – in her adult life – baked so much as a single scone.

Leona, perplexed, picked up the card and read the inscription aloud. 'So much to look forward to?'

On the far side of the coffee table, his fingers steepled beneath his chin, her former psychologist looked on with a slightly pained expression.

'What does he think I'm going to do, Cameron? Make him bloody *cupcakes*?'

— PART TWO —

Sunday

'Come over in the morning.' That's what Saski had said. 'Come over in the morning and we'll take a look at the figures together.'

Now, it was the morning. Definitely the morning. There could be no argument about that. But Marnie was aware that Saski would have been using the word 'morning' in the way it was defined on the weekends by normal people. People with actual lives, who spent their Saturday nights eating at groovy little Japanese restaurants, lounging at rooftop cinemas, or quaffing sangria at neighbourhood barbecues. Not sitting up late on a foldaway bed with a laptop computer, desperately searching the internet for the clues to the unknowable sum that would need to be raised in order to take possession of an old shopfront at the Alexandria Park end of Rathbone Street.

Obviously eight o'clock would have been too early to land herself on Saski and Mo, but now it was just past nine, and Marnie – who'd been sitting in her parked car outside their inner-city terrace for over half an hour – felt sure she had already exercised quite a bit of patience. Plus, she came bearing pastries. From Rafaello's. Who could be pissed at her?

Mo opened the door after Marnie's third spate of knocking. Her long freckled legs were bare, her dark hair tousled with sleep, and her baggy T-shirt blared the slogan, 'I can explain it to you, but I can't understand it for you'.

'Really?' Mo said. Her voice was low and flat, with undertones of growl.

Marnie winced. 'Too early?'

'Saski said you had your knickers in a twist.'

Marnie held out the box of pastries in entreaty.

'Hm.' She was a sucker for a fresh custard Danish. 'All I can say is that it's lucky you make good coffee. Go on through. She'll be down in a minute.'

Marnie and Saski's friendship had been born from the cacao bean. Back when Marnie was running her coffee van, and Saski was a young accountant trying to drum up business, Saski – wearing Carmen Miranda-esque fruit-print overalls, and with artfully messy platinum hair wrapped in a bandana – had leaned on Geraldine's retro linoleum countertop and flourished a business card. This had been just before Easter, so Marnie had been serving coffee wearing a pair of fluffy rabbit ears.

'I want to do the figures for businesses I like,' Saski had announced. From there it was a short hop to nicknames. Peach and Bunny. And to holding business meetings, with shandies and salt-and-vinegar chips, at the Strumpet and Pickle. Marnie had been there on the other end of the phone to hear every detail of Saski's early dates with Mo and had been there to help unpack the removalists' van the day Saski and Mo, and Gershwin the cat, had moved in together, to this very house.

In the narrow galley kitchen, Marnie bent to pat the ageing tabby-cat before firing up the coffee machine like the pro she was. She loved this room, with its hanging plants and earthenware beakers filled with the neighbourhood flowers that Saski inveterately picked as she strolled the streets. The stove, the sink, the coffee machine, the utensils – all clean but clearly well used. When Marnie was here, she had the feeling of being in a real, proper home.

Soon the pastries were on a plate and three coffees, topped with perfectly symmetrical milk-froth hearts, were set out on the bench – strong as it came for Marnie and Mo, baby-strength for Saski. Alongside them was Marnie's laptop, with a slew of spreadsheets open on its screen.

'Beware the giant Peach,' Saski said, coming down the stairs, looking every inch of the seven months' pregnant she was.

'Whoa!' Marnie said. 'It hasn't been *that* long since I saw you. You have seriously popped out!'

When they hugged each other, Marnie felt the surprising firmness of that belly. And there, all of a sudden, scuttling around in Marnie's pre-frontal cortex, was another one of those thoughts. The kind that Marnie knew were nothing more than a trick of evolutionary biology: the kind that needed to be chased out of her brain-space with a large and uncompromising broom.

When Marnie had first learned that Saski was pregnant, it had taken a lot of restraint not to throw herself to the ground and weep. She was no slouch with figures herself, but Saski was so much more than just a regular accountant. Having her on Team Wish & Co had meant Marnie could delegate the lion's share of the financials and concentrate instead on other aspects of her business. A full year of Saski on maternity leave? It was going to be a nightmare. And no, there wasn't anybody else who could just step in. There wasn't anybody else who knew Marnie's business like Saski did, nobody who'd been there – from the start – right alongside Marnie, the way Saski had been. There just wasn't anybody else like Saski, full stop.

Saski, the roots of her perennially scruffy mop of hair showing a good inch and a half of her natural mid-brown for the first time Marnie could remember, sat at the bench and took a cherry Danish. Through her first mouthful, she said, 'So, tell me.'

Marnie didn't need to be asked twice. In a rapid spill, she went through the whole thing, starting with the call from her uncle's PA and her meeting with the real estate agent at the old Fairchild & Sons shop. She was up to the part about how she'd spent the last two nights scouring the internet, researching property prices in Alexandria Park, when Mo came down the stairs, fully dressed this time. She pottered about in the kitchen, putting away dishes and watering plants, but Marnie could tell she was listening in. Mo was a scientist, not an accountant, but Marnie was always glad to have her capacious brain applied to a problem.

'So, the shop. What's it like inside?' Saski asked.

'It's divine,' Marnie said. 'A lot bigger than I remembered. There's a whole other room out the back that I'm not sure I've ever been in before. You could use it for storage, or – you'd like this – maybe even rent it out to another little business? I ran some figures on that, see here? Or, I know, I could pop some hot-desks in there for a little co-operative workspace? Maybe four desks? Peach, it's perfect. I can just imagine how it's going to look once I've —'

'Okay, okay, but what kind of condition is it in *now*?' Saski asked.

Marnie made a *más o menos* gesture with her hand. 'The fire damage in the middle section is worse than I thought. You can't even go upstairs – the staircase is just . . . gone. But, you know, maybe that will keep the price down?'

Saski frowned. 'Possibly. But on the other hand, you're going to have to borrow more for the renovation.'

'There's only going to be a limited pool of buyers. Because of the heritage listing,' Marnie said, hopefully.

'Sure,' Saski said, 'but there are a lot of intangibles here. The location is exceptional. And Fairchild and Sons is an Alexandria Park landmark. Someone who really wants it will be willing to pay.'

Marnie felt a stab of wanting, fierce enough to bring on a wave of panic. 'There's nobody in the world who wants it more than I do.'

'I know, Bunny,' Saski said. 'But there are people in the world who have more money than you. A lot more. What's the sale strategy?'

'Auction, of course.'

'Shit. And I don't suppose they're going to take offers beforehand?'

Marnie let out a crestfallen sigh. 'The agent said there was nothing he could do to stop me putting in an offer, but that his client – aka my uncle – was convinced he'd get the best possible price at auction.'

'So, when is it?' Saski asked.

'Not until November. The agent said they're going to stretch out the advertising period. Allowing time for interest to build, I suppose. Peach, am I going to be able to do it? Please tell me I am. Please?'

'Well, you've got an impressive savings record on your side. You can liquidate your shares pretty quickly if you need to, and your figures have been on the up, especially from the gift-buying sector of the business. All of that is positive too. But we're talking commercial real estate, here. Within spitting distance of Alexandria Park. We don't know who could turn up at this auction, nor do we know what kind of price they'd be prepared to go to.'

Marnie loved it when her friend began to deploy the pronoun 'we'. It made her feel so much less alone. 'But we can work out what we can borrow, right? We can work out our very, very, very top price?'

'Y-e-es, but what that figure is will depend on who we ask. We're not even going to bother with the banks – they're too conservative for this. We're going to want to go to a broker. Maybe the one who did your last loan. There are a couple of others who are good too. But even the brokers are twitchy these days. They're going to want to see your last few tax returns, obviously, but they're also going to want to see this year's figures. As recent as last month's. They're going to turn you upside down and shake out every last bit of proof you've got that you're good for the repayments. There are firms that are willing to take on more risk, but they charge higher interest on the repayments, so we don't want to go down that track.'

'I don't care what I have to go without.'

'Come on, Bunny. Think with your head. The amount you can convince someone to lend you is only part of the equation. You don't want to push yourself to the wall. You have to think about your actual life, and what you want it to be like.'

Now Mo piped up. Coffee cup in hand, she said, 'Seems to me what you two can do is come up with a figure. Which is the absolute most Marnie can pay back per month, based on the current state of play.'

'Okay,' Marnie agreed, cautiously. 'But can we be . . . optimistic? Business is good. It's only going to get better. I'm prepared to give it everything I've got.'

Mo took a bite of her custard Danish and gave Marnie a serious look. 'You work harder than anyone in the known universe. We all know that. And you're frugal. But I see it. Saski deals with it all the time. Small businesses are crushed by debt every day of the week. You don't want that. It's ugly.'

Marnie let out another sigh. Mo, as usual, about almost everything, was right.

'You ready?' Saski asked, and literally rolled up her sleeves.

For the next couple of hours, Marnie and Saski swam in figures. At every opportunity, Marnie cut her projected expenditure to the bare bones. But each time she did so, Saski patiently returned the flesh. She was a stickler for built-in buffers. To allow, as she always said, for a degree of chaos. They argued over a few points, but Saski won almost every battle. She was just so bloody sensible. When they were done, and a figure was reached, Saski wrote it down on a bright orange sticky note and circled it firmly.

'This is your monthly limit,' Saski said. 'We can talk about it again if things look up. Or down. But for now, this is it. So, my job over the next fortnight or so is to pull together all your data and scope out the loan situation.'

Marnie leaned over and kissed her friend on the cheek. 'You're a legend.'

'Yes, yes. What would you do without me, et cetera, et cetera. Flattery isn't going to change the fact that I'll be looking for the most amount of money we can get, but where the repayments won't exceed this figure. Here.'

Saski waved the orange sticky note at Marnie until she took it. Marnie didn't like it. It was clear and precise. No elasticity, no wriggle room. 'Thanks, Peach.'

'I'd say "anytime", but God knows what hour you'd get me up.'

At the front door, Marnie hugged her friend goodbye.

Saski said, 'Hey, a couple of Mo's work friends are coming over for dinner tonight. She's doing pulled pork tacos. Your fave.'

It was tempting.

'Mo's got a new lab assistant, by the way. His name's Jack. And she doesn't hate him, so you know he's got to be all right. Very smart. Very nice. Very single. He's coming tonight.'

That was also slightly tempting. Though, to be honest, not as much as the tacos.

'I love you,' Marnie said, 'but I've got a wrapping workshop this afternoon. Then, I need to do a bit of . . . you know.'

'Client stalking?'

'Yep.' It was the way Marnie usually spent Sunday evenings: trawling around social media keeping tabs on her portfolios, being both horrified by and grateful for how lax most people's privacy settings were.

Saski made a sad face. 'All work, no play, Bunny.'

Marnie thought. Dinner, or work? Work, or dinner? When faced with a choice, where either one was less than ideal, there was – Marnie believed – always a third possibility lurking somewhere in between. 'How about I drop in after dinner? I could pop in for dessert and a drink? What about that?'

Saski crossed her arms over the top of her ballooning belly and narrowed her eyes meaningfully at her friend.

'What?' Marnie asked.

'I'm worried.'

Marnie was perplexed. 'Why?'

'About you and this shop. What if it just doesn't work out? It could turn out to be out of your league, honey, and I'm worried about how you're going to be if that happens.'

'Pessimist,' Marnie said, with a smile.

'No, realist,' Saski said, without.

'Peach, it has to be possible. It just has to be. There's always a way.' The words sounded as true coming out of her own mouth as they had so often done coming out of her grandfather's. 'I just have to find it. That's all.'

Just before her guests arrived, Suzanne Charlesworth – in a new dress that did as much for her figure as any garment could be expected to do, her hair still puffed up from the blow-drier – stood in the formal dining room and sighed. She had always loved this little slice of time. Ever since she had become adept enough, organised enough, to make it happen, she had savoured this held-breath moment, when everything was ready, everything was done, everything was perfect.

Twelve cut-crystal glasses marched down the table in perfect proximity to twelve gleaming sets of silver cutlery, twelve Royal Doulton side plates, twelve pressed linen napkins and twelve printed place cards. Seating arrangements were not left to chance. Not at one of Suzanne Charlesworth's parties. Posies of roses and daphne from her own garden were stationed down the centre of the table. In low crystal bowls. Because floral arrangements were never high enough to impede conversation. Not at Suzanne Charlesworth's table.

Sentinel to the door that led through to the kitchen were a pair of matching sideboards. Atop one of them was a gingerbread house so beautiful that surely every child in the world would want to nibble its iced windowsills. Next to it was a space where the croquembouche, whose staggering dimensions were currently taking up one of the spare fridges in the larder, would eventually be placed. On the other sideboard were two gifts – Suzanne's to Brian, his to her.

The gift she had bought for him was smaller, by far. Wrapped in olive-green paper and tied with a tartan bow, it was a fly-fishing reel. Fishing was still a relatively new interest for Brian, but Suzanne was all in favour of hobbies that kept him out of the office on weekends. At the fishing store, Suzanne had been about to buy a mid-range reel for Brian – after all, he wasn't *that* serious about fishing – but then a chatty young salesman had talked her into a more expensive model by giving her a well-targeted spiel about how this particular reel was a 'classic', the sort of thing a fly-fisher would pass on to children and grandchildren.

Suzanne had no idea whether or not the reel would improve Brian's fortunes at the lakes. The last time he'd gone on a trout-fishing expedition, he'd brought home two lovely little rainbow trout for her to cook. It wasn't until the day after she'd served them, simply and delicately oven-baked with lemon and dill, that she'd stumbled upon the white paper wrapping, complete with the fishmonger's price sticker, in the wheelie bin. She'd stood there in her slippers and giggled. Poor Brian, not wanting to admit that he hadn't caught a thing. Men! Honestly.

Suzanne ran a hand over the thick handmade paper in which Brian's gift to her had been wrapped. Exceptionally wrapped, she noticed. Although, she'd never have chosen black paper herself. And, if she had, she'd certainly not have added a black ribbon. So gloomy!

The box was too big for jewellery, thank heavens. There had been years, *years*, during which Brian had bought her necklaces and bracelets and rings to mark their special occasions. But, after being seen to wear them once or twice, Suzanne would put them away in the dressing-table drawer to live out their inanimate lives, largely forgotten. She hated him wasting money that way, because if Brian had been paying attention, he'd have known she was happy with nothing more than her plain gold wedding band, and the gold chain with the delicate 'S' pendant that her parents had given her for her twenty-first birthday.

In the last few years, though, Brian had apparently had some kind of epiphany so far as gifts went. Instead of the jewellery and perfume he once defaulted to, he'd started giving Suzanne things she really loved. Like soft, possum-merino wraps in colours that toned remarkably well with her wardrobe, weekends at fashionable farm-to-plate cooking schools, and – best of all – the expensive, beautiful kitchen appliances that she could never quite manage to justify buying for herself.

For this anniversary, she'd been quietly hoping for the Smeg stand mixer, the Dolce & Gabbana one that would have completed her collection. But she already knew she was out of luck, for when she'd given the box an experimental nudge, she'd discovered it was too light to contain the mixer. What *was* in there? What *had* he come up with this time?

Well, Suzanne thought – as the doorbell sounded – she would find out soon enough.

Although Luke had spent half the morning cleaning the ute, tossing out all the takeaway coffee cups, brushing the woodchips off the upholstery, vacuuming the sawdust from the carpet, his grandmother sat in the passenger seat with her feet primly together in low-heeled court shoes, her purse clasped tightly on her lap, as if she was trying not to touch any part of the car or allow any part of it to touch her.

Slowly, Luke drove along the western flank of Alexandria Park, giving his grandmother time to enjoy the sight – beyond the park's wrought-iron fence – of the tulips that were blooming around the trunks of the largest trees. At length, he turned a corner into the street upon which his mum and dad lived. On either side of Austinmer Street were substantial houses – brick mansions with sandstone detailing at their windows and balconies, Federation weatherboards in colour schemes that offered a slight twist on the classics. In a nature strip that ran down the centre of the street, a procession of lovely old plane trees shook out the bright green folds of their springtime leaves.

'Well, who'd have thought,' Jocelyn announced.

'Thought what?'

'That they'd make it this far!'

'Who? Mum and Dad?'

'Forty years,' she said, shaking her head. 'I'm amazed, to be honest.' Her tone was conspiratorial. As if this were not the sort of thing she would normally say. Or, at least, not the sort of thing she would say to just anybody.

At eighty-eight Jocelyn Wright was – as her late husband would have said – as sharp as sixteen tacks, but Luke wasn't the only one to notice that her verbal filters weren't quite what they used to be. His mum had picked up on it too. Once the perfect lady, who would no more utter a word out of place than leave the house with a wrinkle in her pantyhose, Jocelyn was now prone to rude comments, which she would deliver – in supermarket queues, at the hair salon – in a clearly audible stage whisper.

'Even before they were married, I could tell,' Jocelyn went on. 'I knew. I knew the way a woman knows. Your father was always charming, of course. But devious with it.'

Luke let out a short laugh. But beneath his amusement at his grandmother's turn of phrase, he felt a slight sting. He remembered all too well that time when his childhood world – which had always seemed so stable – had revealed itself to be built on quicksand. Slammed doors, his mother crying, the invisible but unmistakable sense of wrongness in the house. He couldn't remember how he'd found out the details, but somehow he'd become aware of the existence of somebody called Leona Quick, whom his twelve-year-old self had conflated with the cartoon figure of Cruella de Vil. Luke gripped the steering wheel tighter as the ute rolled past large, beautiful house after beautiful, large house.

'Thank heavens you're not like that. I mean, you were a complete ratbag there for a while. But you did it all out in the open. Never one to be sneaky, not even when you were a tiny thing. What you see is what you get. That's you. That's what I've always loved about you, darling. And you're loving. Like your mother. Even if you're the living spit of Brian to look at, you're all Wright where it counts.' She patted herself on the chest to emphasise the point, rattling her pearls. 'Honourable.'

Luke's smile disappeared altogether. The truth was that, as a teenager, he *had* been sneaky. But the whole point of sneakiness was that nobody was supposed to know about it. Grandparents least of all. What really niggled him, though, was that word. *Honourable.* Even a week ago, he'd have brushed the compliment away as unearned but harmless, nothing more than the biased sentiment of a grandmother who loved him. But today? Today it irritated him. And hurt. Like a splinter under his thumbnail.

Luke parked the ute carefully in the driveway of his mum and dad's house, edging over to the side to give his grandmother plenty of room to step out onto the paving. He glanced up at the house – a tall, gabled weatherboard painted cream with deep green detailing. There, at the second storey, was the exact window he'd climbed out of – as a sixteen-year-old – on the night he'd met Gillian Yip. Just behind the ute was the stretch of street where his friends had waited for him in an idling Jeep that not one of them had a licence to drive.

Today was going to be hard. He'd stayed away from his mother this week, kept their phone conversations short and to the point. Because he knew that she'd try to prise him open the minute she worked out he was troubled and keeping something from her. And because, for once, he found himself almost wanting to be prised open. It would be a relief to tell his mother that she had another grandchild – to tell her about the text message, and what had happened on Friday at the cafe. If anybody could help him work out what to do about Ivy, it would be his mum. Or, at the very least, she'd sit on the other side of the kitchen bench, supplying muffins and cups of coffee, until he'd worked it out for himself.

But today wasn't the day for a disclosure as big as Ivy. Today was about his mum and his dad. It was a day for Luke himself to shake his father's hand and hug his mother and do his best to pretend that he truly thought their marriage was something to celebrate. He hoped, but doubted, that his father knew just how lucky he was.

'I imagine,' Jocelyn said, and unbuckled her seatbelt, holding it away from her pink twinset as it retracted, 'that lunch will be spectacular.'

'Yep,' Luke agreed.

'There will be speeches, I suppose,' she said.

'Yep,' Luke said.

'Elbow me if I nod off, won't you, darling?'

'Yep.'

'Are you all right, Luke?'

'Yep,' he said, and got out of the car to open the door for his grandmother and usher her inside for lunch.

'Congratulations, mate.' Brian's brother-in-law, Clancy – husband to Brian's younger sister, Maeve – grasped his hand and pumped it. 'Forty years married, eh? If it was a job, you'd be onto your second lot of long service leave by now!'

'Yeah.' Brian chuckled.

'So, what are you playing off these days?' Clancy asked, turning the conversation to the safe topic of golf.

'Ah, knocked the handicap down to eight,' Brian said, trying to sound casual about it.

'Maaate,' Clancy said, impressed.

Brian was capable of talking golf with Clancy in the same way that dolphins slept – using only one half of their brains at a time. So while Clancy described a course he'd recently played while on holidays, Brian surveyed the room.

Wait staff moved between the guests with a tray of glasses, one of them having to move out of the way smartly to avoid being bowled over by the human tumbleweed that was Brian's four-year-old granddaughter, Leila. Leila's big brother, six-year-old Benji, meanwhile, sat pensively on Suzanne's lap, gazing adoringly at his grandmother in a way that reminded Brian of Luke.

'. . . lucky I went for the five-wood rather than one of the irons . . .' Clancy was saying, reliving an approach shot complete with arching hand movements.

Luke. Where was Luke? Brian scanned the room, and found his son in conversation by the bay window, beer in hand and shirtsleeves rolled as if he was even proud of those tradesman's arms of his. For the life of him, Brian didn't know why the fool boy had let that German girl go. Annalena had been a beauty. Fit, vigorous, smart. Just the sort of woman to give Luke's life the direction it lacked. As if feeling his father's eyes on him, Luke glanced in Brian's direction. Brian produced what he hoped was a cheerful grin, but all he saw on Luke's face was an infuriating but blamelessly neutral expression – a look that Brian could never help feeling was the adult version of the dumb insolence Luke had practised to perfection in his teens.

Clancy was still talking golf, but Brian was thinking about being a parent, and how it hadn't turned out to be anything like he'd imagined. Even with Caroline, the success story, he didn't feel the way he'd expected to. Where Luke had been sullen and withdrawn, their firstborn had specialised in a kind of light-hearted pragmatism that almost equally infuriated Brian. Faced with his anger, she would simply laugh. Even now, and even after he had given her and Arjun so much, forking out a mint for their wedding, investing heavily in the expansion of their optometry business, she didn't . . . didn't what? Take him seriously? He didn't feel he had . . . what? Leverage? Her respect? It wasn't that she was disrespectful. It was just that Brian had thought there would be *more*, somehow.

Brian was used to feeling successful. This beautiful house, this elegant room, the food that was about to appear on the fine china plates in the other room. His wife . . . *would you just look at her?* That hair. The way it curled, just so, under her chin. The subtle floral wrap dress she was wearing – he was sure he'd never seen it before – that clung to her ample curves. His wife of four decades. His soft, forgiving, generous, beautiful wife. Yes, Brian was a successful man. A wealthy man, forty years married. But when Brian thought about his children, he felt no satisfaction, only a needling suspicion that as a father, he was an also-ran. At best.

That was one thing about Leona. She never made him feel like a loser. How could he be a loser when someone as ferociously smart as Leona Quick had fallen for him? Not just once, either, but three times over. The first time around, they'd been sparring partners, enjoying their verbal stoushes almost as much as the rapprochements that followed. The second time, it had made him feel good to be her rock, a strong and steady presence during the early days of her widowhood. And this time? In his most introspective moments, Brian knew that it had something to do with the greying of his hair, and the way he sometimes felt creaky and sore after a perfectly ordinary round of golf. When he was with Leona it was easier to forget that he was pushing seventy; when he was with Leona, he didn't think about being a father at all, let alone being an ordinary one.

Brian put a hand on his brother-in-law's arm before Clancy could launch into a full recap of his adventures getting out of a sand-trap. 'Excuse me, will you, mate?'

'Yeah, of course,' Clancy said, half raising his glass of rosé. 'This is a nice drop, by the way.'

Brian went through the hall and into the downstairs bathroom. He locked the door behind him and took in the crisp lemon-lime scent of whatever cleaning product it was that had left the tiles so utterly spotless. On the closed seat of the toilet, he sat and breathed until he felt better. And yet, he still needed a little something. He wondered where Leona would be today. He wondered if Leona had liked what he'd given her for her birthday. He wondered what he *had* given her for her birthday.

Of course, Marnie Fairchild would have kept him informed, in one of those email updates she sent out ahead of significant dates. But Brian never looked at those. What was the point of outsourcing things if you were only going to micromanage them anyway? He trusted Marnie to know what she was doing. In the five years she'd been on his books, she'd come through every single time. Heaven help him if she ever changed her line of work, because by now he'd developed quite the reputation as a giver of excellent gifts, and he hadn't the first clue how he'd maintain it without her.

Brian pulled his mobile out of his back pocket and shuffled it from hand to hand, as if it were hot. Just a little something. That was all he needed. A tiny pick-me-up. He swiped open the Scrabble app. It wasn't the same as calling her.

When the quail had been reduced to scatters of tiny bones, the plates were whisked away by the wait staff. Wine glasses disappeared, too, to be swiftly replaced by champagne flutes. While bubbles were poured for the adults and pink lemonade for the children, the croquembouche, set upon a silver platter, was carried through into the dining room. There were *ooohs* and *aaaahs* and applause as the towering dessert was placed upon the sideboard next to the gingerbread house.

Tink, tink, came the sound of Brian's dessert fork against his champagne flute, and a hush fell gradually, rippling down the length of the table. It was not until the quiet was almost complete that Jocelyn leaned towards Luke.

'Don't let me snore, will you, love?' she whispered, over-loudly.

'I got you, Gran.'

Brian, on his feet now, cleared his throat. 'This time of day, forty years ago, I was standing at the altar of St Brigid's Church. Waiting.' He turned to his old friend, Phil Pickett, sitting halfway down the table next to his wife, Wendy. 'You remember, mate – you were there with me. How bad was our get-up?'

The short answer was: very. The two men had worn pale blue jackets with shiny lapels made from the same fabric as their cummerbunds. As children, Luke and Caroline had loved looking at, laughing at, the pictures. Luke remembered the one of his mother and father at the church's arched doorway, which they'd kept framed in the living room. He'd found it one Sunday morning the year he turned twelve, lying on the hearth with the glass cracked. It occurred to him, now, that even when the days of slammed doors and tears had passed into memory, the photograph never had been put back on display.

'But there I was,' Brian continued, 'bad suit and all, waiting for Suzanne to walk up that aisle. There are few men alive who can definitively claim to have found and married their Miss Right. But I'm one of those few, lucky men. The first time I saw Suzanne Wright, I thought to myself, not a word of a lie, I'm going to marry that girl – be beggared if anybody else is going to have her!'

Brian waited for something. Possibly for a laugh that never came. He cleared his throat.

'Over the years, I've watched a lot of my friends' marriages go by the wayside. Not a lot of couples make it, these days, to a milestone like this one. Forty years. I know this is going to be unpopular with my kids – and Caroline, here's fair warning that you should stick your fingers in your ears for a minute – but I can't help thinking that one of the things we did right was to decide on an old-fashioned kind of marriage. Forty years ago, we made the decision that I'd take on the public domain, and Suzanne would be in charge of the home front. Ronald Reagan once said this: "There is no greater happiness for a man than approaching a door at the end of a day knowing someone on the other side of that door is waiting for the sound of his footsteps." And, you know, that's how it's been for me for four decades. For forty years, I've always had a place to come home to where it's warm, and there's good food on the table – just look at this meal today, would you? – and where I've felt loved.'

Caroline caught Luke's eye and made the world's tiniest eye-roll – the kind only detectable between siblings who'd been silently communicating with each other across dining tables all their lives. Luke knew she was biting her tongue to stop herself from calling out his sexist stereotypes.

'I'm a long way from perfect,' Brian said, 'but this beautiful woman has coped, year in, year out, with all of my faults and flaws. Come up here, Suze.'

He held his arm out for her. Bashful and pleased, Suzanne stood and made her way from where she sat at the far end of the table from him. She carried with her a small olive-green parcel, tied with a tartan ribbon.

'A toast,' Brian announced, champagne flute held aloft, 'to my beautiful wife.'

There was an expensive chorus of crystal chinking against crystal, and a murmured cacophony of 'To Suzanne', 'To Mum', 'To Nanna'.

'Anything you want to say, love?'

She seemed to deliberate for a moment, then to decide. She tucked a smooth lock of hair behind her ear.

'It isn't really my thing, speaking like this. But I would like to thank you all for coming to celebrate with us today, and also to say . . . we've been blessed. Yes, we are fortunate to live in this beautiful house, in this lovely part of town, to have nice things. But the true blessing, for me, is in the people around this table and the relationships we all have. This is our wealth: our children, our beautiful grandchildren.' She blew kisses to Benji and Leila. 'Mum. Our siblings. Our dearest, oldest friends. Wendy, Phil, thanks for coming such a distance. Thank you, all of you, for sharing this moment with us. And Brian. Darling, thank you. For this beautiful family we've made. I literally could not have done it without you.'

Wife and husband kissed each other then, and Luke – despite himself – felt a small, movie-theatre wave of emotion rise and crest in his chest.

Suzanne handed her gift to Brian. There was nothing ceremonious about the way he opened it, pulling the ribbon off sideways and tearing at the paper. Luke darted another look across the table at Caroline, who returned it with a knowing grin. How many times had they seen a scenario like this one play out? Their mother's gift to their father would doubtless be something practical. Something serviceable and of good quality, but not decadent. Whatever it was beneath that olive-green paper, it would – Luke knew – be perfectly nice. Their father's gift to their mother, on the other hand, would always be something unmistakably top-shelf.

Luke watched as his father registered the gift, and saw the way he visibly organised his face, pushing away some kind of reaction that Luke couldn't entirely read, but quickly replacing it with one of theatrical surprise.

'A . . . fishing reel!' Brian exclaimed.

Luke was still getting used to the idea of his father as a fisherman. He struggled to imagine him standing knee-deep in a rushing river. For a man as notoriously demanding and impatient as Brian Charlesworth, fly-fishing seemed a particularly odd pastime.

'I hope it brings you luck,' Suzanne said.

Brian smiled at her. 'I already have the best catch.'

'Charmer,' Suzanne accused.

'Open yours, Nanna!' called out little Leila, and as Suzanne walked back down to her end of the table, Maeve transferred the large, wrapped gift from the sideboard to Suzanne's place.

'Card first,' insisted Benji, who was kneeling on Suzanne's seat, eyes wide with the prospect of such a large gift about to be opened.

'Thank you, Benji. Nice manners,' Suzanne said, and as she drew the card out of its envelope, Luke recognised the image on the front as a Georgia O'Keeffe rose. He could never understand how someone as tasteless as his father managed to choose such perfect greeting cards. It was just the sort of card Luke himself would have picked out for his mother. But then, he had taste. Whereas Brian had been responsible for bringing into the house the awful painting of gum trees that took up most of the dining room wall.

Suzanne removed the textured wrapping carefully, as if the black paper was precious.

'Rip it, Nanna!' Leila encouraged, but Benji was content to stand beside his grandmother, to help her prise the paper away without damage. At last, all the joins were undone and upon the table stood a plain, cardboard box. Suzanne unfolded its flaps and lifted out a bag of soft-looking, brown leather. It was what might once have been called a sausage bag, but a very elegant variety. Luke caught sight of the tag, which named the bag 'The Weekender'.

'Oh,' said a surprised Suzanne. 'Am I about to start coming along with you on your fishing jaunts?'

Luke glanced at his father, whose confident expression now looked a little too determinedly held for comfort. The handles of the bag were tied together with ribbon, attached to which was a luggage tag printed with the words 'OPEN ME'.

'Oooohhh,' Suzanne said.

The sound of the zip woke Luke's grandmother from her nodding slumber.

'I wasn't —' Jocelyn protested, but when Luke put a gentle hand on her arm, she fell silent.

Now every single person at the table, including Jocelyn, was watching. Little Leila was bouncing up and down on her chair, with her small hands clasped together, as Suzanne drew out of the bag a rectangular parcel wrapped in white tissue paper. The tissue came away easily to reveal something made from what appeared to be ivory-coloured silk.

'Goodness,' Suzanne said, clearly delighted if a little bashful, 'I feel like this might be a bit private!'

'Geez, Brian,' Clancy said, rubbing his jaw. 'Talk about setting the bar high. Have a heart for the rest of us poor bastards, will you?'

The confident expression on Brian's face was all but gone now, replaced instead with nervousness. Luke peered at the ivory silk in his mother's hands. Mercifully, there was no lace to be seen. But there was a size tag, nestled in the neckline of the garment. Luke didn't consider himself any kind of expert on the size and shape of women, but he knew enough to know that his mother was no XS.

'Mum,' he said. He felt an inexplicable sense of dread. He wanted her to stop, to put the thing – whatever it was – back in the bag.

'Yes, love?'

He shook his head, said nothing. Because what exactly could he say in this moment? Briefly, he considered doing something ridiculous like dashing up to his mother and snatching the silk thing out of her hands, racing off with it, out into the backyard, like an ill-trained Labrador puppy. But then his mother shook out the folds of the garment to reveal that it was a dressing robe, ankle-length by the look of it, with a tie at its impossibly narrow waist. The smile on his mother's face froze into a rictus.

'Mum?' asked Caroline.

Had she seen the size tag? Luke wondered. She must have done. But then, he realised – when she let the robe drop to the table – that there was more. The size tag was only the half of it, because on the pocket was a monogram. Quite large. Two initials embroidered in burgundy thread, the font a swirling cursive. Two very recognisable initials.

LQ

Luke felt his heart drop down through his gut. LQ, as in LQ for Leona Quick. Leona Quick, high court judge. LQ – the woman for whom Brian had endangered his marriage twenty years earlier. But the affair was supposed to have ended. His father was supposed to have stopped seeing her. Twenty years ago. Was it possible? That he'd never ended it after all? That it had been going on all this time? From the way his mother was standing, holding the table's edge with both hands, squinting hard against tears, he gathered she was asking herself the same questions. He wanted to go to her, to put his arms around her, hold her tight enough to distract her from the pain that was showing on her face.

'Darling, does that say LQ?' Jocelyn asked Luke, her whisper clearly audible in the awkward silence. 'I'm sure it does. Heavens above. What a stuff-up!'

'Shhh, Gran.'

'I told you before. Didn't I? Didn't I say? I said your father never could keep it in his pants.'

'Gran. Shhh.'

Brian was ashen-faced. Clancy had leaned back in his chair as if reeling away from this spectacle, his eyes seeming to have doubled in size. Maeve, his wife, had a hand over her mouth. Both Wendy and Phil Pickett were looking down at the blank spots on the table where their dinner plates, at a previous and much more comprehensible moment in time, had been located.

Arjun, baffled, looked from Caroline to Luke and back again, searching for an explanation, or at least a clue. Little Leila was mystified. 'Is Nanna crying?' she bellowed across the table to her mother. 'Mummy, why is Nanna crying?'

For his part, Benji was taking great handfuls of Suzanne's skirts in his fists as his own eyes filled with tears. Luke could see that the little boy didn't know what was wrong, only that something was. Very wrong.

'Go to Mummy, darling,' Suzanne said. Patiently, she unhooked Benji's fingers, and guided him to where Caroline was already on her feet, seeming unsure whether to hold her arms out to her son or her mother.

'Suzanne,' Brian said. 'There's been a mistake.'

Luke heard a sob catch in his mother's throat.

'It wasn't me. I didn't . . . there's been a mistake. Suzanne, I haven't —'

Inexplicably, Suzanne burst out, 'Those bloody trout! And I laughed. *Laughed.*'

Brian started down the length of the table towards his wife.

'Don't you dare think you're going to *touch* me,' Suzanne said, but Brian didn't so much as pause.

'Dad, no,' Caroline said. She and Luke exchanged a hurried glance that told Luke what he had to do. He leaped out of his chair to block his father's way. They were of a size, he and his father. Equal height, equal breadth, equal muscle. But Brian, red-faced and swollen with anger, seemed to loom larger.

'Get out of my way,' Brian said.

'I think you should just leave her —'

'Get. Out. Of my way.'

'No, Dad. Just calm —'

His father barked, 'I want to talk to my wife. Move!'

Brian made as if to push past, but Luke held him by the shoulders. 'Don't embarrass yourself any more than you already have, Dad. Please. The kids, hey?'

Luke saw some of the fight go out of his father's face, felt his shoulders slacken.

Because Luke's back was turned to his mother, he didn't see her leave the room. Instead, he heard a noise come from her, wordless, almost animal. A sound of pain. And then a crash. A clatter of metal on timber boards. And a great, soft *whump*. And then the noise of the kitchen door opening and closing.

Just before he looked around, Luke understood what he would see. His mother would only have needed to give that silver platter a push. One decent shove as she walked out the door. To send that colossal pile of custard-filled profiteroles flying – spraying shards of toffee and dark chocolate – to the floor.

Luke wished his father would just put his bloody seatbelt on. The ute was complaining, its warning bleeps increasing in frequency, a red light flashing insistently on the dash.

'Turn the car around,' Brian commanded, but Luke kept driving. The railings of Alexandria Park's wrought-iron fence flickered in his peripheral vision. The pain Luke had felt on his mother's behalf was gone. Now that he had a task, that he was occupied, he just felt determined. He was doing what needed to be done – driving his father away from the house.

'Take me back home.'

'Mum doesn't want you there at the moment.' *Or ever again, most probably.*

'I just want to get my car. All right?'

Luke shook his head. 'Nope.'

'I want. My own. Car.'

'You've been drinking, Dad.'

Brian sighed in exasperation. 'I haven't had that much.'

Luke didn't respond.

'I can handle a car! I've been driving since before you were in bloody nappies.'

Then you should know better, Luke thought. In his best placating tone, he said, 'I'll go get your car for you tomorrow. I'll bring it to you. For the time being, you just need to leave Mum alone.'

'Bring my car where? Where the hell are we going, anyway?'

Luke didn't know the answer to that question. All he knew was that they were driving away from the house. He swung the ute into Rathbone Street, turning in the direction of the city. The small suitcase into which Caroline had hastily crammed a few of Brian's essentials slid across the tray-back of the ute.

'I said, where are you taking me?'

'You can come home with me if you want,' Luke offered. 'Or I can drop you at a hotel.'

'I don't want to go to any bloody hotel,' his father said, and Luke supposed there was a message implicit in the fact his first offer hadn't even been acknowledged. 'I want to go home. Turn a-bloody-round!'

Luke took a deep breath and said nothing. His father had to have at least six drinks under his belt. There was no point arguing, or even reiterating.

'Shit,' Brian said, apparently in response to something happening within his own mind. He thumped a fist against the passenger side window. 'What a fuck-up.'

Well, he had that part right. Luke's mind brimmed with questions, but now wasn't the right time to ask them.

'Look, I've got to go back. I've got to talk to her,' Brian said. 'I need to tell her —'

'You need to leave her alone,' Luke said.

'She'll calm down. She'll get over it.'

'I don't know, Dad. You drove the knife in a long way this time.'

'Fuck!'

Probably something of an understatement, Luke thought. Where *was* he going to take his father?

'Do you want to go to the Belvedere?' Luke asked.

'Not there.'

'The Windsor?'

'No. It's gone to shit.'

'Where, then?'

'Home. I just want to go home.'

'It's not an option, Dad. I can take you to Leona's if you want to tell me where she lives.' It was a jab. Luke knew it ought to have been beneath him, but he'd never claimed to be any kind of saint. Seething anger had to seep out somewhere.

'She lives down on the Esplanade,' Brian said, looking fixedly out the window of the ute.

Luke raised his eyebrows. As the crow flies, it wasn't far from where he lived in Bankside – just a couple of kilometres along the river, closer to the city. But the place Luke was renting, with its handy backyard workshop, was located in a quasi-industrial stretch of the waterway; the Esplanade, on the other hand, was serious real estate.

Perhaps because his father had not objected to the idea of being taken to Leona's place, or perhaps because his father had momentarily sounded less drunk, Luke couldn't resist asking a question. 'Just exactly how did you expect Mum to react?'

'What? It was a mistake. It's not like I meant that to happen.'

Luke hadn't been talking about the gift. He'd been talking about the affair, full stop. But he was curious. 'Yeah, actually, how *did* you make a mistake like that?'

'I didn't do it! It wasn't me. It was Marnie bloody Fairchild!'

Luke did not compute. That is, he knew the surname; everyone who'd grown up in Alexandria Park knew it. There had been a handful of Fairchilds at Luke's high school, but not a Marnie. 'Who?'

'She's a gift-buyer.'

'She's a what?'

'A gift-buyer. Buys my gifts for me.'

'Is that even a thing?'

'Yes, it's a bloody thing. She was supposed to get your mother's anniversary present, and LQ's birthday present. But she's stuffed up. Royally. I suppose LQ's got whatever your mum was supposed to get.'

'What was Mum supposed to get?' *A size-L silk dressing gown?* Luke wanted to ask. *With SC embroidered on the pocket? Is there such a thing as a wife-and-bit-on-the-side discount? Second item half price?*

'How the hell would I know? What's the point of employing a gift-buyer if you still have to know everything?'

Luke drew the ute to a standstill at a traffic light. To the sound of the motor idling, he said, 'Hang on . . . this gift-buyer. She buys gifts for you to give to Mum? And to give to Leona?'

Brian ran a hand through already mussed hair. 'Why did it have to be the same date? Leona's birthday. Our anniversary. Murphy's Fucking Law. That's why.' And he went on to describe Murphy in the most colourful of terms.

Luke remained on his own train of thought. 'So, *just* for Mum and Leona?'

'No, not just them,' Brian muttered.

'For how many people, then?'

His father gave a deep sigh. 'For everyone. Yes, including you.'

Luke frowned. 'How long have you been doing this for?'

With deep irritation, Brian said, 'I don't know, Luke.'

The light changed to green, and as Luke accelerated away from the intersection, he realised he knew the answer to his own question. It was about five years ago, because that was when his father's gifts to him had, all of a sudden and quite inexplicably, become both expensive *and* tasteful.

During Luke's teenage years, his friends had always thought it was weird – if fortunate – that his mum and dad bought him separate gifts, even though they were still married and living together. To Luke, though, it had always seemed perfectly understandable. They were different people, after all. Always, and consistently, his mother had given him gifts that were modest, thoughtful and useful. His father, though, had been erratic. Sometimes he'd buy Luke a new bicycle that was almost embarrassingly flashy. Or a brand-name wristwatch that would have been more at home on James Bond than a teenage boy. But then, other times, he'd apparently forget, and instead give Luke cash inside a birthday card with a dorky, generic 'Happy Birthday, Son' message inside. The older Luke got, the rarer the presents became, and the more regular the cash.

Then, about five years ago, his father had started giving him things that he actually liked. Beautifully wrapped gifts, with tasteful cards. Luke would never have described himself as a materialistic person, but he could not deny that these gifts had had an effect on him. It wasn't the things themselves, exactly. It was the time and thought that had gone into their choosing, the little thrill of pleasure that his father knew him well enough to be able to work out what sorts of gifts he would deeply appreciate. It was the impression – no, the *illusion*, Luke thought – that his father knew who he was.

'The whole point of the arrangement,' Brian told him, 'is that I don't have to think about it. I don't have to remember anyone's birthday. I don't have to remember anniversaries. I don't have to remember Valentine's Day. I don't have to remember any of it. It's all just taken care of.'

The words echoed in Luke's ears. *We weren't just something that could be taken care of.* That's what Ivy had said to him in the cafe. *We weren't just something that could be taken care of. We were worth more than your fucking money.* He felt the sting of it all over again.

'Don't tell your mum,' Brian said. 'Please.'

'About the gift-buyer?'

'Please.'

Luke considered.

'Promise me?' Brian pushed.

Luke felt like pushing back, but in truth, there was no need to rub salt into Suzanne's wounds. No need for her to know, as he himself now did, that Brian had been lying to them all. 'I won't.'

Suddenly, Brian – who'd been slumped into the seat – sat forward, tense and alert. 'Pull over.'

'What?'

'I said pull over. I want to get out of the car. Jesus, will you stop the freaking car?'

'What for?'

'Just stop, will you?'

'Why?'

Brian took out his wallet, extracted a fifty-dollar note and threw it on Luke's lap. 'Here! Now, stop.'

Luke kept driving.

'Here, then!' Another fifty dollars. 'Now stop the car.'

'Take your money off my lap,' Luke said, his voice low.

'Then stop the car.'

'Where do you want to go?'

'Jesus. Have it all.' Brian tossed his wallet into Luke's lap. 'And this too.' His mobile phone followed. 'Now I can't go anywhere, can I? I haven't got any money, and it's too far to walk home. I'm a captive. You've got me. I'm your prisoner. So, just pull over.'

Now Luke did as he was asked. The vehicle had only barely stopped when his father reefed open the door. He slammed it shut behind him and strode away up the street in the direction they'd just come, hands in the pockets of his beige slacks. Luke returned the banknotes to his father's wallet, noting the small passport-sized photos his father kept in a plastic-fronted pocket – his mother, his sister, himself. In the side-mirror, he saw his father stop and turn, bang with a fist on the door of what must have been a shop of some sort. What the hell did he think he was doing?

It had been a full house at Wish & Co that afternoon: eight women had gathered around the big table to learn some of Marnie's gift-wrapping secrets.

'My worst ever gift?' one of the women had said. 'Get this . . . a decoupage lazy Susan.'

'A *what?*' another of the women had asked.

'Well, that's pretty much what I thought. I was only thirteen, and my godmother had just given me this *thing*. I had no idea what it was. She was asking me "Do you like it, dear?" and I was thinking, what I am supposed to do with it? *Stand* on it?'

Marnie wasn't sure how it happened that her wrapping workshops so reliably produced stories like this one. They usually emerged at the end of the workshop, when she cleared the table and set out pots of tea and coffee, and a platter holding a rainbow's worth of Rafaello's melt-in-your-mouth macarons. One of the women – and, always, it was women who came to Marnie's workshops – would start it, and then they'd all be off, telling their tales of best and worst gifts ever received.

'You're not going to believe this,' another woman had said. She'd booked the workshop as a bonding experience for herself and her teenage daughter, who'd arrived in a sulk before being incrementally won over by the manifold possibilities of beautiful paper, scissors and tape. 'I was once given a single toothpick.'

'You're right. I don't believe that,' her daughter had said.

'I swear. It's true. You know Auntie June. She'd just been overseas. And when she came around to our place she gave me this toothpick, still wrapped in its little cellophane pouch with the airline logo on it. Like she thought it was actually a souvenir, or something. I had absolutely no idea what to say.'

The stories had rolled on. A Christmas Day, when a grandmother had remembered all her many grandchildren but one. Then, for the forgotten granddaughter, she'd hastily wrapped up some magazines . . . with the puzzles already filled in. The oldest woman in the group told the story of discovering a tiny MADE IN INDIA tag on a woollen scarf that her friend had given her, having claimed to have hand-knitted it herself. As market research went, these conversations were gold. In between the stories about the totally bizarre and the utterly inspired, she picked up a surprising amount of intel about what was in and what was out, what people liked, what they resented.

'Marnie, what's your position on cash as a gift?' one of the women had asked.

Thankfully, another participant had jumped in – 'I *hate* being asked to give cash. You know the way people do at weddings these days' – which let Marnie off the hook. Tact was important in her line of business, and workshops were hardly the venue for her unexpurgated opinions on bad gifts. Bath products? In Marnie's world there was nothing that so eloquently screamed, 'I just bought the first generic thing I saw in the first shop I walked into; I wasn't thinking about you at all!' Gift cards? Not opposed to them, per se, but they were never an option for a Wish & Co gift. Cash? Seriously? No. Just, no.

Now that the last of Marnie's wrapping workshop participants had departed – happy with her newfound skills and also with the extravagant number of add-on purchases she'd been unable to resist – Marnie surveyed the shop. Teapot, coffee plunger, used cups and plates were clustered together on the countertop, scissors and tape dispensers were scattered across the table, and little triangles of cut paper littered the floor around the wrapping table.

Since she'd woken at 5 am, it was hardly surprising she felt tired. Probably, she looked it, too. Wisps of hair that had escaped her braid hovered annoyingly around her face, and she had the slightly shaky feeling of a person whose only nutritional intake for the day had involved coffee, tea, an apple Danish and a magenta macaron.

Marnie flirted with the idea of leaving the mess where it was and heading upstairs, where she could flop on her bed and lose herself in the productive procrastination of stalking her quarries on Facebook and Instagram. But before she could take a step in the direction of the back door, she heard Archie Fairchild's voice inside her head. *A job's not over until the tools are put away, my girl.*

On Friday, at the old shop, she'd seen the charred remains of the shadow-boards upon which her grandfather had once upon a time, meticulously, hung his hammers and pliers and awls.

He was right. Of course. And so, with a sigh, she set to, returning the scissors to their caddy, and the tape dispensers to the right shelf on the equipment trolley. She stacked the dishes into a basket to take upstairs for washing, brushed off the table and swept the floor. She had just bent to scrape a tab of double-sided tape off the lino when she heard it. *Thump, thump, thump* – a series of knocks so hard that it sounded more as if somebody wanted to break down the front door than get her attention. She glanced up, and there – on the other side of the glass – was a man who looked a lot like Brian Charlesworth. A man who, she realised with a sudden fizz of adrenaline, *was* Brian Charlesworth.

No crisp white business shirt, today. No perfectly knotted necktie. No tidily swept back hair. But they weren't the only differences. There was something messy about him, other than the hair, something disorganised about his attitude. No, Marnie realised, not disorganised. Angry. And now that she understood that fact, she felt a cold wash of fear run through her. Time slowed, almost to a stop, and a series of images clicked through her mind. The two parcels sitting side by side on the collection shelf by the door, waiting for the courier. The two consignment notes. The way she had kissed Owen in thanks before hastily matching the consignment notes with the gifts. Her own reflection in the shop window as she shrugged on her coat, all the while ignoring the nagging question her subconscious had so diligently raised. *You were careful, weren't you?*

Marnie went to the door, but even before she unlocked it, she knew. Even before she turned the door handle, she understood what was coming. Even before the door swung inwards – and a rush of cool, afternoon air disturbed the stillness of the shop – she had braced herself.

Brian's face was red. Marnie could smell the sourness of wine on his breath as he shouted, 'Do you know what you've done?'

He took a few paces into the shop, so that now he occupied the only stretch of open floor in the entire place, as if he were commanding the centre of a stage. Hands on hips, he glowered at her.

'I have to assume it was a screw-up,' he said. 'Not some sick little joke.'

Marnie breathed, let the door fall closed, concentrated on keeping the pitch of her voice low. 'Brian, are you okay? What's happened?'

'I am a very, very long way from okay. And what's happened is that you stuffed up.' He was almost shouting. 'Somehow, my wife ended up standing in front of a gathering of her family and closest friends, opening a parcel that contained a silk dressing gown . . .'

Marnie closed her eyes.

'. . . with another woman's initials monogrammed on the pocket.'

Now Marnie felt as if somebody had thrown icy water over her, but instead of it pouring over her clothes and skin, it was sluicing down through her veins. She wished she could rewind herself to the moment she'd placed the cards and consignment notes on the parcels. Carelessly. Shit! How could she have been so slack? She wished she could go back to the moment she'd ordered that bloody monogram.

'But . . . the monogram. Couldn't it have been . . . just a brand?'

Brian let out an explosive, bitter laugh. 'Let's just say that there's history. You can be assured that Suzanne was in absolutely no doubt who that gown was meant for.'

Gesticulating strongly, his face growing redder still, Brian described the scene at the anniversary lunch so that Marnie felt as if she had been standing at the table, watching it unfold. She'd been into enough houses of the kind in which the Charlesworths lived to be able to imagine it all. The plush carpet, the pastel furnishings, the fine china dinner service, the expensive-but-dreadful art on the walls, the silver polished to a gleam by a husband-and-wife team of cleaners called something like Barry and Cheryl.

'You stuffed up my anniversary,' he accused. 'You've stuffed up my marriage. Actually, you've stuffed up my life. That's what's happened.'

As she listened, Marnie crossed the room to take up a position behind the wrapping table, feeling a little safer with a substantial obstacle between herself and Brian. She crossed her arms tightly over her chest, but then remembered. It was one of the things you learned in Dealing with an Angry Customer 101. Don't get defensive. She unfolded her arms and rested her palms on the tabletop.

'Brian, I'm so sorry this has happened —'

'Sorry? You're *sorry*? What good is sorry? You think your sorry means anything right now? My wife has thrown me out of the house. Do you understand? She has thrown me out of the house!'

Marnie was great with angry customers, an expert at easing them down from their outrage. She went through the steps. Remain calm (she was doing her best). Apologise (she'd done so). Tell them you understand and reassure them that you'll fix the problem.

'I unders—'

'Understand? No, I don't think you do. My marriage is on the line. Probably over. Because of you.'

Reassure him that you'll fix the problem, then. But how? This was not something that could be remedied with a refund or a replacement product. This was way beyond any of the sweeteners she could think of. Right now, the situation was looking pretty much unfixable.

'I'm so sorry,' Marnie said, helplessly. She understood; he didn't want her apologies. But what else could she offer him? 'It's my fault. Absolutely my fault. I'm so sorry.'

'Damn right it's your fault. You've done well out of me. I've been recommending you left, right and bloody centre. I've —'

Brian's tirade was interrupted by the sound of the door opening for a second time. It was a younger man, in a white shirt, sleeves rolled to the elbows. He leaned a shoulder against the open door, twirled his car keys noisily in his fingers. It took only a few seconds for Marnie to register that she knew exactly who this was. After all, she'd been buying his birthday and Christmas gifts for years. In the framed photographs Brian kept on his office desk, she had more or less seen him grow up – from toddler to primary schooler, teenager to young adult.

This was Luke Charlesworth, born 20 February, age thirty-two years. His girlfriend was Annalena Pfeiffer, a triathlete whose preferred confectionery was Turkish delight and whose favourite flowers were white irises, who'd come to Australia from Germany as a backpacker and stayed, but who did not live with Luke in his rented worker's cottage at 243 Fielding Street, Bankside – a suburb yet to be gentrified, where cottages like Luke's sat cheek-by-jowl with industrial complexes on a stretch of the river that Brian considered undesirable.

Yes, this was Luke – a semi-prodigal son, from the way Brian talked about him. 'Determined underachiever' was the expression Brian had used in relation to Luke, a timber craftsman by trade, with a weakness for chocolate-coated coffee beans and Caribbean rum, but few hobbies outside his work. Which was a quality that Marnie related to – even liked – despite the fact it had made buying gifts for him quite a challenge.

He was the same height as Brian, and had the same easy, symmetrical features, the same hazel eyes, the same shapely lips. And yet, he was entirely different. Not just because his hair was sandy, while his father's was silver. And not just because he was sober, while his father was drunk. It was something else. Something about the attitude he gave off, about the way he occupied space. Brian put Marnie in mind of an over-inflated balloon, lurching around the room on unseen currents. Luke, in comparison, seemed entirely grounded.

'What's going on, Dad?'

'Marnie and I are in the middle of something,' Brian said, as if Luke were five years old and irritating him. He turned back to Marnie. 'We're discussing her little screw-up. I'm telling her that there'll be consequences for it.' Now, he pointed a finger. 'You should have to pay for what you've done. You've cost me my marriage. Probably my home as well. You shouldn't be able to get away it.'

Marnie opened her mouth, but it was Luke who spoke first. 'That's not fair.'

Brian fired up as if someone had thrown petrol on him. 'It's absolutely fair. I pay her good money. Very good money. I don't think it's too much to expect that she can put the right address on the right box. Do you?'

'Brian, I —' Marnie attempted.

'Incompetent,' Brian interrupted. 'And when I think of all the business I've sent your way. Shit! My friends. My colleagues. I'm going to have to call them. Warn them.'

'Please don't,' Marnie said, at the same moment that Luke said, 'Dad, stop.'

'Stop what?' Brian raged. 'Stop telling her what her mistakes have cost me? My wife. Has thrown. Me. Out. Of my own. House!'

Luke had stepped into the shop by now, allowing the door to swing closed. 'Yeah, but that's not Marnie's fault. That's your fault. You're the one who cheated on Mum. Marnie wasn't the one banging Leona Quick. That was *you*.'

'I paid her to do a job. She had a job to do, and she stuffed it up.'

'He's right, you know,' Marnie said.

'No,' Luke said, shaking his head like his father was so deluded it was almost funny.

Brian turned the heat directly on his son. 'You cannot be running a business like this one and be so bloody cavalier. She's ruined my life.'

Luke seemed unperturbed by Brian's anger, making Marnie wonder how many times he'd seen it before in his life. 'No, Dad, you ruined your own life.'

'She admitted it herself,' Brian said, sounding childish. 'You heard her. She admits it's her fault.'

'Look at her, Dad. She's shaking.'

Was she? Stretching out her hands, Marnie saw that he was right.

'I'm so sorry,' Luke said. 'He's had a bit to drink. In a day or two, I'm sure he'll call you and apologise —'

'Like hell I will. She shouldn't get away with this.'

'Don't say any more now, Dad.' He made a gesture out towards the street. 'Let's just —'

'Don't tell me what to do!' Brian thundered, but despite his fury he did what Luke had been about to suggest and stalked out of the shop.

In the wake of his departure, the air itself seemed to settle. Marnie took an audible breath, let it out slowly.

'Sorry, he's —'

'No, no, it's not —'

'Really, I am sorry he behaved like that. It's all pretty raw.'

'I can't believe this,' Marnie said.

'I'm Luke, by the way.'

She allowed herself a half-smile. 'I know.'

'Are you okay?' Luke asked.

Elbows on the table, she let her forehead fall upon her folded hands. 'I have never made a mistake like that. Not ever. I just don't. It doesn't happen. Not to me.'

The worst of it, Marnie ruminated, was the monogram. And she had tossed up whether to get it done or not. She'd not been able to decide if it was too much, or just the right thing. What had made her think of it in the first place was that Brian had told her, in passing, that he'd been the one who'd given Leona the nickname of LQ. Gesturing towards a detail like that was just the sort of thing that made the difference; it was the sort of thing that took a gift from ordinary to special. Even so, Marnie now bitterly regretted her decision.

'Your poor mother,' Marnie said. 'Is she all right?'

Luke made a noncommittal shrug. It was strange, having him here in her shop. Although she had known him for years, she knew him only in theory, not in practice. And now here he was taking a turn around the shop, running his eyes over the contents of the shelves.

'What did you mean for Mum to get?'

'A stand mixer,' Marnie said, miserably.

'The Smeg one? With the Dolce & Gabbana patterns?'

He inspected the paper racks, and it was not lost on Marnie that he brushed a hand over the same black, handmade paper with which she'd wrapped the gift intended for Leona.

'Yes.'

Luke nodded. 'Exactly what she wanted.'

'It's my job to know exactly what people want,' Marnie said.

'Like that pair of antique Tasai chisels, for instance,' he said.

Marnie studied him, trying to work out if he was being playful, or bitter. Or both.

'Precisely,' Marnie said. It had been so satisfying, sniping in to win those chisels on eBay in the dying seconds of a late-night auction. She tried to stop herself from asking but couldn't help it. 'Did you like them?'

He looked at her, his face in neutral. She held her breath.

'Loved them,' he admitted.

'What about the furniture atlas?' she asked. A doorstop of a book, and fiendishly expensive, she'd found it at the Art Gallery gift shop – one of her favourite haunts for finding unique items. 'That one was a bit of a risk.'

'Keep it at my bedside, actually.'

Marnie watched as he absentmindedly straightened a sheet of paper that had been hanging askew. He really was uncanny. So much like his father, and yet . . . not like him at all.

'You know what was best about them, though? About the chisels? The book?' Something else occurred to him. It was like watching a child realise that if Santa was a lie, then the Easter Bunny and the Tooth Fairy were too. 'That slab of queen ebony. Far out.'

'I'm sorry,' Marnie murmured.

'You know what made them really special?'

'What?'

'That they were from my dad.'

He looked directly at her. And she at him. As they took each other in, the hurt in his hazel eyes transmitted itself to her. When she flinched in response, he saw it. She knew he did. For a moment, it seemed to Marnie that he and she were looking directly into each other, seeing each other's bruises. But then he offered her a wry smile, as if to say that it didn't matter. That none of it mattered.

'Your father,' she said, looking in the direction of the door, and the street beyond. 'Do you think I'll be able to fix it with him?'

Luke exhaled heavily. 'As messes go, it's a pretty big one. And let's just say that taking responsibility isn't his strongest suit.'

'But it's not really over between them, is it? Just like that?'

'This wasn't the first time,' Luke said. 'And it wasn't the first time with Leona.'

Marnie winced. 'I didn't know.'

'Yeah, well. I guess it wasn't a detail Dad felt he needed to divulge.'

'He loves your mum so much.'

Luke raised his eyebrows. 'Strange way of showing it. And you knew more about what was really going on than any of us did.'

His words stung a little. She deserved for them to. 'I'm so sorry, Luke. Your mum seems like such a lovely person.'

'She is,' he said, unequivocally.

Marnie pressed the heels of her hands into her eyes, hard. But regret over Suzanne's feelings wasn't the only cause of the sinking feeling in Marnie's gut. It was coming home to her now that she had just lost her best client. Who was the conduit to several of her other best clients. And on a sticky note in the pocket of her dress was Saski's magic number, circled in firm, clear, uncompromising black ink. She couldn't afford to lose any clients. Let alone her very best. Not now. Of all times, not now.

'Hey,' Luke said, his tone softer. 'Mum's hurting right this minute, but I have a feeling this might just turn out to be the best thing that's ever happened to her. It's going to be hard for her. Really hard. But a life beyond my dad? Who knows what she might do with it? And, really, it wasn't your fault.'

Marnie knew that Luke didn't fully understand the nature of her distress. And she knew she didn't deserve his sympathy. Even so, it was nice to have.

'Don't beat yourself up,' he said.

Marnie said, 'Oh, I think I will.'

'Well, at least go easy on yourself. Try to keep the beating, you know, gentle.'

Marnie smiled through her almost-tears.

Luke rattled his keys again. 'I should go. Get him sorted out.'

Marnie went to the door, took hold of the edge of it as Luke stepped out into the street. 'Thank you. For standing up for me. You didn't have to do that.'

'Welcome.'

She wanted to say it was nice to meet him in real life, even in such strange circumstances. That she was glad he'd liked the chisels. To tell him all about how she'd found that slab of ebony, serendipitously, at a farm-gate auction in a country town where she'd gone – not even knowing the auction was on – to pick up an antique lamp for another client. All she said was, 'Bye, Luke.'

He gave her a little salute of a wave and stepped out into the street. When he was out of sight, Marnie slumped, face-first, against the inside of the door, her weight pushing it closed. Without looking, she reached up with one hand and turned the lock. After a while of just standing there, feeling the glass against her forehead, she turned so that her back was against the door as she eased herself down to sit on the floor. From her pocket, she took Saski's bright orange sticky note.

For quite some time, she stared at the number Saski had circled. Calm, clever Saski. Saski, who always made good choices. Saski, who had some preternatural ability to know her own limits, who never overreached. Saski, who always managed to keep herself in balance. Saski, who had said she was worried about Marnie.

The truth was that Marnie was worried, too. Normally, when she wanted something, she knew exactly how to get it. She could work out the steps she needed to take, the knowledge she needed to acquire, the skills she needed to build, the contacts she needed to cultivate. But with trying to buy the old shop, she felt like she was attempting to take possession of something that existed only in the world of dreams, something she could only touch with her imagination, never her hands. And now, she had screwed up the Charlesworth account. Her most valuable account. With her own carelessness, she had pushed the world of dreams even further away, perhaps out of reach.

There's always a way. I just have to find it. That was what she'd told Saski. That was what she believed. Wasn't it? If so, why did those words now feel so thin and brittle? Marnie closed her eyes and breathed, trying to will away the lead-heavy feeling that she was already defeated. That there was no point continuing to try. That it was already obvious, to sensible people like Saski and Mo, to her uncle, to the real estate agent, to everybody . . . that she was trying to compete in a game being played way out of her league. The thoughts were heavy. And they hurt. She just needed to set them down, get away from them for a while. She needed today to be over, to stop. Which was why she went to the counter, found her phone and scrolled down her contact list.

Until she reached 'Owen Kingston'.

You busy tonight? she messaged.

Three tiny dots pulsed at the bottom of her screen while she waited for his reply.

Not too busy for you x

2.30 am

The time of night best beloved of doubts and demons, the hour custom-made for dark and circular thoughts, rumination and regret: 2.30 am found Suzanne lying in her grandson's bed, at the home of her daughter and son-in-law. Benji's blue walls, so much nearer than Suzanne was used to, seemed almost close enough to touch. In the light of the waxing moon, a mobile – of a hot-air balloon – cast a soft-edged shadow across the ceiling. The clean flannelette sheets, which Caroline – in a reversal of roles – had pulled right up to her mother's chin, had the comforting feel of childhood.

Earlier in the night, Luke had called Caroline to debrief, but all Caroline had passed on to Suzanne was that Brian was all right. Perhaps Caroline had been deliberate in failing to mention where Brian was spending the night. Perhaps he was with that woman, Suzanne thought, and a vengeful fantasy exploded in her mind like a firework. She thought of how, as a girl, she'd helped her father castrate the male poddy lambs. They'd used tiny, fat green rubber bands and a special set of pliers to stretch them open. Doubtless, such things were available for purchase in an agricultural store.

But who was she kidding? She would no more hurt Brian than harm her own children or grandchildren. For forty years she'd brought Panadol for his headaches and made him keep his regular doctor's appointments. She'd nursed him through bouts of man flu and the aftermath of surgeries. His body – she had spent so much of her life close to it, tending to it, caring for it, that it almost felt like an extension of her own. She only had to think of what it would really be like to see him hurting, to imagine the look on his face, to feel distress of her own. Even now. Yes, even now that he had betrayed her. Again.

If Brian really knew her, then he'd know that unfaithfulness was the thing she could not bear. For all their married life, she had tolerated his flaws so patiently, withstanding his bouts of self-absorption and thoughtlessness, his workaholism, his habit of talking over the ends of her sentences, assuming he knew what she was going to say. It was what marriage was about, wasn't it? Not about finding somebody perfect, but about hitching your wagon to somebody as imperfect as you were yourself and not minding the way you gradually grew into a shape that accommodated their bumps and burls. If he really knew her, then he'd know how much she could take, and he'd know that the one thing she couldn't was the knowledge that he'd shared with another woman not just his body, but the intimacy that was supposed to be hers alone. If he really knew her then he'd know that for her, their marriage was the bedrock upon which rested everything she loved – her family, her children, her grandchildren. Did he know her at all?

All this thinking was not helping, so Suzanne tried to stop it, to disappear into her senses. To feel the warm weight of the coverlet on her body, to appreciate the numbness that had descended upon her after the tears were – at long last – done, to breathe in the lavender scent that was seeping into the room from the diffuser in Leila's room across the hallway. But her mind was too noisy. Up in her head, there was a war going on, battalions of thoughts and feelings cascading down opposite slopes to clash on the field in the middle.

So, your marriage is over, but don't worry! Life's an adventure, said one of the forces. *A solo adventure now. And that's a little frightening. But you can do it! Be brave, Suzanne. After all, there's plenty of money. You'll never want for anything. This is your chance! You're only in your sixties. It's never too late to start again. Think of it as a chance to reinvent yourself. To try new things. To be somebody else. To have a completely different life.* But somehow, she wasn't quite convinced by these thoughts. There was something tinny, something forced, something too bright and shiny, about their optimism.

The opposing forces sounded quite different, and they were easier to believe. *Your marriage is over. You're going to be alone, Suzanne. Sleep alone. Eat your meals alone. Go on holidays by yourself. No more special occasion dinners around that big table. At least, not with everybody there. And all of your special family occasions from now on? They'll be spoiled. Imagine Benji's birthday party. Or Leila's. And there's you on one side of the room and Brian on the other. Tension tainting the air between you. Because that's how it is in families torn down the middle. Loyalties divided. Every festival of the year negotiated, tiptoed through, managed, survived. And what if Luke gets married? Can't you just see Leona on Brian's arm at the wedding? Her elegant clothes on that whip-thin body. You and he should be standing together. At all the special occasions of Benji's life, of Leila's. But you won't be. Not now. You'll be old, and alone, with nobody to love you.*

Suzanne emitted a small, bitter laugh into the darkness. If either of her children went on like that, she'd tell them to cut it out. That's all in the future, she'd say. You don't know any of that is true. Not yet. Just be in the here and now and go off to sleep.

Morning is wiser than evening. That's what she'd tell them.

She tried to clear the battlefield, to send all of the thoughts away – the ones that were too bright and shiny, and the ones that were dolefully full of despair. But as quickly as she forced them out of her mind, new thoughts came. She thought about how it had been only twenty-four hours ago that she'd been drifting off in her own bed, looking forward to the party, switching her wedding ring over from one hand to the other to serve as a reminder to put out the best hand towels in the downstairs bathroom. And now her house was empty. Brian was . . . where? Probably with that woman. And she was here at Caroline's, sleeping in her grandson's bed. Had anyone cleaned up the croquembouche?

She thought of the phone lines around Alexandria Park tonight, could almost see them glowing hot with the gossip. There was no way what happened was going to stay private. Even if the guests kept it to themselves, there was also the wait staff at the party. They were the almost-adult children of the neighbourhood. Oh yes, the word would spread soon enough. Did you hear Brian Charlesworth gave Suzanne a present that was supposed to be for Leona Quick? A silk, monogrammed dressing robe and a fancy leather bag for going away on dirty weekends! Suzanne could imagine the pity on the faces of the women she was bound to meet, in the markets or at the hairdresser. She knew what it would be like to suffer their platitudes, to be able to detect the tugging undertow of their schadenfreude, dragging her down into . . . what?

Shame, she realised. That was what lay underneath it all. She remembered it now, from the last time Leona had been on the scene. She remembered the all-consuming, toxic depths of it. Shame for being too silly and trusting to know or even suspect that her husband was having an affair, and for being naive enough to believe in the power of wedding vows. Shame over being the boring wife at home while her husband was off with another woman who was more exciting, more intelligent, more erudite, more independent, thinner. Shame for being unsexy and insufficient.

There were things she could add this time, too. Now, twenty years later, there was shame over her hair going grey in an uninteresting way, over the way she sometimes woke in the night knowing that she'd been snoring, over the way she put her arm into the sleeve of a jumper and a version of her own mother's wrinkled hand somehow emerged from the cuff. Shame that she'd been stupid enough to be deceived more than once. Shame that she'd failed to see those bloody trout for what they were. Evidence.

There was shame, too, for the ditzy, delighted way she'd spent weeks organising every last detail of their anniversary lunch. It had all been over the top, hadn't it? The height of the croquembouche, the number of different wines, the hired wait staff – who did she think she *was*? Shame over the way she'd believed in the words of Brian's speech. Shame that she'd been stupid enough to stand there, glowing with happiness and pride, and talk about the wealth of family. Wealth that had turned out to be an illusion, something borrowed from a life she only imagined was truly hers.

Some long time passed this way, the relentless thoughts coming too thick and fast for sleep to be possible. And so, she gave in to the fact that she would lie here, watching Benji's bedside clock tick through the early hours of a Monday that was, whether she liked it or not, the first day of the rest of her life.

Two-thirty am came to Brian Charlesworth in Leona Quick's kitchen, where a Smeg stand mixer rested on the bench in a striped shaft of moonlight that sifted through the venetian blinds of the twelfth-floor window. Hands wide apart on the lip of the bench, Brian hung his head.

'Stupid, stupid, stupid bitch,' he muttered, but when he reached for the righteous, incandescent rage that he'd felt towards Marnie Fairchild when he'd hammered on the door of her shop, he found it had subsided to little more than a glow.

He shivered. It was cool in the early morning kitchen, and he wore only his jocks and a T-shirt that Caroline had packed for him. As if he were a child, she'd selected all the things she'd thought he'd need: spare socks, toilet bag, jumper, phone charger, reading glasses, the Wilbur Smith novel that had been stationed at the side of his bed. All of it neatly packed into the small suitcase – the overhead locker-sized one – that he took on overnight business trips. He'd been trailing that suitcase as he walked through the doors of Leona's apartment block and greeted Geoff the concierge. It had been at his side as he'd ridden the elevator to the twelfth floor, watching himself in its mirrored walls as he'd tried to erase the anger, shame and irritation from his face, and to replace them with a jocular smile. He had been leaning, rakishly (he hoped), on the extended handle of the suitcase, when Leona had opened the door to him, all silver curls and thick-rimmed glasses, wearing a huge cashmere jumper over the top of her girlishly thin legs.

'Brian!'

'Birthday surprise,' he'd announced.

'It certainly *is*.'

He'd leaned in to kiss her, but she'd reeled back. 'Goodness, how much have you had to drink? I hope you didn't drive here.'

He'd followed her into the elegance of her grey-black kitchen, where the bright-coloured mixer was plonked on the bench like a clown who'd been mistakenly parachuted into a funeral.

There had been nothing for it, he'd supposed, but to bald-face it. 'Do you like it?'

Leona had tilted her head, thought. She'd seemed to be trying out words, one at a time, discounting them until she found the right one. 'It's . . . remarkable. Coffee?'

And so, the evening had progressed. He had drunk the strong coffee that she made him, but even a large dose of caffeine had proved unequal to his day's quotient of stress and alcohol. While Leona was in the kitchen putting together a platter of nibbles for dinner, Brian – settled into the big, deep couch – had begun to nod. Now and again, he had woken himself with loud snores. At length Leona had shaken him into sufficient wakefulness that he was able to find his way into the bedroom, change into a T-shirt, and fall into her big, king-sized bed, where he'd slept until his bladder had woken him.

And now he was here. At 2.30 am, contemplating a stand mixer.

Its carnival colours were dim in the moonlight, but Brian knew the scarlet, the yellow, the aqua, by heart. They were the colours of Suzanne's kitchen. His kitchen. The heart of the house. His house. Where he was no longer welcome.

Brian closed his eyes, but more images were waiting there on the undersides of his eyelids. His grandson, big dark eyes full of tears and confusion, and yet knowing enough to look at Brian with reproach. His mother-in-law's eyebrows, arched in I-told-you-so amusement. Caroline taking a deep breath, readying herself to manage the situation. Luke, implacable as a wall, in front of him. Defending his mother. Marnie Fairchild in her shop, holding out her visibly shaking hands. Leona leaning back from Brian's drunken breath. But most of all, there came images of Suzanne. Shock on her face. Pain. Determination. Finality.

'Brian?' Leona padded into the kitchen, a narrow figure in white pyjamas. 'Are you all right?'

Brian gulped. He felt Leona's small, light hand between his shoulder blades. He couldn't even remember the last time he'd cried.

'What's the matter?'

'I can't . . . I can't . . .' Was this what crying felt like? Like choking, and having hay fever, all at once? His nose was tingling; he was sure it was swelling.

'What on earth has happened? Lord, you're not having a heart attack, are you? Brian?'

'She . . .'

'What? She, who?'

'Suzanne.'

'Yes?'

'She . . . found . . .' Brian attempted.

'She found what? She found *out*? About us?'

'Yes. She threw me out of the house. She . . .'

'Oh, Brian.'

Now he was sobbing in earnest. He couldn't make it stop. 'I . . .'

'Yes?'

'I . . .'

'You what?'

'Don't want to lose her,' he said, the truth leaking out in a rush between sobs.

He was not crying like a baby, Leona observed. Neither was he crying like the twenty-two-year-old university student she remembered, who had once produced a tiny drizzle of tears during a debrief about the ending of their first and most tempestuous love affair. Nope. He was crying like a sixty-seven-year-old man with lachrymal ducts rusted shut from years of disuse.

So, his wife had found out. Well, now things made more sense. Leona had wondered why he had turned up, suitcase in hand, unannounced. That was not Brian's style at all. Neither was it his style to fall asleep, snoring, on the sofa, and require shepherding to bed.

It was over between them. This, Leona knew for certain, even as she rubbed sympathetic circles on his back with the palm of her hand. Brian didn't want to lose his wife. He had said so. Quite clearly. Now the affair must end. If he didn't finish it, then she would do it herself.

Leona made one more circle on his back and gave him a couple of soft, final pats on the shoulder. Then she flicked on the kettle, put chamomile tea bags into two wide porcelain cups, and considered. Why wasn't she devastated? Why wasn't she gutted? Why was she feeling strangely light of heart? Had Cameron been right to suggest that her attraction to Brian had less to do with the future than with rosy memories from the past? What was it she was feeling? Was it, possibly, relief?

'Can I ask a question?' she asked, when Brian's sobs had subsided.

He turned his face, blotchy from crying, to look at her in assent.

'Did you really intend to give me that hideous thing for my birthday?'

Leona watched him consider telling her a lie. Then, with a wince, he shook his head.

'Mix-up?' she suggested.

'Today was our fortieth wedding anniversary.'

'And that,' she said, waving a hand at the mixer, 'was for Suzanne.'

'Yep,' Brian said.

'And she opened a gift that was meant for me?'

Brian nodded.

'Ouch.' Leona had more questions – including what had been in that other parcel – but for now she only said, 'Come and sit down.'

He followed her to the couch obediently and submitted to her settling a throw rug over his bare legs. A few moments later, she returned to hand him his cup of chamomile tea. She took a seat opposite him.

'You're giving me the judge look,' he said. 'Like I've just done something unbelievably stupid and you can't wait to hear how on earth I'm going to explain it.'

That was fair, Leona thought. 'Well?'

'I don't know what to say,' he admitted.

'Well, why don't you start by telling me what we've been doing all this time? You allowed me to have the impression that Suzanne was one of those wives who, you know, didn't really mind. Happy enough with her lot in life. So long as you were discreet.'

'Did I?' Brian's face was all innocence.

'You did,' Leona said, definitely.

'Well, no. That's not her.'

Leona thought. All that questioning she'd been doing. She'd gone through her dilemma, thoroughly, with Cameron. The whole 'do I want him/don't I want him' routine. Somehow, she'd locked herself into the idea that she had to choose, when in fact the choice was never hers to make. She felt that sense of lightness bubbling up through her again. There was no decision to make.

She was released. 'So, what did you think you were doing? With me? Again?'

'You're talking as though I was the only one involved.'

Leona's eyebrows shot up. 'You called me. You began it. I didn't come looking for you.'

That roused him. A hint of criticism and he was biting at the bait like a blowfish. 'We have fun, don't we?'

'Yes, we do,' Leona agreed.

'When we're together, it's like old times. Isn't it?'

'Just like old times.'

'I've worked hard, LQ.'

'Which means – what? That you deserve nice things? That it's only right for you to have a little break every now and then?'

'Christ! I've given her everything a woman could want.'

'Except your fidelity.'

Brian set his jaw. 'You're giving me the judge look again.'

She was. 'If I ask you a question, will you tell me the truth?'

'Shoot.'

'This wife of yours, who you love so much,' Leona began, trying to control the quantity of acid in her tone. 'How many other times have you cheated on her? How many other women have there been?'

'No others.' He said it solemnly.

Leona raised an eyebrow.

'It's true. When it comes to being a philandering husband, I'm a pretty loyal one,' he said, with a sideways smile that was almost enough to get her to smile along with him. 'It's only ever been you, LQ.'

'Suzanne and me,' she corrected him, drily. She drew her feet up under her, tilted her head enquiringly. 'Out of curiosity, just how *did* you manage to mess things up so spectacularly?'

Brian grimaced, swirling the tea in his cup. 'Employed the wrong gift-buyer, apparently.'

A gift-buyer, Leona mused. Well, that explained quite a lot. Being good at selecting gifts was something Brian had seemed to acquire in older age, along with his nicely silvered hair and well-chosen spectacles.

'Who is . . . she? I mean, I assume it's a "she".'

'Marnie Fairchild. At Wish and Co.'

Leona knew the shop. It was on Rathbone Street. Nice things; ugly building. Well, she had to admit the woman had taste. For Leona's last birthday, there'd been a pair of Issey Miyake gloves. Terribly chic. And for Christmas, a framed print of a bird in high-heeled shoes by an up-and-coming local artist whose work she'd been admiring for months. Leona had not had the first idea how Brian had known she was coveting that particular artist's work, and when she'd asked, he'd only looked self-satisfied and told her that he had his 'ways and means'. Ways and means, indeed.

Brian made a solemn face. 'I'm sorry I ruined your birthday.'

Leona smiled over the top of her chamomile tea. *Such hubris.*

Marnie Fairchild, at 2.30 am, slid out of Owen Kingston's bed and got quietly dressed in the darkness. For a moment she stood at the second-floor window, gazing out over the night-shrouded faces of the townhouses on Owen's fashionable inner-suburban street: some old, others sleekly new, but all worth a bomb. Marnie wondered what it would have been like – who she would have been – if she, like Owen, had grown up in a world where you always knew your father would buy you a townhouse for your twenty-fifth birthday. A world in which failed exams and aborted university degrees just made for funny dinner table stories; a world in which a failed business would be a minor blow, easily absorbed by the cushion of an endlessly giving trust fund.

Owen slept atop his sheets, and by moonlight she could make out the contours of muscle and bone in his naked torso.

'Leaving?' he murmured, sounding less than half awake.

'Yeah. I can't sleep,' Marnie whispered.

'Are you worrying?'

'And then some.'

'Don't worry,' he said.

Helpful.

'Kiss goodbye?' he asked, and Marnie leaned down to touch her lips to his.

'So, I'll see you . . .?' Marnie began, just a little hopefully.

'. . . when I see you,' Owen finished.

No change, then. Things were the way things had always been. But then, what had she expected? Marnie studied him. He was beautiful. He was fun. And, for now, that was enough to ensure he was never lonely. But what would happen to this particular Peter Pan when the effortless definition of that torso suddenly required some discipline? When that dark hair, now long and shaggy against the pillowslip, began to recede? For how long would beautiful last? For how long would fun be enough?

Leaving Owen to his sleep, Marnie picked her way through his bedroom, dodging bath towels and discarded clothes. In the living room, pinpricks of green and red lights from a state-of-the-art sound system flashed and glittered in the darkness. She couldn't remember when it was that Owen had stopped playing music himself. Once, he'd loved noodling on a guitar, striking jazzy poses with a saxophone, impressing her with his virtuosity on a harmonica. The last time, though, that she'd heard someone ask if he played music, he'd shrugged and said, 'Only the stereo.' She supposed he'd sold his guitar and his saxophone on Gumtree, along with his dreams.

The front door creaked as Marnie edged it open and stepped out into the cool night air. She sat on the veranda steps and pulled out her phone to order a Shebah – safest, she always thought, when she was travelling alone at night. There, in her messages, were a series of texts from Saski.

> What time we expecting you, Bunny?

> Are you far off? Should we put dessert in the oven? Sticky-date pudding!!

> We'll keep yours warm. You okay?

> Jack was so looking forward to meeting you. I thought he was going to weep into his Brandy Alexander when you didn't show. ☹

Marnie felt a nauseating wave of self-recrimination. She had forgotten. In all the chaos of Brian Charlesworth, she had entirely forgotten. That was shitty of her. It was the kind of thing only a shitty friend would do. And she couldn't even apologise right away, because Saski hardly needed an apology so much that she'd want her phone pinging on her bedside table in the wee, small hours.

Feeling heartsick, Marnie ordered her ride. Before long, a quiet little hybrid glided down the street and stopped at the base of the stairs. As the small car carried her homewards, she rested her cheek against the window and watched the moon thread its way through scraps of shredded cloud. She thought of Mo and Saski, waiting for her. She thought of the old shop, of Saski's ultimate figure written down on that orange sticky note, of Brian Charlesworth standing in her shop, pointing the finger at her, furious and threatening – all the things she'd managed to forget in Owen's arms. In Owen's bed. But now the forgetting was over.

Closing her eyes, she brought the old shop into sharp focus in her mind. Not in its current state, with its windows boarded up and its interior charred and vandalised. But how it would be when it was hers. Owen had done the easiest thing; he had let his dreams go. But she was a Fairchild. A real Fairchild, whether anybody else believed that or not. And she did not do what was easiest. She had to come up with a way to fix things with Brian Charlesworth.

— PART THREE —

Monday

With precious few hours of sleep under her belt, and a strong coffee in hand, Marnie went down to the shop, before opening time, to think. She spread a large sheet of paper on the wrapping table and set down a pot of freshly sharpened coloured pencils. In bright green, she wrote: *How do I fix it?*

In blue, she drew a large circle, and inside it she wrote down everything she knew about Brian. Yes, he was egotistical, ambitious, competitive and controlling. Despite his outward shows of power, though, he was painfully vulnerable to criticism. He liked material markers of prosperity: fancy car, big house, vast polished office desk. Equally, though, he was drawn to other signs he considered indicators of a successful life: an intact family, high-achieving children, a loving wife, a large circle of friends. He could be ruthless in business but to those he liked, he was generous – ostentatiously so.

And Suzanne? Marnie picked out a bright fuchsia pencil and made another circle. The core of Suzanne's life was her family: her husband, her children, her grandchildren, her mother. Sure, she liked nice things, but not nearly so much as Brian did. Despite her wealth, she still got a kick out of a bargain. She bottled her apricots, preserved her lemons and mended her clothes. Unlike many of her contemporaries, Suzanne wasn't actually a big spender. Exceptions included food, wine, fresh flowers and her garden; these categories of expenditure seemed to be exempt from her natural restraint. Suzanne, Marnie noted, was sentimental. She treasured her memories, surrounded herself with evidence of special moments from her past.

What about Leona? With a purple pencil, Marnie drew a third circle, smaller than the others, and wrote Leona's name inside it. She thought. When Brian had stood on the far side of this table and shouted, Leona had not featured in his rage. It had not appeared to worry him that Leona had received the wrong gift; Leona had not apparently been on his mind at all. In a gesture that might have seemed ruthless, Marnie drew a large cross through Leona's circle. Leona, she thought, was not part of the equation she had to consider in order to put things right. It was Suzanne and Brian, their marriage, that she had to try to fix.

'Small job then,' she murmured to herself.

Feeling overwhelmed by the size of the task, Marnie was momentarily pleased when the phone rang. At first, she thought the call would be a pleasant distraction, but when she looked at the name on the screen – Lloyd Sherwood – she knew immediately in the pit of her stomach what was coming.

She forced a smile before she answered, 'Good morning, Lloyd!'

Lloyd Sherwood was a retired barrister and mentor to Brian Charlesworth, owner of an E-type Jaguar, a Hummer and a late-model Tesla. He was married to the significantly younger Katharine (that there was an 'a' in the middle was important to her), who took pleasure in buying gifts for the Sherwood clan, which included not only the children she'd had with Lloyd, but also the stepchildren from Lloyd's two previous marriages. It was Marnie, however, who was responsible for buying gifts for Katharine herself, as well as for Lloyd's two ex-wives (he regarded it as strategic to keep things cordial), as well as gifts for three other women, who were about as different from each other, and from Katharine, as you could get.

'Marnie,' Lloyd said, and the premonition churning up Marnie's stomach grew stronger still.

'How can I help?'

'Actually, I have some concerns. And I've rung to say that I'd like to terminate our arrangement, effective immediately.'

Usually, Lloyd was charming to the point of flirty. But today, the man on the end of the phone was the court-hardened lawyer, not the connoisseur of women and cars. Exactly what had Brian told him?

'Lloyd, this comes as a big surprise to me,' Marnie said. 'We've always worked together so well. Is there a problem I'm not aware of?'

'Not . . . that has affected me. As yet,' Lloyd said. 'But let's just say I'd like to avoid any future problems.'

'Would you like to share with me these concerns of yours?'

'I've decided that I simply cannot countenance the risk, to the harmony of my life, if you were to . . . make any unfortunate errors in my portfolio.'

Marnie wanted to scream in frustration. She wanted to slap Brian Charlesworth around the face. She wanted to slap herself around the face for her carelessness. Just how big, how consequential, was this mistake going to get?

'Lloyd, I'd love the chance to reassure —'

'Marnie, my mind is quite made up. All I need today is for you to invoice me for any sum that is outstanding, and assure me, please, that all records pertaining to me, and my portfolio, will be summarily destroyed?'

There was no point arguing. 'Of course. If that's what you wish.'

'It is.'

'And should you, at any time in the future, decide to re-establish your portfolio, I'll be only too happy to —'

'Thanks, Marnie. I must go.'

'Lloyd,' she said, sharply, before he could hang up.

'Yes?'

'Just one thing. Have you been speaking with Brian Charlesworth by any chance?'

There was a brief silence; Marnie could imagine him deliberating with himself in his lawyerly fashion about whether or not to tell her what she wanted to know. 'Matter of fact, I rang him this morning to talk through the details of our annual golf trip.'

'I see,' Marnie said. *Great.*

'Right you are. Bye, then.'

The phone went dead. Marnie let it fall to the table. *Shit, shit, shit.* Lloyd was only a medium-sized fish in her client pool, but there were several more over whom Brian would have the same swift and decisive influence. She turned back to the sheet of paper on the desk and violently underlined Brian's name. She had to get him to stop.

Suzanne, through the passenger window of Caroline's car, studied the facade of her home. Late morning sun touched the poplars and roses in the front yard, the curtains were opened at all the front windows, and there was not a thing apparently amiss except for the rolled-up newspaper still lying, at 11 am, on the path. She had deliberately stayed away until now, not wanting to be present when Luke came around to collect Brian's Mercedes, more of his clothes, his medications, a bottle of his favourite gin, and a canister of his preferred coffee. Apparently, so Luke had told Caroline, Brian was installing himself in a serviced apartment a couple of blocks away from the office.

'Are you sure you don't want me to come in with you?' Caroline asked. 'I can clear my afternoon appointments.'

Forty years, and this was how it ended. With Luke calling Caroline, wanting to know which cupboards to look in, and Suzanne herself in the background providing the answers Caroline couldn't supply. Now, sitting here looking at the empty house, Suzanne felt strange, disassociated, as if her body were some kind of automaton, still going through the motions – a brittle vessel within which she was only partially present. Though where the rest of herself had gone, she hadn't the least idea.

'Really, it's no trouble. Everyone can just be rescheduled,' Caroline insisted.

Suzanne put her hand on her daughter's knee. 'No, you go to work, darling. I'll be fine.'

'You're really sure? We could curl up on the couch? Watch a movie together? Arjun can pick up the kids.'

'You're sweet. But I've got to face this at some point. Might as well be now.' Suzanne leaned over to kiss Caroline's cheek. 'Love you, darling.'

'Love you, Mum.'

Suzanne got out of the car and made her way to the front door, scooping up the newspaper as she went. At the door she turned to wave to Caroline, who pulled her neat little Audi out into the tree-lined street and drove away.

Alone, Suzanne thought. *Alone.*

She unlocked the door and stepped inside. Keys still in hand, her own reflection hovering at her side in the hallway mirror, she stood and listened to the silence. A new kind of silence.

She was accustomed, of course, to the quiet of being alone during the day when Brian was at work, or away on business trips, or for weekends. Away 'trout fishing', she thought, bitterly. Those silences, being only temporary, had felt both safe and familiar. But this? This was a deep silence. A permanent one. Vast and cloudy, it was full of the prospect of lonely days and lonelier nights. Empty rooms, empty hours, empty arms.

Was she really, *really*, going to go through with this? Was she really, *really*, going to dismantle everything they had built together, everything they were to each other?

She moved through the downstairs rooms – kitchen, den, living room. At the door to the formal dining room, she stopped, took a breath, and then turned the handle. Tidy to the point of immaculate, the room hummed with silence. In the corner where she had detonated the croquembouche, no sign remained. There was not so much as a speck of cream on the carpet, nor a blob of custard on the walls. The crystal glasses had been returned to their cabinet and the dinner service put away. The dining chairs had been pushed in, the floral centrepieces removed, the table wiped down. There was only one thing out of place. On the sideboard was a leather bag with a tag that said OPEN ME.

Fury percolated in her belly, providing an answer to the questions she'd been asking herself. Was she going to go through with this? Hell, yes.

Tuesday

Marnie, in a GoGet car she'd collected before dawn, drove along Rathbone Street in the opposite direction of her ultimate destination. The approaching dawn had begun to colour the sky, but the streetlights had not yet switched off. Signs of life were limited to the few other cars on the road, and flickers of movement within a bakery's glowing windows.

As she drove, the nature of the shops changed, growing gradually less shabby, more chic. Block by block, they morphed from the takeaway kebab joints and old-fashioned bridal-wear shops, outlet stores and second-hand bookshops that characterised the neighbourhood near Wish & Co, to the high fashion boutiques, vegan grocers, gourmet bakeries and fancy homewares emporia of Alexandria Park. Reaching Fairchild & Sons, Marnie reefed the tiny car into a U-turn and parked directly in front.

Standing on the street, arms wrapped around herself against the early morning chill, she saw that the shop had been cleaned up a bit. The worst of the graffiti had been scrubbed away, and the weeds that had flourished in the cracks between the pavement and the shop's sandstone footings had been removed. Also, the ever-renewing drift of waterlogged junk-mail that usually lay on the steps and around the base of the front door had been cleared away. But the biggest change was the sign, affixed to the front window. FOR SALE.

Splashed across its centre was a sepia-toned photograph that Marnie knew well. It was the same one that she kept, framed, on the countertop at Wish & Co, showing her grandfather Archie Fairchild standing in his leather cobbler's apron at the top of the steps to the shop's front door. Originally taken for a local newspaper at the time Archie had reinvented his own father's grocery shop to sell high fashion footwear, it had also featured on the back cover of the Alexandria Park Historical Society's pictorial book, *The Verdant Heart*.

So, Marnie thought, the marketing strategy was to play on the shop's place in Alexandria Park's collective imagination. Smart, she thought. Since the heritage listing couldn't be wished away, it made sense to portray the building's history as an asset. Marnie's eyes skipped over the text – *Alexandria Park landmark . . . steeped in history . . . oldest weatherboard building in this sought-after neighbourhood* – to the fact she considered most important: the auction had been set down for Saturday 16 November. Just over two months away. Which meant for that amount of time at the very least, come hell or high water, she had to keep her business figures stable. Or improve them. She could not allow them to go backwards. She was up for the challenge. She could do it. She was, after all, a Fairchild.

The real estate agent, Mark Wigston, shown on the FOR SALE sign wearing a rather self-congratulatory smile, had remarked upon the family resemblance. When she'd met with him at the shop, she'd recognised him as a true Alexandria Park type, his ruthlessness concealed by a gentlemanly and genial charm. He was the type who kept working into late middle age not because he needed the money to maintain his lifestyle, but because he enjoyed the cut and thrust of the property game; probably, he'd been the type of kid who'd routinely trounced all his siblings at Monopoly. His handshake, firm and warm, had drawn Marnie's attention to the family signet ring she doubted was ever again going to come off his chubby pinkie finger, and to the equally tight fit of his fat, gold watch. He'd been slow to release her hand, not holding on to it in an inappropriate way, but seeming rather to appraise her with genuine fondness.

'You're so like your father,' he'd mused. 'That Fairchild hair. But then, look at you from another direction and you're actually more like your mother. I remember them well. I guess a lot of people do. It was quite the wedding. Don't think I've ever seen a more beautiful bride than Christine. How is she these days?'

Poor, Marnie had felt like saying. Extracting her hand, she'd settled for, 'She's well, thank you.'

'Please give her my regards,' Mark had said, and of course, Marnie had promised she would, never meaning it for a second. Bringing up the past was a recipe for her mother to launch into one of her diatribes about how life wasn't fair. That was true, of course. Life wasn't fair, but unlike her mother, Marnie didn't believe there was any point bitching about it.

Yes, if her father had taken his opportunities instead of squandering them, Marnie's life would have been very different. Yes, if her father hadn't been such an idiot, then perhaps she, like Owen, would have been raised in wealth and privilege, rolling around in opportunity, rather than being raised by a dreamy, disappointed mother in a shabby house in a sad little town like Casterbrook.

It had been Marnie herself who'd found a way in through the side door of a good private school in the city, begging her grandfather – the only one of her relatives who bothered with the daughter of the prodigal Rory – to supplement the half-scholarship she'd been offered at Meltonside Grammar, but only after its original recipient had turned it down. Yes, if Marnie's father hadn't thrown it all away, she might not have had to be the kid with the fourth-hand uniform and the beaten-up early-edition textbooks – the ones whose contents were slightly outdated and their page numbers different from everybody else's.

If. Oh, yes. If.

If wishes were horses, my girl, her grandfather used to say to her, *beggars would ride.*

She missed him. Why was it, she wondered, that grandparents tended to die before the time of our lives when they were most needed and wanted? Just once, even, she would like to go back in time to one of those summer afternoons, when school was over and she'd catch the bus to Alexandria Park, and trot up these very steps to that very front door, to hear the bell tinkle as she pushed it open. She remembered: the rich scent of her grandfather's russet-coloured leather apron, discoloured at the middle with a starburst of black shoe polish; the crisp sound made by the mint-green shopping bags when he, standing behind the counter, would sharply snap one open in order to slide in a mint-green shoebox; the way he'd wink at her as he tossed her one of the mint chocolate truffles that he kept on his counter; the snug pull against her instep when he'd re-lace her school shoes after taking them off and shining them for her. Shoes that he gave to her. Her brown lace-ups were just about the only thing she ever wore to school that started out brand new.

If she couldn't go backwards, then she wanted to go forwards. To the day when this window was no longer boarded up but restored. When customers would be able to peer through its many panes, past a display of exquisitely wrapped gifts, to catch sight of the spacious, gracious interior of the new and improved

Wish & Co. When she would serve the customers, and create beautiful displays, and keep the place tidy and ordered, and feel the contentment of having arrived at precisely where she was meant to be.

'Wish me luck today,' she whispered – perhaps to her grandfather, perhaps to the shop itself. Then she got back into the car.

Despite the detour, it was still very early when Marnie arrived at her destination. After taking the elevator to the top floor of the building in the city centre, she found she could do nothing more than stand by an unyielding set of glass sliding doors – etched with the Charlesworth Group's stately, royal blue logo – and wait. She did not take out her phone to check emails or read the news. She did not so much as put down her messenger bag. Because if Brian Charlesworth was the next person to walk out of that elevator and into the twenty-fourth-floor lobby, she wanted him to find her unshaken and standing to attention, perfectly upright in the highest of her high heels. She wanted him to find her with her chin up and her shoulders back, her olive-green skirt suit unwrinkled and her make-up unsmudged.

Her outfit, so different from the flowing skirts and dresses, the felted clogs and linen aprons that she wore in the shop, felt almost like a costume. And in a way, she supposed, it was. If she was going to get what she wanted from Brian Charlesworth today, then she needed to look the part of a woman who meant business.

When a chime announced that the elevator doors were about to open, Marnie prepared her face. Serious, without looking morose. Warm, though not exactly smiling. But the person who stepped out through the sliding doors was not Brian Charlesworth; it was his PA, Gina, her blunt-cut bob styled into its usual superhuman smoothness, her lipstick the glossiest and reddest in the known universe. In the three years since Gina had joined the

Charlesworth Group, Marnie could not recall ever having seen that pillar-box colour looking anything less than freshly applied. Marnie and Gina were not on hugging terms, but their relationship was absolutely in the realm of effusive greetings.

'Hello, lovely!' Gina said. She had the kind of British accent that Marnie found hard not to imitate. 'I didn't see you in the calendar for this morning?'

'Looking gorgeous, as ever,' Marnie observed, gesturing at the trim houndstooth-check dress.

'Why, thank you! Come on through, sweet.'

Marnie didn't need any further encouragement to make her way past the long, sleek reception desk. In the worst-case scenarios – the ones she'd imagined in painstaking detail while concocting her plan – she'd fallen at this first hurdle, being turned away virtually at the door. But thanks to Gina, she was at least going to make it this far. To the CEO's waiting room, where all the light was filtering in through deep, wide windows that offered a spectacular view over the western and southern quarters of the city.

Under the overcast sky, the river wound through the suburbs in a series of steel-grey curves. Amid the maze of streets Marnie searched out Rathbone Street, with its distinctive dogleg, following its traffic-choked trajectory until she located the block where Wish & Co stood, and where Alice should by now have arrived to prepare the shop for opening. Marnie let her eye continue on, all the way out to just shy of the spot where Rathbone Street met the leafy green expanse of Alexandria Park, and where she pinpointed the rooftop that belonged to Fairchild & Sons.

When Gina switched on the lights, the room brightened, and the world beyond the windows receded into dimness. Behind her desk, Gina peered at her monitor.

'You sure you've got the right day, Marnie? I can't find you anywhere.'

'I don't technically have an appointment,' Marnie said, and gave a guilty smile, 'but I figured you'd be able to squeeze me in.'

'We-ell,' Gina said, 'his morning's not *packed*. Why don't you grab a seat, and we'll talk to him when he arrives? But hey, while I've got you . . . my best friend is getting married. I can't think what on earth to get for a wedding present. She and her fiancé, they're into the minimalist thing. You know – they do all their shopping at places that have no packaging. I mean, it's amazing. But what do you do? What do you buy for people like that?'

Marnie nodded that she understood the predicament. 'Don't buy them anything.'

'I can't do that!'

Marnie smiled. 'If they've got an attitude about owning stuff at all, they're going to be super particular about the kind of stuff they want to accept into their lives,' she said, realising her intonations were sliding towards Gina's. Since when did she use a word like 'super'? 'So don't get them any*thing* at all. Give them an experience. Something they'll always remember.'

'O . . . kay,' Gina said. 'What do you suggest?'

Marnie blinked. 'It really depends.'

'Any ideas at all?' Gina begged.

Ideas? For a couple she knew nothing about? It never ceased to amaze Marnie that people seemed to think gift ideas could be summoned up so easily. But this was not the moment to try to educate Gina on this point. This was a moment to be helpful. 'Well, there was one couple I bought for, who were a little like your friends. I chose them a weekend together on a whisky distilling course.'

Gina shook her head. 'She doesn't drink.'

'Scratch that one, then. Are they foodies?' Marnie asked, thinking of the cooking school experience to which she'd sent Suzanne Charlesworth.

'No. They subsist on lentils and pak choy.'

'Are they adventuresome?'

'Absolutely. Mad mountain bikers, hikers. You name it.'

'So, they're getting married, which means you could pitch it along the lines of "taking the plunge" and get them a scuba class? Or "taking the leap", and give them a tandem sky-dive?'

'Sky-diving?' Gina's eyes lit up. 'That's actually genius.'

'Aim to please.'

'Can I get you a coffee while you wait?'

'Thank you, but no.' Marnie didn't want to have a cup in her hands to fumble with when Brian arrived. Nor did she want to take even the tiniest risk of spilling coffee on her cream blouse.

For half an hour she sat – back straight, bag on her knees – studying the flower arrangements until she understood they were extremely accomplished fakes, and that the water in the glass vase was not water at all, but resin.

At last, Brian arrived, and as she watched him stride down the hallway, her pulse kicked up a notch. Today he looked the way she was most accustomed to seeing him – his suit well cut, his white shirt crisp, his tie a sober shade of silver-blue. He carried a slender briefcase in one hand and a folded newspaper in the other. His hair was brushed back, his glasses fashionable. Not for the first time, she observed that he had done well to keep his good looks. Good looks, Marnie recalled, that he had passed on to his son.

Marnie rose. In heels, she was almost exactly Brian's height, so that when their eyes met, they were on the level. His were cold.

'What's she doing here?' he accused Gina.

The poor woman looked utterly perplexed. 'Marnie? Sorry... what?'

As professionally and calmly as she could manage, Marnie said, 'I'd like a brief meeting if possible.'

'What on earth could you have to say to me?'

Gina was watching them with widened eyes, but Marnie didn't want to give away too much more in front of the PA. The last thing she needed was gossip.

'I have a proposal that I think will interest you,' she said, keeping her voice calm, and hoping that her neck was not betraying her by going red and blotchy.

Brian thought, slapping the newspaper against his thigh in a way that made Marnie feel like a puppy that might be just about to get a thwacking.

'Ten minutes,' Brian said. His tone was magisterial, benevolent.

He continued on to his office and Marnie fell in behind him, avoiding Gina's bewildered gaze. Brian closed his office door behind her, and she waited, standing, while he – unhurriedly – took off his jacket and hung it in a narrow closet behind his desk.

Marnie was familiar with the framed photographs that decorated each end of the desk. Studio shots, all of them, Suzanne's hair always the same shade of blonde, its style varying over the years only by inches in length and slight degrees of curl. It was Brian's hair that had changed more, the cuts getting shorter, the shade less sandy. And then there were the children, Caroline and Luke. The pictures showed them with baby teeth, then missing teeth, then brand-new, gappy incisors that looked too big for their young faces. In every photograph, Caroline's expression was natural, sincere, but Marnie could see that while Luke's teeth were always on show, he hated posing for the camera.

Suzanne, Luke, Caroline. For years they had been to Marnie like characters in a sit-com. As with the royals, they were people she studied from afar, about whom she developed opinions and theories. Buying gifts for Caroline had never presented much of a challenge. She was an accessory girl, always thrilled with a brand-name handbag or wallet; there was barely a hat in the world in which she did not look stunning. She also loved perfume. Marnie had picked her as the type to prefer something spicy like Salvatore Ferragamo Pour Femme, and . . . bullseye. Marnie had done a little dance in her apartment when Caroline, on her birthday, had posted on Instagram an image of the bottle with the message, 'So lucky to have a father classy enough to pick just the right scent!'

To buy for Luke, though, Marnie had always needed to think outside the square. He did occasionally use social media, but only for the purposes of profiling his hand-crafted furniture. Still, Marnie was accustomed to taking what information she could get. In order to figure him out, she'd visited an exhibition in which several of his pieces had featured, and she'd gone to a Designer Makers Co-operative where one of his rustic-but-elegant 'Winnipeg' chairs, made from rare blond sassafras, had been included in the permanent display. She'd examined the hand-crafted construction, the way the timber's spectacular grain was showcased along the chair-back. She'd known, then, that she was dealing with somebody who liked quality and paid close attention to fine detail. Somebody who valued tradition but understood how to update it.

She knew, too, from previous conversations with Brian, that Luke had made the imposing desk behind which the CEO now took a seat. Marnie continued to stand, her gaze slightly lowered.

'Please sit,' Brian said, although his tone indicated that he considered this display of good manners to be undeserved.

Marnie sat, and for the moment said nothing. It wouldn't hurt Brian to feel that he was in charge of the encounter.

'Well?' Brian asked.

She met his eye. 'The mistake I made was unforgivable.'

Brian nodded, as if this were obvious.

And now came the careful playing of her hand. Before there was any point laying her cards on the table, there was one thing she needed to know. 'Did you tell Suzanne? That the fault was mine?'

Brian hesitated. 'I did not.'

Marnie breathed a sigh of relief. 'And that was because . . .?'

Brian cocked his head, raised a single eyebrow. 'I have something of a reputation to maintain now. Thanks to you.'

'A reputation for . . .?'

'You want me to piss in your pocket, do you? Well, thanks to you I now have a reputation for being very bloody good at buying gifts for people.'

'And you didn't want to give that up,' Marnie said, knowing there was only so much further she'd be able to push this line of conversation.

'I did not.'

Don't rush, don't rush. 'Then I would like an opportunity,' Marnie said, as calmly as she could manage, 'to help you keep that reputation. And, to keep your business. By rectifying the damage I've done.'

A harsh syllable of laughter came from Brian. 'Rectifying the damage?' He made a sweeping gesture encompassing the framed photos. 'This is what you damaged. This. My family. My life.'

Marnie glanced at the oldest photo-Luke, who smiled out at her, grimly, from in front of a mottled blue studio backdrop, his striped school tie knotted high and tight at his throat. He seemed almost ready to speak, to say something along the lines of what the real Luke had said, in her shop, two days earlier. *No, Dad, you ruined your own life.* But even if he had, this time Marnie would have shushed him. She couldn't care less, right now, about where the responsibility lay. Whether it was Brian's fault that he was in the doghouse, or Marnie's, was irrelevant to her. All that mattered was keeping his business. Whatever that took.

'Look! Look!' Brian said. He flung open a desk drawer and brought out more photographs. Not stagey, over-posed ones like those in the frames. Among the stack that he scattered across the surface of the desk were a handful of old Polaroids and some small, matte-textured photos with rounded edges. As Marnie ran her eyes across them, she saw a succession of candid images. A young Suzanne with a pregnant belly under a flimsy summer top, standing at an easel and poking out her tongue at the camera. Caroline and Luke running through a sprinkler on a patchy lawn. Caroline on a tiny, carnival pony. Luke in a shortie wetsuit with a surfboard under his arm, his smile utterly genuine this time. Suzanne with her arms around a young Caroline, bright blue icing around Caroline's mouth and daubed on Suzanne's nose. A very tanned Brian water-skiing in yellow boardshorts. Luke lying on the carpet, asleep, with a dozy Labrador pup sprawled across his outflung arm. Brian in the hospital, beaming, and holding a pink-swaddled baby that must have been Leila.

Fragments of a life, a story.

'Forty years married, and she won't even pick up my calls. Won't respond to my messages. Nothing. I'm in a serviced apartment. Did you know that?'

Marnie imagined it was a nice serviced apartment. She also imagined that this was only a temporary measure until he had the opportunity to move on the tenants from one of the many other properties he owned. And, if push really came to shove, there was always the beach house an hour and a half out of the city. Many people's commutes were worse.

'The kids are barely talking to me,' he went on. 'I mean, they've done all the right things, bringing me my car, my clothes. But Caroline's down to monosyllables. Which I probably prefer to Luke's little barbs. As if he knows anything about relationships.'

Marnie gave him a quizzical look.

Brian took off his glasses and polished them rather aggressively with a cloth he took from his desk drawer. 'It was on my mind to tell you to scratch Annalena off my recipient list.'

'Oh? They're not together any more?'

'Idiot. He should have married her, not just let her jet off back to Europe.'

Interesting, Marnie thought, and then mentally erased Annalena from her list of concerns – Turkish delight, white irises and all. Probably, the break-up had been predictable. Even though Marnie had never been on more than stalking terms with Annalena, the German woman had never struck her as being entirely Luke's type. There had been something unyielding about Annalena, and Marnie didn't say that only because of the way she looked in Lycra. Luke, she'd always thought, would be better suited to someone a little softer, a little more sentimental, a little more creative.

Brian, hands on his hips, scowled at the photographs scattered across his desk as if willing the pieces of a broken vase to magically reunite themselves. If this life, this story, was so important to him, then why on earth, Marnie wondered, had he betrayed it with Leona Quick? But fundamentally, the answer to that question didn't matter. All that mattered was somehow getting Brian Charlesworth to stick with her services. If she could just do this one thing, if she could just keep him onboard, stop him from doing any more damage, then Fairchild & Sons might still be within her reach.

'You want your family back together,' Marnie said softly.

It was a strategy. One the experts called 'affect labelling', and it was the oldest trick in the pacify-the-angry-customer handbook.

'You feel unfairly treated,' Marnie went on, following her instincts as they led her one step deeper. 'You feel misunderstood.'

'Damn straight I do.'

You feel vulnerable, Marnie didn't say. *You feel lonely and lost.* This may well have been true, but even so, it was a step too far. Instead, she asked, 'May I make a proposal?'

Although Brian gave a 'be my guest' gesture, he set his face in an expression that said he had no intention of believing a single word she said. Marnie felt self-doubt creeping through her, but she couldn't allow it to take over. She had to look confident, even if it was possible that she had totally deluded herself this ploy could ever work.

'I am a very good gift-buyer,' she said, confidently but – she hoped – not arrogantly. 'And I think what we've already established is that until this error of mine – this very serious error – you have always been happy with my services.'

Brian nodded with exaggerated magnanimity. 'Go on.'

'I propose that I choose, and purchase at my own expense, a series of gifts for Suzanne. By which means, she will . . .' At this point, Marnie lost her nerve. She'd rehearsed the words 'forgive you', but now that she was face to face with Brian, she couldn't quite bring herself to say them. It sounded too much like she was blaming him. And that, she did not want to do. But where else to steer that sentence? She will . . . 'take you back'? No. That didn't make him sound powerful enough. She will . . . 'back down'? No, this wasn't a fight. It was a misunderstanding. Marnie's mind was accelerating through options but failing to find the perfect one. Fortunately, Brian broke in.

'I see what you're thinking.'

Holy shit. He was actually tempted. Marnie pressed her lips together tightly. *Let him get himself over the line*, she counselled herself.

'You really think you could do it?' he asked.

Don't be too eager, don't be too eager. Don't overpromise. Be confident, but not cocky. 'I believe I can. I believe she loves you. I believe you love her. I believe this is fixable.'

Marnie didn't know if this was true or not. She only knew that if she lost her best client, and if he decided to badmouth her to other clients, her borrowing power would be diminished. Which could put Fairchild & Sons out of her reach. She didn't know if she could really win him his wife back, even with the cleverest gifts in the world, but if she could just keep Brian in the game, keep him believing, for a few months at the very least, then she might be able to hang on to her dream.

'How many gifts are we talking?'

'Unlimited,' Marnie said, boldly. *Or until you admit defeat*, she didn't say. 'I do have one condition, however.'

She knew she was taking a risk here, but a hard nut of a businessman like Brian Charlesworth wouldn't want to deal with someone who didn't exhibit strength, and smarts.

'You? You have a condition?'

'Yes. My condition is that all other aspects of our business relationship remain unchanged. You continue to pay me the same service fee, and . . .' She swallowed. She'd thought long and hard about how to finesse this next part. She needed no more repeats of yesterday's phone call from Lloyd Sherwood, but it was important to keep this conversation positive. 'You will continue to recommend my services to your colleagues, as you see fit.'

'As I see fit?'

'Yes.'

'Hardly an enforceable condition,' he said, raising a single eyebrow.

'That's true,' Marnie conceded.

'I take it you heard from Lloyd.'

Marnie tried not to show even the faintest glimpse of anger. 'I did.'

Brian shrugged as if to indicate to Marnie that all was fair in love and business. He said, 'I, too, have a condition.'

Marnie braced.

'You will choose the gifts. The wrapping will be at your expense,' he said. 'But as for delivery and the items themselves? I will cover those costs.'

Marnie frowned. 'The mistake was mine, though. I ought to pay.'

'True,' Brian agreed. 'But this isn't about money. In this matter, money should be no object. I don't want you skimping. Fair?'

She was tempted to tell him that expense was not necessarily the measure of a good gift. There was a lot more to it than that. But there was no denying that a Charlesworth-sized budget could buy the realisation of a lot of creative ideas.

'More than fair,' she conceded.

'Then it's a deal,' Brian said, standing and reaching out a hand.

As she got to her feet, she had to fight to keep the relief off her face. Her knees felt precarious, as if they might buckle. She wished she was not wearing high heels. Concentrating on remaining upright, she looked Brian Charlesworth directly in the eye. She took his hand.

'Deal,' she confirmed.

Marnie got into the back seat of her tiny share car, laid her forehead against the headrest of the driver's seat, and took several deep breaths. Holy shit. She'd actually done it.

'Yes!' she whispered to herself. And then a little louder, 'Yes!'

She'd talked him into it. He'd said yes. If mixing up those two gifts had been the board-game equivalent of slipping down an enormous snake, then she had just hauled herself back up a stubby little ladder. There was still a way to go, but at least she was headed in the right direction.

In the relative privacy of the car park, Marnie contorted herself out of her suit and heels and into a dress and clogs, altogether more suitable for shopping. Which was how she planned to spend the rest of the day. She released her hair from its tight, high bun and restyled it into two low braids. That was better; and much more Marnie. Once she was transformed into the regular version of herself, she checked the list she'd made the night before – an ambitious list, it had to be admitted. An optimist's list. But it was with enormous pleasure that she ticked off the first item: *Meeting with Brian Charlesworth*.

Five hours later, the little GoGet car had been on a comprehensive tour of the inner-city suburbs, its boot having accumulated a wealth of parcels, and Marnie was on foot in the CBD, her forearms striped with red marks from the many shopping bags she carried. From a boutique papeterie she'd picked up a fountain pen, several bottles of coloured ink, and a large quantity of beautiful, blank paper for a client to give to his wife, who had recently let it slip on Facebook that she was rekindling a fondness for writing poetry. In a sports store right in the heart of the central business district, Marnie had selected a top-of-the-range baseball glove for the grandson of one of her elderly female clients, who was in a nursing home and now found shopping too difficult. She'd collected a bottle of eighty-year-old Portuguese port, a (very heavy) box set of the cloth-bound editions of Jane Austen's works, and a child's bedside light with interchangeable silhouettes showing scenes from fairy tales.

Of course, Marnie could simply shop online and have all her goods sent to Wish & Co for wrapping and onward delivery, but it was her usual practice – when feasible – to collect the items herself. For one thing, this saved quite a bit on postage and freight. But that wasn't the only reason she shopped in person. Turning off one of the city's main streets, Marnie entered the cool of an old-fashioned shopping arcade, its walls embellished with mirrors and mosaics, and remembered that other reason: inspiration.

In the window of a hat shop, an array of delicate felt trilbies had been placed at perky angles on their stands. Nearby, in the doorway of a yarn shop, hanks of spun merino – in springtime shades of marigold and parsley green – nestled together in cosy baskets. Retail, for Marnie, was a kind of theatre, where all the details mattered. How the shop was lit, the way it smelled, the kind of music that drifted through the air; the way merchandise could be made to look like the answer to a problem, a signifier of identity, or a guarantee of delight.

In the well-dressed displays of clothing boutiques and gift stores, kitchenware shops and bookstores, Marnie found both pleasure and ideas. Her journeys out into the shops of the city not only helped her work out what to buy for some people, it also told her what *not* to buy for others. Such as Saski. Because if an item was on-trend, then the chances were, it was not right for the unique and precious Peach.

This coming weekend was Saski's baby shower, and since most of Saski's relatives and friends had rung Marnie to ask for gift advice, Marnie had been able to make sure that her friend would be given all the things she would need – like a state-of-the-art nappy bag – but none of the things she wouldn't – like more than one or two items of exquisite baby clothing that were so small they'd be outgrown in a matter of hours. Marnie would have been loath to admit it, but she was feeling a bit of performance anxiety around the baby shower. Being both Saski's closest friend and a gift-buyer, she knew she'd be expected to seriously come up with the goods. But she was fairly sure she had it in hand.

In fact, she did have it in hand, quite literally. In one of the large bags Marnie was carrying was a quilt. But not just any quilt. It had been sewn from fabrics that Marnie had begged from Saski's mother, who'd sewed for all her children when they were young. Georgie had handed over a crazy mix of materials, including lightweight summer cottons and heavier pinwale corduroys, remnants of the curtaining from Saski's childhood bedroom and a swatch from Georgie's mother's wedding gown. The quilt-maker had done a beautiful job, creating something that ticked all Saski's boxes – aesthetically pleasing, non-wasteful, sentimental and unique. Marnie was sure it was going to go down a treat.

Emerging on the far side of the arcade, Marnie now stood across the road from the elegant, white-pillared entrance to the Art Gallery. Her last job for the day was to duck into the gallery shop and see what she could find for the sister of one of her wealthy male clients. Perhaps a pair of artisan earrings, or maybe one of the beautiful little ceramic vases that were sold there, made by a local artist to resemble lengths of birch tree trunks.

Crossing the road, Marnie glanced up at the colourful banners that hung from poles spaced along the gallery's facade. The current exhibition, called *Life Going on Without Me*, was by an artist called Cassandra du Plessé, who'd been barely recognised in her lifetime as the surrealist talent that she was. Marnie had read in the weekend papers about Cassandra – how she'd suffered burns as a child, how she'd never married or had a partner, how she'd painted self-portraits, with something bordering on brutal honesty, throughout her short life. The journalist who wrote the article had called her 'Australia's Frida Kahlo', and Marnie had made a mental note to see the exhibition. Which closed, Marnie now read on a banner, tomorrow.

'Shit,' Marnie said. She was going to miss it. Unless . . . did she have time? Today? Not really. But then, it might never happen again that all of Cassandra du Plessé's major works, most of which were owned by private collectors, were shown together in the same place at the same time. Reaching the forecourt of the gallery, Marnie put down her bags and checked her watch. She needed to be back at the shop to relieve Alice at 4 pm. But, if she were to put off buying that one last gift until another day, then she could spare half an hour. It wasn't really enough time to do the exhibition justice. But it was all she had.

Marnie sighed as the classic devil–angel combo popped up, one on either shoulder. *Just get through your list, Marnie,* whispered the insufferably responsible angel. But the devil murmured, *You've been working so hard lately. You can afford to do a little something for yourself.* As if the angel was going to take that lying down! *Marnie, dearest,* it said, *having just made the biggest mistake of your career, do you think you really deserve a treat at the moment?*

The devil was a cunning beastie, though. Doing a rather good imitation of Saski, it simply murmured, *All work, no play, Bunny.* And just for a moment, Marnie wondered if she had it straight which one of them was really the angel, and which the devil.

The gentleman at the cloakroom, bemused by the number of bags Marnie set down on his counter, gave her three tokens for as many lockers. Her arms now empty, Marnie felt light – in body and spirit – as she hurried into the exhibition's first gallery. It had been a long time since she'd allowed herself, even for half an hour, to do something as frivolous and wonderful as wandering into an art gallery in the middle of a working day. The hush, the low light, the tape on the floors that indicated how far a viewer should keep from the artworks, the uniformed guard standing, stone-faced and with hands behind his back, all combined to make Marnie feel as if she were doing something faintly but delightfully illicit.

The walls of the gallery were painted charcoal and each of the artworks had been spot-lit so that they popped – oil-bright colours gleaming, almost as if the paint was still wet. Marnie strolled from image to image, and as she did so, she felt some of her worries and cares peel away. She had a sense of being pulled out of her own life, her own time, and into that of Cassandra du Plessé herself. Some of the paintings were still-lifes, small studies of plants and fruits of weird varieties that Marnie was fairly sure had come, not from real life, but from the artist's fertile imagination. However, it was du Plessé's own image that dominated the walls. In each of her self-portraits, her long red hair – rather like Marnie's own – framed a pale narrow face with huge, brown eyes and an angry burn scar running across one side of the forehead and down one cheek as far as the jawbone.

Marnie stood for a long time in front of a haunting image of the artist holding her hair up on top of her head, the expression on her face bold – almost angry – as if daring the viewer to find her ugly. Gradually, Marnie became aware of someone standing in her peripheral vision: a man, studying the neighbouring painting. There was something about him, though she wasn't exactly sure what, that made her think of Luke Charlesworth.

Obviously, it was a case of the Baader–Meinhof phenomenon. She had Charlesworths on the brain, and so now she was seeing them everywhere. Probably, it was just the man's height that had done it, combined with the white linen shirt she could see out of the corner of her eye, its sleeves rolled to the elbow. But as she moved on to the next painting, she took the opportunity to glance at him a little more directly, just to be sure it wasn't actually Luke. Except that, *oh crap*, it was.

Before he could feel her eyes on him, Marnie hastily turned her gaze back to the work in front of her. Then angled herself just a little so that if he looked her way, he'd see more of the back of her head than her profile. Her heart was thudding just as it had done when his father had stood in her shop, yelling at her that she'd ruined his life. All the feelings flooded back – the guilt, the regret, the irritation of having got something so badly wrong. She'd made a massive mistake, and he knew it. She hated making mistakes only slightly less than she hated being caught out making mistakes. And here was Luke Charlesworth, right beside her, as a life-sized reminder.

She tried to concentrate on the painting before her – in which du Plessé had painted herself in her adult form, even though she was confined to the hospital bed she'd occupied for so long as a child. The red tendrils of her hair had woven themselves between the industrial bars of the bedhead, knitting her in place. Marnie tried simply to look at the artwork, to ignore Luke's proximity, but now that her mind was all stirred up, she'd lost her clarity of vision. Without permitting her gaze to stray in Luke's direction, she searched out the room's exit, and found it, to her right.

Slowly, casually – she hoped – Marnie executed a neat half-turn, spinning away in the opposite direction to where Luke stood and headed purposefully but not hurriedly into the second gallery of the exhibition. She didn't pause there, though. She kept going, right through the centre of it, and into the third gallery, which was full of cabinets containing the artist's early drawings and sketchbooks. At that room's far end was an exit that led to the building's central hall. Marnie made for it, but it felt disrespectful to simply walk past all this work – all these gorgeous sketches – without looking at a single one. So, she paused at one of the display cases, trying to cram into her memory the illustrations of Cassandra's childhood bedroom, her cat, her dog, her sister, as if she might, somehow, be able to take possession of them now and look at them properly later. But it was no good. She couldn't concentrate. The spell had been broken.

Back at the cloakroom desk, Marnie exchanged her three tokens for her many bags. Dividing them evenly between left forearm, left hand, right forearm and right hand, she headed for the gallery's main doors, where afternoon light streamed through tall glass panels to fall on the black-and-white chequered floor. The angel had been right, of course. She shouldn't have even attempted the du Plessé exhibition. She should have just gone into the gallery shop, like she'd planned. *Stupid, lazy, undisciplined . . . did I mention stupid?* As she made her way towards the doors, she gave herself a silent but thorough ticking off. And then, there he was again. Luke. Crossing the foyer from the opposite direction.

Thinking like an ostrich, Marnie put her head down and walked more slowly, counting on Luke to keep going, straight ahead, on his present trajectory. If he did that, he would reach the door first and their paths would not cross. It was a plan that might have worked. Except that she made the mistake of glancing up. Ever so briefly. But that was all it took. She saw him, and he saw her, and more to the point, he saw her see him, and there was no longer any possibility of pretending she had not.

Now they were inside one of those moments, each of them trying to read the other's body language, trying to work out whether or not the other person expected that they would stop and talk, or merely smile and carry on. Marnie, although she had just bolted out of an exhibition to avoid him, now found that she didn't want Luke only to smile and walk on. Perhaps something in her face communicated this fact because he stopped walking, waited for her to reach him.

'I thought it was you back there,' he said. A little awkwardly, he gestured over his shoulder in the direction of the gallery. As if either one of them needed to be reminded where it was. 'Great exhibition, isn't it?'

To be standing so near Luke was like coming across a statue that had just softened from marble into flesh, or a portrait that had suddenly stepped out of its frame. But he was very real, entirely corporeal, smelling faintly of wood shavings and something that might have been mineral turps. His hands – browner and rougher than his father's – had the slightly dusty look of unvarnished timber.

Marnie hated that when she was nervous, she had a habit of speaking too fast, saying too much, being too eager. Over the years she'd tried to teach herself to slow down, to switch herself to a lower speed, the way you could with a record turntable. It helped, she'd discovered, to ask questions rather than answer them. 'Doing the last day rush, too, were you?'

'This is my third visit, actually.'

'You're a fan then?'

'It's my mother who's the serious du Plessé fan.'

Somewhere in Marnie's brain, that morsel of information dropped into the file labelled 'Suzanne Charlesworth'. As it landed, it brushed up against Marnie's memory of one of the photos she'd seen on Brian's desk – the one of a young Suzanne, painting.

Luke went on, 'I come here a lot, so I tend to go through most of the exhibitions a few times. You see a bit more on each pass, I reckon.'

'You would,' Marnie said, thinking regretfully of the paintings she'd ignored in her haste to get out of the gallery. 'I wish I had more time, you know, to be a human being instead of a human doing.'

Luke looked at her questioningly, waited for her to go on.

'Oh, you know. It's so easy to get caught up in the details of your little ant-life. Hurry, hurry, hurry. Art reminds you to look up, look out, look around. That there are things beyond your own little concerns.'

In the silence that fell between them, she wondered – and she guessed Luke did, too – whether or not they were going to address the real subject.

'So, did you beat yourself up?' he asked.

It seemed they were. 'Comprehensively.'

'Much damage?'

Marnie shrugged to suggest it wasn't so bad. And it wasn't. Not now that she'd managed to stitch up a deal to stay in business with his father. Although she had no intention of telling Luke about that. Now she thought about it . . . Luke was going to be a problem. This was, she realised – her mind going swiftly into overdrive – the first time she'd been outed by somebody who'd been on the receiving end of her gift-buying services. Brian had agreed to keep their current arrangement in place, and not to tell Suzanne. But what about Luke? He might easily confide in his mother. And what about buying gifts for him, henceforth?

'Can I ask you a question?' Luke asked.

In Marnie's experience, when people asked such a question they rarely waited for an answer. But Luke actually did.

'If you like.'

'I've been wondering about your job. How you got into it. I mean, it's not exactly a primary school job, is it?'

Marnie furrowed her brow. 'A primary school job?'

'You know: police officer, firefighter, teacher, doctor. The kind of thing you might have said you wanted to be when you were in primary school. I'm guessing eight-year-old you didn't say, hey, what I really want to be when I grow up is a personal gift-buyer.'

At eight years old, all Marnie had wanted was to own a shop. She'd had no definite idea about what that shop might sell, only that she wanted to make it as completely beautiful and inviting as Fairchild & Sons. Maybe she had a touch of OCD, but she'd always had an unreasonable love of things being displayed in an orderly fashion. She loved the illusion of everything being in its place, of there being a place for everything; it made her feel calm and in control.

Luke didn't jump in. He left her plenty of room to say any or all of what she was thinking. But if she did, he'd probably think she was shallow, materialistic. Some kids grew up wanting to save the world; she'd grown up wanting to make sure all the buttons of the world were displayed in accordance with the colour spectrum, and that the spines of all the books in the world were lined up flush with the edge of the bookshelf. She shifted her bags so the handles cut into other parts of her hands and forearms.

'You probably didn't grow up wanting to be a furniture maker either,' she observed.

'Fair,' he admitted. 'All I knew when I was at school was that I was better at those subjects, you know – art, woodwork, science – where you get to do things with your hands.'

'You are. Good, I mean. With your hands,' she said. And then, realising how that might be interpreted, she blushed. The way only a true redhead can. The fact that she was now blushing made her blush even hotter. Why did she have to be a blusher? Why did she have to have the kind of fair skin that broadcast her emotions for everybody to see? Luke's boots, she noticed, while trying to stop looking at his hands, were a beautifully rustic Danish brand. 'I mean, I've seen your work. Your furniture. In your dad's office, and in galleries. I love that chair of yours. The one at the Designer Makers Co-op.'

She was babbling, trying to scramble back onto solid ground. Luke smiled, but to himself this time. He had the look of someone only just now realising that a magic trick was actually a very simple sleight of hand. 'That's how you do it, is it?'

'Do what?'

'That's how you work people out,' he said. 'You stalk them.'

'I wouldn't say "stalk", exactly.' This was a blatant lie. It was exactly the word she used for the kind of research she did on the gift recipients in her clients' portfolios. Truth be told, she set aside two blocks of time each week specifically for the purpose. It was even what she wrote in her diary. *Stalking*.

'Well, whatever you call it, you're good at it. That queen ebony was really something.'

This time Marnie's flush was one of pleasure. She fought the desire to say, *You see? You see? That is why I do what I do! That's the joy in it. The challenge, the chase, the time when you get it exactly right.* Instead, she asked, 'What did you make with it?'

'Nothing yet. I'm too scared.'

'Scared?'

'Of wrecking it. Doing the wrong thing with it. Once I cut it, then I'm committed. So, for now, it's just sitting there where I can look at it and dream.'

Marnie knew what he meant. She'd felt much the same with sheets of scandalously expensive paper. Sometimes it was nicer to let a really beautiful thing retain all its potential rather than limit it to being just one thing. 'I'm glad you liked it.'

'You know a fair bit about us all, don't you? Me, Mum, my sister?'

Marnie shrugged. 'Did you tell your mother? About me? That the mix-up was my fault?'

Luke thought; Marnie waited nervously.

'I don't mean to be dismissive, but you, the mixed-up gifts . . . all of that was only the sideshow. The main game was the affair itself.'

'Does that mean you didn't?'

'No point. Why hurt her more?'

So, he hadn't told her. But that didn't mean he wouldn't in the future. Now that she thought about it, Luke was even more of a problem than she'd first realised. When gifts started to arrive for Suzanne in the coming weeks, would Luke put two and two together and get Marnie Fairchild? She had to hope not. Or that even if he did work it out, he would continue to think that there was no point hurting Suzanne with the truth.

'So, is it a common thing?' Luke asked. 'Among your clients? That they have somebody on the side?'

In his tone, Marnie caught a note of judgement. Stiffly, she said, 'It might surprise you, all the different reasons that people employ me.'

This was not an untruthful statement. He might indeed be surprised. Some of her clients employed her because they were too old and frail to get to the shops and didn't feel confident with internet shopping; she was employed by a few working mothers who simply didn't have the time to run errands, and also by a couple of men who had plenty of time but felt unequal to the task of buying the right thing for wives to whom they were scrupulously faithful. But Luke was onto something; it was true that the highest proportion of her clients were wealthy men with complicated arrangements.

Luke smiled, as if to soften the blow he was about to deal. 'It can't feel good, though. Surely. Helping men like my father to cheat.'

Marnie raised her eyebrows. Was he flirting with her? 'I thought you said it wasn't my fault.'

'No, not your fault. But you did a certain amount of aiding and abetting.'

'I'm a gift-buyer. Not the infidelity police.'

Luke folded his arms, rocked back on his heels. 'But even that? The gift-buying? Do you really think it's right? Buying presents that somebody else pretends are really from them?'

His tone was light-but-not-light.

Provoked, she matched it. 'Were you so very disappointed to learn that your dad had a bit of help?'

And there it was again. The pain she'd seen in his eyes when he'd been at her shop. She wished she could take back that last jab. He really did have some daddy issues; she hadn't meant to poke him where it hurt.

'Not half as disappointed as Mum was with her anniversary present.'

Whoa, Marnie thought. If they were flirting, then it was with live ammo. She felt her temper rise a little. 'Think of it this way. If you want your hair cut, chances are you're going to go to a professional. You want your taxes done? Just like your hair, you *can* do it yourself, but it might just be easier to go to an accountant. Not to mention that you might get a better result. You're not going to represent yourself in court, are you? You're going to get a lawyer. If you want —'

'Okay, okay, surgeon, plumber, gardener, teacher, electrician, tree-lopper, I get it. But gifts are . . . well, you'd know better than me. Aren't they supposed to be part of the fabric of our relationships? Isn't that what they're for? Don't we use them to establish and maintain bonds?'

Well, well. Somebody had read a little bit of sociology somewhere along the line. 'They're exactly that. All the more reason to make sure you do it well. Surely?'

'But aren't there things that are too personal to outsource? Like . . . sex, for example. When you outsource your sex life, well, we have a name for that, don't we?'

Marnie laughed, more in shock than amusement. 'You're saying my business is a form of prostitution?'

'No, no. That's too strong. But paying someone else to buy your gifts for you? It's cheating. It's a form of emotional fraud.'

Emotional *fraud*? If they had been flirting, then it was time to stop. Luke Charlesworth was the son of one of her clients. Her very best client. In a way, Luke himself was a client. An unhappy one. It was time to pull out the affect labelling. 'You're angry.'

'No,' Luke said, 'not angry exactly.'

She would need to refine, then. 'You're hurt.'

'I wouldn't say that either.'

At this point, Marnie was far from sure he was in touch with his true feelings, but clearly, he needed her to use a word he was more comfortable with. 'You're disillusioned.'

Luke kicked lightly at the chequered floor with the toe of his boot. 'Yeah. Yeah, I am. I hate that this is the world we live in. I hate that money buys everything. Time. Love. Gratitude. It's not right.'

Speaking of the correlation of time and money, Alice was once again covering for Marnie in the shop and the clock was ticking expensively. It would be for the best when she went back to normal, seeing Luke Charlesworth only on social media channels or through the medium of his timberwork in galleries.

'I really should get going,' Marnie said, holding up her bags by way of explanation, 'before my arms drop off.'

'Of course. Sorry. Sorry, I should have offered to take them for you. Where are you headed? Can I help?'

Marnie smiled tightly. For a moment she seriously considered telling him that she wouldn't want him to aid and abet an emotional fraudster. 'Thanks, but I'm pretty used to it.'

'It was nice to see you.' He looked like he didn't want her to go.

She turned away from him and adjusted the bags again, swapping the heaviest from one hand to the other in order to share the pain around. As she walked away, she felt self-conscious, as if he might still be watching her. *Emotional fraud*, she thought as the wide glass doors opened at her approach. She was grateful for the gust of springtime air from the outside, cool against the angry blush that was creeping steadily up her neck.

Thursday

In those first few long, slow days of aloneness, Suzanne resisted the temptation to make the radio her companion, or to turn on the television. She left the stereo untouched. Instead, she tried to learn how to get along with the silence that lurked like a shadow beside her, how to go to sleep with it lying beside her at night. The hardest part, she was discovering, was waking up each morning to find that it was still there.

That morning, though, the silence was disturbed just after eight o'clock by the doorbell. Suzanne got out of bed, drew on her dressing gown and peeked out the window to see a hot-pink delivery van – its doors wide open – haphazardly parked at the edge of her lawn, one wheel on the kerb. When the doorbell rang a second time, Suzanne descended the stairs.

On the doorstep, with a blonde ponytail captured under a hot-pink cap and an enormous fitness tracker dwarfing her tiny wrist, a delivery driver jogged on the spot. The bouquet in her arms jiggled, sending the heady, tropical scent of the flowers in Suzanne's direction. It was the perfume of her wedding bouquet, of the Mexican nights of her honeymoon, of the arrangement at her hospital bedside after Caroline's birth. So often, too, the fragrance of frangipani had been the olfactory backdrop to Brian's apologies, to the make-up sex that followed. Sweetness, sauciness, happiness, nostalgia, regret, grief. Suzanne's senses reeled.

'Mrs Charlesworth?' the delivery driver asked, her voice as perky as her ponytail.

Suzanne blinked. Her name, she supposed, was yet another thing she was going to have to think about. She'd liked, once upon a time, being Suzanne Wright. But she'd been Mrs Charlesworth for so long now that she was almost entirely convinced that's who she really was.

The driver peered at her notes. 'Suzanne?'

'That's me.'

The young woman beamed. 'Beautiful, aren't they?' she enthused, handing over the bouquet. 'And a long way from home. Somebody loves you to go to all that trouble!'

Suzanne wondered if Brian had paid extra for the lip-service. 'Thank you,' she managed.

'Well, have a nice day,' the young woman said, now empty-handed, then took off down the path at a trot.

Suzanne fished the card out of the wrapping. The sight of Brian's own handwriting was enough to make her feel as if her heart had just been applied to a lemon juicer.

Suzanne, it read, *I'm so sorry. Please can we talk?*

The second bouquet arrived just after 9 am, and the third, an hour after that. The fourth didn't come until noon, but the fifth arrived only five minutes later. Each time, a different delivery company; each time the flowers were differently wrapped – the paper either glossy or matte, the bow tied either in thick brown string or satin ribbon. But every time they were frangipanis. *Plumeria alba.* Suzanne's favourite, with their white, waxy, overlapping petals; their tiny yellow hearts, so perfect it was hard to believe they were even real.

Each time the note was in Brian's handwriting, and each time the note said the same, simple thing. *Suzanne, I'm so sorry. Please can we talk?* Each time Suzanne cut the stems and filled a vase with water, carefully folded the wrapping paper for future use, and tossed the note in the bin.

Throughout the afternoon, the frangipani assault continued, causing Suzanne to downshift from her best vases to her second-best. Soon there were frangipanis in the kitchen and frangipanis in the front hallway, frangipanis in the living room and the bathroom, in the back hallway and the study, on the landing of the stairs, in the bedroom and even the ensuite.

Several times, Suzanne went out into the backyard just so that she could come back inside and discover, all over again, how the scent of her favourite flowers permeated the house, threatening to overwhelm even the silence itself.

When the twelfth bouquet arrived, it was after 7 pm, and the sky above Alexandria Park had deepened to cloudy violet.

'Been a long time since I've delivered a bunch of frangipanis,' the delivery driver confided. An older man, tired-looking despite his schoolboy shorts, he found himself unable to resist putting his nose to the flowers. Wistfully, he said, 'Nights in the Pacific. They smell just like this.'

'Keep them,' Suzanne said.

'Oh, I couldn't do that.'

'Really. Please have them. I have . . . more than I need.'

'Do you know how much these would have cost?'

'I can imagine, but I don't need them. Really, I don't. Give them to your . . .' But maybe he didn't have a partner, or a lover. Maybe he was alone, just like her. The last thing she wanted was to cause him pain. 'Just keep them.'

The debate went on a little longer, but when at last he walked away, he held the bouquet tenderly in his arms. He'd made sure, though, to leave Suzanne with the card. Which read: *Suzanne, I'm so sorry. Please can we talk?*

In the kitchen, she opened the bin drawer. She held the card poised and ready to be deposited on top of eleven others the same. She hesitated. Read the words again. She was going to have to call him at some point. It wasn't as if she could ignore him forever. These thoughts, and other small tendrils of temptation, uncoiled around the edges of her mind, but before Suzanne could reach for her telephone, she caught herself, scrunched the card and let it drop. *No.* Because *just no* and *never, ever again.* Did she need reminding of the details? Perhaps she did.

She pushed open the door to the dining room. With nobody to see, and before she could lose her nerve, Suzanne yanked on the zipper of the leather bag on the sideboard. The offending garment was still there, neatly folded into a square of ivory silk. Suzanne drew it out and held it up, confronting herself with its expensive shimmer, its dainty proportions, its damnable monogrammed pocket. She felt once again the undoing of the bag's high-quality, heavy-duty metal zipper. But this time it was her heart, her lungs, her liver, her guts that she felt pouring out through the gaping hole. *Never again.*

Suzanne took hold of the robe in a clenched fist, as if by its throat. Past the frangipanis in the kitchen and past the frangipanis in the back hallway, she carried it out to the garage and threw it into the wash trough. Silk, she remembered, wasn't the easiest of fabrics to burn – it had a tendency to self-extinguish if you didn't keep the flame steady and hot. Well, she had an answer for that. Out here in the garage, in tidy plastic tubs, was where she kept some of her cake-decorating equipment. And the small, yellow chef's blowtorch she used for scorching crèmes brûlées.

When she pressed the lever, the nozzle spouted instant, bright blue flame.

She turned the heat on the bundle of ivory silk in the trough, aiming the flame directly at the embroidered monogram on the pocket, and then at the insufferable rudeness of the XS size tag at the neck. The torch felt like an extension of herself. Blasting out fire and fury.

Saturday

Outsourcing sex. Emotional fraud. Far out. Had he actually said those things? Oh yes, he had. Although he'd gone over his exchange with Marnie multiple times these past days, his own words were still embarrassingly fresh in his memory.

The world beyond his bedroom window was dark as he pulled his shirt over his head and lobbed it in the direction of the laundry hamper, took off his jeans and draped them across the arm of a chair, which was an early and imperfect example of the 'Winnipeg'. Then, in the ensuite bathroom, he confronted his idiot self in the mirror above the basin.

'Dickhead,' he accused his reflection.

Why had he said that stuff to her? *Why?*

Brushing his teeth more vigorously than strictly necessary, he replayed the whole thing in his head yet again. They'd been having fun. Debating, bantering. Possibly flirting. He'd even been thinking about suggesting that they continue the argument over a glass or two in the fancy new wine bar down the road from the gallery. But instead, he'd gone and taken things too far. Marnie had laughed at his jibes, but her laugh had come out tinny and forced. And he'd seen the flinch in her eyes, the slight physical recoil. That had been the end of it, really. After that, she'd started looking for a way to say goodbye.

Luke spat toothpaste froth into the basin. He glanced up at himself again, shook his head. If he'd had the sense to pull that punch instead of landing it square on her jaw, things might have been very different. Instead of coming home that afternoon and opening a beer, alone, he might have found himself sitting with Marnie Fairchild at one of the wine bar's high tables with their rough-hewn tops and tall stools. Maybe, just maybe, instead of throwing together a pasta dish involving a random selection of leftovers from the fridge, and spending his night watching reruns of *Grand Designs*, maybe, just maybe, a couple of drinks at the wine bar could have segued into wood-fired pizza down by the river.

He and she had talked a decent while at the gallery, and yet – Luke knew – he hadn't even begun to get past the surface of her. Marnie struck him as something like a well-crafted puzzle box – all smooth, polished planes and invisible joins. He knew how such things worked, though. You just had to figure out the trick, find the exact place to push or twist. There was always a way. It was only a matter of finding it. But accusing a woman of emotional fraud? That was most certainly not it.

Luke flung back the covers and got into bed, wedging all four pillows behind himself for a back-rest. When he picked up the book on his bedside table, a droll laugh escaped him. Because just when he'd rather have stopped thinking about Marnie Fairchild, and how badly he'd made a knob of himself in front of her, there on his lap was a 1028-page, fully illustrated, hardback reminder of her in the shape of the *Atlas of Furniture Design*.

Luke turned to his bookmarked page and took in the iconic shape of George Nelson's multi-coloured marshmallow sofa, and although his eyes roved over the words that described its history and significance, none of the details made their way into his preoccupied mind. How, exactly, did Marnie do it? What was the exact sequence? Had she decided upon buying him a book, then gone hunting for the ideal one? Was that how it worked? Or had she come upon this book, perhaps even in the Art Gallery shop – which was where he'd first seen it, but been too frugal to fork out the hundreds it would have cost to buy it – and known that he'd love it?

How, without ever meeting him in person, had she worked him out so well? The chisels, the ebony . . . she'd picked him like a nose. So she'd seen his work in galleries, and his father must have told her some things of course, but even so, her choices of gifts for him were almost too perfect. There were so many things he'd have liked to ask her. But after he'd insulted her, she'd done exactly what he would have done himself. She'd walked away.

He closed the heavy book, rearranged the pillows and flicked off the light. But even as he closed his eyes and hoped for sleep, he was still picturing her. The back of her, two long dark-red braids trailing over her shoulders as she strode off, carrying a mountain of shopping bags that he'd failed – until it was too late – to notice were hurting her arms.

At first, the ringtone incorporated itself into Luke's dream, chiming out through the PA system of the misty gallery through which he was walking – alone, mercifully, since every image on the charcoal-coloured walls depicted Luke himself, often naked, and always in a less-than-flattering pose. But as he drifted up into sleep's shallows, he came to understand that his telephone really was ringing, and that the sound was coming from the jeans he'd slung over the chair.

He moved quickly, getting out of bed and fumbling the phone out of a pocket with sleepy fingers. *Ivy*, the screen said. Luke felt a sudden spike in his pulse, swiped to take the call. 'Ivy?'

But the voice on the other end of the phone was that of a young man. He spoke loudly, almost shouting over the pulse of music. 'Hey, are you the dad of the girl who owns this phone?'

Luke opened his mouth, but no words came out. What? Was he Ivy's dad? That was complicated. And it hardly seemed fair that he was being called upon to answer such a thorny question when he was only half awake. Seconds ticked by as he tried to marshal his thoughts.

'Hello? Are you the dad?'

'Is Ivy all right?' Luke asked. 'Where is she?'

'Ivy, cool. She's a bit of a mess. I don't know her or anything. Her friend was here, but she . . . went, I think. So, Ivy, right? Yeah, I got her phone and scrolled through her contacts. You're her dad?'

'Can you tell me where you are?'

'What?'

Of course, the music. Luke spoke up. 'Can you tell me where you are?'

'You won't, like, come down hard on her? I didn't want to get her into trouble or anything, but the girl she came with? She's left with some guy. And Ivy's a bit . . . well, she's had a bit to drink.'

The young man was, Luke realised, a little drunk himself. 'Can I talk to her?'

'Sure. Hang on. Ivy? Ivy? I've got your dad on the phone.'

He heard Ivy's voice at a slight remove. 'My dad? My *dad*? What the fuck did you do?' And then, right into his ear, 'Hello?'

'Ivy, hi. It's Luke.'

'Why are you talking to me?' She sounded shrill. And very drunk.

'Where are you?'

'I'm at a party. What are you doing calling me?'

'Do you need help getting home?'

'Um. Persia . . . she just went. My wallet's in her bag. I've only got, like, my phone. Don't tell Mum. Please don't. She'll kill me.'

'Ivy. It's all right.' Tentatively, he asked, 'Do you need me to . . . to come and get you?'

'Shit,' Ivy said, and Luke heard the noise of retching. Splashing. Reflexively, he held the phone a little further away from his ear.

Then the young man was back on the phone. 'She's not really looking that great.'

Luke made up his mind. 'I'll come and get her, okay? Just tell me where you are.'

It took some time for the young man to be sure of the street and certain of the house number, but at last Luke had extracted and memorised the details.

'You'll stay with her, until I get there. If she passes out or anything, you'll stay with her,' he said, pitching his tone somewhere between request and command. 'Do you know what to do? If she passes out?'

'Yeah, I'll watch her.'

'Turn her on her side, remember? You don't want her on her back if she spews again. And don't —' Don't what? Don't do anything to her? Don't touch her? Luke wanted to say something in that ballpark, but he pulled himself up, remembering he was talking to a kid who, even when tipsy himself, had demonstrated the good sense to scroll through a drunk girl's phone and call her father. Her *father*. Shit. 'Don't worry. I'm on my way.'

He dragged on his jeans, found a clean shirt and a jumper. Two jumpers. Ivy might need one. He grabbed a couple of towels and an empty ice-cream bucket, too. His ute was no limousine, but he'd been around the block enough times himself to know just how easily vomit could find its way into the deepest, most uncleanable crevices of a vehicle.

As he slid behind the wheel of the ute, Luke tried to identify what he was feeling. He was worried, for sure; awful things happened to drunk girls at parties. But he was also heightened. Was he excited, almost? Maybe. And there was something else, too. It made him feel a bit of a sap to admit it, but he was pleased. Proud, even. His daughter was in a spot of bother. She needed him to come and get her. She needed him to do a thing that a regular father would do. And, even more than that, she had filed his phone number not under 'Luke', but under 'Dad'.

He drove quickly, intensely, tapping the wheel when he had to stop at red lights, getting irritated with the leisurely attitude of other drivers on the road. It took half an hour and Siri's assistance to get him to the right street, but the house itself was easy to find thanks to the police car parked on the verge. As Luke made his way into the house, two officers – their vests and holsters giving them an intimidating bulk – were firmly but calmly discussing the noise with a pack of teenagers.

Inside, the house had an emptied-out feel; it seemed that the music had already been turned down. Luke followed the layout of the house, through a bottle-littered living room to an open-plan kitchen that smelled suspiciously of weed, out to a covered patio. And there she was, curled into the foetal position on the cushions of a two-seater sofa. So vulnerable. Sitting on a nearby chair was a young man who appeared to be watching over her every bit as carefully as Luke had asked him to.

'You're her dad?' the young man asked.

This time, he didn't agonise over the answer. 'Yep.'

He stood for a moment, hands on hips, taking in his daughter's shaggy black hair, and her long eyelashes, which lay in two impressive curls against her cheeks. Were they real? He thought probably not. One of her long rainbow socks was scrunched down to her vomit-splashed Converse while the other was pulled up over her knee, close to the hem of a black skirt. He saw how her David Bowie T-shirt had been inexpertly turned into a midriff top by way of a rubber band that held together all the unwanted fabric in a bunch at her spine. Her belly button was pierced, he noted. There was so very much about her that he didn't know.

Luke crouched at her side, laid a hand on her shoulder, gently rocked her.

'Ivy?'

She made no response.

'She's been out cold since she threw up,' the young man said. 'I'm Cody, by the way.'

'This your place?'

'Nah. It's Richo's. His parents are away.'

Luke felt sure they'd be thrilled when they got back.

'Here's her phone,' Cody said, handing over an early-model iPhone in a Moomintroll case.

Luke thanked him and tried once again to wake Ivy.

'I reckon you might have to carry her,' Cody offered.

Luke felt his eyes go wide. Carry her? Would she be okay with that? Was he okay with that? What was okay, and what was not, in this situation? What was the acceptable code of conduct for fathers meeting their hitherto-unknown daughters for the second time when said daughter was hammered to the point of unconsciousness?

'Ivy?' He shook her a little more firmly this time, but there was still no response.

'Yeah, she's not waking up anytime soon, I don't reckon.'

Luke sighed. Picking up girls, bodily, off couches, wasn't something he did every day. One arm under the shoulders, one under the knees, he supposed. A fireman's lift might be easier on his back, but probably less dignified for Ivy. He didn't know why, precisely – maybe it was just to buy himself some time to think – but he started by pulling up her scrunched-down sock until it almost matched with the other.

'Thanks for keeping an eye on her,' he said to Cody.

'No worries, man.'

To Ivy, as he slipped his arms under her sleeping form, he whispered, 'Come on, you.'

She wasn't light, exactly, but neither was she especially heavy. The smell of spew was present, but not overpowering. As Luke walked through the house and across the lawn, he held Ivy so that her head was supported against his shoulder. It took a little ingenuity to get the ute door open and slide her into the passenger seat. She half woke, murmuring, as he reached the seatbelt across her body and latched it. Luke jogged around the car and got into the driver's seat. He draped his spare jumper across Ivy's upper body, tucking it around her bare arms. He placed a towel on her lap and wedged the ice-cream bucket into the console where he could grab it quickly if necessary.

And now what, genius? He'd been so keen to get here, to pick her up, to make sure she was safe, that he hadn't thought any further ahead. Even if he knew where she lived, with Gillian – which he didn't – he assumed that he'd be landing Ivy in hot water if he took her there. Should he take her to his house? No, that didn't feel right.

He could take her to his own mother's house. That would be more appropriate. And Suzanne had any number of soft beds she could tuck Ivy into. But he didn't think Ivy would thank him for introducing her to her grandmother while comatose and smelling of vomit. Caroline's house? Obviously they'd be welcome there, too, but Luke didn't want to do anything that would cause Ivy to be embarrassed in front of a brand-new aunt and cousins. What options did that leave him with? Unable to come up with any, he turned the key in the ignition.

'Looks like we're going on a bit of a road trip.'

By the time dawn came, Luke's ute had an extra 320 kilometres on the clock.

Ivy had missed the drive through the outer suburbs that crept up the foothills of the mountains to the city's west. She'd missed the owl that had flown low across the road, right in front of the windscreen. She'd missed the fuel station Luke had called into just after she'd spewed again, too unexpectedly for the ice-cream bucket to have been of any use, and where he'd slung a mucky towel into the tray-back of the ute, then gone into the bathrooms to rinse the vomit off his jumper before tucking it around her once again. She'd missed him pulling to a stop right outside the cafe where they'd first met, and where he'd sat for a while, arms folded and head nodding, before tilting back his own seat and closing his eyes.

He slept only lightly, and at the first sound of Ivy's stirring, his eyes were open. She was staring at him in horror.

'Oh, God,' she said, covering her face with both hands.

'Nope. Only me.'

She peered at him through outstretched fingers. 'This is not good.'

Luke shrugged noncommittally and gestured in the direction of the cafe. Sometime in the last half-hour, an OPEN sign had appeared on the door and a sandwich board on the pavement. 'You want something to eat? A coffee?'

Her eyes narrowed, and a memory seemed to come to her. 'He called you. That guy.'

'Cody,' Luke supplied.

Ivy peeled away the jumper and towel and looked down at herself. 'Where's my stuff?'

Luke handed over her phone. 'This is all there was. Your friend? Persia, I think you said? Sounds like she's got the rest of your things.'

Remembrance dawned on her face. 'Great.'

'I could do with a coffee.' Luke yawned. 'It's been a long night.'

Ivy sighed. In frustration? Annoyance? Luke couldn't quite tell.

'I don't have any money,' she said.

Ah . . . pride.

'Well, we're all sorted then,' Luke said, and opened his door. 'Because you paid last time.'

Inside the cafe, Luke led the way to the same booth as before. Ivy tried ordering nothing more than a short black coffee, so in addition to his own coffee, Luke ordered two serves of the breakfast with everything and two freshly squeezed orange juices. When the plates landed on the table, Ivy attempted to ignore the one set in front of her. But the bacon was nicely crisped, and the avocado slices on the side were perfectly ripe, and before long she relented.

'So, did you give my letter to your mum?'

'No.'

'Does she know we've met?'

Ivy shook her head.

'Are you planning to tell her?'

Ivy shrugged. 'Not sure yet.'

That was fair. After all, that's all he could ever have been to Ivy – just some idiot who'd once abandoned her mother. He took a deep breath. 'You were right the other day. My age . . . it was no excuse.'

She looked up at him, those long eyelashes making an impressive frame for dark eyes that, he thought now, contained a little glimmer of new interest.

'I was clueless,' he said. 'And what is worse, gutless. But for the record, I never thought you were just something to be dealt with. I just tried not to think at all, and I was pretty successful.'

Her eyes didn't leave his face. Luke could almost feel it, physically, the way they were examining him, probing, searching his expression for any sign of falseness.

'Ivy, you came and found me, so you must want something from me. Even if it's just to satisfy your curiosity. But if you'll have me, I'd really like . . . you know, to do dad things for you. Like come and pick you up from parties when you've spewed all over your shoes.'

A smile twitched around the edges of Ivy's eyes and lips. At length, she stopped trying to prevent it from spreading across her face. 'I am never drinking tequila again. We did that thing, you know?'

'Lick, sip, suck?' Luke suggested.

'With the salt, and the lemon?'

'Yep. It allows the alcohol to pretty much bypass your tastebuds. Really easy to drink too much that way.'

'Turns out, right?'

For a time, they ate together in companionable silence. Gradually the eggs and bacon, toast and mushrooms restored some colour to Ivy's cheeks.

Luke laid his cutlery across his almost-empty plate. 'So, this friend of yours? Persia? Tell me, how do we feel about her?'

Ivy gave a wry smile. 'How do *we* feel about her?'

Luke nodded seriously.

'You? You're really going to pass judgement on her for skipping out on me?'

'Fair cop,' Luke said. 'The question remains. How do we feel about Persia?'

'We like her. Most of the time. But we don't trust her as far as we could kick her.'

'You were supposed to stay over at hers?'

'Uh-huh.'

'And she was supposed to stay over at yours?'

'Don't tell me you never did it,' Ivy said.

'Of course I did it. But would we agree that if you're going to take risks – like, say, going to a party that your mother doesn't know anything about – Persia is not your ideal wing-woman?'

Ivy tilted her head and raised a single eyebrow. Luke knew that facial expression. The single-eyebrow hitch was something his father could pull off. And Caroline, too. But not Luke himself. 'Shouldn't you be telling me not to go to parties like that? Or not to deceive my mother?'

'Hey. I've known that I'm a father for – what? Just over a week? I haven't had time to read the entire manual. So, until I'm across the fine print, I'm going to stick with saying if you're going to do that kind of stuff, you want to do it with the kind of friend who's going to have your back, the way you'd have theirs, right?'

Ivy sized him up. Smiled. 'Okay, *Dad*.'

Luke suppressed a grin. She'd said it deliberately. She'd said it ironically. But whichever way you looked at it, she'd said it.

Sunday

When all the baby shower guests – except Marnie – had left, Saski flopped down on the couch, and put her feet up on a crochet-covered cushion. Mo, having massively overdrawn on her reserves of social energy, knelt at the side of the coffee table, wearing a huge pair of over-ear headphones while she carefully peeled tabs of tape off salvageable sheets of gift wrap, folded the paper into squares and rolled lengths of ribbon into tidy little skeins.

Stacked neatly by the fireplace, but spilling out onto the hearthrug, were the gifts themselves. Almost every one of them, Marnie had been pleased and proud to note, were thoughtful, tasteful and appropriate. Probably, though, it was fair to say that Marnie's quilt was the biggest hit. After pulling it out of its wrapping, Saski had sat with it for ages, remembering, telling the small, funny stories that went along with the yellow poplin printed with tiny white poodles, and the watermelon-coloured seersucker that had come from a childhood dress she'd loved so much that she'd worn it into her teens, by which time it was a crop top, and the corduroy that came from her favourite pants, out of which her mother had made a coat for their actual white poodle. At length Saski had draped the quilt over the back of the couch. Now, as she reclined, she rested one hand on her belly, and trailed the other across the mixed textures of its squares.

'Thanks, Bunny.'

Marnie, tired from a morning in the shop followed by serving tea and cupcakes to Saski's guests, sat on the hearthrug. 'I'm so glad you like it.'

'I don't just mean the quilt. Don't think I can't see your fingerprints all over this lot.' Saski gestured to the pile of gifts for her baby.

Marnie gave a noncommittal shrug.

'Don't be like that. Come on, tell me. How many of the people here today called you up and asked you what I'd like?'

Marnie made a mysterious face. 'A lady doesn't tell.'

Marnie was good at secrets. While there was nothing Saski didn't know about her friend's financial situation, there were things Marnie kept strictly to herself – like the identity of her clients, and recipients in their portfolios. *Three people*, her grandfather used to say, *can keep a secret. Provided two of them are dead.*

'All right, Miss Secret Squirrel-pants. Have it your way.'

Absentmindedly, Marnie unfolded two tiny for-best playsuits and refolded them the way you might for a shop display. She stacked the board books together and the picture books in a pyramid pile – largest at the bottom.

'Peach,' she said, 'do you think there's anything wrong with what I do?'

'What do you mean?'

'I mean the gift-buying. Is it wrong? Would you say I was committing some kind of emotional fraud on people?'

'Hmmm,' Saski said, looking at her friend diagnostically. 'Who said that?'

Marnie looked up, taken by surprise at Saski's accurate assumption.

'Oh, Bunny in the headlights!' Saski said with a laugh. 'Who was it?'

'Just some guy.'

Saski looked rather too interested. 'What guy?'

Marnie changed tack. 'Okay, forget emotional fraud. Let's talk about aiding and abetting.'

'What's this about, Bunny?' Saski looked worried.

'Let's say, just for argument's sake, that I have a client who's a wealthy man.'

'Your favourite type, in other words. Useless at buying gifts for himself, just wants the whole sticky, risky mess taken care of by somebody else.'

'Correct. So, he gets me to buy for his wife, for his kids, his sister, his godchildren —'

'Hang on,' Saski interrupted. 'If there is a wife, why doesn't she buy for the kids and the sister and the godchildren? It's the sort of thing that pretty regularly does fall to the wife.'

'She does buy presents for their kids and grandkids, but they're not joint presents. They're only from her.'

'That's weird.'

'Yeah, it is a bit unusual. Apparently, they could never agree on what to get their kids. He's all about the big gesture, but even though she's a wealthy woman now, she's still got a frugal streak. Rather than argue, they just get their kids separate presents.'

'Okay, got it. So, where were we? He gets you to buy for the wife, the kids, the siblings, the godkids . . .'

'. . . and the mistress.'

'Of course. There had to be one of those.'

'So, back to my question. Is there something wrong with what

I do? I'm just doing what he asks, right? I'm just providing a service. I'm not the one cheating. I'm not making him cheat. I'm not asking him to cheat. I'm not suggesting he cheats. I'm just buying gifts for a woman who's on his list.'

'Sounding a little defensive, Bunny.'

'Am I?'

'Yep.'

'But is what I'm doing *wrong*? Am I aiding and abetting a cheater?'

Saski adjusted her position. With her huge belly, it didn't look that easy. 'I don't know, honey. You've got to do what feels right to you, I guess.'

Marnie studied Saski carefully, but she could see not the faintest trace of judgement in her expression. All she saw was Saski's usual forthright, honest kindness, and the round mountain of her growing belly beneath the drape of a riotously colourful maternity top.

'What does it feel like?'

'What? Being pregnant?'

Marnie nodded.

Saski thought. 'Do you really want to know, or do you just want me to put you off by talking about the constipation and the heartburn and the piles?'

'I really want to know.'

'Because I don't want to be one of those women who goes on about it to their childless friends. I don't want to be a bore.'

'I mean it. I really want to know.'

'Okay, then. It's a fucking miracle. It's totally amazing. I could lie here all day and just watch my stomach move around. Here, put your hand here.'

Marnie laid a flat palm against Saski's stomach. At first, she felt nothing. But then there was a twitch, something that might have been a nudging elbow. Then a larger movement, like a shoulder rolling under a tight, heavy blanket.

'Oh my goodness, there's a real live human in there,' Marnie said with a nervous laugh.

'I know, right! And we don't know who it is, yet. I already know I will love this person unconditionally, no matter who they turn out to be. It's like giving out a blank cheque, but somehow I'm not even scared.'

'Wow,' Marnie said, a touch wistfully.

'Yeah,' Saski said, meeting her friend's eye. 'Wow.'

Monday

Had you asked Marnie when she first became interested in gift-wrapping, she'd have been able to identify the moment with pinpoint accuracy. It was the day of Katie Nettlebeck's ninth birthday, for which Katie's parents had done something never before seen in Casterbrook, and brought in a professional balloon artist and a face-painter to entertain the kids at the party. They'd even paid someone to take the blue heeler out for a very long walk so it didn't nip any of the party guests on the ankles. Marnie's mother – who'd burned quite a few of her bridges back in the time when she'd thought she'd escaped the town via marriage to Rory Fairchild – had not come inside for tea and chit-chat with the other mums. She'd just dropped Marnie at the letterbox and handed her a gift for the birthday girl.

It wasn't until Marnie put her offering down on the table, the one set aside for the purpose, that she realised: her present was a mess. The gift wrap was cheap, and it had torn in a couple of places to reveal the low-quality pencils and colouring-in book within. Not only was the sticky-tape showing, but it was put on crookedly. The more comparisons little Marnie made, the worse her gift appeared. There was no ribbon. Nor any rosette. Not even a card. Her mum had written *For Katie, from Marnie*, in black

Texta, directly on the gift wrap. In that moment, Marnie made a decision. Her mother was sacked. From now on, Marnie would do the gift-wrapping herself.

More such decisions followed over the years. Chrissie was the type to turn an entire load of laundry pink with a single red garment, or to convert a nice woollen jumper to felt. So, before she even reached her teens, Marnie was washing all her own clothes. Chrissie's version of ironing left wrinkles in the difficult places around cuffs and collars. So, Marnie took over that task, too. About the only thing Chrissie did better than other mums in Casterbrook was make-up. That, she did really well.

Marnie, one eyelid already delicately outlined in black, leaned in close to the mirror of her tiny bathroom in the flat above Wish & Co. Without breaking a sweat, she drew a liquid-liner pen across the second lid so that it perfectly matched the first, and silently thanked her mother for the skill. Her mother. Who lived mostly on unemployment benefits, although she pulled in a bit of extra cash doing tarot readings behind a saffron-yellow curtain in the back room. Extra cash that she deposited, one coin at a time, time after time, into the slots of the poker machines down at the local club.

When Marnie, at fifteen, had started making the one and a half hour each way commute to the city for the upper years of high school, Chrissie had started spending more and more time at the pokies. Soon, Marnie stopped going home so often, preferring instead to stay weeknights in the city with Owen at his father's house. It had been no skin off Gerry Kingston's nose – the house had rooms galore, the housekeeper made sure the fridge was stocked, and a bonus of having Marnie around was that it kept Owen out of his hair. On the weekends, when Marnie went home, she'd walk down to the Casterbrook RSL to find her mother wreathed in cigarette smoke, moodily lit by the screen of a poker machine, her make-up done to perfection, sitting on a high stool with the air of an actress on a film set.

Marnie sketched in her lip-line with a reddish-brown liner and rehearsed the smile she would use, today, on her potential new client, Hugh Cosgrove. He was an orthopaedic surgeon, the newest partner in the practice started by Owen's father, who had referred Hugh to Marnie. If she could snag Hugh, she'd make up for the loss of Lloyd Sherwood; another small ladder climbed. Unlike most of Marnie's clients, Hugh Cosgrove was young. Few people of Marnie's own age had yet come into the kind of wealth that would enable them to afford a professional gift-buyer. She wondered how extensive a portfolio he was after. Just a couple of recipients, or – like Brian Charlesworth – a bucketload.

For today's meeting, their first, she hadn't gone as far as to dress in her olive-green skirt suit, but neither had she defaulted to her regular in-shop wardrobe. She'd picked a middle path, choosing a linen shirtdress with sober navy and oatmeal stripes, and fixing her hair in a French roll.

Emotional fraud, Marnie thought as she applied her lip colour. She scoffed, aloud. Buying gifts for people, buying appropriate and well-thought-out gifts for people – that was not emotional fraud. It was just a sensible use of resources. It was wasteful to give people crap they didn't want. For that matter, it was wasteful to give people beautiful things they didn't want. And her service circumvented that. The gifter used their money wisely, the giftee appreciated a well-chosen present, and, in this way, relationships were enhanced. Marnie was sure about that much. But the question of infidelity. That was a little bit different.

Surely Hugh Cosgrove wouldn't have any delicate arrangements. That sort of thing had to be getting less common, didn't it? The married men of her age, that she knew, were the type who worked four or even three days a week so they could spend one or two days with their kids: way too dedicated to their families to be having extramarital affairs. According to Owen's father, Hugh Cosgrove was married to Alyssa Whittaker, who'd been a year ahead of Marnie at school. Marnie remembered her as blonde, petite and sporty, the kind of natural conciliator who hated it when the other girls in her circle were out of sorts with each other. Marnie could imagine her as the wife of an orthopaedic surgeon. Probably, she and Hugh were already well on the way to breeding half a soccer team's worth of bouncy little moppets. Marnie didn't want to be asked to do anything behind Alyssa's back. Other than buy gifts for her, of course.

Marnie looked at herself in the mirror, rubbed her lips together, pinched her cheeks lightly and tucked a wisp of hair behind her ear. Nice.

She'd arranged to meet Hugh Cosgrove at Rafaello's, a block or two along Dufrene Street from his Alexandria Park surgery. She arrived first, exactly as she had intended to do, and took a corner seat at the table she'd reserved. Her vantage point gave her a moment, when Hugh strolled through the door, to study him.

She saw that he was tall and well-muscled, and that he clearly wanted people to know this, since both his open-necked short-sleeved shirt and business pants were tightly fitted. His shoes, exaggeratedly long and narrow, were the kind of shiny of which Archie Fairchild would have approved. His near-black hair was just a little too perfect, his watch a colossus. His slick style was not one she especially liked; she much preferred Luke Charlesworth's look – his shirt looser, the leather of his boots not so shiny, his smile less practised than the one Hugh now turned on her.

'Marnie?'

She stood, shook his hand. In best-behaviour tones, she said, 'Lovely to meet you.'

It took them about ten minutes to dispense with the small talk – the weather (still very cool for spring), isn't Gerry Kingston a wag (yes, absolutely, they agreed), whether Hugh had been busy in his surgery (end of the football season; he had) – and to order their coffees. Then Marnie shifted herself into gear, unfolding her iPad case, sliding her stylus out of its holder, readying herself to take notes.

'So, I understand you'd like a little help with gift-buying,' she began.

'Yes. Absolutely, yes. Please. Tell me how it works.'

Marnie embarked on a well-rehearsed spiel. It was simple, really. He provided her with a list of people he wanted her to buy for, and of the occasions that were important in his relationships with those people, and he nominated a price ceiling for each person's gifts. She would bill him directly for the cost of the item, wrapping and delivery. She would give him a quote for portfolio management and gift selection, based on his needs.

'I would need a little of your time, once you decide to go ahead' – she used the word 'once' quite deliberately – 'for us to go through each person on your list and capture all the relevant details. After that, the only work you have to do is sit down every now and then with a handful of greeting cards – don't worry, I provide them – and write your personal messages in them. Return the cards to me, and I make sure they turn up with the perfect gift, guaranteed to arrive on time, and beautifully wrapped. Of course, I send you an email ahead of each occasion, so you can keep abreast of what's in each parcel if you want to, but other than that, it's "set and forget". Everything fully taken care of.'

She saw it land with him, the idea of outsourcing all his

gift-buying needs. Inwardly, Marnie high-fived herself; she had him in the bag.

'It's such a bloody headache. I don't know how people do it. Do they just, I don't know, wander around shops, or what? I don't even know where I'd find the time for all that.'

Marnie gave an understanding smile.

He went on, 'No sooner have I got my wife's birthday present sorted out than it's our anniversary. We've only been married six years and I'm already running out of ideas.'

'So, you'd want me to buy for your wife,' Marnie said, without the least intention of revealing to Hugh that she remembered her from school. 'And will your children be on your list also?'

'No, Alyssa buys for the kids, from both of us. And everyone in her family. But she draws the line at my family. Says it's not her job.'

Marnie agreed with her but didn't say so. 'So, your side of the family includes . . .'

'My mother, my stepfather, my sister, her three kids, my brother, his two kids, my father, my half-brother. The kids in particular, yeah? I want them to know that I care, to think I'm a good guy, but it's bloody hard to keep track of them all. There's a whole rash of family birthdays in January and February, and you know what that time of year's like. Crazy. Oh, man, it would be so great if it was all just taken care of.'

He was so much like Brian Charlesworth. Another man who wanted the pleasures that flowed from well-nurtured relationships but wasn't prepared to do the nurturing himself. *Ker-ching*, Marnie thought. Yes, this portfolio would involve a lot of work, but upon the imaginary financial graph in her mind, Marnie saw the income arrow tilting – just a little, but nevertheless significantly – in an upwards direction. She had to pull her thoughts back from the place they inevitably went next: to the 16 November auction and the prospect of the hammer falling in her favour.

Buoyed up, Marnie asked question after question; about the holidays Hugh's family observed and about their gift-giving expectations and traditions. When she felt she had a clear picture, she summed up: 'Well, I've got a good idea of your needs, certainly enough to write you up a quote for my service fee. I have your contact details, so I'll shoot it through to you. It'll be in your inbox by this evening at the latest.'

As Marnie made a move to fold away her iPad, Hugh smiled gratefully, but there was something unsaid skipping around in his eyes. Swiftly, his expression changed, as if a new thought had just occurred to him.

Oh, shit. Marnie tried not to let her trepidation show on her face.

'There is one other thing.'

Let me guess. There's a woman.

'I have a . . . friend.'

Oh, a friend. But wait for it . . .

'She's quite a special friend.'

Imagine my surprise.

'And, ah, a child that . . . well, let's just say . . .'

'Hugh, let me just stop you right there.' Marnie paused herself. She forced herself to think of the excruciating moment that Suzanne Charlesworth opened a gift that had been intended for her husband's lover. She didn't have to force herself to think of her conversation with Luke Charlesworth in the Art Gallery forecourt. She had made her decision; she was quite resolved. But how to communicate it to Hugh?

Warmly, she said, 'I can't wait to get started on the rest of your portfolio, but I don't do "special friends". I'm sure you understand.'

Hugh crossed his arms and tucked in his chin, the look on his face suggesting that she was pulling his leg. 'You're not serious?'

Marnie dialled up her smile to maximum amiability. 'Actually, I'm quite serious. I know this might seem a little airy-fairy, but in a way, I develop a relationship with the people I buy for. Your wife, your mother, your brothers and your sister, your nephews and nieces . . . in order to do my best work, I'll need to get to know them, in a sense. Even if I never meet them in person, I'll care about them. They're your people, of course. But they'll be my people, too. It's part of what makes me good at my job. You're a surgeon. I'm sure you understand about caring for people.'

Hugh looked half amused, his tongue poked firmly into his cheek. 'Gerry led me to believe that complicated lives were, in fact, your specialty.'

I'll bet he did. It was the complexity of Gerry's life that had given him the idea for Marnie's gift-buying business in the first place.

'I'm so sorry to disappoint you,' she said. 'It's just not something I feel comfortable with. But, as I said, I can't wait to start on the rest of your portfolio.'

All traces of Hugh's smile disappeared, from his eyes as well as his lips. His expression was a direct challenge. 'I came here thinking you were offering a service. Not a sermon,' he said.

Marnie put her hands up as if in surrender. 'No sermon. Honestly.' Mentally, she was calculating how low she could go with her service fee in order to keep him in the game. 'Please, just let me send you through the quote for everything we discussed this morning. I think you'll be pleasantly surprised.'

Hugh nodded, but all the enthusiasm had gone out of his eyes. In all but body, he was already out the door. Even so, he had manners. He stood and shook her hand.

'I'll look out for your email,' he said.

But Marnie knew. The bag she thought she'd had him in? It had a big hole in the bottom. One that she'd put there herself.

Thursday

At the wrapping table, Marnie fussed with the pleated folds at the base of a cylinder, now and then glancing over at Saski, who was eating her lunch. A salad sandwich. Which was worryingly full of ingredients that might drip. There was even beetroot, and beetroot and expensive pale pink rag-paper did not mix. With a cheeky smile, Saski brought a tissue out of her pocket and laid it on the surface of the table in front of her as a makeshift placemat, patting it to placate her friend.

'Thank you,' Marnie said, a little more crisply than she'd meant to.

Saski tilted her head. 'You all right, Bunny?'

'Ah, I've had a bit of a shit week.'

'What's been happening, honey?'

'Nothing serious. Just shot myself in the foot with a new client. I so nearly had him, but then I lost him on the fine details. My fault. I was stupid.'

All the way back from Rafaello's, and on and off for the couple of days since, she'd kicked herself for losing Hugh Cosgrove's business. The email he'd sent, sharing his decision not to take her up on her quote, had been polite. But devastatingly brief. She shouldn't even have tried with the whole honourable thing. Why change a winning formula? Why? Just because she'd copped a little bit of criticism from a man with very nice hands and forearms. And good taste in art. And shoes.

Before she started berating herself in earnest all over again, Marnie refocused her attention on getting every single narrow pleat in the pale pink paper to be the same width as every other. Brow furrowed, she tucked the very last fold underneath the first with just a shred of double-sided tape to keep it in place. The whole thing was seamless; perfect.

'Honestly,' Saski said, watching on with an expression of disbelief. 'Why don't you go buy a gift bag?'

'Wash your mouth out,' Marnie said, a little bit of good humour creeping back into her voice. 'I could *make* a gift bag, but even that is tantamount to an admission of defeat.'

'I seriously do not know how you can be bothered.'

'No, but when Christmas comes, you'll be grateful for my superpowers.'

They had a standing arrangement. Mo made Marnie a bottle of something she called Christmas milk, which was wildly alcoholic and very sweet, and which they drank in copious quantities while Marnie wrapped every single one of Saski's and Mo's Christmas presents.

The moment Saski finished her lunch, Marnie swept up her sandwich wrapper, binned it and wiped her hands on her apron. Saski, amused rather than perturbed by Marnie's fastidiousness, pulled a folder out of her bag.

'You ready?' she asked Marnie.

'Hit me with it.'

'Right, so I've talked with three separate brokers, and there's very little difference between the products they can offer you. This is how much you can borrow.'

Saski affixed a sticky note to the surface of the table. Marnie looked at the figure. It was about what she expected, but not quite what she'd hoped for.

'This is really the most? The absolute most I can borrow?'

'Full disclosure: no, it's not. They have higher risk products, which would enable you to borrow more.'

'How much more?'

Saski pulled a sheet of paper out of her folder and indicated a number. It was quite a lot more. 'But because this loan would be considered a much higher risk, the interest rate is higher, which means the repayments would be higher. And we've already determined the most you can repay. Remember?'

Marnie pulled Saski's first sticky note out of her apron pocket and waved it about as proof.

'Excellent.'

Marnie studied the second sticky note. 'Is it going to be enough?'

'There's no way of knowing. We just don't know who else is going to be in the market. But when you go to that auction, this is your top dollar.' She rapped a stern finger on the written figure.

'Unless my sales figures miraculously double, or unless I can find some magical way, between now and the sixteenth of November, to come up with more money,' Marnie said.

'Correct.'

Into the disconsolate hush that fell across the table, the shop's telephone rang.

'Good afternoon, this is Wish and Co.'

'Hello, Marnie?'

Did she recognise that voice? *Could it be?*

'It's Luke Charlesworth.'

'Hi, Luke.' Oh crap, had that come out sounding squeaky?

It had. Marnie knew because of the way Saski looked up from her paperwork, curiosity piqued.

'I wanted to ask you something,' Luke said. 'It's a little bit out of left field, though.'

'O . . . kay?'

'There's somebody I need to buy a present for,' he began, and Marnie was surprised to feel a little sting of disappointment. What had she thought he was going to ask? To the left of which field, precisely, had she been hoping his query would come?

'A birthday present,' he went on.

Wow, Marnie thought. It hadn't taken him long to replace Annalena, then. But why did she care? Luke = client. Nothing more.

'I have to get this gift right. I really need to make an impression.'

Marnie couldn't resist. With a smile in her voice, she said, 'And you want me to commit some emotional fraud on this person, on your behalf?'

If such a thing were possible, Saski perked up even more. Marnie could virtually see the antennae shooting from the top of her head.

'Touché,' he said. 'But no. I want something else, actually. So, here's my left-field enquiry. I don't want to pay you to choose the gift, I want to pay you for a lesson. I want you to teach me how it's done.'

Marnie burst out laughing. 'You think I can teach you that in one lesson? Ever tried to learn a musical instrument?'

'Yeah, yeah, okay, but I'm assuming this is more like learning the recorder than the French horn.'

'The recorder? Wow, you really do know how to flatter a girl.'

Marnie glanced over to see Saski sitting with her hand on her chin, grinning, and with her eyebrows halfway up her forehead.

'Look, sorry. That all came out wrong. Can we wind it back?'

'You can try.'

He affected a courtly voice. 'Ms Fairchild, if you please, would you consider teaching me a little something of the art of gift-buying? Understanding that I will be unable to attain anything like your standard in a single lesson, my aspiration – at best – would be to acquire some of the rudiments. One lesson in stalking, Marnie Fairchild-style. That's all I'm asking for.'

'I do not stalk,' Marnie insisted. 'I research.'

This was becoming less of a lie. In the pages of her diary, she had erased the word 'stalking', and replaced it with the more honourable alternative.

'Will you show me how to do this particular kind of "research"?'

'People think they want to know how a magic trick's done. But they don't; not really. They just want to enjoy the show,' she said. It was her stock answer when people pressed her for details of how she did what she did.

Luke, however, was not deterred. 'I guess I'm not most people. So, what do you say?'

'I'm not sure.' One part of Marnie told her that this was a bad idea. The last thing she needed was to further complicate her entanglement with the Charlesworth family. But another part of her was sure, certain, that she was capable of compartmentalising; Brian over there, and Luke over there. And, in any case, it was only one lesson. 'How much do you expect to pay for me to simply hand over trade secrets to you?'

'I'll leave that up to you. Needless to say, I value your time.'

Marnie thought. 'I'll tell you what – let's trade. Skill for skill. You make me something that you think is worth a lesson.'

'Done,' he said. He didn't appear to even have to think about it. 'So, when are you free?'

'On Saturdays closing time is four pm. You could come to the shop then?'

'Perfect.'

After they'd said their farewells and Marnie had put down the phone, Saski said, 'Ooh la la! What was that all about?'

'Just business,' Marnie said, though she'd have been unable to deny that the phone call had left her feeling a little bit fizzy. She knew she was smiling like a nitwit.

'I'm guessing that was Mr Emotional Fraud. Also known as "just some guy". I'm all ears, Bunny.'

'Nothing to tell,' Marnie insisted. Still, the smile refused to die down.

'Bullshit.'

'He wants me to help him work out how to buy a gift for somebody else, Peach,' Marnie said, serious now.

'What kind of somebody else?'

'A girlfriend. Obviously.'

'Oh, I think not "obviously". Somebody who made up half of the conversation I just heard does not have a girlfriend. Or, at least, they shouldn't have one.'

Marnie looked at her friend and considered. Luke wasn't the duplicitous type. She knew that about him already. And his tone had been distinctly flirtatious. 'Do you think?'

'I shall tell you what I think,' Saski said. 'I think my dear friend Bunny has got a little crush.'

Saturday

The weekend took forever to come, but – at last – it did. Throughout the morning, between the intermittent customers who dropped by for party supplies, and those who came in to get gifts wrapped, Marnie had killed time by redoing her window display to advertise the just-delivered products in her cheerful new colourway, Peaches and Cream, named in Saski's honour. From the storeroom at the back of the shop, she'd pulled out one of her most prized possessions – an antique French dovecote – and to sit inside the arched pigeonholes, she'd made an origami peace dove in each of the new, coordinating wrapping papers.

The dovecote was the real deal. There was nothing fake about the distress to the cream-coloured paint, and the wear and tear to the shingles on the steeply pitched roof was the result of honest-to-goodness weather. To one side of the dovecote, Marnie had placed a wicker basket and filled it with rolls of paper – spots, stripes, florals, fleur-de-lys. Scattered about the scene were gifts in all sizes and shapes, wrapped in those same designs. Her favourite flourish, though, was the small table she'd set to the other side of the dovecote that held a cluster of pillar candles, a large enamel jug and a single fresh peach. While she'd shifted these objects around, she'd found herself using Luke as a reference point, wondering if the arrangement would strike him the way she intended: as being rather like the composition of a classic, still-life painting.

That task complete, she was now wrapping a medley of gifts for Suzanne Charlesworth – a long rectangular box, several cylinders and a stack of flat square parcels. Once each was wrapped in yellow paper, Marnie added a length of white satin ribbon and a spray of fabric flowers: yellow-hearted frangipanis, to create a unifying link back to the deluge of fresh flowers.

Suzanne had not rung to thank Brian, nor acknowledged the flowers' arrival in any other way. But neither, as Marnie reminded Brian over the phone, had she arranged for the whole job-lot of them to be sent back to his office to wilt on his desk. He'd sounded a little disappointed that Operation Frangipani had failed to return an immediate and positive result, but not particularly surprised. He seemed to accept Marnie's counsel that their mission could take some time. As well as some teamwork. She'd asked him to fish out one of the photographs from his desk drawer and leave it for her to collect. Then she'd taken it to a print shop and had it copied for a greeting card, which she later took back to the Charlesworth Group offices for Brian to inscribe. Marnie did not want to even begin to calculate the amount of time she was losing to her one moment of carelessness.

Wrapping complete, Marnie assembled all the elements of the gift in a basket and propped the card in a prominent position. To finish, she twisted ribbon around the basket handle and fixed fabric frangipanis at either end. The effect of the whole was rather lovely. If Marnie did say so herself. *I defy you, Suzanne Charlesworth, to remain unmoved.*

Marnie walked the basket over to the delivery shelf by the front door. And then remembered. Probably best not to leave a gift for Suzanne in a place where Luke could see it. Even the undershelf of the wrapping table, or behind the counter, would be a risk. So, she ran it upstairs to the flat, safely out of sight.

The warm afternoon dragged on, even more tediously than the morning. By two o'clock, Marnie was checking her watch to discover that only five minutes had passed since her last glance. Each time this happened, she reminded herself that there was no cause for this nervous anticipation. Luke was coming to seek her advice. On buying a gift for a special somebody. A special somebody else.

When at last closing time came, Marnie made herself go through her usual routine – locking the door, swinging the sign to CLOSED, and switching the ambient shop music to something a little livelier while she cleared the wrapping table and set to work sweeping the floor. Her only concession to her visitor's imminent arrival was that she ducked into the back room to tidy her hair and touch up her make-up. Other than her lipstick and mascara being a little fresher than they would normally be at 4 pm, she looked entirely natural – apron still on, dustpan and brush in hand – when Luke knocked at the front door. As she went to let him in, she realised that all of her self-talk about calm had been for naught; on the inside she was fizzing like a midnight sparkler.

His shirt, this time, was a deep blue, made of linen with a faint sheen that held the hint of other colours – deep purple, drake green. The sleeves were, again, rolled to the elbows, and in those articulate brown hands of his, Luke held a parcel that was wrapped – passably wrapped, Marnie decided – in white tissue paper.

'Payment,' he said, handing it over.

'In advance?' she asked. 'Should I open it now?'

'As you wish.'

Marnie was curious. And so, at the wrapping table, she peeled away the tissue paper to find herself holding a small cube.

A light timber – blond sassafras, she realised – had been inlaid with dark timber in the manner of a ribbon around a gift. But it wasn't just any dark timber.

'Oh, good grief, you cut the ebony!' Marnie wasn't sure if she was flattered or devastated.

Luke shrugged. 'Didn't use much of it. And anyway, I had to do it some time. I've never cut anything like it before. Like cutting iron.'

Marnie turned the cube over in her hands. This was not something he'd thrown together. It was a piece of exquisite, polished craftsmanship.

'It's a puzzle box,' Luke explained. 'It does open.'

Marnie studied the smoothly joined surfaces. 'How?'

'You think I'm going to give away my trade secrets? Just like that?'

'Which part moves?' Marnie said, already frustrated.

'Work on it,' he said. 'If you haven't figured it out by the next time I see you, I'll show you then.'

The next time I see you. Marnie felt it, the thing with feathers – hope – flap its wings inside her, and looked over at Luke to scan his face. His expression, though warm, betrayed nothing more than friendliness, and, perhaps, habitual good manners. She seriously needed to stop with the hopefulness. Hope, in this situation, ought to be irrelevant. In fact, it should have been non-existent.

'Thank you,' she said. 'It's beautiful. Shall we start?'

'All good with me.'

Marnie made tea for them both, and spread out a large sheet of plain white paper and a bunch of freshly sharpened coloured pencils. She could not help but arrange them in rainbow order.

'Okay, who is our subject?' Marnie asked.

'Her name is Ivy.'

As Marnie wrote the name in thick black strokes at the top of the page, she felt the hope inside her – the supposedly non-existent hope – lose altitude. Determined not to show it, she selected a shade of green and sketched some appropriately shaped leaves on either side. 'And Ivy is . . .'

'Ivy is . . .' Luke took a breath. 'Whew. This is kind of hard. You're actually the very first person I've told.'

So, the relationship was new. Very new. New enough to cause the sweating palms that he now rubbed on his denim-clad thighs. By now, Marnie's non-existent hope was plummeting earthwards.

'She's my daughter.'

'Your *daughter*?' Marnie had not managed to keep the genuine shock out of her voice. A daughter. Not, therefore, a girlfriend. The thing with feathers caught an updraft.

'Yeah, one of those daughters. The type who show up when they're almost sixteen and let you know there were big consequences for some of the dumb stuff you did when you were sixteen yourself.'

'You didn't know anything about her? Back then?'

Luke looked slightly uncomfortable. 'Nope.'

Marnie stared, trying to come to grips with the idea of Luke as the father of a sixteen-year-old child. It was hard to think of him as old enough for such a thing. If he was old enough, then she was, too.

'How long since you found out?'

'A couple of weeks.'

'Wow. And you haven't even told your folks?'

'It doesn't seem like the right time, somehow. Mum and Dad are both . . . well, they're pretty preoccupied at the minute.'

Marnie felt a sting of guilt over the role she'd played in that preoccupation. But then, more strongly, she felt a pang of sorrow for Suzanne, whose life revolved around her two grandchildren, and didn't even know she had a third.

'Right,' Marnie said. Recovering her professional veneer, she turned her attention back to the sheet of paper before them. 'So, her name is Ivy, and she's about to turn sixteen.'

'Yes, and I need the perfect sixteenth birthday present for her. Trouble is, I've only met her twice. I barely know her, but I want to get this right. I've thought and thought, and I just keep drawing blanks.'

'Okay, so tell me everything you do know.'

Luke started to talk, and Marnie – picking up different coloured pencils – jotted down the things he told her. Her full name was Ivy Juliet Yip. She had dark hair, like her mother, Gillian, and light-brown skin. She was slender. She was not exactly short, but neither was she tall. Marnie stood so he could compare, and he decided Ivy was a little shorter.

'Are her ears pierced?' Marnie asked.

'Yes, and her belly button too.'

Marnie blinked, but Luke charged on. He told her the name of Ivy's school, said it was possible she was a fan of David Bowie, described her rainbow socks and Converse high-tops. She was into ceramics; she was part of a climate action group. She played the clarinet. Of the bands he listed as Ivy's favourites, at least half were foreign to Marnie. Her birthday was less than a month away, on 20 October.

'Which makes her a Libran,' Marnie calculated. 'An air sign, like you.'

Luke looked perplexed. 'How . . .?' And then, 'Oh. Of course.'

'Do you have a photo of her?'

'Just the one,' Luke said, and scrolled on his phone.

The girl in the image radiated intelligence, and Marnie could see traces of Charlesworth genetics in her lips, her eyebrows.

'She's stunning.'

Luke's attempt at a neutral expression failed to entirely disguise his pleasure at the praise. 'So, what next?'

Marnie opened her laptop. 'We Google her. But surely you've done that already.'

Luke shook his head.

'Really?' Marnie had thought it was standard practice with anybody one was curious about.

The search returned a handful of hits. In one photograph, from the website of Ivy's school, she was shown as part of a music ensemble, wearing her school dress baggier and longer than many girls of her age would have done. In another, a picture from a newspaper story about a student climate strike, she was wearing heavy eye make-up and a Nirvana T-shirt, exactly like the one Owen owned.

'What are you looking for, exactly?' Luke asked.

'Clues. I'm looking for her style, for what she says about her identity by the things she wears, the items she surrounds herself with, the causes she associates herself with.'

Then began the trawl of social media sites. It wasn't, Marnie explained to Luke, just a matter of looking at Ivy's own profiles, which – to Luke's shock – seemed to be almost completely devoid of any privacy settings. By looking at her friends' profiles, Marnie went on, you could learn a great deal more. Luke watched as Marnie produced more and more pictures of Ivy; holding placards at rallies, in bright T-shirts helping out at market stalls for good causes, at parties – usually in short skirts and with knee-high socks.

'So, what are you seeing?'

'Well, like most teenagers, she's a bit of a chameleon. She's got a few personas, but she's on the edgier side of things. She's not the kind of girl you're going to give a designer handbag or a jewellery box. Ethical choices are going to be important to this girl. Like father, like daughter, hey?'

'So, I'm not imagining it. Gifts really are loaded?'

Marnie continued to note down some of her observations on the big sheet of paper. 'Of course. When people give you gifts that are just not you, it makes you wonder who they're seeing.'

Luke raised an eyebrow meaningfully.

'What?' Marnie asked.

'It's a curious statement, that's all. Coming from the woman who once told me that outsourcing gift-buying was just like . . . what was the example you gave? Employing a tax accountant?'

Marnie flushed. 'I suppose that in a perfect world, everybody would just instinctively give each other perfect gifts. And I'd be out of business.'

'So, do you come from a long line of excellent gift-givers?' Luke asked.

'Ha!' Marnie said, with a touch of bitterness.

'I'm going to take that as a no, then.'

'For my last birthday, my mother bought me tarot cards.'

'Well, they're not something that you're supposed to be able to buy for yourself, are they? Aren't you supposed to get tarot cards as gifts?'

'If you even read tarot cards. Which I don't. But even more off the mark is the fact that she always puts a TattsLotto ticket in my card. I never even check the numbers. I just throw them away. Oh, listen to me. I sound like such a brat! She doesn't have much money. I don't want her spending it on rubbish. On rubbish for me. It's not about the expense. I just wish she knew me. That's all.'

Luke took a swig of his tea, which, if it was anything like her own, would be cold by now. 'I know what you mean. My dad? Sometimes he just used to give me a wad of cash inside a card. I don't know whether he really couldn't think of anything I'd like, or whether he just ran out of time to give it any thought at all, but it just didn't mean anything to me. I don't want to complain either. Heaps of kids would love that. But for my dad, money's always been the thing you use to solve your problems. The easy option, you know?'

Marnie did know. The belief that money could solve any problem was one widely shared by her wealthy male clients.

'Dad's sister tells this story. When I was born and Mum was still in hospital with me, Dad took my sister to a picnic, and while they were there she had one of those explosive accidents that toddlers do.'

'Ah, the poo-nami,' Marnie said.

'That's the one. Dad took Caroline, holding her out at arm's length, dripping, to his sister, and said, "I haven't got another nappy in me today. Please, if you'll just change the nappy, I'll give you five hundred dollars."'

'That's a lot of money for one nappy.'

'Yeah, I know. It kind of puts the fifty-dollar notes in my birthday cards in the shade.' Luke laughed. 'But I'm not complaining about the amount. That wasn't the problem. The problem was that it was a pattern. He paid someone else to teach me to play cricket – and, you know, he was a good batsman in his day. He paid someone else to help me with my homework. He outsourced me. He outsourced us all. So, when I found out he paid you to buy his gifts, it just seemed like more of the same.'

'I get it.'

'I'm really sorry I was so rude the other day,' Luke said. Then, looking Marnie directly in the eye, 'I am glad, though, that you're not working for Dad any more.'

Marnie, her conscience pricked, thought of the basketful of gifts upstairs in the flat. The one that she had, quite deliberately, hidden from him.

Luke went on, 'My mother's always babied him, making his favourite meals, booking his dentist appointments, organising all the family events.'

'Emotional labour,' Marnie said.

'Is that what you call it? She's always done it all. I can't wait to see him forced to do things for himself for once. He can't pay for everything.'

'Your mum didn't seem unhappy with her life though,' Marnie said, feeling oddly defensive on Brian's behalf. 'I always thought they were quite the love story, actually.'

'Do people in a love story cheat on each other?'

'You'd probably be surprised how often.'

'So, I was right? You do have a lot of clients with a bit on the side?'

Marnie sketched another scroll of ivy along the edge of the paper, avoiding Luke's direct gaze. 'I think things are changing.'

'Really?'

'Yeah, I turned someone down this week.' This was only, Marnie told herself, an exaggeration of what had transpired between herself and Hugh Cosgrove – not precisely a lie. It was true that she had established a boundary, and that it had cost her his business.

'Why?'

'It might have had to do with how I felt about your mum getting the wrong gift. Or it might have had to do with how I felt when' – she took a breath – 'you called me out on it.'

'Well, that pleases me.'

Marnie bristled. Just slightly. She didn't need his seal of approval on the way she did business, with whom, or why. 'Not so good for the bottom line, though.'

'Does it matter so much? A client here and there. Surely that can't make or break your viability?'

'It's not about viability.' Marnie went to the counter and returned with her framed photograph of Fairchild & Sons. She passed it to Luke. 'It's about this place being up for sale.'

He studied the photograph. 'I did wonder if you were one of those Fairchilds. I went to school with Charlie and Ava.'

'Second cousins,' Marnie explained. 'Not that I've ever met them. Not properly, anyway.'

The note of bitterness in her voice didn't appear to land upon Luke. He was still examining the picture. 'And you want to buy it?'

'Yes, but I don't know if —'

'Your name, you being part of the family, that's got to give you some kind of inside running, surely?'

Marnie shook her head regretfully. 'Long story.'

Luke seemed to reappraise her, and to be surprised. 'That's serious money.'

'I'll be borrowing. Obviously.'

'Even so. To be in a position to do that. Are you buying with . . . a partner?'

Marnie looked at him closely. Yes, she thought, it had cost him something to ask that. He had put himself ever so slightly on the line. 'No. No partner. In business, or in life.'

Her words were forthright, but once she'd said them, she found herself unable to hold Luke's intense hazel-eyed gaze. She let out an uncomfortable half-laugh. 'We're a bit off track, aren't we?'

With a *let's-get-back-to-work* air, Marnie drew three overlapping circles on an empty stretch of the sheet of paper.

'A Venn diagram?' Luke asked.

'You bet. There are three main things. One is the person. Two is the occasion.' In one circle, she wrote 'Ivy'. In the second, she drew a cake with sixteen candles. 'A sixteenth birthday is significant. It doesn't signify adulthood, per se, but it's close. It's certainly when a gift ought to gesture to the adult future, not the childhood past. It's a time to give someone something a little more grown-up than they've ever had before.'

'And three?' Luke asked.

'Three is the relationship.' Marnie made a rough sketch of a father and a daughter inside the third circle. 'The perfect gift constitutes a memorable episode in the story of your relationship.'

As Marnie said this, she remembered – ruefully – that Suzanne Charlesworth would never, ever forget the gift she got for her fortieth wedding anniversary. 'For you and Ivy, it's like a first episode. This is the first birthday of her life that she'll get a gift from her father. The person, the occasion, the relationship – you'll find your perfect gift right here.' She tapped her pencil in the space where the three circles overlapped.

'Does the gift have to be only one thing?'

'No, of course not,' Marnie said, and was about to add that a collection of things, joined by some kind of theme, could make a wonderful gift. But then she remembered that the present Suzanne was about to receive operated on this principle. So, without saying anything more, she closed her laptop, rolled the paper, and found a rubber band to keep it secure.

She handed it to him. 'Good luck.'

When she showed him to the door, Marnie noted that the sun

was already quite low in the sky, and that although the warmth of the day was ebbing, the air still held the promise of a mild, springtime evening. Among the people out on the street were couples, hand in hand. On their way out for a meal or a drink, Marnie supposed.

'Today was great,' Luke said. He was leaning against the open door, half in, half out of the shop. 'Really helpful. Could we do it again?'

Marnie was surprised. 'You think you need another lesson?'

'I could bring you my ideas. You could critique them.'

'Wouldn't that be sailing dangerously close to a situation where I was actually helping you choose?' She'd not have been able to deny that she was flirting, now.

Luke's smile matched hers. 'The ideas will be mine. And so will the final decision.'

Marnie considered. 'Okay, then.'

'Same time next week? Here?'

'Sure.' Marnie nodded as casually as she could manage.

'Same payment?'

'Oh, I couldn't.' Marnie glanced back over her shoulder at the puzzle box on the table. 'The time you must have spent . . . it wouldn't be a fair trade.'

'Don't sell yourself short,' he said. 'I've learned a lot today.'

'Well, there is something,' Marnie said, surprising herself. She'd meant to continue insisting that he shouldn't bother, but these quite different words had come out of her mouth almost before the thought appeared in her head.

'Yeah?'

'Don't suppose you'd take a walk to Fairchild and Sons with me? Give me some advice? I mean, I don't know if I'm going to be able to buy it or not, yet. But it would be great to have an educated idea of what kind of work's going to need to go into the timber-work on the facade.'

Luke seemed pleased with that idea. 'Advice for advice? Brilliant.'

'We could meet there?'

'Sounds like a plan.'

Luke stepped out the door, holding up the scroll of paper in a gesture of farewell.

A week.

It felt, to Marnie, like a very long time to wait.

— PART FOUR —

PART FOUR

Monday

For Suzanne, it had been one of those mornings: the slow kind that involve a dressing gown and the studious evasion of mirrors. Not a glamorous dressing gown, either. Not silky, not slinky, but one of the plush, mumsy sort you'd see advertised in gift catalogues for Mother's Day. Still wrapped in a good half-acre of mid-pink fleece at around noon, Suzanne sat on the living room sofa, regarding the thing on the coffee table that had just been delivered by courier – a frangipani-trimmed basket of gifts, each one wrapped in soft-yellow paper.

The basket seemed to emit a pulse of life and energy. Implicit in this offering, Suzanne knew, was a question. A plea. But for now, that plea was contained – beautifully wrapped, trussed in white satin ribbon – and Suzanne found that she both wanted, and did not want, to let it loose. So, she settled for counting the number of parcels. Eight. Consciously, she allowed herself to feel all the things that flooded into the empty parts of her when she looked at her own name written in Brian's assured handwriting on the front of the envelope that was invitingly angled amid the parcels. Then, with a sense of triumphant restraint, she stood up and walked away.

The following day – Tuesday – Suzanne returned to the sofa. Once again, she could feel how the basket radiated a kind of life-force, like a gentle fire to which she might hold up the palms of her hands. After thinking for a while, she lifted out the envelope and turned it over in her hands. She slipped a finger under the envelope's flap, felt the glue loosen and give. Then, she remembered all the promises she had made to herself, and all the resolve she had already invested.

She had managed not to call Brian after he had filled the house with frangipanis. She had managed, also, not to call him in the middle of that awful night when she'd woken from a dream about Brian dying, only to find his side of the bed empty. Heart thumping, mouth dry, it had taken her a moment to come back to earth. He had not died. The reason he was not in her bed was because she'd asked him to leave. Although she had cried, and although she had desperately wanted to speak to him, she'd stopped herself. She wasn't going to give in and call him now, just because he'd sent a basket of gifts.

She would have to call him eventually, of course. And soon, she would have to call her solicitor, and start the process of disentangling her legal and financial affairs from his. The task felt monumental, but she didn't have to do it yet. She was still bruised and aching and vulnerable – still much too fragile, she realised as she held the envelope in her hands, to cope dispassionately with whatever Brian had written inside it. So, she folded the flap down again and shoved the envelope back into its place. When she left the living room, she closed the door firmly behind her, pulling on the handle until she heard the final, definitive click of the latch.

On Wednesday, Leila woke with a slight temperature, and rather than send her to childcare, Caroline brought her to her grandmother for the day. Beneath the noise of Leila's chatter, complaints, laughter and fussing, Suzanne could still hear the subtle, buttercup-yellow call of the gift basket in the closed-off living room. To block it out, she threw herself with a passion into meeting Leila's desires – making playdough in no fewer than six colours, sitting down to an elaborate dolls' picnic on a rug out in the back garden, reading *Where Is the Green Sheep* so many times that, at last, in a totally unprecedented move, Leila herself closed the book and put it aside.

But then came Thursday, and Thursday night, ever since Caroline and Luke had left home, had been Suzanne and Brian's night. While Friday nights had a habit of filling up with family occasions, social engagements and Brian's work events, Thursday nights were an oasis. Brian would come home a little earlier than usual and open a bottle of good wine while Suzanne broke out the best cheese. Sometimes they'd watch a movie on the small television in their bedroom. Other times, they'd run a bath, bubbles as high as their armpits, and sip wine while they chatted, planned and reminisced. How she missed him. And all the while, on the coffee table in the living room, was a parcel, singing out to her that she didn't have to be without him. Not if she didn't want to.

She slept for a good part of that Thursday, telling herself Leila had worn her out the day before, but in truth she was just trying not to capitulate. So long as she was asleep, she didn't have to discipline herself to stay out of the living room, to leave the phone alone. At last, when she couldn't sleep any longer and after she'd come to the last page, on her Kindle, of *All Men are Bastards* by someone calling themselves 'Myra Venge', she got up. Then, without ceremony, and without any anticipation of pleasure, she yanked open the living room door and confronted the basketful of gifts.

This time, she did not start with the card. Screw manners. Instead, she went first for the largest of the parcels – a long rectangular box. She did not take the paper off carefully so that it might be re-used. She tore it away. Inside was a plain cardboard box that reminded her painfully of the last plain cardboard box she'd opened. But she persisted, opening it to reveal an easel. A fold-out *plein air* easel, its brand synonymous with quality.

She did not slow down. Ripping at paper and cardboard, she discovered that the flat parcels contained canvases, a palette, and a sumptuous graduating rainbow of oil paints. In the cylinders were brushes, and more brushes, and still more brushes – their tips ranging from impossibly narrow to stubby and plush. It had been a long time since she'd painted. Such a long, long time. Just looking at these implements made her fingers twitch with anticipation. Part of her was already out on the back lawn with the easel unfolded, and with the colours to render the blossoming apple tree squeezed in bright worms of pigment onto the palette. *Bastard*.

Soon all that remained in the basket was the envelope. Suzanne tugged out the card. *Oh*. The image on the front almost hurt her with the saturation of its vintage colours, with the force of memory. It was a copy of an old photograph that dated from their Kelsey Street days. Of her. Hair a light and natural blonde, the summery, too-short top a bright turquoise, the underpants a scrap of pink beneath the rosy and voluptuous pregnant belly. That was Caroline, unborn. Suzanne and Brian weren't even parents at the time, just parents-in-waiting, and she was standing at her easel – the old rickety one she'd bought second hand when she'd been at art school – poking out her tongue at the person holding the camera. Who was, of course, Brian.

She remembered that day. A summer's day. Suzanne's studies were over by then, and all she had to do was wait for Caroline to arrive. It was the last of their days before the routines and the responsibilities set in. Suzanne had been painting Brian; he'd been posing, nude, on their bed. He'd had such a beautiful body, though he'd been absolutely useless at keeping still. At one point, she'd looked up to find him holding not his pose, but their camera. He'd said something good-naturedly lewd. The sort of thing lovers say when they're alone and slightly off their scones with lust. *Double bastard.*

Inside the card, there were words. It was a struggle for Suzanne to focus on them. *I want to go back to the good times. With you. I'm sorry. Love, Brian.*

'Triple fucking bastard,' she whispered to herself, and hurled the card. Although, as angry gestures went, it wasn't that satisfying; the card travelled hardly any distance at all before fluttering to the floor.

She missed him, she wanted him. She hated him, she would never forgive him. She was hurting. She wanted him to hold her, to make it better. She wanted to hurt him, to slice him open with words, to freeze him with indifference. She wanted to scream, she wanted to cry, she wanted to curl up in a ball on the living room floor and sleep it all off. She wanted the feelings – all of them – to, just, stop.

Leaving the basket and whole mess of yellow paper and fabric flowers behind her, she collected up the components of her gift and went into the formal dining room. There, on the sideboard, was the leather bag – the Weekender. *Z-i-i-i-p*, she opened it, and shoved the paints, palette and brushes inside. Then, before she could change her mind or think, she took the bag through to the kitchen, dumped it on the bench and found her phone. What was the name of the bloody place? The trout-fishing lodge? Watersmeet. That was it.

'Hey, Siri,' she commanded. 'Call Watersmeet Lodge.'

For once, Siri seemed to grasp the urgency of the situation and didn't ask any irritating supplementary questions. As the phone began to ring, Suzanne jittered her fingernails against the benchtop.

'Good evening, this is Watersmeet Lodge.'

'I'd like to make a reservation, please.'

'Of course! Which dates did you have in mind?'

'Tonight,' Suzanne said.

'To . . . night?'

It was past seven already, and to drive there would take three hours, at least. But what else, now, did her Thursday nights have in store? She could eat on the way and still be there before midnight.

'Yes,' Suzanne said. 'Tonight.'

Friday

Marnie strolled through the sliding doors of the Charlesworth Group offices, first thing, and approached the desk where Gina, red lipstick as glossy as ever, sat upright at her terminal, immaculately turned out in a vintage pinafore that reminded Marnie of something Ray Eames might have worn.

'For you,' she said, and handed over a gift pack of smaller wares – tealight candles, mini-napkins, notepaper and envelopes – from the Peaches and Cream colourway. 'I just wanted to thank you. You know, for all the things you do.'

'Marnie, thank you!'

'No, thank *you*, for always being so helpful. Is he ready?'

'This time you're right here in the calendar. He's waiting for you, so you can go on in.'

Gina emphasised the words 'this time'. Clearly, she was dying to know the cause of the frostiness she'd previously witnessed between Marnie and Brian, but Marnie had no intention of sharing. A warm smile, some words of appreciation and a little bit of lovely merchandise ought to be enough to keep Gina sweet, even if it didn't sate her curiosity.

Brian was standing at the window.

'Marnie.' He held up the coffee mug in his hand. 'Shall I have Gina get you one?'

'No, no. I'm fine, thanks.' All she really wanted to know was whether or not Suzanne's gift basket had netted a response. 'So . . . how did we go?'

He shook his head despondently. 'Nothing. Not a peep.'

Marnie let out a long, slow breath. It was disappointing news, but probably to be expected.

'I thought she'd at least send a text,' Brian said. He sank into the chair behind his desk and gestured for Marnie to sit across from him. 'It's the not-knowing. That's what I really hate.'

'I'm sorry,' Marnie murmured. Since they had begun working together in earnest on Project Suzanne, Marnie had become aware that there were more sides to Brian Charlesworth than she'd originally thought. Yes, there was the ego, and yes, the quick temper. But Suzanne's protracted silence was killing him, and not only because he hated the idea that there was anything in the world he couldn't get to bend to his will or respond to his purchasing power. There was more to it than that. A lot more. Without Suzanne, Brian was lost, adrift, lonely, bereft. There had been barely a trace of regret in his demeanour when he'd asked Marnie to remove Leona from his gift portfolio. It seemed to Marnie that for as long as Brian had been able to have both women, he'd been content to do so, but when forced to choose, he was quite certain. It was his wife he really wanted.

'So, what do we do now?' Brian asked.

'We stay the course,' Marnie said, trying to sound confident. 'This was always going to be a tough gig.'

'What's your next idea?'

Marnie drew her laptop out of her messenger bag and clicked open the file called 'Suzanne Ideas'. It was a living document of long standing in which Marnie kept track of the gifts Brian had already given his wife, and noted any wishes that Suzanne expressed on social media, or trends that interested her. Over the years, Marnie had trained herself to capture those fleeting thoughts that popped up when she was out and about shopping, flicking through magazines or people-watching in a cafe. If ever she thought 'Suzanne might like that' or 'that's very Suzanne', Marnie would make a note in her document. Prior to her meeting with Brian, she'd highlighted several ideas, but hadn't yet decided which to present.

In one way, it didn't matter which idea she settled on. They were all good ones, and from an entirely selfish point of view, Marnie knew that all she really had to do was keep Brian convinced that their efforts would eventually pay off. She had to keep him in the game until Fairchild & Sons went to auction. She was surprised to discover, though, that the nature of her investment in this mission was changing. There was part of her now that truly felt sorry for Brian. That wanted him to find a way to be redeemed in his wife's eyes. But how exactly was she going to help him make that happen? She was looking not simply for something Suzanne would like, but something that would really touch a nerve.

'Should we be thinking jewellery?' Brian suggested, waving his coffee cup around. 'A ring, maybe? Rings, commitment. They go together, don't they?'

Marnie glanced up at him, brow furrowed. The man had been married for forty years and not noticed that his wife barely wore jewellery? He was out of his depth, and from his jesting, uncertain tone, Marnie could tell that he knew it, too. Summoning her tact, she said, 'So, I've never met Suzanne in person, but you know that I've seen a lot of photographs of her, yes?'

Brian nodded.

'I've noticed that she doesn't seem to wear a lot of jewellery,' Marnie said. 'Not even on special occasions. Some women are all about the bling. But not your wife.'

'What *is* she all about, then?'

'Come on, Brian. Think,' Marnie said, then wished she had not. She should not allow herself to betray frustration. After all, this kind of cluelessness was a cornerstone of her gift-buying service. Without it, she'd be just a shop owner who tied pretty bows on parcels.

'I thought that was what I paid you for,' he said, and although he was still being light-hearted, Marnie detected a hint of steel in his voice.

She gave him a confident smile, designed to reassure him. She needed him to believe that she knew exactly what she was doing. 'The thing about gifts is that people want to feel seen. They want to feel known.' *It's about paying attention*, she wanted to say to him. *It's about being specific. Not generic.* 'The art supply gifts were about telling Suzanne that you see who she was, as well as who she is now.'

'It didn't work, though,' Brian said, a touch petulantly in Marnie's view.

'I think we have to take a multi-faceted approach. And, for our next trick, I think we need to shift closer to home. Because if Suzanne is "about" any one thing, it's her family. And for her, that means her home, her kitchen, her dining table. Her garden.'

'So, what exactly do you suggest?'

'A rose.'

'A rose?' He sounded underwhelmed.

'As you know,' Marnie said, unsure whether or not Brian actually would know this fact, 'quite a lot of the roses in your garden at Austinmer Street are from the same breeder. What you might not know is that the breeder has a relatively new cultivar that you don't yet have in your garden. And it's called, wait for it . . . "Suzanne". Very pretty. Two-tone petals – white with pink tips.'

'Luke gave her a rose bush last Christmas,' Brian objected.

So, Luke gave his mother a rose, did he? Well, great minds thought alike. And so did theirs.

'Ah, but was it her very own rose?' she countered.

'The frangipanis didn't work. Why would a rose bush?'

'Oh, I think we can do a little better than *a* rose bush, don't you?'

'What do you have in mind?'

'What if you were to give her an entire bed of her own roses?'

Marnie watched Brian consider that while he took a deep sip of his coffee. She continued, 'What I'm wondering is whether there's room in your back garden for a whole bed of "Suzannes"? If so, we could consider, maybe, twenty rose bushes?'

'Ye-e-es,' Brian said. And then, more definitely, 'Yes, I like that idea. She does love her roses. I'll send you the number of our regular gardener, Vincent. She trusts him. But make it forty bushes. One for every year of our marriage.'

'Nice thinking!' And she was, quite genuinely, impressed with his sense of scale, and occasion. It must really be something, she thought, to live a life in which money was no obstacle. 'But . . .'

'Yes?'

Marnie knew she really shouldn't do it. She shouldn't use information gleaned from Luke in the service of Project Suzanne. Although, she rationalised, all Luke had really done was put into words something Marnie would have been able to work out for herself anyway, which was that Brian's habit of outsourcing didn't always sit well with his family.

'Is it really the best move to send the gardener?' Marnie hinted.

'It would be a lot of work for her, digging in that many roses,' Brian said.

'I wasn't thinking that Suzanne should do it.' She looked at him with raised eyebrows.

Brian's eyes went wide. 'Who? Me?'

Yes! Marnie thought, watching as her own thought blossomed in his head.

'You want me, me personally, to dig in forty rose bushes? Suzanne's more likely to be able to do it than I am. I can't even remember the last time I picked up a shovel.'

He was not an unfit man, but even so it was an effort to imagine him in shorts and a pair of elastic-sided boots, digging in the dirt. 'But you could do it. If you wanted to. And would a practical demonstration of devotion really be such a bad thing right now? She's worth the effort, isn't she? I mean she's worth *your* effort.'

Brian leaned back in his chair, steepling his fingers. He nodded. 'You order the roses. I'll think about how to get them in the ground.'

'It shall be done.' Marnie snapped her laptop shut and stood in readiness to leave.

'One more thing,' Brian said, still in his chair.

'Yes?'

'Something I've been wondering about is . . . why are you doing this? Why are you busting your backside to fix this?'

Marnie blinked. She wondered if Brian had forgotten the shot he'd sent across her bow in the form of that phone call from Lloyd Sherwood. She wondered if, now that they were working together so closely, he'd failed to remember he'd been willing to use his power to damage her reputation. If he had forgotten, then that could only be for the good. She would leave it in the past.

'I'm only one client,' Brian said. 'Why not just put the whole sorry mess down to experience and move on? Find yourself another customer?'

This, Marnie realised, was something quite new. Curiosity was hardly one of Brian's strong suits; in all the time they'd worked together, he'd shown zero interest in finding out more about her. She was both flattered and nervous. Was he the sort of person to whom she really wanted to reveal herself?

'Honestly?' Marnie asked.

'Honestly.'

Marnie felt an impulse to be truthful. But was that wise? Or would it turn out to be something she would regret? She didn't know, but even though she wasn't completely sure she knew what she was doing, she found herself saying, 'I can't afford to lose you right now.'

Brian nodded, as if this was something he could understand and respect. 'Because?'

'My shop needs a new home. There's a property I want to buy. I need my figures in the best possible shape if I'm going to borrow enough to get what I want.' Marnie herself had heard the steel in her voice as she said that, and she could see from the look on Brian's face that he had too.

'What's the property?'

'Fairchild and Sons.'

'The old shop?'

'That's the one.'

'So, you are one of those Fairchilds,' he said.

'Archie was my grandfather.'

'I remember him. He was a good bloke. Honest, hardworking.'

'Yes,' Marnie said.

'But you're buying it? Alone?'

'Yes.'

'No family support?'

Marnie shook her head. 'I'm Rory's daughter.'

A flicker of sympathy rippled across his face, along with a dawning of understanding. He sat forward, elbows on the desk. 'It's Lewis who owns it now, isn't it? Well, it's about time he let someone else do something with the old place rather than have it sit there half burned – Archie's memory deserves better. So, can you afford it?'

'I don't know yet. There'll be an auction.'

Brian pressed his lips together. 'Not ideal. And it's not a good time to buy. Prices are high.'

'I know.'

There was something new in Brian's gaze now. A kind of respect, as if he'd just realised that Marnie was a serious businesswoman. He stood and came around the front of the desk.

'I can imagine your business in that place,' he said. 'I really can.'

Marnie, feeling a surprising prickle of tears at the back of her eyes, hoped he had not noticed, but seen only her smile. 'Thanks, Brian.'

He walked her to the door, but before she stepped out into the waiting room, he said, 'This will work, won't it? With Suzanne? We will get there in the end, won't we?'

'I'm sure of it,' Marnie lied.

Marnie hurried past Gina with a wave and a smile. She kept the smile on her face all the way to the elevator, and it was only once she was inside that she let it fall. Was it going to work? If she and Brian, together, were going to break Suzanne's resolve, then Marnie was going to need more ideas. Good ideas.

Maybe the roses would work, but what if they didn't? What

was *the* idea? The one that would turn the tide and deliver the result she needed? What, on earth, would prove to be the magic bullet?

Ivy wasn't used to being here. School bag at her feet, the sun cooking her hair, she observed some of the younger boys larking about, squirting each other with the warm, smelly water from their drink bottles. She kept herself slightly apart from the girls in her own year group, who leaned against the afternoon heat of the brick walls, gingham dresses hitched up so the hems sat around the tops of their thighs, and talked in conspiratorial tones about their plans for the coming weekend.

She supposed it was just normal for these kids to hang out here, killing time at the top of the school's big circular driveway, until they caught sight of the car that was coming for them. Then they'd sling their school bags in through the rear door of some hulking great SUV, and slide into the passenger seat without so much as turning to look at their mum, or dad, behind the wheel. In all her years of high school, Ivy had never been picked up here. Her mum had always worked long hours at the nursing home. Usually, at the end of the day, Ivy would leave campus in the other direction, on foot, making her way along the main road to the train station. But today was different. Today was something new.

Across the curve of the turning circle, in the gap between two cars in the inching conga-line, she caught sight of Persia – dip-dyed hair so aggressively straightened that it looked like nylon. Persia waved furiously, then pushed through the crowd.

'Ivy!' *Mwah, mwah.* 'What are you doing here, hon?'

Ivy affected casualness. 'Just waiting for my dad.'

'Your *dad*? What the actual fuck?'

Don't smile, don't smile. 'Yeah, my dad.'

'Since when do you have a dad?'

Persia could be fun, but when it came to the Book of the Self, she was the sort to whom you showed the cover, and not the inside pages.

'Since I was conceived, I suppose.'

'Oh. I thought you only had a mum.'

Ivy squinted into the sun behind Persia's ironed hair. 'I'm not sure they had the technology for that, back when we were born.'

'For what?' Persia looked confused, but Ivy didn't care, because nosing in through the school gates was a dusty white ute. There were still four or five cars ahead of it in the queue. The kids stood around, waiting until their rides made it to the top of the turning circle. Partly, she wanted to do the same. Partly, she wanted to see Persia's face when her friend looked through the window of the ute and caught a glimpse of her dad. Her young, fit, good-looking dad, who gave off the vibe of a cultivated tradie. It turned out, though, that the stronger part of her just wanted to skip down to where the ute waited, and to keep her dad – for now – all to herself.

'Gotta go,' she told Persia. *Mwah, mwah.* 'See you Monday.'

The books in Ivy's bag hammered against her spine as she jogged past the idling cars and wrenched open the passenger door.

'Hey,' her dad said. Her *dad*.

'Hey, Dad,' she said. And for a minute they grinned at each other like a pair of idiots. They'd agreed to catch up for a coffee after school. Just a regular father and daughter, hanging out together.

'So, where are we going?' Luke asked. 'Usual place, or do you fancy a change of scene?'

Ivy honestly could not care less. 'You choose.'

'Right then,' Luke said. 'I have a plan.'

As Luke drove across town, elbow on the frame of the open window, they talked – about school, about Luke's new commission to make a set of dining chairs for a well-known television actor, about some recent developments in the news on the politics of climate change. With each passing block, Ivy felt as if she was settling deeper into the car seat. The sunny afternoon, her dad's company . . . it was all so freaking comfortable.

At length, Luke nosed the ute into a car park that abutted a riverside reserve. They were going to Clockwork? Cafe by day, cocktail bar by night, it was perched right on the river, and known to Ivy as the kind of place well-heeled mummies took their girls for complicated milkshakes after they'd been out on mother-daughter mani-pedi dates. Ivy felt slightly light-headed with happiness.

They grabbed a table out on the deck, and before long they each had in front of them a milkshake embellished with shards of flavoured chocolate – peppermint for Ivy, honeycomb for Luke. Although the conversation ticked along cheerfully enough, Ivy couldn't shake the sense that her father was slightly distracted, as if one section of his brain was still working on a problem in the background. It was the sort of thing she could easily have ignored, but if the point of these get-togethers was for them to really find out about each other, then honesty was going to be the best policy.

The next time she saw Luke's attention waver, she asked, 'So, you going to tell me what's up?'

'What do you mean?'

'I mean, something's bothering you.'

'How can you tell?' Luke asked, and Ivy smiled. She was sure she had his full attention now.

'Just a hunch.'

'I'm sorry if I've been a bit vague. It's something I'm doing tomorrow.'

'What kind of something?'

He ran a hand through his hair nervously. 'I have a meeting with this woman.'

'Woman, or *woman*?'

'Officially, it's business.'

'But you're interested in her?'

'Hard not to be. She's a very interesting woman.'

'Interesting, how?'

'She's smart. Really perceptive, you know? Creative, has great taste.'

'You can say she's attractive,' Ivy said, with a grin. 'I won't deduct points. Promise.'

Luke blanched. She'd sprung him again. 'She is,' he admitted. 'Attractive. Very.'

'So, why are you nervous?'

'Well, what do I do?'

Ivy looked at him mock-seriously and flexed her fingers as if warming up. But despite her jokiness, she was thrilled to be asked to dispense a little advice.

'Let's go back a bit,' Ivy said. 'What do you usually do wrong? With women?'

'What makes you think I do anything wrong?'

Ivy lifted a single eyebrow. Meaningfully.

'What happened with your mother was a very long time ago,' Luke said.

Thinking of her mother, Ivy felt a sting of guilt. She'd told her she was going to spend some time after school hanging out with a guy she was getting to know. Which wasn't untrue. Soon, though, she was going to have to find the courage to tell her mother who the guy actually was.

'Okay, but more lately? What gets in the way?'

Ivy watched her father think. 'Probably, I'm . . . slow to trust. I suppose I leave the walls up. Hold a bit in reserve, just in case.'

'What, and wait for someone to prove you right by disappointing you?' Ivy asked.

That had landed, Ivy saw. 'Ouch,' Luke said.

'Sounds like you're into self-fulfilling prophecies. You think everyone will disappoint you, and so they do.'

'What's the answer then, Clever Clogs?'

'Don't you have to start every new relationship as if it might be the one that never ends?'

'I don't know, do you?'

'Love's the hokey pokey, Dad.'

'What do you mean?'

'You've got to put your whole self in.'

Luke leaned back in his chair, put his hands on his head. 'Oh, the bravery of the young!'

'Come on! What kind of love story do you want to tell my future little half-brothers and half-sisters?' Ivy noticed the embarrassed expression that took over his face. 'Do you want to have to say, "Yeah, your mum and I dated in a kinda half-arsed, walls-up way for a while, and then we thought, oh, right, we don't exactly hate each other, so we got married." Is that the story you want to tell?'

'Not really. But other than having my heart surgically removed and affixed to my shirtsleeve, what should I do?'

'What's this woman's name?'

'Marnie.'

'And what did you say about Marnie? That she's really

perceptive? Creative? Has great taste? Level *up*, Dad. You're all those things too. Show her. If you like her, don't play it safe.'

'Love's the hokey pokey?'

'That's right. Do something bold.'

'Are you sure?'

Ivy smiled. She was out, at a fancy cafe on the riverfront, with her dad, advising him on his love life. She was happy. 'One hundred per cent.'

Suzanne hardly knew how to take it all in, let alone how to capture it in paint on canvas. The way the two rivers flowed into each other, forming a stretch of herringbone wavelets and creating ribbons of creamy foam; the way the distant and mottled mountains folded over each other in the manner of a stage setting; the way the gum trees stretched out their pale limbs to dangle plumes of leaves, like long green fingers, into the rushing water below. Once she had begun to look, every aspect of the scene seemed to invite her, or command her, to look harder, deeper, more closely.

Her skills, rusty with disuse, were profoundly unequal to the task. Yet, she had persisted. Perhaps the best she could say, as she packed away her equipment, was that she had – for the first time in decades – felt like a painter. In her striped, collarless shirt and broad-brimmed sun hat, standing at her easel on the riverbank, her palette covered with mixings of various olives, browns, creamy whites and inky blues, she had opened her eyes in a particular way, felt her pupils dilate to absorb it all. She had tried, haltingly, to find a language of shape and tone and texture to say what it was that she'd seen. Just to try had been a thrill. Even if the daubings on her canvas were an amateurish mess, she had loved the attempt.

Dappled light fell across the damp and leaf-littered track as Suzanne, feeling the pleasant tug of tiredness that comes from spending an entire day out of doors, made her way back to Watersmeet Lodge. She passed the main building, whose stony walls glowed with a moss-green patina in the afternoon light, and followed the track to her cabin, nestled in lush stretches of man fern, pandanus and rhododendron.

It wasn't until she reached the cabin door that her thoughts returned to the murky places they'd gone when she'd first arrived, very late the previous night. Was this cabin the same one to which Brian had brought Leona on one or more of their clandestine little jaunts? Was she about to sleep in a bed in which her husband had made love to another woman?

She reaffirmed to herself, once again, that even if it was the very same cabin, and the very same bed, she would not be daunted. The leather bag that lay open on the luggage rack belonged to her now, and not to Leona Quick. It was she, Suzanne Charlesworth, who would tonight occupy the cabin, sleep in the bed, fill the bathtub and sip the best wine.

An hour later, washed and dressed for dinner, still feeling the pleasant tightening of the skin on her face from a day in the open air, Suzanne went down to the lodge, where she was shown to a table that was – although she would not allow this to upset her – set for one. The high-ceilinged dining room was decorated with plush plaid carpets, fishing trophies and paintings of swirling, rushing rivers. Within a fireplace that was nearly large enough to accommodate entire trees, a modest blaze took the edge off the late September chill.

When Suzanne looked around at the other diners, she found she was less bothered by the young couples holding hands across the table than she was by the multi-generational families – older couples surrounded by their adult children and grandchildren. It was the sight of those that hurt her heart. The diners at the table beside hers were two men whom she might have described as old, until it occurred to her that they were most likely her contemporaries. Out of the corner of her eye, she watched them put away hearty starters before steadily consuming the enormous main meals the server set down in front of them. When one of the men clattered his cutlery together on an impressively bare plate, Suzanne found herself unable to resist comment.

'You two must have hollow legs,' she said.

'We've been on rations for a week,' said one.

'Oh?'

'We've been paddling,' said the other. 'Started at the headwaters of the Davenport. It's taken us a week. Some of the campsites were a bit ordinary, so staying here with a restaurant and nice soft bed? It's our little treat.'

And then the conversation was off and running. They were both farmers from up towards the state border, and every year since they'd each lost their wives, they'd taken a river trip together. They came across as gentlemen, Suzanne decided. The sort who'd open doors and pull out chairs. The sort who'd have conservative views on politics and religion, but good enough manners not to be overly opinionated in the course of polite, dinnertime conversation. Suzanne developed a preference for Tony, who had a mischievous smile, over Rod, who seemed tired, possibly because he'd drunk a little too much of the excellent wine.

When Rod, after finishing his meal with an enormous slice of cheesecake, announced he was calling it quits and heading off to bed, Suzanne and Tony settled in with a nip of cognac by the fire. It was four years, he told her without prompting, since his wife had died.

'What about you?' he asked. 'Widowed? Divorced?'

'Separated,' Suzanne said. It was, she realised, the very first time she'd said it out loud. It was the first time her ears had heard it spoken as truth, and her eyes moistened with tears that Tony didn't fail to observe.

'Still pretty new, hey?'

Suzanne nodded, smiled weakly, then steered the conversation back to safer territory. They talked about paddling conditions on his journey, about her painting, about the horrors of leeches, about the effectiveness of alpacas as guardians for sheep. He was, she supposed, a good-looking enough man, although when she watched him walk to the bar to fetch them both a second cognac, she observed that he had developed the disappearing backside of an old man – a fate that had not, as yet, befallen Brian. When he returned, they talked more. About her grandchildren, about his dogs, about the book on tree communities that they'd both recently read.

The warmth of the fire on her face, the relaxing effect of the alcohol, the softness of the chair, the pleasantness of the conversation – it was all so very nice. And yet.

'It does get better,' Tony said.

Was she really so transparent?

He went on, 'Once you learn to shop for one, cook for one, you don't throw out so much food. And the silence in the house gets quieter.'

That got her attention.

'Ah, you know that one,' Tony observed, with a wry smile.

'Your wife. What did she die from?'

'Yeah, the Big C. Three times she had it – a different part of her body each time. Got her in the end.'

'I'm so sorry.'

'She was a bright spark. Full of life, you know. It wasn't right that she went so early.'

Suzanne swirled her cognac. 'Tony, you seem like a fairly forthright person.'

'I am that.'

'Can I ask you a personal question?'

'Shoot.'

'Were you ever unfaithful to your wife?'

The way his eyebrows shot up indicated to her that this wasn't the question he'd been expecting. He breathed all the way out. 'Well, I'm not going to lie. Yes, I was.'

'Only when she was ill?'

Tony shook his head. 'Actually, no. Not when she was ill. Not at all, then. But a long time before that, I was.'

'Why do men do it?' The question came out sounding angrier than Suzanne had intended, but Tony didn't appear to take it personally.

He thought for a time. Then said, 'I think some men feel like they should. It's like fancy cars, you know. You don't really need them. Maybe they turn you on, but even if they don't, there's the world telling you that you should want one. The message is that having a fancy car broadcasts the fact that you're a successful man. I think, maybe, for some men, having an affair is a bit like that.'

Suzanne thought. Brian was one for trophies. Expensive watch, expensive car, expensive shoes, expensive suits, expensive art – even if it was hideous. Was that all Leona had been to him? A luxury item he could afford? But what was the use of arm candy if you had to keep it hidden from sight? Surely there had to be more to it than that.

'Was that how it was for you?'

'Maybe a little bit,' Tony said, narrowing his eyes as if he had to squint to see that far back into the past. 'But it was also exciting, you know? To have a secret. The affair was like a doorway out of my ordinary life and into a place where I could reconnect with parts of myself that I'd lost. For as long as I could keep the guilt at bay, I could feel, just for a little while, like somebody who hadn't already fenced himself in with choices. I could feel, I don't know . . . free, I suppose. Young.'

Brian had not chosen a younger woman, but in Leona, he had chosen a woman from his youth. Had the affair been his way of fighting the ageing process? Again? Suzanne realised she was trying to understand, to have compassion. To forgive him. But why should she?

'Doesn't cheating just come down to selfishness in the end? I want it, so I should be able to have it? No matter who it hurts?'

Tony shrugged. 'There's always the illusion that you'll get away with it. That nobody will be hurt. But the truth has a way of getting out of the box.'

Literally, Suzanne thought, remembering how she'd lifted that leather bag out of its cardboard carton.

Tony said, 'Look, Suzanne. You were right. I am pretty forthright. So, I'm just going to say it, all right? You're here. I'm here. It's a beautiful night. And the first time's the hardest.'

It took her a moment, but then she realised what he was asking her. She watched him patiently wait, empty glass in his hand, for her response. She wondered whether – at some level – this was in fact why she had come here, to Watersmeet Lodge. To see what would happen. To see if something just like this might.

Suzanne nodded, just ever so slightly. Tony stood. To the few people remaining in the dining room, Suzanne realised, he would look like a man reaching out his hand to his wife, and she – taking his hand – would look like that wife, on her way to bed with her husband after a few quiet drinks at the fireside. Was she really going to do this?

They went out into the cold stillness of the night. As they walked towards his cabin, hand in hand, Suzanne was aware of the bright, bright stars overhead, the smell of the wet forest, the sounds of the creatures in the darkness of the garden.

Saturday

For Marnie, it was something of an effort not to show up early, or to arrive right on time, at Fairchild & Sons that day. It was only by stopping off in one of the boutiques at the Alexandria Park end of Rathbone Street, where she tried on a couple of pretty skirts, that she managed to get the timing right – not late enough to be rude, not punctual enough to give away the fact that she'd been waiting for this moment all week.

As she strolled the last block towards the old shop, she caught sight of a dusty white ute parked out the front; the signwriting down its side read 'Luke Charlesworth Timber Design'. That he'd arrived first was perfect. But even more perfect was the fact that parked right behind Luke's ute was a snub-nosed car painted in the burgundy-and-white livery of Parkside Realty. Marnie had thought she and Luke would only be able to look around the exterior of the place, but it appeared as if they'd chanced to turn up at the same time as the agent, and – given that the front door of the shop was open – it seemed that Luke had already been shown inside.

She quickened her pace and hurried up the front steps of the shop. The main showroom, where the solid old counter still stood, was empty, but Marnie could hear voices from further inside. She went through into the mid-section of the building, where the arsonist's fire had consumed the old timber staircase that led up into the living quarters. Although the floors had been cleared of rubble, and the graffiti on the walls whited out, the space was still a scene of destruction. The charred beams overhead, the remains of the shadow-boards on the walls, the fire-chewed planks on the floor: they could do little more than gesture to the building's original glories.

In the centre of this accidental atrium stood a young woman in a skirt suit holding a burgundy clipboard, and a sleek-looking young man. Although he wore jeans and a knitted jumper, he retained the aura of someone accustomed to wearing a suit. Luke was standing at the window, experimentally poking at a patch of raw, flaking timber on the frame. Catching sight of Marnie, he shot her a wink.

She looked at him questioningly. What was he up to?

'. . . the oldest weatherboard building in Alexandria Park,' the young woman was telling her customer. 'It's a really important part of the mercantile history of this part of town.'

The woman turned to Marnie.

'Jodie Bainbridge,' she said, offering a slim, manicured hand.

'I'm Marnie,' she said, taking Jodie's hand, but not supplying a surname.

'She's with me,' Luke said, with a winsome smile to Jodie. He beckoned to Marnie. 'Have a look here.'

Through one of the many gaps in the historic lathe and plaster walls, Luke pointed out some strands of electrical wiring. 'I guess it's what you'd call vintage. But, yeah, we'd be up for rewiring the entire place.'

Okay, Marnie thought, so that was the game. Luke was going to play the role of the unimpressed customer, and she his offsider.

But the use of the 'we'? It was nice. Extremely nice. Though she felt like smiling, she managed to produce a worried frown. 'Does that mean the plumbing's likely to be in the same sort of shape?'

'Every chance,' Luke said, arms crossed as he surveyed the room critically.

Poor Jodie Bainbridge was only young. She had no strategy for redirecting her sharply dressed client as Luke went on to express his concerns about the load-bearing capacity of fire-damaged beams overhead, and the advanced state of the dry rot in the windowsills and frames.

When Jodie set off on her tour of the property with the young man in tow, she could find no way of preventing Luke and Marnie from joining them, and she didn't seem to know what else to do but chew her bottom lip when her client began to tune in to Luke's commentary on the building's quirks and flaws. In the large, empty back room – the one Marnie had thought she could potentially rent out to another business, or set up as a hot-desking space – Luke squatted down to examine the skirting boards. In places they had been burned; other sections of them had been hacked away.

'There's nothing off-the-shelf about these. They were handmade. If you're going to meet the heritage requirements, you can't just replace them with modern skirting. You'll need to cut out the damaged sections and have new pieces specially fabricated. That's the kind of thing that gets expensive with these old places,' he said, matter-of-factly.

Out on the street, the little party looked up at the old shop's decorative facade. Luke pointed out to Marnie, and by extension to the other potential buyer, the missing parts of the scrollwork on the crown mouldings. He noted the missing carved rose from the left-hand side of the signwriting above the main window. 'Just that feature alone would be a significant job for a skilled timber craftsman.'

'So, what do you do for a living?' the sleek young man asked Luke.

Luke gestured to the ute parked at the kerb behind them. 'Timber craftsman,' he said, his manner so nonchalant that Marnie was forced to swallow a giggle.

Convinced by Luke's credentials, the young man started to ask questions of his own. Soon Luke was pointing out to him that even the weatherboards on the outside of the building were custom-moulded, explaining that they would need to be replaced like for like, and describing the mammoth amount of work involved in glazing the big, mullioned window at street level, and the arched windows on the second storey, all of which were presently boarded up with plywood. This led on to a discussion about the amount of rain damage that would surely have been sustained by the window frames after so many years without paint. Neglect was like negative compound interest, he said; it had exponential results.

'Buildings like this one are like very old cars: all very romantic until they fall to bits, and you discover that there's no such thing as spare parts unless you get them custom-made.'

'Yeah,' the young man said, seeming to take in the old shop's facade with fresh eyes. 'Might be a bit out of my league, I suspect.'

'It'd be a labour of love, that's for sure,' Luke said. 'Anything else you want to look at, Marnie? Or are we done?'

Marnie shrugged as if to say she was satisfied. She followed him to his ute, sure he'd give her a fuller assessment once they were alone.

'Give me a lift back? I walked,' she explained.

Luke squinted. 'I can. Of course. But if you fancy a drink while we talk, it occurs to me that the Strumpet and Pickle's only a couple of blocks that way.'

There was a little extra bounce in Luke's step as he and Marnie walked the short distance between Fairchild & Sons and Alexandria Park's cosiest, best loved old pub.

'Those were some nice theatrics back there, Mr Charlesworth,' Marnie observed. 'Wherever did you learn your trade?'

'Let's just say I spent some time in car yards with my dad.'

'Do you think we scared him off?'

'I think we did our darnedest,' Luke said, trying not to look too pleased with himself.

'Just how insurmountable is it, though? Truthfully?'

What could he tell her? It was a gorgeous place, full of beautiful old timbers and quirky details. A true one of a kind. To fix it up, though, was going to be a massive job, fraught with challenges: bureaucratic, practical and financial.

'I'm not going to sugar-coat it. A lot of what I said is absolutely true. It's a big job. You know that, right?'

She nodded.

'But it's also gold. The timbers? You just can't get materials like that any more. And the features that weren't destroyed, they're truly beautiful.'

'But to restore it? Am I out of my depth? What do I need to know?'

'The first thing's going to be getting your renovation plans past the heritage people. You'll need to be really clear in your plans about where you can't do anything else but replace the features, and you'll need to keep absolutely everything you can. A delicate business – and heritage experts can be hard to please, believe me.'

'What about the cost?'

'It won't be the materials that will be the killer. It'll be the labour. It's really specialised work, not the kind of thing you can get any old tradesman to do. What I can say from having a good look around the place is that the main potential buyers will either be heritage enthusiasts with very deep pockets who don't care what they have to pay for the renovation, or people with the skills to do quite a lot of the work themselves.'

Marnie went quiet.

'Or very determined granddaughters of Archie Fairchild who love the place enough to make it work any way they can,' he added, and was pleased to see he'd managed to coax a small smile onto Marnie's face.

As they walked, Luke watched their reflections materialise and dematerialise in the windows of the shopfronts. Today was the first time he'd seen Marnie's hair completely loose, and it was longer than he'd thought, reaching right down her back and forming a striking contrast against the green wool of her coat. It was a little fluffed-up, too, as if freshly washed; around her face, shorter lengths framed her wide cheekbones, her hazel eyes, her fair, redhead's complexion.

Without exactly meaning to, he examined his own reflection too. Jeans (his best), shirt (his favourite), boots (actually polished, for once), hair (tidy, without being obviously brushed). Slung across his body was a leather bag, the main compartment of which contained things he'd brought to show Marnie – sketches and gift ideas for Ivy that he hoped would meet with her approval. But in a smaller front pocket was something else, to which he had pinned an entirely different kind of hope. Two tickets to *Lux*, an installation of light-based artworks out at the Hearst Hill Gardens in the hills. Tonight. He hoped he'd been right to take Ivy's advice about surprising Marnie with a bold gesture.

At the Strumpet and Pickle, Luke held the front door for Marnie and followed her through into the beginnings of a Saturday evening crowd. The bar stools were fully occupied, and a small crowd of patrons tapped their toes to the music of the Celtic folk band that had taken up residence on a small, triangular stage. Luke and Marnie gravitated without discussion to the quieter end of the pub, where they took a booth seat positioned beneath a stained-glass window.

'What can I get you?'

'Gin and tonic, thanks,' Marnie said, over the music.

While he waited at the bar, Luke felt his nerves start to build. At the old shop, comfortable in the presence of the weathered cedar and celery-top pine and busy with the task of talking up the building's problems, he'd been in his element. Then, as they'd walked to the pub, he'd basked in the role in which Marnie had cast him: that of expert. Now, not only had they stepped back into her territory, where he would reveal to her his ideas for Ivy's birthday present, he was also going to have to pick the right moment to produce the tickets to *Lux*, take the risk of revealing an attraction, an interest, that he wasn't entirely certain she shared. Had he done the right thing? Had it been presumptuous to buy the tickets on spec? Would she like that, or would it make her feel pressured? He had no idea.

By the time he returned to the table, the nervous anticipation had tightened his throat, but then he saw, in Marnie's hands, the puzzle box he'd given her the week before.

Grateful for the easy conversation-starter, he asked, 'So, did you work it out?'

'Curse you, no,' Marnie said. 'I worked out that this bit – here – slides. But then what?'

'Do you really want me to show you?'

'It's driven me crazy all week.'

Luke held out his hand for the box, comprised of panels of pale timber crisscrossed with bands of ebony in the manner of a ribbon-wrapped gift. He held it up to his ear while he pushed on the moving section of ebony that Marnie had already discovered, sliding it until he heard a tiny click. Then he showed her the sequence of subtle slides, back and forth, that eventually led to the box springing open. Inside were pale sassafras sides and a dark ebony floor. She watched intently, and when she took the closed box back and tried to copy his moves, she got nearly all of them on the first try.

'Now like this?' she asked.

'Almost,' he said, reaching over to help. 'Like this.'

When the box popped open for a second time, they both laughed, and Luke felt the tension ease away.

'So, how did you go? With ideas for Ivy?' Marnie asked.

'Good, I think.' Luke extracted from his satchel a glossy magazine: the next year's program for the city's symphony orchestra. He handed it to Marnie. 'I'm thinking about one of the multi-concert packages. It's an experience, not a thing, so that means no clutter. Therefore, it ticks the ethical box. No plastic. No exploitation. I hope. And going out for the evening to the orchestra is a chance to get a little dressed up, maybe have a sneaky sip of champagne in the concert hall foyer before the concert, so it's got that grown-up vibe about it that we were looking for. But see here' – he flicked to a page at the back of the magazine – 'there's a package called "Experimentalists", and it includes the edgier concerts. One is all about percussion, one has a guest artist who made his name in death metal.' In a spirit of self-mockery, he said, 'I want her to think I'm cool. Obviously.'

Marnie took the magazine from him and leafed through the sumptuously designed pages. She squinted, seeming unconvinced, and Luke's spirits dived. He'd really thought she'd like this idea.

'You don't think it might be a little lonely?' she said.

'Aha! But no! Because here's the thing. I thought I'd buy two tickets to all those concerts. And I'll make a deal with her. I'll put aside each of those nights in my diary, so I'm free to go with her if she doesn't have someone else she'd rather take.'

Now Marnie was nodding, smiling her approval. Although there was something else in her expression, too. Something slightly pained, perhaps.

'No expectations,' he went on. 'I'll make that totally clear. I'll be there if she wants and not if she doesn't.'

'I think that's perfect.'

Now Luke was certain. Sadness. That's what he could see in Marnie's face. But what on earth had he said to make her feel like that?

'It's a beautiful idea,' she added, forcing an extra degree of brightness into her smile.

'But wait. There's more. I thought that while an experience is all very nice, I'd also like to give her something she might potentially keep. Something tangible.'

Luke brought a spiral-bound sketchbook out of his satchel and flicked through pages covered with pencil-sketched diagrams, design ideas, measurements. When he reached the right page, he held the book to his chest, so Marnie couldn't yet see what he'd drawn.

'Remember when we were looking at all those internet pictures of Ivy? Well, I went back over them, and I noticed that in quite a lot of them, she's wearing this particular style of earrings.'

He revealed the picture: a side-view of a girl's face, framed in jagged-cut hair like Ivy's, but tucked behind the ear, which was the focus of the picture. Following the ear's curve, up from lobe to helix, was a climbing earring that clung like his daughter's namesake. Ivy.

'Oh, Luke.'

There was more. He tugged his wallet out of his back pocket and turned it upside down over the page. Sprinkled over the paper like table scatters were tiny ivy leaves, exquisitely carved from ebony. Marnie picked one of them up to examine it.

'I found a jeweller who can do the silversmithing to create the vines and the fixings,' he said, wondering if he was being a bit too keen, too much of a show-off. Maybe he was coming off like a small boy displaying an artwork of which he was perhaps a little too proud. He looked to Marnie for a response, desperately wanting her to like his idea, but when she looked up at him, he instantly felt ashamed that he'd been thinking of himself. Because her lower eyelids were brimming with tears.

'Sorry,' she said. She squeezed her eyes shut, brushed away the tears.

'No, I'm sorry. Are you all right? What did I say?'

'Nothing. Nothing at all. No, nothing!' she insisted. She wiped her eyes again. 'I'm sorry. I'm being stupid.'

Luke instinctively reached across the table to put a hand on her upper arm, wanting to comfort her. 'I didn't mean to upset you.'

'You didn't.'

'What's going on?'

'Oh, it's nothing. Just . . . when I was sixteen? I'd have given anything for my dad to come out of nowhere and buy me tickets to concerts, and a pair of earrings that he designed himself.' She shrugged resignedly. 'I didn't have anyone to give me such nice, thoughtful things. I would have loved it. When people say, "it's the thought that counts", this, *this*, is what they ought to mean.'

He couldn't help it; his mouth twisted into a wry smile.

'What?' she demanded.

'You don't think it's a little ironic? You admit it's the thought that counts, but your clients don't have to think at all.'

Marnie shrugged. 'I don't think it's ironic. My clients know the thought counts, too. They also know that they don't have the time or the ability to do the thinking themselves. So they employ me.'

Luke shook his head. She had a real blind spot on this point, but the last thing he wanted to do was argue. Gently, he asked, 'So what was the story with your father?'

'Oh, you don't want to hear my poor-me story.'

'Tell me?' he offered.

'No, you didn't come here to —'

'Please,' he said. 'I'd love to know.'

She looked him full in the face, and Luke had the feeling that if Marnie Fairchild was a puzzle box, he'd just inadvertently found the first moving part.

'Please. I'd love to know,' Luke said, and as Marnie met his eye across the table of the Strumpet and Pickle, she was surprised to discover that she was actually tempted to tell him.

'Why do you want to know?' she asked, cautiously.

Luke smiled knowingly. 'Yeah, I know that one too. If someone asks you a question you don't want to answer, you ask "Why do you want to know?"'

Marnie, caught out, began once again to fiddle with the puzzle box.

Luke went on, 'I'd like to understand. What it is with you and that shop. When you were walking through it today, you were a special kind of dreamy.'

Marnie gave a wry smile. He had seen her. *Seen* her. Which both pleased and pained her. To be unseen meant freedom, but loneliness. To be seen meant connection, but vulnerability. Why was nothing easy?

'You already know some of the story,' she said. 'You went to school with Fairchilds.'

Luke nodded.

'My great-grandfather, William. My grandfather, Archie, his brothers. They worked hard. Honest trades, you know? Grocers, cobblers, haberdashers, printers. But always quality, and always in Alexandria Park, and there was always real estate involved. The next generation – my father, his siblings, his cousins. They grew up to be lawyers, mostly, and financial advisers. It was a story of evolution, yes? Each generation getting a leg-up from the one before, climbing the social ladder.'

'Yeah, I know that story. My grandfather was a miner. My father was a property developer. I was supposed to be something better than that. And instead . . . here I am.'

'You're not happy?'

'Yeah, I am,' Luke said, though his tone indicated a qualified happiness. 'But my dad's got a special way of pushing the buttons in my mental mechanics. It would be so much easier to be satisfied if he wasn't always telling me how unsatisfied I ought to be.'

Marnie saw the opportunity to change the subject. She knew from experience how easily people could be redirected if you gave them an opening to talk about themselves. 'Do you think he means to do that to you?'

Luke gave Marnie a look that said *nice try*. 'We both know about my dad. I'm asking about yours.'

'His name was Rory,' Marnie said. 'Youngest of three. Naughty, apparently. Out of those kids, he was the one with the reddest hair, the biggest smile. He had everybody by the heart. Scraped through economics at university on charm and luck. I gather his assignments had to fit in around surfing trips and drinking binges. But somehow, he graduated and then he went into business with his older brother, Lewis, and one of Lewis's best mates.'

'What kind of business?'

'Financial advisers. My dad was great for them. He had the charm, you know? Grew the client base, pulled in bigger and bigger fish, got those fish to invest more and more.'

'And your mum?'

'Ah, Chrissie. They met over a blackjack table at the casino. She was a croupier. A lot of people were surprised at his choice, but then Fairchilds had working-class roots, so why not a pretty girl from a small town? It was a big wedding. They were a beautiful couple. I was born not long after they were married.'

'And then?' Luke asked.

'Everything seemed fine. That's what my mum says. He seemed happy, they were living in a nice house. Just a small one, but in Alexandria Park. This neighbourhood's a long way from where my mum grew up. From where I grew up.'

'Where was that?'

'Casterbrook. It used to be a farming town, but now it's just the arse-end of nowhere. The kind of place people live when they can't afford the city. The poker machines do well out of the locals' unemployment benefits.' Marnie was aware she was sounding bitter. 'Mum says she didn't have a clue about my dad, and I believe her. My grandfather wouldn't talk about it with me much, but the one time I did manage to get him talking, he said that nobody saw the signs.'

'Signs of what?'

Marnie took a sip of her gin and tonic. 'Gambling with clients' money.'

'Shit.'

'Lots of clients. Lots of money.'

'Uh-oh.'

'I don't know what happened, exactly, when Lewis found out and confronted him. Mum said my dad just came home that night like nothing was wrong. Next morning, he got up and put his surfboard on the top of his car and headed off. Early, the way surfers do. Nothing unusual about the time he left, or how he said goodbye. Mum waited for him to come home. I suppose I did as well, although I was only two.'

Luke was watching her, closely. 'Where did he go?'

'Just his regular beach.'

'And?'

'Nobody really knows the truth. It could have been an accident. His surfboard was found around the headland, smashed on the rocks. It could have been a shark. Or, it might have been that he didn't feel like there was any way back from where he'd found himself. I don't know. I'm only guessing. I don't remember him at all.'

'What happened then?'

'My mother and I moved back to Casterbrook. The proceeds from our house went towards paying back some of the clients.

I gather it was an uphill battle for Lewis to recover his reputation. In the middle of all that, I guess, the rest of the Fairchilds were too busy to wonder what had happened to us. My mother and I, we just faded conveniently out of existence.'

'But you knew your grandfather?'

'I had to introduce myself.'

'Ouch.'

'I walked into that shop, off the street. That first time, when I told him who I was, he looked at me like I'd just dragged my father's body into his shop. We got there, though, Archie and me. He helped me through school, and he taught me a thing or two. And he kept me in school shoes. I think he'd have been proud of me, of how far I've got on my own. He liked grit. At his funeral, Mum and I stood at the back, and . . . you remember Ava? My cousin? You went to school with her?'

Luke nodded.

'As she walked past us, on the way in, she looked over at us, and asked her mother, "Are those the con artists?" She said it so quietly that to start with I wasn't sure whether I'd imagined it or not. But Mum heard it, too. And for her, it wasn't the first time.'

Marnie, not quite believing she'd been so unfiltered as to divulge all of this information, watched as Luke absorbed the impact of her story. He was a good listener, a disarming one. He had drawn out of her way more than she was used to disclosing, but somehow it didn't feel unsafe.

'Ironic, isn't it?' Luke observed. 'There you are, longing for a father to give you a leg-up into the world. I have a father who offers me help, and I won't take it.'

Marnie wasn't sure what it was that made her look across the room, then. Perhaps it was a lull in the music coming from the band, or perhaps she'd caught sight – out of the corner of her eye – of some familiar detail of hair or clothing or manner. But there, coming towards their table through the crowd, was Owen Kingston.

Something – someone – had caught Marnie's eye, and Luke watched her face close over into an expression of manufactured, but quite convincing, cheerfulness.

'Hello, you,' she said.

'Hey,' said a man. In his early thirties, Luke estimated, he wore skinny black jeans, and an authentically beaten-up denim jacket over the top of a Cypress Hill T-shirt. His longish dark hair swayed as he slid into the booth seat next to Marnie. The smile he gave Luke was easy, friendly, and utterly devoid of meaning.

The trace of puffiness around Marnie's eyes would have been hard to pick, Luke realised, and he figured this new arrival would have no way of knowing where Marnie's mood had been less than a minute earlier.

Brightly, she gestured to each of them in turn. 'Owen Kingston, Luke Charlesworth. Luke, Owen.'

Owen glanced at the sketchbook on the table in a way that made Luke want to close it, but it was Marnie who flipped the cover over and pushed the book in Luke's direction.

'What're you up to?' Owen asked.

'Just a little work meeting, actually,' Marnie said.

Luke felt as if she'd slapped him. What was that expression Luke had heard Ivy use? 'Friend-zoned'? Well, he was pretty sure he'd just been categorised even more impersonally than that. He'd been 'work-zoned'.

'Oh, you're one of her clients,' Owen said.

'Not exactly,' Marnie said.

Not exactly. What did that mean?

Owen put an arm proprietorially around Marnie's shoulders. 'Three times in as many weeks,' he remarked to her, as if Luke didn't exist. 'I'm starting to think you're stalking me!'

'You should be so lucky,' Marnie said, drily.

Luke remembered, quite clearly, that Marnie had said she didn't have a partner. Not in business, or in life. That was what she'd said. Who was this guy to Marnie? *What* was this guy to Marnie? And why could Luke detect the unmistakable scent of competition in the air? *Three times in as many weeks.* Who said something like that? Not a boyfriend. There was some kind of intimacy between them, though. That much was obvious. The signals were all scrambled; Luke couldn't work it out.

'So, what are you up to later?' Owen asked Marnie.

Luke focused on scooping up all the little ivy leaves and returning them to his wallet, but when he stole a glance at Marnie's face, he found it unreadable.

'Not sure yet,' she told Owen. Her tone gave away no more than her face.

'We could go grab some dinner if you want?' Owen suggested. 'You know, when you're done here, of course.'

Luke took this window of opportunity. 'I think we are, aren't we? Done?'

Marnie said nothing. But the look she gave him . . . what was it supposed to mean? That she was disappointed he was leaving so soon? That she was politely refraining from insisting that he stay, because she really did want him to go now? Or that she was politely refraining from insisting that he stay even though she really did want him to? He didn't know, couldn't tell. Owen's body language, though, was explicit. He was already on his feet, holding out his hand to Luke to shake in farewell.

'Nice to meet you, man,' Owen said, and there it was again, that content-free smile.

Luke stood too and accepted the handshake, which was neither too firm nor too limp, but perfectly correct in every way.

'You too.' Luke hoisted his bag onto his shoulder.

'The gift ideas are perfect. Absolutely perfect,' Marnie told Luke. 'Her birthday's going to go really well. She's a lucky girl.'

'Thanks. For the meeting,' he said, wondering if he'd sprinkled just a little too much saltiness on the word 'meeting'.

'You're so welcome.'

Luke settled the strap of his bag across his body and threaded his way through the crowd, dodging a cheerful bloke carrying two sloshing pints of beer and an older woman in a twirly skirt, clearly enjoying the music. Unscathed, at least on the outside, he reached the front door and stepped out into a mild, cloudless dusk. There wasn't a breath of wind. For walking through gardens, looking at light-art in the dark, it would have been the perfect night.

'Well, thanks for that,' Marnie said.

Owen had sat back down, but opposite her this time. Eyes all wide and innocent, he said, 'Oh, I'm sorry. Did I interrupt something?'

'I don't know,' Marnie said, truthfully. 'But did you have to be so —'

'You said it was a work meeting,' Owen protested, his eyes now gleaming with mischief. 'Surely, Ms Fairchild, you wouldn't countenance the idea of mixing business with pleasure?'

'Actually, I was considering it,' she said, seriously.

'Oh, come on. Lighten up, Kiddo.' He brought out the smile.

The thousand-watt one that had, for as long as they'd known each other, fairly reliably overridden her good sense.

'It's not something I'd have done to you,' Marnie said, no less seriously. 'If you'd been sitting here with a woman? I might have come over to say hello, but I wouldn't have draped myself all over you and invited you out for dinner.'

'That guy? Marnie, Marnie. There are plenty more where he came from.'

Maybe it was Owen's experience that one girl was much the same as the next, that they came along like the buses on Rathbone Street – not exactly on schedule, but often enough that you never had to wait long in the cold. It wasn't how things were for her, though. It had been a long time since she'd come across anyone even remotely like Luke Charlesworth.

'Can you just let me decide? Rather than doing it for me?'

'Guys like that, they come and go. But you and me – we're a constant.'

A flash of anger rose in Marnie, staining her cheeks. 'Is that what you really think? That in twenty years from now, you'll still be swinging by the shop for a quick shag whenever you're bored? That's what you think . . . of me? That I'll just be there, waiting for you?'

Owen was unperturbed. 'Probably. We're not the settling type, you and me.'

Marnie realised he genuinely thought he'd just given her a compliment. 'Not the settling type?'

'You're too ruthless for all that domestic bullshit. It's one of the things I love about you.'

'Ruthless?' she echoed.

'Luke, was it? He'd soon find out.'

'What do you mean by that?' Marnie asked, incredulous.

'So, what was the last one's name? Chris? Setting up a new life in Switzerland, spare business class ticket sitting right beside him. And you blew him off.'

'Yeah, that was *his* new life in Switzerland. What about my life? My business? Everything I've worked for?'

'And, um, Jamie? You literally, *literally*, put all his stuff out on the street. Someone stole his freaking Xbox.'

She had. That was true. Jamie had lived with her, in a house she'd owned at the time, spent his days on the couch she'd bought, eaten the food she'd cooked when she got home at the end of the day, tired. It was after she'd thrown him out that she'd decided to sell that little house, invest the money and move to the apartment over the shop, a decision that had been good for the bottom line. 'Jamie was almost thirty, and surgically connected to that fucking toy. He wouldn't have worked in an iron lung.'

Owen leaned back against the leather of the booth seat, his face set in an expression that clearly said 'QED'. 'You're an uncompromising woman, Marnie Fairchild.'

'What's wrong with that?' Marnie demanded.

'Nothing. Not a thing. But you've got to admit, it doesn't leave a lot of room. Except for the occasional little stroll down sideshow alley.' He fixed her with a look that usually ended up in only one place. 'With me. For instance.'

For once, she didn't feel tempted. Neither did she any longer feel angry. Now, she just felt sad – for Owen, for herself, for the scotched opportunity that had walked out the door of the Strumpet and Pickle in the shape of Luke Charlesworth. She reached across the table for Owen's hand. It was warm and familiar, the olive of his skin pronounced against the paleness of her own.

'Are we friends?' she asked him.

'Duh.'

'If that's true,' Marnie said, 'then start behaving like it.'

'What's that supposed to mean?'

'What you did tonight?' Her gaze was level, steely. 'Don't do it again.'

That was when she saw it. Camouflaged against a dark streak in the grain of the timber table lay one tiny little ebony leaf. She picked it up. It was so delicate, so small.

'I have to go,' she said, impulsively.

Owen squinted. 'Aren't we having dinner?'

Marnie collected up her things, buttoned herself into her coat, dropped a friendly kiss on the top of Owen's hair. 'Be my friend. And I'll be yours.'

Was this a good idea?

In the back seat of a Shebah ride, Marnie discounted this question before she had considered it for even a moment. Because whether or not it was a good idea, she was doing it. She was heading in the direction of 243 Fielding Street, Bankside – an address she had written many a time on consignment notes for couriers, a small worker's cottage that she may once have driven past, slowly, in the course of her 'research'.

What if he's not there?

What if he is there, but he's not alone?

What if he is there, and he is alone?

What will he think about me turning up, unannounced?

The questions came thick and fast, filling her mind like an irretrievable tangle of yarn, until before she knew it, the Shebah driver had arrived in the industrial precinct of Bankside, with its mixture of dilapidated old houses, shiny new plumbing businesses, fabrication workshops, cyclone-fenced boat retailers, marinas, and empty blocks sprouting thistles and dock.

Luke's house, its exterior grey in the last light of the day, had the look of a child's drawing – two square windows symmetrically placed on either side of the front door. Where once there might have been a lawn there was only concrete, although two small brick-rimmed circles had been left as homes for straggly fruit trees, their limbs sparsely dotted with blossom. Apricots, Marnie thought, or peaches. What was she doing here? No light shone in either of the windows, and the gust of wind that came in off the river lifted the skirts of her coat and seemed to push her backwards. Away.

Regardless, she rang the doorbell.

Tick, tick, tick. Time passed and nothing happened. No sound of footsteps, no sudden bloom of light behind the frosted-glass panels on either side of the door. She could walk away now, really quite easily. If she were to order a rideshare, it might even happen that the same driver who had just dropped her off would do a U-turn in some nearby street and cruise back to collect her. Right on the edge of her hearing, though, was a sound. The faint hum of machinery.

Marnie went to the side of the house and followed her ears and her instincts down a path to the backyard, where a rectangle of yellow light appeared in the doorway of a large, corrugated-iron shed that had been built only metres from the back door of the house. Her pulse racing, she went to the door, and there was Luke. He was wearing a flannel shirt now; the handsome, patterned shirt he'd been wearing at the pub hung on a hook to the side of the shadow-board, on the back wall, where his hand tools rested in perfect order.

Beneath the shadow-board was a desk covered by sketchbooks and dog-eared sheets of paper, fat rectangular pencils, rulers and set-squares. Marnie noticed that the antique chisels she'd chosen for him were set out on a bespoke stand that Luke had likely made for himself. Around the workshop were racks upon racks of timbers, large black bins full of smaller lengths and offcuts; there were huge saws and serious-looking lathes and other machines whose precise uses Marnie could not have guessed at.

In the centre of the room, at a large worktable, Luke – clear safety glasses across his face – was bent over a slab of timber, methodically going over its surface with an electric sander. His sleeves rolled to the elbow, he guided the sander with one hand, and with the other, brushed away the powdery sawdust which made low clouds in the air before settling on the tabletop. He was totally absorbed in his work, which meant that it was not, even now, too late for Marnie to walk away.

Then, it was too late. Because Luke glanced up and saw her in the doorway. For a moment he seemed to look right through her before realising she was real. He turned off the sander, though it took a moment for its motor to spin down to silence. He pushed the safety glasses up onto the top of his head.

'You left this at the pub.' She came to where he stood and tipped the tiny carved ivy leaf into his dusty, outstretched palm.

'Thanks,' he said.

And now, Marnie realised, she was marooned. Because this was where her plan ended. She had wanted to give him back the leaf. She had wanted to see him, to be in his presence. Now, those objectives had been achieved, and she felt like she was standing at the top of a staircase that led to nowhere. Just space. Luke wasn't helping, either. He was just standing, hand closed around the leaf she'd brought, saying nothing.

Be brave.

'About Owen,' she blurted.

'You don't have to ex—'

'No, I want to. He's a friend. A very old friend. But just a friend.'

Luke appeared unconvinced. 'But also *not* just a friend, I suspect.'

'Is it that obvious?' Marnie asked.

'I think he wanted it to be that obvious.'

'Maybe he was a little jealous,' Marnie said, tentatively.

'Did he have any reason to be?'

She considered deflecting, but what was the point of being anything other than forthright? She had come this far. 'Yes.'

'Marnie, why are you here?'

Marnie blushed. 'To give you that.'

'And?'

On the inside, she was squirming like a worm on a hot pavement. Did he have to be so direct? She searched for words to explain. 'I didn't feel like we were done. I didn't feel like that was the way it should have finished.'

A silence started. And stretched out. Continued a little longer. Marnie stood there, feeling foolish.

'There was something I wanted to give you today, actually,' Luke said. 'A gift, I suppose. But the right moment never happened.'

With the tip of his finger in the fine sawdust that lay on the surface of his worktable, Luke drew three overlapping circles.

'One is the person,' he said, pointing to a circle. 'And that person is someone who once told me that looking at art made her feel like less of a human doing and more of a human being.'

He'd remembered. A detail from their conversation at the Art

Gallery, and he'd remembered it. A shiver ratcheted its way up the back of Marnie's neck.

'Two is the occasion.' Luke pointed to the next circle. He paused, then, and Marnie could see that he wasn't entirely sure how to proceed. 'The occasion, at least my intention, is that it's a first date. But one that's memorable, not ordinary.'

A first date. Marnie meant to keep her smile small, but she wasn't sure she was managing it.

'Three is the relationship,' he said. He looked up at Marnie now. 'That remains a mystery, I guess. But I'm open to possibilities.'

Now, she was beaming, could feel herself lighting up with anticipation. 'So what's in the middle?'

Beneath the shirt hanging on the hook was the leather bag he'd been carrying; he took something out of the front pocket.

'These,' he said. He dropped the contents of his hand onto the table, blurring the edges of his diagram.

They were tickets, Marnie saw, to *Lux*. The art installation show out at Hearst Hill Gardens. For tonight.

'It starts in half an hour,' Marnie said, deflated. 'We won't make it.'

'Not all the way out to Hearst Hill. Not in half an hour,' he said.

Marnie felt ripped off, and angry with herself that she hadn't found a better way to manage Owen's unexpected appearance. 'I'm so sorry.'

He gave a shrug. 'Maybe the thought will have to count.'

Marnie didn't want to give up that easily. 'Would it matter so very much?'

'What?'

'If we were just a little late?'

It didn't matter. In the darkness, the gardens were a labyrinth, navigable only by the light of the tiny lanterns, shaped like the soft peaks of beaten egg-whites, that were spaced out on the grassy edges of the pathways. Though Marnie and Luke were given a map that showed the location of each artwork, there was no need to see them in order. Patrons were free to wander as they wished.

To Marnie, the night-time gardens felt like a different dimension, one in which the anxieties of everyday life had been suspended, but even if that had not been so, Luke had been clear. A first date, he had said, and it had seemed so easy, so right – almost as soon as they set off – for her to reach out and take him by the hand. His skin felt just the way she had thought it would: the kind of gentle-rough that would catch on the fabric if he were ever to run his hands up her stockinged legs. Even in the darkness, the skin felt brown – like a fine and supple layer of tree-bark.

They were standing underneath the umbrella of a massive fig, its branches flickering with pinpricks of green light and a soundscape falling like rain into the under-tree space, when Luke lifted Marnie's hand to his mouth and gently kissed the back of her fingers. His lips were as soft as his hands were roughened.

Although other people walked ahead of Marnie and Luke, or behind them, stopping just as they did to look at the artworks along the ways, in the low light they were nothing more to Marnie than shapes and sounds, and it seemed to her that the only real people in the shadowy gardens that night were her and Luke. The only face she saw properly, all night, was his.

For much of the time, they really were alone. There wasn't anyone else around when they stood on the shores of the lily-pond, pressing their hands onto a sensor pad so that the shape and pressure and warmth of their fingers and palms were broadcast in auras of red and pink, green and yellow, purple and electric blue on the surface of the water.

They were alone, too, in a darkened conservatory, where images of savage-looking mermaids were projected onto the curving sheets of water produced by the fountain at the top of a wishing well. For as long as Marnie could remember, her wishes – made in wells built for the purpose, or just before the blowing out of candles – had belonged to her plans for Fairchild & Sons. But tonight, when Luke fished a coin out of his pocket and handed it to her, she hesitated. In the end, she decided that since the coin had two sides, it would surely allow her two wishes – one for the shop, and one for the way the rest of this night would transpire.

Even if it did rely on the strength of only half a coin, it didn't take long for her second wish to come true. Beyond the arched doorway of a glowing egg-shaped pod, Luke pressed the small circle of a sensor pad against Marnie's chest, so that the pale yellow light all around them pulsed in time with her heartbeat. Fast. Because Luke was standing right in front of her, the fingers of one hand just lifting the curving neckline of her dress, and that was where they were when they kissed each other for the first time, the light inside the thick, opaque walls of the pod fading in and out quicker and quicker as Marnie's body responded to his. She thought of going back to the wishing well to toss in another coin, just to make sure that the idea didn't occur to him to go home to his own bed, alone.

Sunday

Marnie woke at the time, and in the way, that she usually did – with the sounds of Rathbone Street's early morning traffic filtering into dreams that became thinner and thinner, as they prepared to evaporate altogether. She became gradually aware of the insistent bleeping of a reversing truck, the wail of a distant siren, and the chittering of the sparrows who perched in the street's plane trees.

All of this was quite usual, but there were other things that were not – things that Marnie could discern even before she opened her eyes. For one thing, she was naked, nothing against her bare skin but her bedsheets. For another, she felt . . . what? A vague looseness of her limbs, and a sense that the chemicals floating around within the crucible of her skull were all the benevolent and joy-inducing ones. Usually, Marnie woke in a neutral state, ready to hope the day would be a good one, or fear that it would not. Today, though, she had the sense that it was already decided: the day was good, and she – for whatever reason – was disgustingly, extravagantly, ridiculously happy.

Ah. Well. That would be the reason, then.

There, asleep in her own bed, was Luke.

Marnie rolled onto her side where she could look at him,

stubble just beginning to emerge on his sculpted chin, those articulate, work-roughened hands resting on the outside of the sheets. It was a curious thing, how some humans were just so beautifully made.

Watching him sleep, Marnie could see the likeness to his father: the well-shaped lips, the arching eyebrows, the easy-going symmetry of his features. It was courtesy of Suzanne, though, that all the parts of him were just a little more generous – the lips a little fuller, the eyes a little larger, the chin a little rounder. Marnie got a mischievous buzz from wondering what Brian would think if he knew where his son and his gift-buyer were right now.

It was a pure pleasure to Marnie to have this moment to observe Luke without feeling studied, or judged, in return. When his eyes were open, they missed nothing, but with them closed she could relax, take in all the details of him, and remember. She recalled that there hadn't been much savouring the first time around; it had all been a bit too urgent. The second time, though, they'd slowed down, learning their way around each other. She smiled, perhaps a little smugly. But then, why not? Bit by bit, they had tested out the delicate and private boundaries of how far, how hard, how soft, how quiet, how loud, how dirty, how sweet. It had been the kind of sex that sent feeling flooding not only through her body, but all the way to her brain. The kind of sex that even sent its tentacles close to her heart, the kind of dangerously overwhelming sex that, before you knew it, if you weren't careful, could end up with the words *I love you* falling right out of your mouth.

Marnie would have been happy to lie there and look at him, remember, for quite a bit longer, but now his eyes flickered open, and he smiled at her.

'True then,' he said.

'It would seem so.'

Luke, eyes soft with sleep and affection, reached out to tuck a tendril of her hair behind one of her ears so he could see her face more clearly. Men could be such tender things, really. It was so easy to forget that. She kissed him softly, and then a little less softly, feeling how ready all the parts of her were to do it all again. She wasn't alone.

'More?' he asked, as if he couldn't believe his luck.

'Yes, please.'

It turned out to be the kind of morning-after that Marnie hadn't experienced in forever. The sort where she and Luke couldn't let go of each other long enough to shower separately, and so stood together, letting the pitiful flow of Marnie's fitful shower spray needles of water, alternately too hot and too cold, onto their pressed-together chests; the sort where Luke, wearing one of Marnie's old robes that didn't quite fit across his chest, dried Marnie's hair gently with a towel, and then combed it through while she sat cross-legged on the bed; the kind where they went to the kitchen together and kissed while the coffee brewed, then went back to bed to drink it.

Wish & Co opened on Sundays only once each month, for wrapping workshops, and by a stroke of luck, today was not one of those Sundays. Although Marnie usually spent her Sundays doing chores, as well as a few hours of research, there was really nothing so pressing that it couldn't be deferred. The day stretched emptily out ahead of her – ahead of them. Maybe they could go out to breakfast? Maybe they could take a trip back to the Art Gallery and wander about, slowly this time?

Luke took in every detail of Marnie's apartment, apparently as curious about her surroundings as he was about Marnie herself. He studied her sketches of Fairchild & Sons that were Blu-tacked to the wall behind the foldaway bed, looked closely at the photographs and postcards she kept pinned up on a corkboard, and examined the titles of the books on her shelves. It was there that he found the unopened deck of tarot cards that Marnie's mother had given her for her last birthday.

'May I?' he asked.

Marnie, sitting on the bed in her robe, hair still wet, laughed. 'If you really want to.'

He tore the plastic off the deck and began to shuffle, then tied his patterned shirt into a turban around his head and found an ungainly way of fixing one of her huge, hoop earrings to his unpierced ear.

'Are you about to reveal yet another talent?'

Luke gave her a knowing look and continued to shuffle the cards. At last, he waved a hand – magician-style – over the full deck before splaying it into a wide fan.

'Three cards, if you please.'

Marnie burst out laughing. 'What is that meant to be? Spanish? German?'

'Transylvanian. Come along, please.'

Marnie did as she was told and took three cards, which she laid upon the deliciously crumpled bedsheets.

'Have you ever actually read tarot cards before?'

'No,' he said, in his regular voice, 'but I had my cards read once. Is that the same thing?'

'Not remotely.' Marnie leaned over and kissed him; she couldn't help herself.

'Please, not to be distracting the reader,' he said, returning to his bizarre accent. 'This card, here, represents you. This one here, me. This one here, us.'

'Not bad.' It was the kind of simple three-card spread her

mother might have done on a rickety little table at the town fair.

'Please, if you would be so kind, turn over just this one here.'

He had tapped the card that was supposed to represent herself. Marnie flipped it to reveal the Ten of Wands.

'Ah, yes. I could have predicted this,' Luke jested. He lifted the card and turned it to read the tiny gold writing at the top. 'The Ten of Wands.'

When he set it down, it was upright, but Marnie had not forgotten that it had been dealt out reversed.

'So, this person, here,' Luke said, faux-mystically, 'is holding a bundle of sticks. Very heavy sticks, it seems. And she, that's you, is walking up a hill with these sticks. And this is because she, like the second pig in the tale, is going to build a house of sticks. So, somewhere in your future is a very nice house.'

'I see,' Marnie said, amused.

Knowledge of the tarot was not something she had deliberately gained, but growing up with her mother it had been impossible to avoid. Her mother would have said that the Ten of Wands, reversed, could be a warning that you were carrying too much, all by yourself, trying to heft the burden of those sticks to the top of the hill while wilfully refusing to ask for, or accept, any help. Or else, it could indicate another kind of burden – a secret. Remembering that, Marnie felt a tiny sting of guilt. She was going to have to tell Luke about the arrangement she still had with his father. But not today; not on this perfect morning.

'Next card if you please, lovely lady,' Luke said. Marnie turned it over to reveal the Seven of Cups. 'Ah, yes. Again, I am unsurprised by the appearance, here, of the . . . seven? Of cups. This card indicates to me that I am very lucky. I have seven whole cups in front of me and many of them are overflowing. It also indicates that in the very near future I will go out drinking with a very beautiful woman, and between us, we will drink seven cocktails.' Dropping the accent, he said, 'What is your favourite cocktail, by the way?'

'Margarita,' she said, unequivocally. 'And don't hold back on the salt.'

'Right. Let's go out for Mexican. Tonight?'

'Absolutely,' Marnie said. She was trying to remain buoyant, but the cards were rattling her. It was just a game, she reminded herself. Luke was only mucking around, trying to delight her, with a deck of cards that meant nothing. Nothing. But why the Seven of Cups? Had Luke looked more closely at the card, he'd have seen that while some of the cups contained good things, like jewels and a victory wreath, others contained curses: a snake, a scorpion. It was the card of illusion, of wishing, of falseness. Marnie's mother would have read it as a warning. Do not be taken in.

'And now, if you please, this final one. The us card.'

Don't, she wanted to say. *Leave it where it is*, she wanted to say. *Let's go out for breakfast*, she wanted to say. But he was just having fun. She needed to calm down and play along. So, she turned the third card. It was The Lovers.

He tugged the shirt off his head. Without any trace of an accent, he said, 'That has to be a good sign, doesn't it?'

Marnie was disarmed by the hopefulness in his expression. She wished she could return it honestly, but here was the thing. The most apparently obvious cards, her mother always said, were the ones that had the least straightforward meanings. Death wasn't death, it was new beginnings. And The Lovers? It wasn't simply about falling in love but about becoming absolutely naked in the eyes of another, hiding nothing. Often, it signalled a choice. A difficult one, that could only be made with reference to who you really, truthfully, were and wanted to be.

Luke leaned across the three cards on the bedsheets and kissed her, and although a sweet and delicious current flowed through Marnie's veins, an undercurrent did also.

— PART FIVE —

Marnie knew she had to tell Luke she was still in the employ of his father. It was just a matter of picking the right moment. While she waited, though, for that right moment to present itself, time continued to pass. That wasn't her fault. It was just that the sun continued to go down each night, and to rise each morning, and that each new day seemed to come with its own special reason for avoiding the issue.

She was hardly going to bring it up on the day she first introduced Luke to Saski and Mo. Although she didn't tell him in as many words that this meeting with her friends was more important to her than taking him to meet her mother, she was fairly certain, as they sat together in the back of an Uber on their way to Saski and Mo's place, that she was giving the game away in any case.

'They don't know the sex of the baby,' she told him. 'It's not a question they like being asked.'

'Baby is not a boy. Baby is not a girl. Baby is a baby,' Luke said. 'Got it.'

'And it's probably best if you don't hug Mo. She's not really a hugger.'

This was an understatement. While Saski was affectionate and effusive, and would happily absorb any amount of interpersonal sharing, Mo had clearly defined boundaries and a hatred of social hugging that bordered on a phobia.

'Handshake only. And not even that, if it doesn't seem appropriate,' he said, managing to keep a straight face.

Given how different Saski and Mo were from each other, it was a tough gig for anyone to play them simultaneously. It involved being demonstrative and restrained at the same time. Or, at least, switching quickly between modes. Marnie considered telling this to Luke, but she didn't want him to become as nervous as she was herself.

'The cat is called Gershwin.' Anxiously, she picked a spot of lint off her tights. 'He's old, and a little bit deaf.'

'I will take care to enunciate clearly when I speak to Gershwin,' Luke said, doing less well this time with the straight face. Marnie swatted him, then quickly steadied the bottle of tequila that had nearly rolled off her lap.

'Mo loves margaritas as much as I do,' Marnie said, although she'd already mentioned this at the bottle shop. And again at the supermarket, where they'd stopped to pick up limes. She so badly wanted this night to go well.

When they arrived, Saski – whose belly now looked as exaggerated as a theatre prop – welcomed Luke as if she'd known and loved him for years. Mo, meanwhile, was in the living room trying to put together a complicated self-rocking bassinet that had arrived in a flatpack with instructions that comprised vague sketches and icons, but almost no words. The project seemed already to have gone well over its time-budget and still to be a long way from completion. A highly intelligent human, Mo did not like to be defeated by any kind of technical or mental challenge. She was, therefore, in the kind of quiet fury that created a radioactive halo about her person, although she did manage a peck on the cheek for Marnie, and a half-hearted hello for Luke.

'I think I'll get started on the cocktails,' Marnie said to Saski.

'Strategic,' Saski agreed.

'I've got the fixings for a virgin version for you, my love.'

'O joy, o rapture,' Saski said, drily.

For a time, Luke observed the bassinet dilemma in silence, and Marnie was grateful that even though he was the hands-on, practical type, he didn't attempt any heroics. Instead, he watched carefully, and thought long and hard, before quietly asking Mo if it was possible that one of the components went the other way around.

'Like this, maybe?' he suggested.

Marnie was even more grateful that he turned out to be absolutely right, and that half an hour later, the bassinet – complete with a rack of bright and dangly toys – was all put together.

'Fully operational,' Mo said, hands on hips.

'Just like the Death Star,' Luke said.

'Quite so,' Mo agreed, and gave Luke the kind of smile that – Marnie knew – was reserved for those rare people she was actually prepared to befriend.

By the time Marnie and Luke ended up back at Luke's place, full of Mo's excellent pulled pork tacos and Marnie's equally excellent margaritas, having laughed themselves stupid over a game of Cards Against Humanity – which Saski, despite her sweet nature, had won with her filthy sense of humour – Marnie was beyond happy.

Her state of mind was only intensified when she discovered that Luke had stocked up on her favourite brand of tea and bought in almond croissants for breakfast. He was a man with an eye for detail. Also, a man with a king-sized bed and several acres of clean cotton sheets just waiting to be messed up. All things considered, Marnie decided, it was definitely not the night for uncomfortable truths.

Within two weeks of their love affair's beginning, there was a toothbrush belonging to Marnie in Luke's bathroom, and a toothbrush belonging to Luke in Marnie's. Spray cans of deodorant and items of underwear were migrating freely between Luke's house on Fielding Street and the apartment above Wish & Co. Extra covers had piled up on Luke's bed for Marnie; spare keys had been cut. For this is how it is, sometimes, when two lovers find each other – they just fall into each other's lives as easily as into a highland lake on a warm, springtime day.

Which was something Marnie and Luke did, when the October sun was shining to just the right degree that they impulsively decided to climb Chiron Peak. There was plenty of time to talk in the car as they drove out through the suburbs and into farmlands where young crops had turned the fields bright yellow and gold, and yet more time as the road twisted upwards into slopes richly forested with dark, dripping trees. For that matter, there was plenty of time to talk on the track itself, though talking became less easy when the narrow duckboarding gave way to a rocky track so steep that Marnie's thighs burned from exertion.

Although she recovered her breath quickly when they emerged onto the unexpected shore of Vanishing Tarn, it just didn't seem the right moment for a difficult conversation. The water was so clear, and the pebbles on the lakebed were so beautifully coloured in shades of toffee and amber. Her sweaty clothes came off so easily and the cold knocked the breath right out of her when she dived under. It wasn't exactly possible to talk while she was in the water with Luke, her legs wrapped around his torso, and her mouth busy with kissing him. With one thing and another, she never did manage to tell him the truth that day. They never made it all the way to the top of Chiron Peak either.

Obviously, Marnie couldn't risk telling him on the morning they had their first disagreement. It was over Marnie's habit of idly switching off the radio in Luke's kitchen when she wandered through, barefoot and wrapped in a towel, in the morning. When he got annoyed by this, she stared at him in puzzlement. Who the hell thought it was a good idea to listen to the news in the morning?

'Well, me, actually. I like to know what's going on in the world.' He switched the radio back on.

She switched it off. 'Sure, but not first thing. That's just a recipe for depression! If I listened to the news in the morning, I could end up in the foetal position unable to do anything all day.'

When she followed up the radio thing by unilaterally deciding to fast-forward to the next track on his playlist in the car as he drove her back to the shop, he became quite terse.

That evening, she appeared straight after closing time at his workshop to put things right with a bottle of nice red wine and an apologetic speech about how she'd clearly lived alone for too long and would try to be more considerate. It was, she decided, much too delicate a moment to complicate with talk about his father.

The day Luke introduced Marnie to Ivy was, clearly, not a day to create any extra stress. While he kept saying he wanted to keep it all very low-key, he nevertheless put an awful lot of thought into art-directing the moment. Would Marnie consider getting Alice in for a couple of hours on a Saturday morning? Luke had asked. That way, he and Marnie could casually swing by the market stall where Ivy was volunteering, selling merchandise and collecting donations for an anti-logging campaign. They could turn up just as she was finishing her shift and take her out for lunch.

One thing that Luke had not factored in was how hard it was going to be to get a park in the crammed streets around the market. In the ute, he gridded the narrow thoroughfares again and again, one eye on the clock. Despite Marnie's silent pleas to the Parking Goddess, no spaces appeared. Eventually, unable to bear his nervous tapping on the steering wheel, Marnie said, 'How about you jump out and go find Ivy? I'll get us a parking spot, and then catch up to you.'

Luke grumbled. It wasn't the way he'd wanted it to go.

'You'll make more of a mess of your day by being grumpy than you will by being alone when you get there,' Marnie pointed out.

Once Luke got out of the car, and it was just between herself and the Parking Goddess, a space appeared almost immediately. Only ten minutes behind Luke, Marnie arrived at the stall, which was surrounded by impressive pictures of the tall trees of the Vale of Nekeyah. Marnie bought a calico bag and a bunch of badges and fell easily into conversation with Ivy about the time Marnie had visited the vale, although it had been a while ago now. It wasn't long before they were promising each other to go there together for a hike.

'I have to say, I'm glad you took my advice,' Ivy said, cheekily, to her father, over the wreckage of their restaurant lunches.

'Don't know what you're talking about,' Luke deadpanned.

Ivy turned to Marnie. 'If he hadn't taken my advice, we might not all be sitting here. He'd have been too chicken to ask you out.'

'Excuse me?' Luke said, eyebrows high on his forehead.

'It was me who suggested he ask you out on that light show date.'

'Hey, hang on,' Luke protested. 'That is not strictly true.'

'Okay, but I did tell you that a bold gesture was required.'

'Sure, but I decided on the exact nature of the bold gesture.'

'The exact nature, Dad,' Ivy said, seeming to enjoy the use of the word, 'was less important than the quantity of the boldness. Don't you agree, Marnie?'

Marnie, who'd been watching this exchange as though it was an entertaining rally in tennis, said she couldn't possibly adjudicate. Instead, she ordered hot chocolates all round and when they arrived, she felt warm and happy. Much too warm and happy to take the risk of sitting Luke down to a serious conversation about the secret she wished she was not keeping from him.

She couldn't tell him about it on the day he arrived at her shop, unexpectedly, at lunchtime with a bouquet of sunflowers, nor on the day he took away the rickety timber stool that she was worried would collapse under the weight of one of her workshop guests, and returned with it later that same day, made solid and serviceable. Nor on the day that they barely saw each other because they were both so busy with work, and then he had an arrangement with Ivy in the evening, which was really just as well, because Marnie was falling horribly behind in all her bookwork and needed to catch up. And not, either, on the evening he went out to the pub with a few mates, leaving Marnie to have an early night, but then used his spare key to let himself in at about one in the morning and slid into bed beside her to spoon the warmth of his slightly beer-scented body around hers.

Wrong days accumulated, and as they did so, Marnie continued to deny to herself the horrible truth: she could wait all she wanted for the perfect moment to tell him. It was never, not ever, going to arrive.

Saturday

Through a gap in a twitched-back lace curtain at the dormer window of the upstairs bedroom that had once been Caroline's, Suzanne looked down into the backyard where Brian was digging. He'd been at it for several hours.

It *was* Brian. That was the shape of him, the height of him, the way he walked, the angle at which he held his head. He was deeply familiar, yet at the same time . . . unfamiliar. The confusion she felt reminded her of the time her father had shaved off the beard he'd worn for her whole life up to that point, and she'd found herself sitting across the dinner table from a man she knew extremely well, and yet did not know at all.

For one thing, Brian did not wear shorts. Or elastic-sided boots. And here he was, wearing both, with a winter-white stretch of leg between them, glowing brightly in the spring sunshine. For another thing, he did not dig. Especially not for hours, in the heat, until a Rorschach blot of sweat formed down the back of his blue T-shirt. He was not practised at digging, which was why it had taken him such a long time to grub out the lavender bushes that grew in a straggly hedge around the pergola.

It was past time those bushes were pulled out, but Suzanne had been waiting for an inspired idea of what to plant in their place. In so far as she'd thought about it at all – and in recent times she'd had rather a lot more on her mind than the state of the garden – she'd assumed it would be roses. It wasn't possible to have too many roses, really, nor too many varieties, and there on the lawn behind Brian, delivered right to the spot by a nursery truck earlier in the morning, was an entire hedge's worth of rose bushes. Although, at the speed he was managing to turn over the earth in the garden bed, it would be after dark before he got them all in the ground.

Brian – her version of Brian – did not attempt feats like this one. He worked hard at the office so that he could afford to pay someone else to dig over his garden. If he had one skill above all others, it was outsourcing. Had there been such a thing as the Australian Outsourcing Team, then he would have been both its captain and its coach. It was his creed in life that when it came to manual or domestic labour, he did not do it himself.

Perhaps the strangest thing, though, about this Brian – this boot-wearing, digging, sweating, DIY Brian – was that although he had come to the property, he hadn't actually come to the house. He'd neither knocked on the door, nor – so far as Suzanne had observed – looked up to the windows to check whether or not she was watching, reacting, being impressed. He had simply arrived, selected a shovel from the tool shed and begun to dig.

She watched him stab into an unyielding patch of earth, inexpertly putting his weight on the step of the shovel blade to drive it deeper. Brian, her Brian, did not tolerate being inept at anything. He didn't play any kind of game unless he had a reasonable chance of winning it, take up a sport unless he expected to be good at it, or have a tilt at a business deal unless he was pretty certain it would come off. He hated to fail. Even to struggle. And yet, here he was. Struggling.

Suzanne let the lace curtain fall back into place and went down the hall to her bedroom. On the ottoman at the end of the bed lay the Weekender, unzipped and emptied of all the things she'd taken to Watersmeet Lodge. Less important, perhaps, than what she'd taken on that journey were the things she had brought back. The tangible things were three paintings in the early stages of their development and a plethora of photographs that would enable her to go on with them. The less tangible thing was the night she'd spent with Tony the farmer, surname unknown.

It was something that even a month ago, she wouldn't have imagined having the courage to do. Before she was married, she'd had sex with precisely two people other than Brian. She'd been so very young back then, and that world had been a very different place. The furtive little rendezvous she'd shared with her boyfriends had been tense and impersonal – the twin objectives were to say you'd done it, and not to get caught. For forty years after that, for four whole decades, there had been nobody but Brian.

She and her similarly faithful girlfriends talked about it sometimes, about what it would be like to sleep with somebody new. Before her night with Tony, she'd imagined the experience would be rife with awkwardness and potential humiliations. In her own head, she belonged in some way to Brian, having been shaped to him emotionally, physically, sexually.

It wasn't as if the sex with Tony had been tectonic in its amazingness. It hadn't. But she had done it, and perfectly well, too. After a while, she'd even managed to relax enough to enjoy herself. If ever she decided to tell her girlfriends about the experience, she'd be able to say that, actually, it was perfectly possible to waltz with a partner other than one's own. It was reassuring, and liberating, to discover – or really, to prove – that even after all these years her body belonged to nobody but herself.

Suzanne had declined to give Tony her own phone number, but had agreed to accept his, making no promises. It was scrawled on the sheet of notepaper that she now fished out of a pocket in the bag and scrunched in her fist. There was nothing more she needed from Tony the farmer, surname unknown. She tossed the crumpled page into the bathroom bin and changed her clothes from skirt and blouse to gardening pants and a flannel shirt.

Downstairs, she poured a tall glass of cold water from the fridge, then stopped by the mudroom for gloves, sun hat and rubber gardening clogs. Brian turned at the sound of the back door opening, and rested for a moment, leaning on the handle of the shovel. Even if he was a philandering snake, he was a good-looking one. Even if she was not going to forgive him, the least she could do was help him to plant the roses. And keep him hydrated.

She handed him the water. 'Don't say a word,' she told him, then strode past him in the direction of the tool shed. Returning with a shovel of her own, she got to work. Before long, he was doing better, having begun to figure out where Suzanne was putting her weight to make the shovel blade slide more easily into the earth. Working together, side by side – in silence – they picked up the pace. Soon the entire bed was turned over and ready for planting. Brian dug the first pot-sized hole, and Suzanne picked up one of the potted rose bushes. When she flipped the tag, she saw that not only had it come from one of her favourite breeders, but it was also one of their newest cultivars, the 'Suzanne'. They were all Suzannes. Every one of them.

The tears that welled in her eyes appeared to give Brian a touch of courage.

'I got forty,' he told her. 'One for every year.'

'Shush,' she reminded him.

Suzanne eased the rose out of its pot and gently teased out its roots before handing it to Brian so that he could set it down in place. She supposed it was the fruit of forty years together, the way they easily found a rhythm. Dig, extract, pass, plant, settle, pat. When all the planting was done, Brian collected the plant tags and threw them in the bin, collected up the empty pots and shovels and took them to the tool shed. Suzanne turned on the garden tap and unwound the hose to water in the bushes. The job was complete.

'Suze—' he said.

She held up a hand as a stop sign. 'Don't.'

She loved him. She was furious with him. She was touched by his gesture. She was not letting him get under her skin.

After scooping up his empty water glass, she headed for the house. She closed the back door behind her. Inside the kitchen, she braced, wondering whether or not he would knock. She wanted him to; she did not want him to. She hoped he would; she dreaded that he might. After a few minutes waiting, she heard his car pull out of the drive. She was relieved; she was desolate.

Sunday

'So, are you game?' Ivy asked him.

Luke, sitting behind the wheel of his idling ute, took in the facade of the unprepossessing suburban brick bungalow in front of which they were parked, and considered.

'Come on,' she urged, from the passenger seat. 'You can do it.'

Her birthday lunch – at a very fashionable Turkish restaurant – had been delicious, and Luke's gifts had been a spectacular success. Though he had no intention of holding her to her promise, she had vowed she would take Luke himself to every single one of the symphony orchestra concerts. And, no sooner had she unwrapped the earrings than she had dashed off to the bathroom to put them on and admire them in the mirror.

Ivy. His daughter. At sixteen years old, she was witty, she was kind, she was forthright, she was principled, and Luke was totally charmed by her. To her mother, he owed an apology, as well as a huge debt of gratitude for the spectacular job she'd done of raising this child on her own. Was today the right day to take a risk? Or ought he leave Ivy and Gillian on their own on this special day? He wasn't sure what was the right thing to do – come to the door or say goodbye now and drive away – but Ivy, her seatbelt already unbuckled, was appealing to him, wide-eyed, her hands clasped together beneath her chin. How could he possibly say no to her?

'I'm game,' he confirmed. 'But are you sure your mother wants to see me?'

'She's counting on it,' Ivy said, her face full of mischief. 'She's got the baseball bat stashed by the front door and everything.'

Luke reeled just a little. 'That's not actually funny.'

'Oh, come on. Lighten up. She does want to see you. I know she does. Even if she does chew her lip every time I mention you.'

'Okay then,' Luke said, unclasping his own seatbelt and switching off the engine. 'Let's do this thing.'

The bungalow's front door was already open by the time Ivy was halfway up the path, and Luke felt a tide of nerves surge up into his throat as he registered that standing on the front step – in jeans and a simple red T-shirt, her small feet in white sneakers, her gleaming black hair pulled back into a girlish ponytail – was Gillian Yip, whom he had last seen half a lifetime ago, when he was the same age as their daughter. She was nervous, too. Luke could see tightness in her shoulders and at the corners of her mouth, even though she smiled as she admired the earrings that Ivy was showing off by tucking back her hair and tilting her head.

Without rushing, Luke arrived behind Ivy. He stopped himself from putting a hand on his daughter's shoulder, not wanting to do anything that might be construed as possessive. Yes, she was his daughter, but for the majority of Ivy's sixteen years, she had been only Gillian's.

'Luke,' she said.

'Gillian, hello.'

A silence followed in which they regarded one another. He wondered if she was feeling much the same as he – a little freaked out that she was, fundamentally, unchanged; slightly unmoored in time and space, as if he wasn't quite sure if he was sixteen or thirty-two, or some indefinite age in between; unsure of how to proceed, what to say. Even if she was feeling all of that, too, Luke knew there were also some feelings that were his alone to bear. Guilt, shame, sorrow, regret. Taken all together, they were too big to get out all at once, and so he found himself unable to say anything at all.

Ivy glanced from one of her parents to the other and back again, apparently trying to read their faces. Luke wanted to reassure her that everything was all right, but no useful words made their way down from his brain to his mouth. In the end, it was Ivy who spoke first.

'You know what?' she said, cheerfully. 'I'm going to get out of the middle of whatever . . . this . . . is. Why don't you two say whatever you have to say, and then give me a call. I'll put the kettle on, yeah?'

Once Ivy had withdrawn into the house, the awkwardness seemed only to intensify for a moment, before – at last – Luke landed on the first sentiment he wanted to express.

'She's remarkable, Gillian,' Luke said.

Gillian smiled. 'Isn't she?'

'Thank you,' he said, wondering if she had any way of understanding that those two words might as well have been a great, big, fat overflowing suitcase, or travelling trunk, there was so much stuffed into them. And then he wondered if he knew, himself, just how much he had to thank her for. After all, he had never raised a child. He decided to name just the biggest ticket items. 'Thank you for ignoring my assumption, all those years ago, when I sent that money. Thank you for raising her. For doing such an incredible job of it.'

Gillian's mouth twisted and straightened before she spoke. 'Thanks. It's nice to have that acknowledged, but . . . look, I don't mean to be cruel, Luke, but it was actually your loss.'

'You're right,' he said. 'You're absolutely right.'

Another silence followed. It lasted until the pressure of Luke's feelings became too intense.

'I'm so sorry,' he burst out.

Gillian looked to be trapped between tears and anger. 'I'd like to say there were no hard feelings, but there are some, if I'm honest.'

'That's fair. Did Ivy ever give you my letter?'

'She did, yes. I was pretty surprised that she'd gone and found you. Without telling me. That was hard. But your letter was . . . very reasonable. Thanks.'

'So, someday – not today, obviously, but one day . . . could we talk? I know I've got a lot to make up for. With you, with her. Maybe that's not even possible, but I can at least try. It would be great to have a talk about how I could contribute. How we could work together. As her parents.' Hearing himself say those words made him feel as if he had crossed a threshold. He'd thought he'd acclimatised to the notion of being a father, but standing here talking to Gillian had made it feel even more real.

Gillian thought. Seconds ticked by. Eventually, she nodded. 'Okay. Yes.'

'Thank you,' Luke said. 'I only want what's best for Ivy.'

Something approaching a smile tugged at the corners of Gillian's mouth and eyes.

He smiled back, knowing that – somehow, and in time – it was all going to be all right.

'Well, then,' she said, 'are you coming in for a cup of tea?'

Marnie snatched up the phone the moment she saw Luke's name appear on its screen. Probably, he was already driving in the direction of Wish & Co, but he'd developed the habit of calling when he was on his way, just to chat, staying on the phone until he was standing right at the front door. Often, he'd ring just after closing time, and Marnie — who loved their companionable little debriefs — would sweep the floor while they talked, phone tucked under her chin in a manner that could not possibly be good for her neck. Today, though, was Sunday, and Marnie was upstairs in her apartment, struggling bravely through a choppy sea of paperwork.

'Well?' she asked. 'How did it go?'

'Which part?' he asked, and Marnie was relieved to hear the trace of a laugh in his voice. He sounded relaxed, which meant things had likely gone well.

'All of it! Any of it! Did she like her present? How did you find Gillian?'

'Ivy loved her present,' he said, and Marnie could tell how pleased he was. 'She's totally stoked about the concerts, but I think the really key thing was telling her that I'd set aside the dates to go with her if she wants.'

'Oh, that's so great. And the earrings?'

'She put them on straight away. Couldn't wait to show her mum. I think she really, *really* liked them.'

'Well done, Daddy-O.' Marnie sighed with pleasure. There were few things in life she loved so much as a happy ending to a gift-giving story. 'And Gillian? How did that go?'

'I think it's fair to say it was a good start. She's agreed to meet up, just the two of us, and talk about future stuff. You know, I want to give Ivy a bit of a start towards buying a car, one that we can say is from both of us, even if Gill hasn't got the money.

I want to help support her through school and uni, but make sure it's a joint effort. So, there's a long way to go yet, but it all feels pretty good. What about you? Good day?'

'Absolutely nothing to report except invoices and emails and filing,' Marnie said. 'I don't even want to talk about it. Tell me more about you.'

There was a brief silence. 'Well, Mum called.'

'Yes?' Marnie said, trying to retract the antennae that automatically popped up each time Luke mentioned Suzanne.

'You'll never guess what my father's done now,' Luke said.

Marnie winced, for the truth was that she could make a very good guess indeed. Earlier in the day, she'd taken a call from a triumphant Brian. Suzanne had come out of the house to help him plant the roses, he'd reported. A real breakthrough, he'd trumpeted. Marnie was a genius, he declared. He was sure, now, that the frost was starting to thaw, that they were making progress. Marnie hoped he was right. Did she dare hope that Luke's parents might reconcile before she had to confess?

For now, though, her only option seemed to be to play dumb. 'I don't know. What's your dad done?'

'He's tracked down some rose bush called "Suzanne" and bought enough of them to fill the entire bed around the pergola. Can you believe that?'

She could. It made her feel sick that Luke was such a trusting soul that he didn't appear even to have considered that Marnie had been involved in the purchase of the roses. The clock was ticking, and Marnie knew it. She had to tell him, before he guessed or found out.

'Luke, there's . . .' she began. But no. Just no. Not over the telephone.

'Marnie? I think you dropped out.'

That was not what had happened. She had lost her nerve, was all.

'I don't know what happened there,' she lied. 'What did your mum think of them? The roses?'

'Mum loves roses.'

'Enough to forgive your dad?' She hated herself for lying to Luke, but she hated herself even more for being unable to resist the temptation to pump him for information.

'I don't know about that. I feel like she's just starting to find her feet. You know, she's painting again. Maybe she'll even find someone else. Someone who'll love her the way she deserves to be loved.'

Marnie, feeling the bizarre instinct to put in a good word for Brian, to protest that she was only painting again because Brian had sent her paints and canvases and an easel, kept herself from saying anything.

'You there?' Luke asked. 'Did I lose you again?'

'Yeah, I'm here.'

'You okay?'

Deep breath. *Be brave.* 'Luke, there's something I have to tell you.'

'Whoa. That sounds serious.'

'It is a bit.'

'But we're okay?'

'I hope so,' Marnie said. 'I want us to be.'

'Right, okay,' Luke said, a worried note in his voice. 'Look, I'm almost there. I'm just a couple of blocks away. How about we talk about it when I get there?'

'Okay.'

'All right. See you in a minute.'

Love you, she didn't say. That was a threshold they had yet to cross.

Marnie got up from her paperwork-covered table and went to the window. Rathbone Street was Sunday-afternoon quiet. Any minute now she would see Luke's ute coming from the direction of the city, and she'd run downstairs to let him in at the front door of the shop, and then . . . then, what? How did she even start?

I made a deal with your father, and . . .

About those roses that your father planted . . .

You know how much I want that shop? Well . . .

I never meant to lie to you, but . . .

Nothing sounded right. There was the ute. She watched Luke make several attempts before at last he successfully backed it into a snug parking spot just across the street. She padded down the steps in her socks to open the door.

Luke's expression was as worried as his voice had been over the phone. He kissed her, and she kissed him back especially tenderly, trying to communicate with that kiss that when she'd said she hoped they were okay, she had been telling the absolute truth.

'You all right?' he asked.

'Yes, fine.'

He followed her up the stairs and into the unusually messy apartment. Piles of papers covered the table and kitchen bench. More piles had formed on top of the hurriedly pulled-up duvet. Marnie quickly tidied these into one big pile that she landed on the floor, and pulled Luke down to sit with her on the bed.

She did not want to tell him. *You have to.* She did not want to have to tell him. *Yes, but that's the way things are.* Maybe it was the wrong time? *There is never going to be a right time.* What if he walks away from you? That last thought hit her like a punch. She could already feel the ache of its impact. When she opened her mouth, even she was surprised by the words that came out.

'You remember Owen?'

Luke squinted. 'Yes, I remember.'

'Well, next month is his father's wedding.'

'Yes, and?'

'I said I'd go with him.'

There was a short pause, and then Luke gave a small laugh, relieved. 'That's what you had to tell me? You had me worry for three whole blocks, and make a mess of my reverse parking, because you're going to Owen's father's wedding? You goose.'

He kissed her on the forehead, and the papery, resiny smell of sawdust filled her nostrils, making her feel like crying. She rested her head against his chest, not wanting to move. 'I just thought you should know.'

Luke, stroking her hair, said, 'Some kid once told me that you have to take down the walls and trust people if you want a relationship to work.'

'Wise kid, that one.'

'I trust you, Marnie.' Luke lifted her chin to kiss her on the lips. 'Oh, and I forgot to tell you, on the phone. Mum's invited us for dinner on Thursday night.'

Marnie pulled back from Luke's embrace, her eyes suddenly wide.

'Problem?' Luke asked.

'I don't think I can do that.'

'Meet my mother? What? Ever?'

'I mean, obviously I want to meet your mother, but —'

'Marnie, she'll love you. You'll love her,' Luke insisted.

'But —'

'But what? So, you used to buy gifts for her. That's all in the past now.'

Except, of course, that it wasn't. Marnie let her mind wander back over the last couple of weeks – introducing Luke to Saski and Mo, meeting Ivy, walking in the mountains, sharing each other's beds. He and she had been busy with all the easy parts of falling in love. Now life was going to make her pay the price. She sank back against Luke's chest.

'What are you thinking?' Luke probed.

'About your father,' Marnie said.

'Yeah, I guess I don't have to introduce you to him. We just have to work out how to tell him.' He didn't sound as if it was something he was in a rush to do, but even so, Marnie heard the distant ticking of a time-bomb.

'I'd really like you to come to Mum's on Thursday,' Luke said, simply. 'I think it's time.'

'What will you tell your mum if she asks how we met?'

'We can just tell her that we ran into each other at the Cassandra du Plessé exhibition. She'll like that.'

'You hate lying,' Marnie said, flatly.

'For you, beautiful,' he said, chivalrously, 'I will tolerate this one small deception.'

Marnie knew he had meant them kindly, but his words made her feel like shit. She was nothing more than a grubby little liar. Somebody for whom exceptions had to be made. Somebody who did not deserve the trust they were being given.

Thursday

They ate at a table on the back veranda, just the three of them. Suzanne served an egg and bacon pie with buttery, melt-in-your-mouth pastry that Marnie had immediately known was homemade. In a vase at the centre of the table were the carnations that Marnie had brought, recognising that to bring roses to Suzanne was the equivalent of bringing ice to penguins. She'd also brought a candle from the Sea Glass colourway which Suzanne had asked Luke to light – for the scent rather than for the glow, since the late springtime sun hovered in the sky well into the evening.

It should have been a perfect night. The weather was warm, the wine was chilled, the conversation was effortless, and subtle scents of flowers drifted up to the veranda from the huge back garden that stretched down past the pergola – rimmed with newly planted rose bushes – and a stand of apple trees, to finish in a well-established conifer hedge that Marnie imagined would have been beyond perfect for children's hide-and-seek. It *was* a perfect night, in every detail except for one: Marnie felt like she was taking advantage of a woman who deserved better.

She had always imagined she would like Suzanne, if she ever had the chance to meet her in person, and her instincts proved correct. While it was easy to see the physical resemblance between Brian and Luke, it was just as easy to see the similarity in temperament between Luke and Suzanne. They shared a watchfulness, a way of listening with their full attention, a habit of waiting for a moment to absorb what had just been said, before responding. If Marnie had been asked to describe them in just a few words, she would have said that they took people seriously, and handled life gently.

Marnie observed, too, the comfortable way Luke kissed and hugged Suzanne in greeting, the easy-going way he and she set the table in tandem, Luke laying out the napkins and Suzanne pinning them to the table with cutlery, but without any apparent discussion taking place. At one point, they alluded to their special connection, agreeing that some of their favourite memories had come from the times when Brian and Caroline had both been away from home, taking their noise and demands with them. At the mention of Brian, a small sadness descended over Suzanne, but then she rallied, bringing bowls of fresh raspberries with shavings of white chocolate and dollops of cream, as if Luke and Marnie were not already full to the brim with delicious food.

Over the main course, Suzanne and Marnie had covered all the getting-to-know-you basics. Suzanne, on learning that Marnie ran Wish & Co, said she'd seen the shop but had never stopped by. She would do so, she promised, next time she was passing. It was only now that dessert was on the table that other inevitable questions arose: 'So, Marnie, where do you fit into the Fairchild clan?'

Marnie darted a quick glance at Luke, sitting across from her. His expression seemed to say, *go on, it's safe*. And so, for once, Marnie did not take her usual circuitous route around her family tree but went directly to the heart of the matter.

'I'm Rory's daughter,' she said.

'Oh, Marnie,' Suzanne said. 'I'm so sorry.'

'It was a long time ago.'

'Such a tragedy, I'll never forget it. It was so much in the papers. He was a vibrant-looking young man, I always thought. And your mother? She was so young, and what a terrible, terrible shock for her.'

'We got by,' Marnie said in a small voice. Suzanne's genuine and effusive sympathy had touched a nerve.

Luke said, 'Marnie's hoping to buy the old shop. Fairchild and Sons.'

'Really? How wonderful! It needs some love, the poor old place,' Suzanne said. 'Luke, darling, would you go inside and grab my Alexandria Park book? It's on the living room shelves. You know the one? *The Verdant Heart?*'

Luke came back a few minutes later with the book, a lavishly produced history of the Alexandria Park region that Marnie knew well. Most likely there was an identical copy kicking around in half the houses along Austinmer Street. On the back cover was the image Marnie kept on her counter — her grandfather at the shop on opening day.

'He was a lovely man, Archie,' Suzanne said, running a finger over the book cover. 'And the shoes he made. Just divine! I remember the first time I could afford a pair. I had them resoled twice before they came to the end of their lives. Just look at that architecture. So much character packed into that little building. The arched windows — they really make the place, don't they?'

Marnie felt her heart squeeze. Just three weeks remained, now, until the auction, and it was impossible to know who else was out there, equally set on realising their dreams on that small square of real estate.

When dessert was done, and the temperature of the evening dropped to a few degrees below completely comfortable, Suzanne suggested they go inside. While Luke unsubtly busied himself with examining a section of the veranda railing that needed repair, Suzanne and Marnie cleared away the last of the dishes and took them, together, to the kitchen.

'Just leave them,' Suzanne said, 'I can do all that later.'

'Really, I like to help,' Marnie insisted. 'Many hands, all that.'

In the kitchen was the Smeg coffee maker that Marnie had organised Brian to buy for Suzanne, as well as the matching juicer. And the toaster. And the kettle. Bright against the white cupboards and pale grey marble benchtops, they were missing only their cousin the stand mixer. As she rinsed plates and forks, and loaded the dishwasher, Marnie felt a complicated cocktail of emotions – regret that her mistake had played a role in disturbing Suzanne's orderly life; selfish pleasure that as a result of that mistake she was now here, with Luke.

'Luke seems happy,' Suzanne observed.

Marnie smiled at the sideways compliment. 'I know I am.'

She knew her thoughts were starting to run ahead of her, but for the moment there didn't seem to be any harm in letting them have their way. If her relationship with Luke were to continue, Marnie realised, then this was the house to which she would bring her children to be babysat. This was the woman who would be her children's grandmother. This was the kitchen where she and her mother-in-law would stand, shoulder to shoulder, making salads or peeling potatoes on Christmas morning. She and Suzanne would be tied, part of the joys and sadnesses of each other's lives. These were sweet thoughts, but at some deep level Marnie had the sense they were just a dream. One that would never come true.

On the far side of the kitchen bench was a breakfast nook with tall windows that Marnie imagined would let in the morning sunshine. There, Suzanne had set up her easel, the one Marnie had bought in the city on the fervent recommendation of the young artist serving behind the counter at the art supply shop. Resting on the easel was a painting, not yet complete, of two rushing rivers blending into one. It was slightly inexpert, but there was something energetic and beautiful about the way the water had been captured in its roiling and churning.

'Yours?' Marnie asked.

'Yes,' Suzanne admitted. 'Please don't feel you have to say anything about it. I'm just getting back to painting after a very long time.'

'Luke said you loved art. That you've got quite the collection.'

Suzanne hung her tea-towel and smiled brightly. 'Come, and I'll show you some much better pictures than that one.'

The tour took Marnie down halls and into living spaces, upstairs and into the room that had once been Luke's – street-facing and with a window that gave access to that faithful friend of the disobedient teenager: a downpipe. On every stretch of wall there hung something beautiful, and although some of the works were by well-known artists, many others were by painters of whom Marnie had never heard.

'There's art that you love on the gallery wall. It's striking or thought-provoking or remarkable, but you wouldn't necessarily want to look at it every single day of your life,' Suzanne mused. 'The only sort of art I buy is the sort I truly want to live with.'

Marnie thought of Brian. Had Leona been his version of art on the gallery wall? Striking, thought-provoking, remarkable – but not, in the end, the one he wanted to live with every day?

Suzanne led the way back downstairs and into the formal

dining room. The space – with its long table and neatly aligned dining chairs, the tall cabinets at one end, the polished sideboards at the other – struck Marnie as being rather like an empty stage upon which a famous scene had once played out. The way she sometimes did in a theatre, or when visiting the preserved house of a well-known artist or celebrity, Marnie had the sense of being able to feel, even now, the emotional residue of all that had happened here.

'And then there's this painting,' Suzanne said, her face a picture of amusement.

It was overwhelmingly green, a picture of gum trees in the wind, and the signature in the corner was that of Roger Cubit, a well-known artist who'd lived and worked for most of his life in Alexandria Park.

'It's . . .' Marnie began.

'Ghastly,' Suzanne finished.

Perhaps not 'ghastly', exactly, but it struck Marnie as the sort of mass-produced painting you might see in a hotel room, the kind that magically matched the decor.

'Brian gave it to me. An anniversary gift. Not long after we moved in here.' Suzanne looked at the painting and almost winced. 'I don't know why he thought I'd like it. It's not the sort of thing I've ever liked. Brian just saw the artist's name, I suppose. Poor old Roger – he got a bit slapdash towards the end, but his signature still sold paintings. Brian probably thought he was giving me such a great gift.' She considered for a moment. 'I suppose I can do what I like with it now. Luke will have told you, of course. About the separation.'

Throughout dinner, Suzanne had made vague allusions to Brian's absence, but this was the first time she had approached the subject directly.

'I'm so sorry, Suzanne,' Marnie said, knowing that Suzanne could not possibly understand all the many dimensions of her sorrow. Her guilt at having been part of the cause.

'It's not something I ever imagined would happen to me. To us. I thought the one thing I did well, you know, really well, was being a wife.'

'Is it really over, do you think?' Marnie asked, although she could hardly believe she had dared.

Suzanne, seemingly still caught in private thoughts, shook her head sadly. 'I don't know, Marnie. I really don't.'

That was some distance short of a categorical 'yes'. There was hope for Brian yet; Marnie could see it in Suzanne's face and she wanted to ask more questions. *What would he have to do? What would it take? Where is the magic button? What is the key?* But she also wanted to slap herself around the face. *What the hell are you doing? What are you thinking? Are you even thinking? Sniffing around this lovely woman's house for clues, forming your little hypotheses. What is it exactly, Marnie, that you want?*

The trouble was, she wanted so many things. She wanted Luke to love her, and she wanted Suzanne to be happy. She wanted Brian to win back his wife, and she wanted Fairchild & Sons to be hers. She wanted no secrets, nor any more lies. But all her wants were tangled up together like a messy ball of several different kinds of string. If she pulled too hard or too fast on any one thread, she would only make a mess somewhere else.

If she continued to help Brian get Suzanne back, Luke may not forgive her. If she didn't continue to help Brian, he might put Fairchild & Sons out of her reach. There was a solution to all of it, though. There had to be. There always was.

'There you both are,' Luke said, clearly pleased to see his mother and his new girlfriend getting on so well.

'Marnie's getting the art tour. We're just admiring the Cubit.'

Luke raised his eyebrows. 'That horrible thing. Now's your chance to get rid of it, Mum. It would probably still fetch a reasonable price. If you could take the money in all good conscience.'

All good conscience. Marnie felt those words sting, as if they'd been directed at her.

'It's been a long time since I had an empty wall to fill,' Suzanne mused, and Marnie felt the familiar sensation of an idea beginning to take shape in her mind.

Friday

'Eleanor who?' Brian asked.

'Eleanor-*a*. Eleanora Middleton-Holmes,' Marnie repeated.

'Never heard of her,' Brian said.

In the back seat of the taxi, she handed across a print-out of the late artist's biography. Until two thirty that morning, Marnie had not heard of Ms Middleton-Holmes either. But in the wee, small hours, she'd been doing what she always did when she couldn't sleep: working. In the weeks since she'd met Luke, she'd fallen behind in so many aspects of her business. It was so much more fun to hang out with him than to trawl through social media feeds, scanning for clues. And yet, her research, formerly known as stalking, was a crucial and time-consuming part of what she did.

Curled up on Luke's sofa with her phone and her laptop, she'd checked in with some of her clients' loved ones. On Instagram, the daughter of one of Marnie's clients had expressed deep love for a pair of black boots with leather batwings at the heels. Shoes were always a risky gift – since choosing the right size was critical – but Marnie remembered that this girl had some time ago posted a link to her eBay listings. And there – *Bingo!* – Marnie had found what she needed: pair after pair of shoes for sale, every one of them size 38. The wife of another client professed, on Facebook, a desire to reacquaint herself with the classics of Greek mythology, so Marnie spent some time searching the internet for the most beautiful editions, and most well-regarded translations, of the *Iliad* and the *Odyssey*.

Out of habit, Marnie also checked in on the websites of her favourite auction houses – one that specialised in farm sales and deceased estates, another that specialised in vintage bric-a-brac, antique furniture and art. It was there that she'd found Eleanora Middleton-Holmes. Or to be more specific, six paintings by the little-known Australian painter.

From the auction house website, it had taken only a few keystrokes and clicks to land Marnie on Eleanora's entry in the *Australian Dictionary of Biography*. The daughter of landscape painter John Middleton-Holmes, the talented second child of nine, Eleanora had painted only until her mid-twenties, when she had married. After her wedding, to a wealthy sheep grazier, she had gone on to produce seven children of her own, but no more paintings, so far as anybody knew.

Now Marnie, having collected Brian from his office, was on her way to the auction house while Alice took care of the shop, to see these paintings 'in the flesh'. Three of the artworks were in excess of two metres wide, making them a good size for the large wall in the formal dining room at Austinmer Street. More importantly, Middleton-Holmes painted in a soft-edged, Impressionist style that Marnie knew Suzanne would adore.

While Brian read through the biography, Marnie listened in a desultory fashion to the talkback on the taxi radio, and tried to ignore the nasty chemical smell of the little scent tree hanging from the stem of the rear-view mirror.

'So she was a cousin of Cassandra du Plessé,' Brian noted, aloud. 'Suzanne does like her. I know that much.'

'Eleanora was even less famous than Cassandra herself. Probably because her career was so short.'

'You're sure Suzanne would like one of these, though?' Brian asked.

Cassandra du Plessé's paintings were of the sort you might want to look at on the gallery walls, but in Marnie's opinion, Eleanora's were the kind you would want to live with, to look at every day.

'Quite,' she assured Brian.

'You said you think we should be looking at one of the big ones. Over two metres, right? I'm trying to imagine where in the house Suzanne would put it.'

Now Marnie needed to be diplomatic. 'I don't know, are there any paintings in the house that are about that size? A space that could do with . . . refreshing?'

'Can't think of one,' he said.

Marnie ransacked her brain for the right way to approach this. She needed to remind him about the ugly Roger Cubit painting, but she didn't really want Brian to know that she'd dined with Luke and Suzanne. She was beginning to feel, uncomfortably, like a double agent. 'Are there any outliers in your house? Paintings that are noticeably different, stylistically, from the ones Suzanne has bought for herself?'

Brian shrugged. You could lead a horse to water, Marnie thought. She wondered if it would be too blunt to ask him, outright, if there were any paintings in the house that he had chosen himself.

'You can't have that many really big canvases,' Marnie suggested.

'The only one I can think of is the one in the dining room. That's a Roger Cubit, though. It was very expensive.'

'Not always the most important factor, when choosing a painting.'

'Well, of course not. But Roger was very well regarded,' Brian said, confidently. But then he continued, 'Wasn't he?'

Marnie made a so-so gesture with her outspread hand. 'His later works were generally considered to be a bit . . . mass-produced? But it would still sell. Probably for about what you bought it for.' She'd done her research into that, too. 'Would it be so hard to let it go?'

Brian turned slightly to look Marnie straight in the face. 'I want my wife back. If she wants a picture of a two-headed walrus on the dining room wall, she can have it as far as I'm concerned.'

Marnie beamed. 'Then let's go shopping.'

The Sunderland Auction warehouse was a space well known to Marnie. Past glossy mahogany sideboards and enormous walnut wardrobes, Marnie led Brian to the back wall where the current selection of artworks had been hung on a grid. There were moody seascapes, uninspiring reproductions of colonial pictures of tall ships in harbour, and a handful of still-lifes featuring odd combinations of fruits and dead animals. Hung at the centre of the offerings, clearly signalling that they were expected to be hot items, were the paintings by Eleanora Middleton-Holmes.

In real life, the paintings were more impressive – richer, more detailed, more subtle – than on screen, and they proved unaccountably moving to Marnie. She turned away from Brian, pretending to study one of the maritime scenes, so that he didn't see she was feeling emotional. When she had regained her composure, she rejoined him where he stood, taking in the three largest of the artist's works.

Marnie already knew which one she would choose for Suzanne,

but even before ringing Brian this morning and inviting him to view the paintings, she had decided that she would leave the decision up to him. Little by little, her role as Brian's gift-buyer was changing. Just as she had been for Luke, she was becoming – for his father – more of an adviser and less of a unilateral decision-maker. She had to admit it felt good. But, at the same time, she was practical enough to know that it was no way to do business. The whole reason her clients paid her, in the first place, was so that they didn't have to think. But how nice it was to be here with Brian, and to be doing the thinking together.

'Which one's best?' Brian asked.

'I've brought you this far,' Marnie said, looking at the art and not at Brian. 'The final choice is yours.'

She expected him to object, to make some remark about getting his money's worth out of her services, but he only looked more closely at the paintings.

'How do you do it?' he asked, with a degree of vulnerability that Marnie had never seen in him before. 'How do I do it?'

Marnie pictured her Venn diagram. Person, occasion, relationship. 'You think about Suzanne, Brian. About who she is, what you know about her. You think about how sorry you are. You think about the story of your relationship with her, about the way you want the next chapter to be.'

Brian nodded. 'Then it's this one.'

Bingo, Marnie thought. He had not chosen the painting of the quaint cottage, with its fragile flower garden marooned in a wider landscape of bleached grass. Nor had he settled on the kitchen scene, in which a well-dressed woman – sleeves rolled to the elbows – worked alongside two younger women in calico aprons and plain dresses, who might have been her maids. Instead, he'd chosen the one called *Summer Day at Drowsy Creek*.

It was a group portrait of a family picnicking on a summer's day in long, wheat-coloured grass under a sky of fierce and cloudless blue. But it was not a scene of perfection. The bonneted baby was squalling while two older siblings fought over the right to pull the infant onto their laps. In the distance, children with bare legs and blousy shirts were wading in a shallow watercourse where wet rocks gleamed brightly. In the centre of the image, a man in a white jacket was shooing flies away from what remained of the food, and a woman slept, the brim of a straw hat over her eyes. Perhaps Marnie's favourite detail was that the woman had been painted at an angle that revealed her perfectly imperfect double chin.

Having cross-referenced the date of the painting and the details of Eleanora's life, Marnie felt sure that *Summer Day at Drowsy Creek* was a representation of Eleanora's parents and siblings, and that Eleanora herself, that day, had been the equivalent of the person behind the camera.

'Do you agree?' Brian asked.

'Wholeheartedly,' Marnie said, feeling another tidal wave of emotion. She wanted, she realised, for Suzanne to love it. She wanted, she realised, Brian to win back his wife. Not just for her own reasons, now.

'When's the auction?'

'Next Wednesday,' Marnie said. 'I can manage the bidding if you want, or you can. Or we can come together if you like.'

Brian bumped his shoulder against her, playfully. 'Wouldn't dream of doing it without you.'

'I can't tell you how much interest it's likely to attract, but I can send you the research I've done about the prices of comparable works, and then you can decide how high you want to bid.'

'I think we'll be all right, Marnie,' he said, and his smile was slightly smug.

She wished she could say the same about Fairchild & Sons.

Brian checked his watch. 'Shall we head off then?'

'Sure.'

As they walked back past the wardrobes and sideboards and huge velvet-upholstered chairs, Marnie knew she had well and truly done it now. If – no, when – Brian bought the Middleton-Holmes painting and arranged for it to be hung in place of the horrible Roger Cubit painting, there was no way Marnie could continue to keep Luke in the dark. The painting might or might not turn out to be the gift that would change Suzanne's mind, but it would certainly be the one that forced Marnie to tell Luke the truth.

Monday

Saski set a newly released copy of the *Alexandria Park Star* down on the table at Wish & Co, but when Marnie reached for it, Saski stopped her hand.

'It's not good news, Bunny,' Saski warned her, 'but it may not be as terrible as it first looks, so try not to panic, okay?'

Marnie didn't have to flick far through the magazine to find what she was looking for. Spread across the top of pages six and seven were several pictures of Fairchild & Sons in different phases of its history – in sepia in its heyday, in vintage colour as the backdrop for a royal visit, in pixelated newspaper black and white right after it was burned. The profile picture, though, was a crisp colour shot showing the shop as it looked right now, with a FOR SALE sign dominating its facade. Standing in front of the building, smiling with toothpaste advertisement perfection, a dark-haired woman posed with palpable confidence.

'Carly McCulloch?' Marnie asked. 'Of the wine McCullochs?'

'I'm afraid so,' Saski said.

The headline read: 'Everything happens for a Riesling'.

Marnie scanned the copy. *Wine heiress Carly McCulloch has revealed that she has her eye on the heritage shopfront of Fairchild & Sons . . . auction 16 November . . . happened to come on the market right at the time she was searching for the perfect venue for an ambitious new wine bar and fromagerie . . . 'a privilege to restore this Alexandria Park gem to its former glory' . . . newest branch of the multi-generational wine business that began its life with just a few vines . . . team of heritage architects and craftsmen . . .*

'Shit,' Marnie said. She let the magazine fall to the table and put her hand to her forehead. She was tired, headachy. It had been almost a week since she'd slept through the night without getting up to work in the wee hours to distract herself from her worries.

'It's a risk for them, to announce they're going after a property before the auction,' Saski said. 'It might be part of a strategy to scare off other buyers. Ones like you, who assume they're smaller fry.'

'I am smaller fry,' Marnie said, her voice quivering.

Saski, her belly ballooning into her lap, covered Marnie's hand with hers. 'I'd come around and hug you, but it was quite an effort to get up here, and I don't think I can do it all over again today.'

Marnie went around the table, where Saski was holding out her arms. It was such a good hug – sincere and warm – that Marnie allowed herself to collapse just a little more than usual.

'Hey, it's all right,' Saski said. 'Even if you can't afford it, it won't be the end of the world. It won't even be the end of Wish and Co.'

'But it will be the end of a dream.'

'There'll be other dreams, babe. And this one's not dead yet.'

'It's not just a shop to me, Peach.'

'I know, Bunny. But what would your grandfather say?'

Marnie shook her head, trying to keep in the tears. For the moment, every last one of her grandfather's aphorisms had vanished from the accessible parts of her memory.

Saski said, 'He'd say, "It's the people that make a place, my girl, not the bricks and mortar."'

It was exactly what he would have said. Marnie smiled. The good thing about repeating someone else's words of wisdom was that if you did it often enough, those words would find a way back to you, and right when you needed them most.

Wednesday

Brian was pleased, overall, with the renovation of the reception room at the Charlesworth Group. The work had only just been completed: granite bar at one end of the space that made quite a statement, fashionable polished concrete for the flooring. He'd found the room a bit echoey during the first function they'd put on there, but when it came to cleaning up afterwards, the concrete had proved a total winner.

His footsteps rang out as he strode across the room, Marnie Fairchild following him carefully in her high heels. Behind the bar, Brian opened one of the sleek, black-doored fridges and surveyed the contents.

'Sparkling red, sparking rosé, sparkling white? Which one? Anything you like. We're celebrating,' he said, still fizzing with leftover adrenaline from the art auction.

When they'd first gone together to the warehouse and Brian had seen how the place was stuffed with fusty old furnishings, he'd wondered what on earth Marnie had talked him into. But then he'd seen the Eleanora Middleton-Holmes paintings and known, immediately, that Marnie had struck gold.

He liked the Roger Cubit painting he'd bought for the dining room. It was big, and colourful, and easy to understand. Trees.

In the wind. Simple. Nothing complicated about that. But this painting? It made the Cubit look like a sketch. Here were real people, living and breathing and snoring and squabbling in the kind of sunshine you could feel on your skin, that almost radiated out of the frame. Marnie Fairchild had some kind of rare and special gift. He supposed some people would call it simply 'taste', but he was beginning to think it was something more.

'Marnie?' he called out to where she stood at the window. 'What can I get you?'

There was something a little unusual about her today. She was normally so sparky, so full of energy and optimism, but today it was as if those qualities had been dialled right back, leaving her quiet and pensive.

'Sorry,' she said, and stepped away from the window, appearing slightly wan, as if the vertiginous view over the city had taken a toll. 'White?'

'Your wish. My command.'

When Brian popped the cork it hit the ceiling, but he worked fast, directing the bubbling froth into the twin flutes he'd set out on the bar. When the initial fizz had settled, he passed a flute to Marnie.

'Here's to you, and to me, and to Eleanora Middleton-Holmes, who today fetched a record price for one of her paintings. And here's to *Summer Day at Drowsy Creek*. And to Suzanne liking – no, loving – it.'

They touched glasses, drank.

Brian and Marnie had not been the only ones at the auction with their eye on the Drowsy Creek painting. There had been a number of bidders at the start, but only two who'd given Brian a serious run for his money.

'So, what did you make of the others?' Brian asked.

'I thought the woman was probably an art dealer. A professional.'

'What makes you say so?'

'She was hard as nails,' Marnie said.

Face like a hatchet, Brian silently agreed. 'Wasn't she just? And she wasn't passionate about the painting either. Not at all. She knew when we'd passed the point where a profit was possible and that was when she stopped bidding. Did you see that?'

Marnie nodded. 'The man, though. Do you think he might have been family?'

Brian hadn't thought of that. All he'd seen was a middle-aged bloke with conspicuously large eyes that had far too much fear in them. 'I don't know, but he really wanted it. Didn't he? We pushed him right to his limit. I wouldn't be surprised if, towards the end there, he was actually bidding above his limit.'

'You really enjoyed it, didn't you?'

'Of course! We won! No weeping into the Weet-Bix for us.'

Marnie looked even more subdued than before. 'Brian, what do you know about the McCullochs?'

'The wine McCullochs? Why do you ask?'

'One of them has splashed it all over the *Alexandria Park Star* that she wants to buy Fairchild and Sons for a wine bar and fromagerie.'

Brian observed the accentuated way Marnie rolled the 'r's in 'fromagerie'. 'She declared her hand in the press? Before the auction? Unusual move.'

Marnie shrugged. 'I'm guessing McCullochs have deep pockets and can afford unusual moves.'

So that was what was up with her today. 'She's got you rattled, has she?'

'I could just see myself,' Marnie said, closing her eyes for a heartbeat, 'in the shoes of that poor man today. When he finally realised he couldn't go on, he looked gutted. That's the way I'll look if Carly Bloody McCulloch gets my shop for her wanky fromagerie. Why can't she just call it a cheese shop?'

As Brian let out a laugh, he heard footsteps from behind him. But although he'd told Gina she should come and have a glass of bubbly with them, that wasn't the sound of Gina's clippy-cloppy heels. He turned to see who'd come through the door, and standing there, frozen – as if somebody had pressed pause on him – was Luke.

'Luke!' Brian said, remembering: Luke had said he was going to swing by. There was something he wanted to discuss, apparently. Well, he'd come at the right time, because from the looks of it, Marnie and Brian alone weren't going to do justice to a whole bottle of sparkling wine. He could celebrate with them.

'You remember Marnie, don't you?'

Luke was studying Marnie, and Marnie – looking at Luke – had turned completely ashen. She didn't move, or stumble. She wasn't visibly shaking. But somehow it happened anyway – the half-full wine flute fell clean out of her hand and smashed into tiny splinters on the polished concrete floor.

Later that afternoon, a woman walked up to the front door of Wish & Co. In her market basket was a picture book and a teddy-bear she'd bought for the newborn baby of one of her daughter's friends. She hated wrapping irregular objects. In fact, she hated wrapping presents, full stop. But that lovely red-haired girl at Wish & Co always did such a beautiful job, though she wasn't cheap.

The woman regarded Wish & Co as a nice shop with sensible

opening hours, unlike those other specialty shops that opened late, closed on odd days of the week, and where you could never keep track. Just the one time, the woman had come to Wish & Co and found a BACK IN 15 MINUTES sign hanging on the door, but she'd returned fifteen minutes later to find the girl in the shop unlocking the door, a little flushed in the cheeks as if she'd run all the way to and from her errand. Today, though – and this was most unusual – the CLOSED sign was showing in the middle of the afternoon. The woman frowned and the glass door caught the reflection of her back as she, resigning herself to a prefabricated gift bag, walked away in the direction of the nearest newsagent.

On the other side of that door, the shop was quiet. On the shelves, candles stood silently beside tableware and napkins, invitation cards and envelopes. A few small triangles of pink and paisley wrapping paper littered the floor around the base of the wrapping table, and a couple of tabs of invisible tape stuck out around its rim. A few of the lightweight papers hanging on the racks had their corners lifted by the breeze that came in through the wide-open back door.

Beyond the back door, a set of metal steps led up to the small and shabby apartment where, inside, Marnie Fairchild sat cross-legged on the bed, her eyes swollen from crying. Luke Charlesworth sat at the nearby table, elbows on his knees, head in his hands. For two hours already, they had gone around, and around, and around in circles.

Over and over again, Luke had said: *I trusted you, and you deliberately kept this from me. I went there today to tell him. About us, and you let me go in there totally blind. And, what's worse, you let me take you to my mother's house for dinner. You totally trespassed on her hospitality.*

Over and over and over again, Marnie had said: *I wanted to tell you, I tried to tell you. When I first mixed up the gifts, your father had one of his pals ring me up to cancel his portfolio. I had to worry about securing my loan. I couldn't afford to lose clients hand over fist, but of all the clients I couldn't afford to lose, your father was number one.*

On these points, they understood each other. Marnie understood Luke's hurts, and he understood her reasons. But that only brought them so far, because then came the intractable murk through which they didn't seem to be able to follow each other at all.

'I just don't understand how you can do what you do,' Luke said.

'What do you mean "what I do"?'

'You manipulate people. From behind the scenes. You deceive people!'

'I do not.'

'You do. And you know it. If it wasn't a sham, why would you get your clients to write in their own cards and pretend the gift is really from them?'

'The gift really *is* from them,' Marnie protested, hotly.

'No, Marnie, the gift is paid for by them. Admit it – the gift is from you. You are a professional con artist.'

Marnie felt that blade go all the way in. 'Not that expression. Any other. Not that one.'

'It's accurate.'

'You fight dirty.'

Luke sighed. 'You're right. That was uncalled for. But I still don't understand why you would even want to help him. He cheated on her.'

'He's sorry for that!'

'Just let him deal with it himself.'

'He is dealing with it himself. He's only paying for my advice, Luke.'

'She's better off without him.'

'That's a completely separate issue. And anyway, how can you be so sure? I'm not.'

'What right is it of yours to decide?'

Incensed, Marnie spat back, 'What right is it of *yours*?'

'I just have an opinion. You're the one meddling.'

'It's not meddling. It's just . . . giving.'

'But you're too bloody good at it. It's not fair. It's like selling out your superpower to the highest bidder.'

'That's how the world works! You do it too. You sell your superpower to the highest bidder, except that what they end up with is chairs and tables instead of gifts.'

'It's different,' Luke insisted.

'How is it different?'

In these words, and others, they circled the issues, and with each pass, both Marnie and Luke became more exhausted, less coherent, more emotional, less careful, more confused. Was he right? Was she a fraud? Marnie found herself wondering this, but nothing in the world would make her admit it to him.

'Marnie, this is not getting us anywhere,' Luke said at last, and he stood up to leave. Marnie felt panic flood her body.

'I'll quit,' she said, looking up at him tearfully from where she sat. 'If you want me to, I will go and see your father, and I'll resign. If that's what you need me to do, that's what I'll do. Just please don't be angry with me any more. I don't want to lose you, Luke.'

He ran a hand through sandy hair that was already well and truly mussed.

'I'll go see your dad,' she said. 'I'll tell him I'm done. Please don't tell your mother.'

Luke eyed her, his expression hard. 'I'll leave hurting my mother to you and Dad if that's all right.'

'I would never hurt her,' she said, and something in Marnie's tone appeared to appease Luke a little.

A little more gently, he said, 'Look, I'm going to go. But once you've spoken to him, once you're free of all this mess, give me a call. Okay?'

'Where are you going?'

'I don't know exactly,' Luke said, 'but right now I can't be here.'

There was no point, now, leaving anything on the bench.

'I love you,' she said.

Marnie looked at his face, into his eyes. She waited for a long moment for his response.

'I'll see you later, okay?' he said.

When he walked out the door, she didn't get up from the bed, just listened to the clatter of his feet on the metal stairs. It sounded very much like goodbye.

Thursday

Late morning at Austinmer Street, the flower-lined path shone in the aftermath of a sun-shower, and the jasmine that climbed the trellis at the side of the front door breathed out its rich scent along with the evaporating moisture. Suzanne watched from the living room window as a truck backed into her driveway. It was the second of the day.

Earlier, before the rain, Suzanne had stood in the same place as a similar truck had rolled in, bringing two men who announced they had been instructed to relieve her of *Windy Ridge*, a painting by Roger Cubit. When Suzanne pressed them for details, they told her it was to go to Sunderland Auction warehouse where it would be sold.

Now's your chance to get rid of it. That's what Luke had said, when he and Marnie had come for dinner. Was this Luke's doing, then? That seemed unlikely. He wasn't one for secrets or surprises, usually. Luke would have talked to her about it, and when she'd spoken with him on the phone yesterday, he hadn't mentioned it. In fact, he'd said very little at all, and overnight she'd wondered what it was that had made him sound so bleak, hoping it had nothing to do with that gorgeous girl, Marnie.

'Sorry, who made this arrangement with you?' she'd asked the men.

The driver had consulted the notes on his clipboard. 'Ah, Mr Charlesworth? Brian Charlesworth?'

Suzanne, surprised and amused in equal parts, had shown the two men inside and watched with some satisfaction as they'd taken down the ugly painting, leaving behind a wall that was blank except for two sets of heavy-duty picture hooks and a dusty stripe in the place where the top of the painting had rested for so many years. Once the men were gone, she'd dragged in a stepladder and cleaned up the last of the evidence with a few squirts of Spray n'Wipe.

Now there was a second truck. Suzanne watched from the front door as one of the deliverymen opened its rear doors to reveal a painting-sized shape, sheathed in layers of bubble wrap. What on earth had the crazy man done now? What on earth had he bought? *Please, God,* Suzanne prayed, *let it not be another Roger Cubit.*

Two strong young men carried the painting, still wrapped in its protective layers, into the dining room as directed by Suzanne. She stood back, almost holding her breath, as the bubble wrap came away, so that she saw the painting for the first time in fragments, piece by piece. An antique frame, timber, subtly ornamented with carved flowers. The bright blotch of the sun, high in an achingly blue sky. Children paddling in a creek, bare-legged. Two children bickering over the care of a baby. A man, minding what was left of a picnic. A woman lazing with a straw hat across her face.

Then, as the painting was hoisted into place, she saw it in its entirety. The scene was so vivid that Suzanne was there. She was the woman, breathing that summer air, hearing the buzz of the occasional fly, half aware, even while dozing, of the location of each of her children.

'Sign here, if you wouldn't mind,' said one of the men from the auction house, holding out a clipboard.

Suzanne peered at the fine print on the document. *Summer Day at Drowsy Creek*, it was called. By Eleanora Middleton-Holmes. Suzanne had heard of her. Not that Suzanne had ever seen her work, but she knew Eleanora was a cousin to Cassandra du Plessé. Once upon a time, Suzanne had promised herself that she'd find out more about this artist, who – like Suzanne herself – had stopped painting when the demands of being a wife and a mother had taken priority. Feeling slightly dazed, she scribbled her signature into the blank space, and returned the clipboard.

'Oh, and this is for you, too,' the man said, tugging a cream envelope out from underneath the form she'd signed. 'And if that's all? We'll be off.'

Suzanne saw the delivery men to the door before returning to the dining room, where she stood for a time drinking in every detail of the painting. How had he known? After the Cubit painting, how – but just how – had he got it so right?

In the envelope were two A5 pages of thick, creamy stock, covered in her husband's best handwriting. Even before she had read a word, Suzanne's throat felt thick with emotion.

It had been a long, long time since he'd written her a letter.

Dear Suzanne,

I don't know much about art, so maybe it's a foolhardy thing to do – to buy a painting for you, who knows so much. You don't answer my messages or pick up the phone when I call. I can see you don't want to talk to me, and I guess I don't blame you. But there's so much I want to say.

I want to say it in better words than the ones I can put on paper. I want to say it bigger and more beautifully than any words I could ever come up with.

I love you, Suzanne, and I am so sorry I feel sick about it every day. I betrayed you, and I betrayed us. And what's even worse is that it wasn't the first time. Twenty years ago, I was stupid enough to be unfaithful. You forgave me, gave me a chance, and I took it, and maybe it no longer matters to you, but I want you to know, for the record, that for almost all of the last twenty years, I honoured that chance.

Why did I fall on my face again? Why did I do it? This is the question that keeps me up at night. Not that there are any excuses, only that I'm trying to understand this weakness in me – understand it and fix it. I risked us, I risked you, the love of my life. It was beyond stupid, and it is all in the past.

I want to say all of this in a way that you'll believe. Maybe this painting will speak for me and tell you what I hope is still out there for us, and our family, in the future. Maybe it is too late, and the damage is done and perhaps you will never forgive me, but your forgiveness is now the only thing I want. That, and to be able to come home. To you. Please talk to me, Suze.

I love you,
Brian

She read the letter twice. Three times. Then, just one more time. At last, she folded the letter in two. She ached for him (dear, silly man). She ached for herself (her hurt, hurt heart). She wanted to clasp the letter to her chest and sob. She wanted to crumple it into a ball and throw it on the floor.

In the end, she did neither of these things. Instead, she took out her phone and, for the first time since the day of her fortieth wedding anniversary, she called her husband's number.

'Suze?' he answered. 'Suze?'

'I have only one thing to say, and then I'm going to hang up.'

'Don't hang up. Suze, please.'

'One thing to say, Brian.'

'Yes?'

She couldn't keep the tears out of her voice. 'That painting is the single most beautiful thing you've ever given me. I love it.'

And then, just as she had promised, she hung up the phone.

Friday

The clouds that coasted past the twenty-fourth-floor windows of Brian Charlesworth's office also drifted, in reflection, over the dark, polished timber of his desk. Marnie watched them, rather than Brian's face, as he considered all that she'd just said. When at last he spoke, it was not in the stern, disappointed tone that she'd braced herself for.

'Can I ask you to reconsider?' he said.

Marnie, sitting on the edge of her chair, tried not to fidget with the hem of her narrow pencil skirt.

'I've already done that,' Marnie said, disconsolately. 'I have considered, and I reconsidered. Considered some more and then reconsidered. Believe me, I've looked at this from every angle. Brian, I just can't work for you any more.'

'But Marnie, we're almost there. I'm sure of it. She rang me. For the first time, she picked up the phone and rang me.'

It was hard to believe, but Brian Charlesworth, the CEO of the Charlesworth Group, a man who was used to demanding and insisting, was actually pleading. She stared at him. At his lips, his eyebrows, his cheekbones – all so similar to the ones she knew and loved on Luke's face. It was an unfair advantage.

'I'm sorry, Brian. My mind's made up.'

'Suzanne's right on the brink. I can tell. We're not quite there, but we're so close. Please don't bail on me now. This is my marriage we're talking about. The whole rest of my life. Somehow you just *get* her. I can't do it without your help.'

What about the rest of my life? she wanted to say. *What if your son, of the rough but eloquent hands, is the rest of my life?*

'You actually could, you know,' Marnie told him.

'I can't – you've got a real gift, Marnie.' He smiled. 'A gift for gifts.'

'I'm sorry, Brian. I quit. I have to. I promised Luke.'

Luke, who hadn't so much as called since he'd walked out of her apartment two days earlier, who hadn't responded to any of her tentative text messages. Luke, who'd been quite clear that he didn't want to hear from her until this meeting was done, and she had extricated herself from his father's business.

Brian leaned back in his chair with a sigh. 'It wasn't particularly professional of you. To get involved with my son. That surprised me, Marnie, I have to say. And not in a good way.'

'You're right. It was a long way from best practice. But it just . . . happened.'

'So, you've made up your mind? And there's nothing I can say to make you change it?'

Marnie shook her head.

Brian, taking a sharp breath in through his nose, said, 'I didn't want to have to do this. I really didn't.'

No. No, no, no, no, Marnie thought, remembering the phone call she'd taken from Lloyd Sherwood, that fat spider, sitting there in the centre of the tangled web of infidelities he'd spun for himself, telling her she was a threat to the harmony of his life. Brian wouldn't, would he? He wouldn't destroy her business now. Surely they'd shared too much, come too far, for him to be so brutal. But then, business was business, and Brian liked to win.

'Please. I know you can wreck my reputation. I know you can talk to people. People like Lloyd —'

'Marnie, Marnie,' Brian interrupted. 'I'm not a complete bastard. That business with Lloyd? That was the stick. But a stick's not the only way to get what you want. What I had hoped not to need was the carrot.'

'Carrot?'

'Yes,' he said. 'I'm going to make you an offer now, and I want you to think about what it actually means. For you, for your future.'

What was this? What was he going to do?

'Over this period that we've been working together,' he went on, 'I've developed a pretty good understanding, I think, of what Fairchild and Sons means to you.'

Marnie, feeling shaky, had to clasp her hands together to hide their quivering.

'You're going to auction, in what . . . a couple of weeks now?'

'The sixteenth of November.'

'And unless you've got something up your sleeve that I can't imagine, you're going to get steamrollered by a bigger player. Whether that's Carly McCulloch and her wine and cheese shop or somebody else, I don't know, but it's Alexandria Park and you are not a big enough player to pull this off.'

He knew this business; he knew that neighbourhood. He could easily be right.

'But,' he said, 'I will loan to you, interest-free, the difference between your top dollar – I'm sure you already know what that is – and the price of Fairchild and Sons at auction.'

Marnie breathed. Her eyes went wide. 'You would do that for me?'

'If you'll keep working for me. Yes.'

'Why?'

'I want my wife back.' He rolled his chair closer to the desk and scrawled something on a piece of paper. 'I'm not going to give you an entirely blank cheque, but this is how much I'm prepared to loan you on those conditions.'

He handed her the paper. The figure was staggering.

More importantly, it was enough.

'This is extraordinary,' she told him. 'It's beyond generous.'

'I need you to stay the course, Marnie,' he said, pointing at the piece of paper. 'I need you that much.'

Her mind was humming like a beehive.

'I'll give you a couple of hours to think about it,' Brian said.

Hot afternoon sunshine slid through the windows of the Rathbone Street tram, draping a bright parallelogram across Marnie's shoulder and lap. Slightly disgusted by the felty texture of the upholstery beneath her skirt, sweating in the heat, she sat in the window seat as a succession of different humans – plugged into their earphones, glued to their screens – took the aisle seat beside her for a few stops' worth of their journey.

As the tram passed Wish & Co, she looked up to catch a brief glimpse of Alice moving around inside the shop, and a slightly longer view of the dovecote in the window. With an unusual lack of anticipation or enthusiasm, she realised that her window was almost due for an overhaul. Since it was now November, she supposed it was time to come up with an idea for this year's Christmas display. As the tram rattled on, further from the city, closer to Alexandria Park, the roadside trees grew taller, thicker, older, leafier, until Marnie pressed the button and stepped off near Fairchild & Sons.

At the cafe directly across the road from the old shop, she took a seat at an outdoor table and ordered a chai and a sandwich, which she only now realised would be the first things she had eaten all day. Perhaps hunger was part of the sad, sick feeling that had come over her, but it was definitely not the greater part.

Marnie watched as people walked past Fairchild & Sons, most of them paying no mind to the building, although some stopped to peer at the historic photographs on the FOR SALE sign and read its enthusiastic copy. She could have it. The shop. It could be hers. At auction on 16 November, she could play the part that Brian had played at the auction of *Summer Day at Drowsy Creek*. She could stand there, in full view of the auctioneer, in full possession of herself, knowing there was every chance she'd be the last one standing at the end. The very thing Marnie had wanted for most of her life was now within her grasp. Had this opportunity fallen into her lap even a month ago, she would have been out of her mind with joy, overcome with a sense of victory. So why, now, did it feel like such a terrible loss?

If only she hadn't been stupid enough to get involved with Luke in the first place! But, she quickly realised, that didn't make any sense. Had she not got involved with him, she wouldn't be here, in this situation. Had she not come to know Suzanne better, through Luke, she might not have impressed Brian to the point where he was prepared to make this extraordinary offer. Further, had she not fallen in love with Luke, she'd never have resigned from Brian's employ; he'd have had no cause to pull out such a whacking big inducement for her to stay.

Marnie's mind drifted back to the night she had lit a candle in the shop and manifested her dream future, imagining Fairchild &

Sons into her possession. The final challenge of the process, so the magazine had said, was to believe that the universe would provide. She had not believed, not really. And now it had provided, but at a price. She couldn't help but feel that the universe had played a cruel trick on her, delivering the shop into her hands, but at the cost of the sweetest love affair she'd ever had.

Once you've spoken to him, once you're free of all this mess, give me a call. That's what Luke had said. She had spoken to Brian, but now she had to decide. Was she in, or was she out? Was she going to take the opportunity to buy the shop? Or the chance of fixing things with Luke?

Above the sharply pitched roof of Fairchild & Sons, creamy-white clouds drifted, stretched apart and came back together, burning a time-lapse sequence onto Marnie's retinas as she watched, and thought, and thought, and watched. The shop was what she had wanted for almost her entire life. She dialled Brian Charlesworth's number.

At Fielding Street, Luke opened the door but offered Marnie no kiss in greeting. Arms crossed over her chest as if to stop all of her insides from spilling out, she followed him into his kitchen. In this very room, she had once sidled up behind him and put her arms around him while he was frying bacon and eggs. Here, she had annoyed him by sneaking in to pinch some cheese while he was grating it. She'd sat right there, on that stretch of kitchen bench, and kissed him, wrapping her legs around the backs of his and pulling him closer so that what had begun as warm and cuddly soon shifted gears to hot and delicious and ended up in the bedroom.

Now, he just leaned against that bench. He didn't even suggest she sit down.

'So, you told him you quit?' he asked.

'It didn't quite work out . . . the way I expected,' she admitted.

Luke's face showed disappointment, but a total lack of surprise – the very same combination he had once told Marnie that he hated to see on his father's face.

'What happened?'

'He's offered me a loan.'

'A loan?'

'An interest-free loan. To help me buy the shop.'

Luke gave a droll laugh. 'Yeah, that'd be right. That'd be my dad. If he couldn't have you, he'd buy you.'

Anger flashed through Marnie. 'He hasn't bought me. He's lending me money. A lot of money, interest-free.'

'Right. Sure. So, what's the price?'

'Only that I keep working for him.'

'That you keep playing tricks on my mother, in other words?'

Marnie took a breath, trying to regain her equilibrium. If she explained the situation to him clearly enough, surely he would understand. 'It's not playing tricks on your mother. It's just giving your father some advice.'

'What you're doing is making him look like someone who knows her, someone who cares about her. You're making him look like someone who pays attention, like someone who actually gives a damn. That's a trick, Marnie.'

'But he does give a damn. Really, he does.'

'Since when?'

'Luke, what I'm doing for your father is really no different from the lessons I gave you, for Ivy.'

He made a scoffing laugh. 'It's completely different. What you do for him is make wrapped-up parcels arrive by magic. I bet he never even knows what's inside them.'

'Maybe that used to be true, but not any more. He's coming up with ideas of his own now. Really good ones.' This was almost true. Take the rose bush idea. Okay, she had needed to nudge him towards the idea of planting them himself, but he'd cottoned on almost immediately. 'It's more like a collaboration now. Just like it was when you and I got together to talk about Ivy's present. I didn't choose the painting on my own. I didn't, Luke. Sure, I helped, but the final choice was his. He knew exactly which one was right for her, I'm telling you. Brian and I . . . it's more like we're working together now.'

Luke made a gesture of frustration with his hands, as though he wanted to shake some sense into her. 'He should be made to sink or swim on his own! Not be able to buy his way out of the mess he made by screwing around. He should have to fix it by himself.'

'But it's not that simple. Can't you see? I need him too. I need his business. That shop is the thing I've worked towards for my whole career. I have gone without and saved like a demon. I have worked incredibly long hours, been smart with my investments. Fairchild and Sons is not just any building to me, and you know it. You even said so. Do you remember? That day we were there together. You said I was a special kind of dreamy. Remember?'

Luke narrowed his eyes and fixed her with a disgusted look. 'You really don't care what you have to do, do you? You don't care who you have to deceive. Just so long as you get what you want.'

Anger again, like a bolt this time, forking right through the middle of her. 'What is your deal with this? I have been helping your father buy some gifts for your mother. That's all. I'm hardly selling my soul to the devil here. Your father pays me to do a job, and I need to keep him as a client. That's all.' The red mist upon her, she went on. 'If I had really been prepared to manipulate the situation, do you know what I would have done?'

'What?'

'I'd have told your father about Ivy.'

Incredulous, Luke said, 'You'd have what?'

Marnie knew she should be quiet, but by now her temper had entirely escaped its restraints. 'What does your mother want more than anything else? To have her family together. To have more grandchildren to love. To have big parties around that dinner table with her husband, and her children and their children. That is what she wants. That's the key to your mother – not frangipanis, not art supplies, not rose bushes. Not even great big valuable paintings.'

Luke looked at her with contempt. 'That's disgusting.'

'I haven't done it. And I wouldn't, because it's your place to tell them, not mine. But if I really had been prepared to do anything at all in order to get my way, then I'd have told him about Ivy.'

'I should never have taken you to meet my mother. I can't believe I did that to her. You just size people up and work out how they tick, and then you use that knowledge for your own advantage.'

Desperate for him to understand, Marnie raised her voice even further. 'All your life, Luke, you've had your family's support, right there on tap. You've had the luxury of rejecting it. You've had the privilege of turning your back on serious money. I have had to work really hard for everything I have. Your father would give you anything you asked for.'

'I've never asked him for a thing.'

'I know you haven't,' Marnie said, more quietly. She did not want to fight with him. Really, she didn't. 'But I don't even have anyone to ask. And now your father has made me this offer. Try, just for a moment, to think what it means, for me.' She was pleading now. 'What it means for me to have that property, my grandfather's shop, in my grasp.'

'I can't have any part in that.'

'But —'

'We're done, Marnie.'

'Will you tell your mother?' Marnie could not help but ask.

Luke shook his head. 'You're unbelievable. You really are.'

The wall inside him was now even thicker than it had been two days before. If once it had been timber, now it was iron, and she was banging her head against it. She had no way of getting through to him. She had lost access. He was gone from her.

'Being together,' she said. 'It was nice. Very nice. While it lasted.'

For just a moment, there was a chink in the wall. A brief window of light, of contact, of sincerity.

'It was.'

— PART SIX —

PART SIX

Seven days before the auction of Fairchild & Sons

When the bridal waltz was done, there was a rush to the dance floor that had been set up on the wide lawns of the Kingston house. Owen, though, didn't appear to be in any hurry to get to his feet. With his tie askew and a couple of his shirt buttons already released from duty, he was looking somewhat dishevelled, though that probably wasn't surprising, given the amount of wine he'd consumed during dinner. Marnie wasn't entirely sober herself, having had two glasses of sparkling wine even before Owen twisted the barman's arm to make an exception, for Marnie, to the bar's beer-and-wine-only policy. Already she was one margarita down, and halfway through her second.

Today, she had done all the things that were required to smooth a plausible veneer over the mess of her broken heart. She had been to the hairdresser to have soft, loose curls installed, chosen the perfect shade of silver for her gel fingernails and toenails, and shimmied into a beloved silver-grey dress and strappy sandals. Add a clutch purse, a wisp of an apricot scarf and a credible smile. *Et voila!* Now, though, the alcohol seemed to be exacerbating the contrast between her inner and outer states of being. With every sip she was getting louder, sassier and flirtier, even while the rock-heavy chunks of her internal wreckage seemed to be growing heavier and more painful.

Over the swelling chords of an irritatingly romantic song, Owen asked, 'So, what ended up happening with Mr Tradie Hands?'

Mr Tradie Hands. She supposed he meant Luke.

'Something,' she said, airily. 'And then, nothing.'

Owen gave her a wolfish smile and took a gulp of his wine. 'Told you.'

'Told me what?' Marnie said, trying to sound playful.

'Told you he'd find out.' He leaned in close and put on the attitude of a foppish Romantic poet. Touching her on the chest, he said, 'About the callous heart that beats beneath that white and pretty breast.'

Marnie pulled away from him. 'Actually . . . ouch.'

'Ah. Too soon, then? Oh well, maybe next week. Feel like a dance, Kiddo?'

In the thick of the music, where the bride was whirling about in a white dress that was all skirt and cleavage, there would be no need to talk. Dancing with Owen was always fun, and there was no reason – as, at one time, she'd thought there might have been – to keep things tidy. What would it matter now, if she were to kiss him during a slow dance, and finally end up in his bed?

Before either one of them could make a move, though, a woman in a trim hot-pink suit sat down in the empty chair beside Marnie.

'Well, come on, love. Introduce us,' she said to Owen.

He made the hand gestures that accompanied a courtly bow, and said, 'Audrey Crawford, the first of my two – ah, make that three – stepmothers. Marnie Fairchild, dear friend and proprietor of Wish and Co.'

Ah, Marnie thought. *So this is the famous Audrey.* Although Audrey's marriage to Gerry Kingston had pre-dated Marnie's friendship with Owen, she'd heard plenty about this stepmother. According to the stories, Audrey had taken a fairly laissez-faire approach to step-parenting Owen, once giving him a beaker of gin when she was desperate for him to go to sleep and give her a bit of peace.

'Marnie,' Audrey said, oozing charm. 'How lovely to meet you.'

Marnie braced for the usual business about the Fairchild family tree, but when Audrey announced early in the conversation that she played bridge on Thursdays with Marnie's aunt, Marilyn, it was clear to Marnie that she'd already been well and truly pigeonholed. The conversation traversed the expected subjects – the marriage service (yes, it had been lovely), the bride's dress (certainly daring), their hopes (probably flimsy) that this marriage would prove fourth-time lucky for Gerry. Then Audrey looked over meaningfully at Owen.

'Yes?' he said.

'Well, go on then. Off you go. I want to talk to Marnie.'

Owen made a mock-indignant face, collected up his wine glass and the bottle of red from the middle of the table, and sauntered off, leaving Marnie mildly stunned and without the first clue about what Audrey might want to discuss. Thankfully, she got straight to the point.

'Marnie, about six years ago, Gerry must have been in a particularly good mood, because he included me – I assume he included all his ex-wives – on his Christmas list. He bought me a bottle of Chanel Number Nineteen perfume. I wonder if you knew anything about that?'

It had been seven years. Marnie smiled. 'I couldn't possibly say.'

'Don't give me that, Marnie.' Her tone was sharp, but not unkind. 'You see, the reason I remember this was that for our whole married life, every time he bought me perfume, he bought me Chanel Number Five. When in fact, I prefer Number Nineteen. Always have. I wonder if you can tell me how he suddenly, out of nowhere, and after we were divorced, got it right?'

Marnie shrugged. 'I'm sure I can't tell you, Audrey.'

Of course, Marnie remembered the details perfectly well. At the time of which Audrey spoke, Marnie had just opened Wish & Co, using the proceeds from the sale of the coffee van to start up her new venture. The shop established, she had decided to use Gerry himself as a guinea pig for testing his theory that wealthy men with complicated lives would pay, and pay well, for a bespoke gift-buying service. He'd given her a budget and a list of people to buy for, and she'd taken it from there. As for the precise nature of the Chanel perfume? That had been simple; there had been a bottle of No. 19 in the bathroom cupboard of the summer house that Audrey and Gerry had continued, almost amicably, to share for many years after their divorce, and where Owen and Marnie occasionally snuck off for a weekend.

'You see, I asked Gerry about it once, and here's the thing. It was evident that he didn't have a clue which perfume he'd bought me. I don't think he even knew there was a Number Nineteen. But somebody knew. Then, just lately, I heard a story doing the rounds of the Alexandria Park gossip circuits, that you run a gift-buying service, and I remembered that you and Owen were . . . friends. It made me wonder, all over again, about that bottle of perfume.'

Now that Marnie had listened to Audrey talk for a while, she was beginning to understand. Audrey was hurting, just as Marnie was herself. Weddings were for joy and celebration, yes, but they could also bring heartbreak and loneliness into sharp relief for those who were suffering them. Gently, Marnie asked, 'Is there something I can do for you, Audrey?'

'Actually, yes. I'm on my own now. I feel it most, you know, when birthdays roll around, and so on. Some of my friends have children who give them lovely gifts, but the way my life's turned out, I seem to have fallen through the cracks. Of course, I could buy myself pretty much whatever I want, really, but it's not the same. No element of surprise, you see.

'I wondered if you've ever thought of this little diversification? I could employ you. To buy gifts . . . not for other people. I can do that. But for *me*. My birthday, Christmas, and perhaps, every now and then, just out of the blue.'

It was almost certainly the tequila that made Marnie do it, because reaching out to hug a complete stranger was not a gesture she kept in her regular playbook. Audrey accepted her embrace, though, and returned it, and it was one of those hugs of understanding that said more than words ever could. They were both, that night, loners on the outside of the circle of love.

'It would be my pleasure to work for you,' Marnie said, and from her clutch purse she took a Wish & Co business card. 'I've been making some changes in the way I do business lately, and what you're suggesting is just the sort of thing I'd love to move towards.'

Audrey took the card and slipped it into her own purse. 'So how *did* you know? About the perfume?'

Marnie tilted her head. 'Do people really, really want to know how magic tricks are done? Or do they actually just want to enjoy them?'

'All right then,' Audrey said, standing to go. 'You keep your secrets. We'll talk.'

'I'll look forward to it.'

'Oh, and Marnie, darling,' Audrey said. 'I don't mean to teach you to suck eggs. I'm sure you're a very sensible girl, but' – she nodded towards the bar, from which direction Owen was heading back to the table, carrying a third margarita for Marnie and another bottle of wine – 'that way lies nothing but misery. Try not to end up like me. Hm?'

It was a sobering piece of advice.

By the time Owen returned, Audrey had disappeared into the crowd. He set the margarita down on the table, and the lemony liquid shimmied in the glass until it gradually settled to stillness.

'I must say, you are looking particularly gorgeous tonight, Kiddo,' he told her.

'You're not so bad yourself, Kingo,' Marnie told him. And that was true. His long dark hair brushed his collar in a way that made her want to run her hands through it, and she was in no doubt that he'd arranged his shaving routine so that, tonight, he had just the rock-star amount of stubble on his chin. The tie was gone altogether now, and the half-unbuttoned shirt allowed a glimpse of that olive-skinned chest she knew so well, and upon which she had rested her head so many times.

The margarita in front of her was made just the way she liked it – the rim of the glass thickly crusted with salt; even so, Marnie knew she would not drink it. And neither, tonight, would she end up in Owen Kingston's bed. She would dance with him, she would wish the happy couple well, and in so doing would discharge her duty as a handbag. But Marnie had just taken a good look further down the road of 'third margarita' thinking, and it looked lonely in a pink suit at a wedding. It wasn't where Marnie wanted to be.

Six days before the auction of Fairchild & Sons

'Well?' Suzanne asked.

In the formal dining room at Austinmer Street, Luke stood beside his mother and stared. The painting could almost have been a Renoir, had the scene not been so quintessentially Australian. Even the frame was a treasure. Cherry, if he wasn't mistaken, subtly carved with flowers in an Arts and Crafts style that dated it to somewhere about the late nineteenth century, or the very early twentieth. But who, in Australia, at that time, was painting like *this*? He couldn't think of anything he'd seen that was so accomplished and yet so candid. The late morning light of a slightly overcast, springtime Sunday filtered through the windows from the garden and made the painting glow.

'Was this you?' his mother asked. 'Did you help him pick this out?'

For a moment, Luke almost wished he'd been able to say that yes, he had, because it was hard to imagine a painting more perfect for this space, or more perfect for his mother.

'Because,' Suzanne went on, 'there we were, you and me, and Marnie, discussing that horrible Roger Cubit painting, and then *poof*! Out of the blue, your father sends a delivery truck to take it away, and this arrives. This.'

Luke stared into the painting. He knew those small sticky flies that the man was brushing away, knew how they landed on your face and hands, how insistently you had to swat them away. He knew the mixed-up feeling of having sun on your hair and icy river-water around your feet; he'd felt it himself not so long ago, on that day at Vanishing Tarn with Marnie. His mother's eyes shone as she looked at the painting; this time, Marnie had outdone even herself.

'Luke?' Suzanne prompted.

What was it that Marnie said? People don't really want to know how magic tricks are done. They just want to enjoy the magic.

'You know something about it, Luke,' Suzanne said. 'I can tell. Come on, you're terrible at keeping secrets. You always have been. You'll end up telling me the truth. You know you will, in the end.'

He regarded his mother. A woman of sixty-seven in a pale blue blouse and white pants, carrying a little more weight around the middle than she liked to, her skin showing signs of the punishing sunbathing she'd done in her youth, blonde hair carefully styled, mascara slightly smudged into the crinkly skin beneath her eyes. The lines on her face had settled into the expressions she most often wore – the mildly puzzled frown, the *bless your cotton socks* smile. How could his father have hurt her?

If he told his mother about Marnie, he might only hurt her more. But she was using that look on him, knowing and motherly.

'It was your doing, wasn't it?' she asked. Her eyes expressed the deep knowledge that, one way or another, she was going to prise him open.

He sighed with resignation. 'Why don't you go put the kettle on, Mum? It's a long story.'

Luke carried the tea-tray out to the pergola. Over French Earl Grey and Suzanne's homemade biscuits – the Monte Carlos that

Luke had never been able to resist – he began. He kept to the facts, which were: as well as the shopfront, Marnie's business, Wish & Co, comprised a gift-buying service, which Brian had used for about the last five years. Perhaps Brian and Marnie's arrangement would have simply continued, with no one else being any the wiser, had Leona Quick's birthday not happened to be on 8 September, the same day as Suzanne and Brian's wedding anniversary, and had Marnie not mixed up the gifts.

It was because she had her heart set on buying Fairchild & Sons, and couldn't afford to lose her best client, that Marnie had made a deal. The houseful of frangipanis? Marnie's idea. The painting supplies and the card with the old photograph of Suzanne at the easel? Marnie's idea. The bed of roses? Marnie's idea.

Luke himself may never have known any of this, except that on the day of the anniversary lunch, when he'd been driving his father away from Austinmer Street, Brian had insisted on calling in to Wish & Co. It was then that Luke had met Marnie. He'd not known, he told Suzanne, about Marnie's later deal with Brian. Or else he would never have brought her for dinner. He wouldn't have let Suzanne walk Marnie through the house, opening the doors of her life to somebody who was perpetrating a trick upon them all. He wouldn't have allowed Marnie to stand there and size up the dining room wall. So, as for the Eleanora Middleton-Holmes painting? No, Luke said, not his doing. That was Marnie, too. Although he did remember to mention that his father went along with Marnie to the art auction, and that Marnie had vowed and declared the choice of *Summer Day at Drowsy Creek* had been Brian's and not hers.

He talked for a long time and his mother neither interrupted, nor asked questions, nor supplied further details, only listened. When he had finished, she sat for a moment absorbing all that he'd imparted. To begin with, Luke couldn't read her face, but then a small smile twitched at the edges of her mouth. Then the smile grew and turned into a laugh.

'Well, that explains a lot. A *lot*,' Suzanne said, and laughed again. 'That total ratbag. He employed a gift-buyer? For all those years? And not just any gift-buyer, but a very, very good one.' She thought some more. 'The Smeg appliances?'

'Marnie,' Luke confirmed.

'Those beautiful possum-merino wraps?'

'Marnie.'

Luke watched his mother laugh, and laugh, and laugh some more. 'You don't seem very bothered.'

'Bothered?' she repeated, wiping her eyes. 'There are many things that I am bothered by, my love. I am bothered about your father having an affair. I am bothered about him having an affair with a woman who can fit into an extra-small silk robe. But employing a gift-buyer? That part doesn't bother me in the least.'

'You don't feel . . . manipulated.'

'No, darling. Gifts have never been your dad's strong suit. I used to hate it when he bought me things I didn't like. It was such a terrible waste.' She laughed again. 'Delegate. Del-e-gate. At least he took his own advice!'

Still, Luke struggled to see the funny side of it. 'You don't feel as if you've been lied to?'

Suzanne regarded her son.

'Oh, darling,' she said, a realisation slowly dawning. 'I've just been thinking about myself, haven't I? But it wasn't just my presents, was it? That your father had Marnie buy?'

'No,' Luke replied.

'My sweetheart.'

He looked away, squinting. He peered down into the depths of the garden, where apple trees gave way to the hedge at the fence line. A few moments passed; a blue wren alighted briefly on the railing of the pergola, then flitted away again in pursuit of his little brown mate.

'When you and Caroline were small,' she said, 'one of the things I had to work out is that every child comes with its personality all bundled up inside, ready to be expressed. The things that worked with Caroline didn't work with you, when you came along. Things that Caroline didn't care about, you did.

'If I needed to show Caroline that I loved her, it was all about the words. She needed to be told, again and again, that I loved her, that I was proud of her, that I treasured her. But you? Words bounced off you. Your thing was that you liked to have something you could hold in your hands. If I had to be away from you for a time, I would come home with a little gift. It could be anything. A rock, a feather, a book, a tiny toy. It was like proof to you, that I'd been thinking of you while I was away. You wanted hard evidence, Luke. Needed it. But that's you. It's not everybody.'

Luke remembered those small gifts, how he'd treasured them.

Suzanne said, 'Your father does love you, you know.'

'I disappoint him. I've always disappointed him,' Luke said. He saw that this was something his mother could not refute.

'He expected a son he would understand, effortlessly, and instead he got you. He just doesn't know how to reach you, is all. Truth be told, he feels as if he disappoints you.'

'He does,' Luke said. When the words were out of his mouth, he wondered if he'd said them with vastly too much blunt force.

'You've fought with Marnie over this, too, haven't you?'

'Marnie and I . . . we're done, Mum.'

'No!'

'Afraid so.'

'Oh, Luke,' Suzanne said, her face a picture of sorrow. 'I thought you two were just right for each other.'

'Yeah, me too, but when push came to shove, there were other things she wanted more than she wanted me.'

'You can be very hard on people sometimes, my love.'

'I'm not sure you're hard enough.'

'Sweetheart, have you never done something wrong, that you really wished you hadn't? Have you never done something unforgiveable, but wanted to be forgiven anyway?'

He had. He had sent a wad of cash via a friend of a friend to Gillian Yip, to take care of a difficult situation he had helped to create. And that was a whole other story he would need to work out how to tell his mother, but not – he decided – today.

Suzanne brushed a scatter of biscuit crumbs into her palm and tossed them over the pergola railing. 'Forty years is a long time, Luke. Forty years is a lot of memories. Your father was there with me at all the turning points of my life. The good ones and the shitty ones. There isn't anyone else alive who knows my story as well as he does. Nobody else who was there, except him.'

'What about what he did? With Leona?'

'Oh, I'm angry. Believe me, I'm still very angry. But who in this world is perfect, Luke? And what do I want the rest of my life to look like? How do I want to spend it? Alone?'

'So, what will you do?'

Now it was Suzanne's turn to look away into the distance. 'I don't know what I'll do yet. But I'm sure that he really is sorry. Have you ever before seen your father dig in a whole bed of roses? Have you ever before known your father to go to an art auction, or to take even the faintest bit of interest in what kind of art I like, or don't like? He's trying, Luke. And he's hurting.

I know he is, and I miss him. Without him here, there's this empty patch of air beside me, where there used to be a person I could reach out for. I miss him in bed at night. I miss him beside me on the couch.'

Luke's own bed had been empty these past nights, too. Over the course of just a few short weeks, he'd become accustomed to Marnie's proximity, the warmth of her body, the smell of her hair, the sound of her breathing in her sleep. Now that it was over, the emptiness beside him felt bigger than ever before.

Three days before the auction of Fairchild & Sons

When Marnie arrived at the hospital, she was met by signs that clearly set out the visiting hours, and this time of night – 11 pm – was within none of the acceptable parameters. She pulled her coat around her and made confidently for the elevator, trusting that the reception staff would assume she was an on-call doctor summoned to deal with an emergency. Once inside the lift, she peered at the labels beside the buttons, until she found what she was looking for: Maternity.

It was Mo who'd called her, asking if she wanted to come in, and there she was, waiting for Marnie in the lobby, wearing a T-shirt that said, 'Introverted, but willing to discuss dark matter'. Marnie judged that it was one of those times when a hug would be tolerated, maybe even welcomed.

'You all right?' Marnie asked.

'Just exhausted,' Mo said. 'And kind of awestruck.'

They tiptoed together into the softly lit birthing room, and there – sitting up in bed, her hair an unholy mess, with a white-wrapped bundle in her arms – was Saski. Marnie hurried to her side, kissed her forehead.

'Oh my goodness, Peach. Look what you made.'

Saski passed the small, white bundle into Marnie's arms.

'Hello, little one.'

'Marnie, this is Anouk.'

'Well, of course it is. Hello, Anouk.'

'Anouk, this is Marnie, but we call her Bunny.'

All the adorable parts of a newborn baby were present and accounted for – the tiny fingers, the translucent fingernails, the chiselled lips – all the miniature perfections of a brand-new person. But it was none of those things that took Marnie's breath away. What gobsmacked Marnie was that she could already tell who little Anouk was.

At just a few hours old, she was even now so much more than the combination of genetics that had started her off. There were still details to come, Marnie knew, like the final colour of her hair – which right now was soft and black – and the finished colour of her eyes. Her taste, her style, her likes, her dislikes – all of these were yet to be revealed and it was going to be a joy to watch them emerge, but Marnie could tell that Anouk, already, was purely and completely herself.

Mo said, 'Saski and I, we'd like you to be . . . well, not her godmother, because none of us here is even faintly religious. We want you to be her special person.'

'Me?' Marnie teared up. 'You want me to be her special person? Are you sure?'

Saski gave a low laugh. 'Why wouldn't we be?'

Marnie wanted to wipe her eyes, but she was holding something incredibly precious in her arms. 'Because I'm a shit human being. That's why.'

'You?' Saski asked. 'Are you serious?'

'Owen says I'm ruthless.'

'Marnie, you're determined.'

'Luke says I'm deceitful.'

'No, love. You're discreet. Best secret-keeper ever.'

'I'm a workaholic.'

'Well,' Saski said, 'there's therapy for that.'

Marnie let out a teary laugh. 'And I'm confused.'

'My darling friend,' Saski said.

With Saski on one side of her, Mo on the other, and Anouk in her arms, Marnie felt so insanely well loved that it made the tears flow more freely.

Later, she would be able to say it was in that moment that something inside her broke off and drifted away. Later she would be able to say it was right then, sitting on the hospital bed, that she decided she could no longer hold on so tightly. She had to just . . . let go. She would no longer work for Brian Charlesworth. She would try to buy Fairchild & Sons. At the auction, she would give it every ounce of her heart and soul, but if it was beyond her resources, then beyond her resources it was. The universe might provide, or it might not. She just needed to be okay with whatever it chose.

Because it wasn't the bricks and mortar. It wasn't the weatherboard and the lathe and plaster, however authentic. It wasn't the triple-arched windows, or the carved roses, no matter how beautiful. It wasn't the celery-top pine counter, nor even the proximity to Alexandria Park. With two of her favourite people beside her, and her newest favourite person in her arms, she knew. It was this.

Two days before the auction of Fairchild & Sons

As Marnie walked through the door of Brian's office at the Charlesworth Group that morning, she wondered if she was doing so for the very last time. Today, she wore no suit and no heels, but a long dusty-pink dress and felted clogs, her hair fixed into a crown of braids.

'Morning,' Brian said.

'Morning,' she replied, and took a seat opposite him, where she found herself once again under the watchful eye of the many Suzannes, Carolines and Lukes who filled the frames that were angled, just so, on Brian's desk.

'Problem?' Brian asked.

'Thanks for squeezing me in without an appointment. I wanted to tell you in person.' She took a deep breath. 'That I've decided to withdraw from our arrangement.'

Brian shifted his glasses onto his head and leaned forward. 'You cannot be serious.'

Except that she was. 'The offer you made me – it's extraordinary. If you'd made me that offer a couple of months ago, there's no way I would have even considered saying no. But for much the same reason you're prepared to make the offer, I have to turn it down.'

'I see.'

'You're putting your relationship first. I have to be prepared to do the same.'

Perhaps she had a different kind of energy about her today. Perhaps Brian had been in business long enough to know when it was pointless trying to talk somebody around, because this time he didn't try. He only said, 'You're talking about Luke, of course.'

'I am. I don't even know whether that relationship still exists. But I have to give it a chance.'

'My son doesn't know how fortunate he is.'

'I disappointed him, Brian. Deeply. He has every right to be angry. When you see him next, would you mind giving him this?'

It was an envelope. 'And would you tell him . . .'

'Yes?'

'That I faced my difficult decision. That I made my choice.'

'I'll do that.'

'Thank you, Brian. I should go.'

Half an hour later, Marnie was back at Wish & Co. She swung the door sign to OPEN, dusted the shelves, wiped clean the wrapping table, and straightened the papers on her racks.

So, her little shop might end up having to stay, for the meantime, in this ugly, boxy building. Gradually, she would phase out clients with complicated lives and – who knew? – perhaps even replace them with the wealthy singletons of Alexandria Park, like Audrey Crawford, who needed every now and then to feel loved.

From behind the counter, she watched the mid-morning activity of Rathbone Street. Across the road, the woman in the bridal shop was tizzying up her window with a selection of scarlet frocks for the holiday season; a P-plater in a tiny hatchback screeched to a halt, narrowly avoiding running into the rear-end of a BMW; the grocer over the way placed the last fruit in his cantaloupe pyramid. Life, Marnie decided, would simply go on.

One day before the auction of Fairchild & Sons

At Clockwork, Luke took the corner seat, his back to the water so that the others could enjoy the river view. His mother arrived first, checking her hair, her lipstick and the fit of her fuchsia-coloured dress in a mirrored wall as she passed. He stood to greet her.

'Darling,' she said, and kissed his cheek. 'This is most unlike you to be so mysterious. What are you up to?'

'Dad should be here in a moment.'

Her face froze. 'Your dad? Now you're throwing us together? I can't keep up.'

'It'll all make sense, Mum. I promise.'

Soon after they had taken their seats, Brian arrived, in full business splendour – smart grey suit, white shirt, blue tie, immaculate hair. Suzanne did not stand. If, as Luke suspected, her feelings towards his father were a whirlpool of contradictions, then she hid it well. It was her fundamental politeness that came to the fore.

'Brian,' she said, her tone only slightly chilly.

Overly cheerful from nervousness, Brian asked, 'So, what's this? Family reunion? Are we expecting Caro too?'

'No, not Caro,' Luke said.

A waiter appeared, and this began a spirited discussion of the wine list. Once a bottle of chilled chardonnay had arrived, and three glasses had been poured, Luke decided it was time.

'Mum, Dad, thanks for coming today. I know that things aren't exactly simple between you at the moment, but there's something I need to tell you both, and it seemed like the right thing to tell you at the same time.'

He saw the anxious set of his mother's face and the way his father was bracing for disappointment.

'There was a time, you won't have forgotten it,' Luke said, 'when I was a bit difficult. A little bit out of control.'

Brian nodded. Perhaps a little too emphatically, Luke thought.

'I had a girlfriend there for a while, not that I ever brought her home or introduced her. I suppose I wasn't really into sharing my life with you two, at that point.'

Luke saw that his mother was holding herself conspicuously in check. This next part was going to be hard.

'Dad, I don't know if you remember the time I let you think I'd lost a brand-new laptop on the train? The truth is that I sold it. I'm not proud of that. I'm not proud of deceiving you, and I'm not proud of selling it so I could give my girlfriend money to have an abortion.'

Suzanne closed her eyes.

'She didn't go through with it,' Luke hurried to say, 'although I didn't know anything about that until a couple of months ago. It turns out that you have another granddaughter, because I have a daughter; she's sixteen, and her name's Ivy.'

'We have another granddaughter?' Suzanne looked stunned.

'Whoa,' Brian said. 'Not what I was expecting when I woke up this morning.'

Luke looked from his mother to his father, and back again. Their expressions mirrored each other's in a mixture of relief and joy, surprise and regret, shock and anticipation. The universe was a funny old machine. Had he, at the age of sixteen, told his mother and father that his girlfriend was pregnant, it would have been a crisis. They would have felt the need to make decisions and interventions; the situation would have seemed overwhelming, insurmountable.

He knew it wasn't fair, or right, that Gillian's family had borne all the challenges alone. That he and Brian and Suzanne could receive Ivy into their lives almost fully grown, having taken no responsibility, having borne none of the cost. But they had lost out, too, because Ivy's childhood had gone, and could never be recaptured. Sixteen years of her life had been lost to them. All they could do was go forward, make new memories.

Had he told his parents this news when Ivy was first conceived, it would have been a matter of shame, but that was not the emotion he saw in his mother's eyes as she took one of his hands. Nor was it the emotion he saw on his father's face.

'Dad, I know I'm not the son you wanted, ideally —'

'Luke, no. Please,' his father said.

'Well, I'm not. Am I?'

Brian closed his eyes momentarily. 'Luke, the thing is . . . I thought I knew what would be best for you. I thought what made me happy would make you happy, that it was my job to show you the path that I'd walked. To force you along it somehow. But you knew better than me all along. You're not me. I'm not you. I'm proud you had the guts to follow your own path, even while I was trying to frogmarch you onto mine. I'm sorry, Luke. I wish I'd done better.'

Following his wife's lead, Brian took hold of Luke's other hand. There followed a moment of indecision, but then Suzanne made her choice. She reached across the table for Brian's hand, completing the circle. They stayed that way for a quiet moment, and Luke thought it had probably been decades since he had been in physical contact with both his parents at the one time.

Suzanne asked, 'So, when can we meet her? Our Ivy?'

Our Ivy. He wondered if, once again, Marnie had been right. He wondered if, by sharing this news with his parents, he was giving them a bridge to cross, back to each other. Whether Marnie was also right that they were better together than apart. His mother was correct; he had been hard on Marnie. When Marnie had brought Ivy into the discussion about his parents' marriage, it had angered him. But when he'd thought about it later, he'd realised: just as he had insisted that Ivy was not an object that could be given as a gift, neither could he regard her as his own private secret to keep. She was part of them all.

'She's, um, waiting outside actually. Shall I go get her?'

'You left her outside! That poor girl,' Suzanne said, getting to her feet.

Giving no thought to the handbag she'd slung over her chair, barely waiting for Luke to extricate himself from the table and accompany her, Suzanne made her way out into the car park, where she stood and searched out Luke's ute. Leaning against the passenger door, dressed in a pretty floral frock and huge platform Doc Martens, was Ivy.

Luke thought back to the day he'd met his daughter for the first time, remembering the way he'd spent so long agonising over whether or not to stand up and embrace her that she'd sat down before he'd had the chance. Now, he watched his mother give him a masterclass in the way it ought to have been done, walking towards Ivy with her arms already outstretched, with an attitude of such profound welcome that Ivy would have been justified in believing that there was already a bed made up for her at Austinmer Street, and a mug with her name on it already waiting in the kitchen cupboard.

'Oh my goodness, Luke,' Suzanne said, as he approached them. 'Will you look at her? Will you look at how beautiful she is? Can you believe she's ours?'

Had Ivy harboured any intention of being stand-offish, Suzanne's enthusiasm and affection would have broken them down; Luke was moved to see that Ivy's smile was as stupidly broad as her grandmother's.

'You wait, Mum,' Luke said, proudly. 'How beautiful she is, that's only the beginning.'

It was a lunch they would all remember; not because of the food, although it was extremely good, and not only because it was then that Suzanne and Brian, at the same time, fell in love with their granddaughter. After they had each asked Ivy what felt like several thousand questions about herself and her life, after the main course was done and dessert was insisted upon (by Suzanne), and the coffee arrived, Luke saw a cloud pass over Ivy's face. He was not the only one who caught the sudden change of mood.

'What is it, love?' Suzanne asked.

'I feel like Marnie ought to be here. That's all.'

At the mention of her name, Luke felt like a trapdoor had swung open in the bottom of his heart, allowing all its contents to fall out in a rush. He felt empty. It was hard for him to remember exactly why it was he'd been so angry.

'Oh, shoot the moon,' Brian said. 'I completely forgot – I've got something for you, Luke. The events of the day' – he sent a wink in Ivy's direction – 'somewhat derailed me.'

Brian searched the inside pocket of his suit jacket and drew out a plain, white envelope. He tapped it on the table.

'Suze, how much do you know . . . about Marnie?'

Suzanne raised her eyebrows. 'Interesting woman. *Fas*cinating line of business.'

'I see,' Brian said. Turning to Luke, he said, 'She gave this to me when she quit. And she said to tell you she made her choice.'

'She quit? What? That can't be right. She wouldn't. Not after that offer of yours.'

'Well, she did. Just walked away,' Brian confirmed. 'For you.'

Perhaps Luke ought to have waited to open the envelope later, in private, but in that moment, confused by the news his father had relayed, he didn't pause to think. He tore open the envelope. No note, no words. Just a card.

'A tarot card?' Ivy asked.

Luke nodded. It was a card he recognised: one of the three Marnie had pulled when he had pretended to do a reading for her, the morning after the first night they had spent together.

'Which one?' Ivy asked.

He flipped it around: The Lovers.

'Well,' Suzanne said, one eyebrow meaningfully raised.

'I guess that's a pretty clear message,' Brian said.

'Actually, it's quite a complex card,' Ivy put in, causing her father and grandparents to look simultaneously in her direction, curious and expectant. 'It's a card about choice, really. If you pull it when you're facing moral dilemma, it's supposed to mean that you should take the higher path. The path of, well, love.'

'How do you know this stuff?' Luke asked, bewildered.

'Oh,' Ivy said, a picture of nonchalance. 'I read.'

Luke studied the card, and the dominoes of realisation cascaded inside his head. Marnie had turned down his father's offer of a loan. For him. Tomorrow was the auction of Fairchild & Sons. At tomorrow's auction, she could easily lose. Because of him.

He turned to his father. He wasn't angry, but he was confused. 'And you're, what, going to withdraw your offer of a loan? After everything she did?'

'She doesn't want it, Luke.' His father's eyes were intense behind the glass of his spectacles. 'As I understand it, she's under the impression that it comes at much too high a cost.'

Luke took a gulp of his coffee. Still more dominoes toppled. He had never asked his parents for anything. He had promised himself that he never would. It was a big old chunk of pride that he was about to swallow. And in front of Ivy, too.

'Mum, Dad,' he said. 'There's something I need to ask.'

Saturday

It was like fête day on that stretch of Rathbone Street. The pavement sprouted teardrop banners in the burgundy-and-white livery of Parkside Realty, and generous clusters of helium-filled balloons rose up on either side of the facade of Fairchild & Sons. The shop's front door had been thrown open, and people were making their way up and down the stairs, taking this rare opportunity to have a stickybeak inside, to see for themselves just how bad the fire damage had been, and to make their best guess at just how high the price would go today.

The cafe across the road was doing a roaring trade in takeaway coffees, and a busker – playing 'Somewhere Over the Rainbow', Israel Kamakawiwoʻole-style – had set up with his coin-strewn instrument case and his EFTPOS tap-square, right beside its front door.

When Marnie arrived, having been awake since the small hours, and with her nerves already mostly shredded, she went to greet the agent, Mark Wigston. At his side was his assistant Jodie Bainbridge, and the two were in conversation with the auctioneer, a lanky young man with a blotchily freckled face. He had the look, Marnie decided, of a farm boy. Despite his slightly shiny suit, it was only too easy to imagine him in a pair of shorts and a flannel shirt with the arms cut off, mucking out at the shearing sheds.

'Dave Morrisby, auctioneer,' Mark Wigston said by way of introduction. 'This is Marnie Fairchild, who, if I'm not mistaken, might be one of your bidders today?'

Marnie nodded.

'G'day,' Dave said. 'Family, are ya?'

His accent was as broadly Australian as they came, and he had the smile of a larrikin, but Marnie was not fooled; she could see the glint of intelligent ruthlessness in his eyes.

'That's right,' Marnie confirmed.

'Good luck, eh?'

Coming down the front steps now, in jeans and a black blouse as silky as her hair, was Carly McCulloch, followed by an entourage of her supporters, as well as a cameraman, his equipment bearing the logo of a commercial television station. Marnie had the sinking feeling that today was a fait accompli, and that it was already inevitable that the joyful faces that cameraman would be capturing, later this morning, would be those of the wine heiress and her crew.

Standing quietly to one side of the gathering throng was a rather portly man with thinning salt-and-pepper hair that might have been red before it went grey. At the sight of him, Marnie felt slightly cold, as if a breeze had just brushed over her skin, though none had. It was her uncle, Lewis.

If she did not turn out to be today's winner, one of the many things that were going to sting was knowing that her uncle had watched it happen. That, despite knowing how much she wanted this place, how well equipped she was to make a success of it, how hard she'd been prepared to work for it, their blood connection had not – to Lewis – seemed a reason to cut her even the slightest break, nor even to negotiate with her directly.

Marnie felt in her dress pocket for Saski's sticky note. Although the figure written upon it was burned into her brain, she had brought the scrap of paper for a lucky talisman as much as a reminder of her limits. She did not take it out, though. In her nervous state, she felt as if she was surrounded by prying eyes, and the last thing she needed was for the wrong person to catch a glimpse of her magic figure, her very top dollar.

'Oh, thank heavens, there you are,' Marnie said, finding Mo, who'd come to keep her upright during the auction, no matter what happened, and who was dressed in an unusually cheerful T-shirt that said, 'Never Trust an Atom: They Make Everything Up'.

'Saski said to say, "Go get 'em, girl",' Mo told her.

'How is Mumma? And the gorgeous babe?'

'They're perfect.'

Marnie took Mo on a tour through the shop, pointing out to her many of the small details that she'd never have noticed herself, had it not been for the day she'd come here with Luke. Marnie watched Mo's face as she took it all in.

'I didn't realise,' she told Marnie, keeping her voice to a whisper. 'I thought you were just being romantic. But you're right. You're exactly the person to make this place amazing.'

'I am,' she said, wishing now that she could press pause on time, go away and puzzle out another way of coming up with more money.

'You all right, Bunny?'

'I'm not sure. I can't shake the feeling that I've just come here to get my heart broken into a thousand tiny pieces.' As if the damage to that heart wasn't bad enough already.

Marnie and Mo stood back from the door, waiting while another party of potential bidders, or perhaps just curious onlookers, made their way into the shop's front room. When Mo reached the top of the stairs, she turned to Marnie and said, 'Seems I'm not the only one here to hold your hand today, after all.'

Marnie stepped out beside her, and there in the centre of the crowd she saw Luke. He was quintessentially himself, in jeans and a white shirt, with his sleeves rolled to the elbows. Had Brian passed on her message to him? Was that why he was here?

'I thought it was all over with you two,' Mo said, her eyebrow arched.

'It was, last time I checked.'

'Does that look to you like a guy who thinks it's all over?'

Marnie had to admit that it did not. Clearly, Luke was looking for someone, searching the crowd, his expression slightly concerned until he glanced up to the door of the shop, and saw Marnie standing there. He seemed relieved, happy to see her, and even before Marnie trotted down the steps in his direction, she knew he'd received her message. From his open face, Marnie could tell right away that the walls had come down. She couldn't see even the slightest trace of where they'd been. Now, though, there was the question of the walls she'd begun to build within herself.

'What brings you here?' she asked.

He produced her tarot card, holding it up so she could see the words: The Lovers. She crossed her arms to prevent them from ending up around his neck.

'So, you got my message?'

'I did,' he said.

'Took your time replying to it.'

Luke winced. 'Turns out it's a long way down from a high horse like the one I was being an idiot on.'

'An idiot?'

'A judgemental idiot,' he specified.

'Yeah, you were that.'

'It was a big call. To knock Dad's offer back,' he told her. 'I know exactly how big.'

'And?'

'And I shouldn't have asked you to choose. That was cruel. I was harsh.'

'But you weren't wrong about all of it. You made me do some thinking that I needed to do.'

Luke nodded, but without the least hint of *I told you so*. He looked around at the crowd. 'Are you confident?'

'Not even a little bit,' she said.

'Have lunch with me, after?'

'Even if I'm a crying mess?'

'Especially if you're a crying mess,' he said.

Marnie's internal walls were fighting a losing battle to remain upstanding; her face was struggling at least as hard to remain impassive. She relented, smiling as she said, 'Okay then, I'll have lunch with you after.'

'And stay at my house tonight?'

'I don't know yet,' Marnie said.

'Well, what about tomorrow night as well, then?'

'How does that make sense?'

'What about all the nights? Always?'

He waved the tarot card at her, and she couldn't help it: the smile became a laugh. When he held out his arms to her, she let herself fall into them, felt them tighten low around her back in a way that threatened to melt her entirely.

'We're just about ready to get underway, folks,' cried Dave the auctioneer. Slapping against his palm the rolled-up property prospectus that he appeared to intend to use as a gavel, he called out, 'So, if you're going to throw your hat in the ring today, make sure you find yourself a spot where you can catch my eye.'

'Are you ready to do this thing?' Luke asked.

'There's nothing more I can do now.'

'What's your limit?' he whispered.

Quickly, she walked him to the edge of the crowd, and drew the sticky note out of her pocket, shielding it like an ace in a hand of cards. Although maybe it would turn out to be only a King. Or a Queen. Luke looked at it, winced.

'It's not going to be enough, is it?' she said, the panic rising in her all over again.

It was all right, she told herself. It was all right. She had faced her difficult decision; she had made her choice. She had chosen the man standing beside her, and if she lost today, she would cry her tears on that shoulder, right there.

Luke reached into his back pocket and pulled out his wallet. Inside it was a scrap of notepaper of the kind she recognised from his workshop desk, torn from a small, lined writing pad. He handed it to her. Written on it was a dollar sign, and a figure. A figure almost as great as the one on the sticky note. Marnie's stomach felt like it had just experienced the plummet of a rollercoaster.

'What's this?'

'That's how much you can add. To your price. If we buy the place together.'

'Are you serious?' Marnie thought the insane pressure of the happiness inside her head might burst her skull apart.

'Never more so.'

'What did you have to do?'

'I had to swallow some pride. An awful lot of it, to tell you the truth. And ask my mum and dad for help.'

'And you did that for me?'

'For us.'

From behind them, she heard the auctioneer's carnivalesque voice. 'Right, folks,' he bellowed. 'Let's get this show on the road, shall we?'

With Luke's help, Marnie pushed to the front of the crowd and took up a position where Dave the auctioneer had a clear view of her.

'So, who's going to start me off?' he challenged. Marnie's pulse skyrocketed as he suggested a price; a high price. Clearly, he had no intention of messing around. But then, neither did Marnie Fairchild.

With Luke Charlesworth right beside her, she confidently raised her hand.

Five months after the auction of Fairchild & Sons

Seven blocks made a lot of difference, as it turned out. Now, when Marnie woke with the dawn, it was to the sound of green lorikeets screeching in the stand of old Norfolk Pines that towered over the south end of Alexandria Park, and the clatter of chairs being distributed around the outdoor tables of the neighbourhood cafes. Now, when the morning sun seeped in to touch her eyelids, it was filtered through the glass of a gorgeous triple-arched window and softened by the glow of honey-coloured floorboards.

Today, with a sigh of happiness, Marnie remembered that it was Sunday; that there was no need to rush. Eyes closed, she breathed in the resiny smell of newly varnished timber and the mineral scent of plaster dust – evidence of the renovation's latest leaps forward. The circular staircase now had elegantly moulded railings, and the upstairs rooms, just in time for the approaching winter, had a proper ceiling and actual walls.

Downstairs, although the building was still far from finished, the front room was in good enough shape for Wish & Co to trade, and every time Marnie walked into that space, she felt a rush of satisfaction to see how perfect her wrapping table looked there on the old, polished floorboards, and how perfect her new paper racks – custom-made by Luke Charlesworth

Timber Design – looked against the plaster walls, which she'd painted – in homage to Fairchild & Sons – in a delicate shade of mint green. She felt proud to have brought home to Fairchild & Sons the old photograph of her grandfather at the shop's front door, and it always made her happy to invite a customer to take one of the mint chocolate truffles she kept in a glass bowl on the old celery-top pine counter.

Without fully waking, she wriggled closer to Luke. Instinctively, he shifted his arm so she could lay her head on his chest. There they stayed, while the sun crept a little higher in the sky, and the clock advanced a little further into that autumn morning.

It was past eight when Marnie, still dozing, felt the sandpapery touch of Luke's hand on her hip, his light but insistent tug on the hem of the pyjama top she habitually wore without bottoms. They had been together long enough, now, that there wasn't anything really to discuss. Only four buttons to undo, and two sleeves to slip out of, and Luke's boxers to be discarded, and then the whole length of her, and the whole length of him, was nothing but skin and in every place they touched, she felt the sweet, soft, raw tingle of being completely naked.

There wasn't anything they had to talk about or negotiate; their bodies knew what they were doing. Lips found lips and tongues found tongues, and all the softnesses and hardnesses adjusted themselves to the right degree and slid together, and Marnie loved the weight of him that was enough to take just a pleasurable amount of her breath away from her, although after a time, she rolled him over and sat astride him, settling to stillness for a moment so that she could look properly at the colour of his eyes and touch the curve of his lips and lay her palms on the contours of his chest.

'I love you,' he told her, and she entirely believed him, not only because he'd said so, but also because of the gentle grip he had on her waist with those beautiful hands of his.

'I love you too,' she told him and they started to move all over again, and she smiled at the wilful forgetting in which they had absolutely colluded, this morning, the pair of them, with every one of those foil packets left unopened in the bedside drawer, and there was something about that thought alone that lost her to the inside world of her own body, all full of taut muscle and soft tissue and complete readiness, until twin bombs of stupid-making pleasure went off inside her head and the epicentre of her stomach.

'Did we really just do that?' Marnie asked Luke in the quiet of the afterwards.

'Are you okay with that?'

It didn't make sense. Not now, when all she had was a half-finished shop and all he had was a half-equipped workshop, and together they had a debt the size of your average Egyptian pyramid. But then, Marnie figured, having children wasn't something that ever really made sense. It was just something that she knew would make her feel whole, and home.

'What time do we have to leave?'

'About eleven,' Luke said.

That gave them a couple of hours to sand the skirting boards in the front room. Maybe there would even be time to cut in another coat of paint around the architraves in the middle room as well, before they'd need to shower and dress and jump in the ute to go collect Ivy and head to Austinmer Street for Suzanne's birthday lunch.

There, in the formal dining room, in the presence of Eleanora Middleton-Holmes's *Summer Day at Drowsy Creek*, Suzanne would dish up exquisite food, and Brian would pour excellent wines. After lunch, Benji might induce Luke to play a game of Chinese Checkers with him while Leila dragged Marnie outside to bounce on the trampoline, leaving Arjun and Caroline to catch a quiet moment, just the two of them, in the kitchen while they stacked the dishwasher. Brian would take Ivy for a driving lesson, helping her to stick her brand-new L-plates to the back and front windows of his Mercedes. And this time, every one of Suzanne's gifts would be intended for her, and her alone.

'So, what did you get your mum for her birthday?' Marnie asked, her head on Luke's chest, where he couldn't see the mischief in her eyes. She felt his breath stall.

'Shit, I didn't . . . I thought you . . .'

Marnie laughed then, and Luke – understanding that the joke was on him – tickled her until she laughed even harder.

At Austinmer Street, Brian and Suzanne were also in bed, and they, too, had shared a morning of conjugal contentment. Five months had made almost as much difference to the Charlesworth marriage as seven blocks had made to Marnie Fairchild.

'Happy birthday, love,' Brian said. 'And, thank you.'

'What for?' Suzanne asked, twisting around in his arms to look up at his face.

'For forgiving me. For giving us this chance. I will never screw it up again.'

'I know, darling. I bought some special pliers, and a handful of those little green rings they use on the lambs' balls. Just in case.'

They laughed, although Suzanne did notice that Brian crossed his legs.

'What was it, incidentally?' he asked.

'What was what?'

'The thing that made the difference? The thing that made up your mind?'

'To forgive you? I suppose it was all of it. The day you dug the roses. Your letter. My beautiful Eleanora Middleton-Holmes. And I wasn't going to have Ivy come into half a family. We had to be whole.'

'That crazy girl,' Brian mused. 'Teaching her to drive is going to be the death of me.'

The stretch of sky Suzanne could see through the window was blue with the cartoon-animal clouds of a mild, autumn day. Brian, quite nude, got out of bed and went to the walk-in robe, returning with a gift.

It was not, Suzanne saw, one of Marnie's wrap jobs – just white tissue paper, with sticky-tape clearly visible at the joins and the kind of curly ribbon, royal blue, that you'd pick up at the newsagent. It was all Brian's very own handiwork.

'Go on,' he said.

Suzanne peeled away the paper. Inside was a photo album, its pages full of images that she both knew and did not know. Some were old enough to have been printed with rounded corners; others were Polaroids. They were the cast-offs, she realised, the imperfect cousins – whether slightly out of focus, or someone had their eyes shut – of the photos that had made it into their official albums.

'Where did you get these?' Suzanne asked, turning pages that showed her Caroline and Luke under a sprinkler in the backyard at her mother's house, a grinning Luke at the beach with his surfboard, Caroline at the school fair on that nasty little pony that had later bitten her and made her cry. Herself holding Caroline, blue icing on both their faces. That picture, the one Marnie had turned into a greeting card, of herself at her easel, poking out her tongue at the naked man in her bed. The same man who was still, despite everything, and after all these years, naked in her bed.

'They're the ones that have ended up in my desk drawer. I've amassed quite a collection.'

After the old photos came the newer ones: Brian nursing newborn Leila, Benji trying glasses on at his parents' optometry practice, the selfie of Ivy and Suzanne taken at Clockwork on the day they'd first met, a picture of Marnie and Luke on the front steps of the new Wish & Co, which was also the old Fairchild & Sons, the pair of them posing together in just the place Marnie's grandfather had stood in the famous old photo.

'Won't those two have the most beautiful children?' Suzanne mused aloud.

'Now, now, Nanna,' Brian said. 'No nagging, no hints. They've got plenty of time yet.'

'Oh, I don't think it'll be long, love. I've seen the way Marnie looks at Leila.'

Brian reached over and turned the page. The next one was blank. And, he showed her, so was the next, and the next, and the next. He was happy with himself, she realised, proud of his gift, which held both memories of the past and possibilities for the future.

'There's still so much more to come, my lovely wife,' he told her.

And that was true.

— THAT BIT AFTER THE CREDITS HAVE ROLLED —

A little less than a month after the implosion of the Charlesworth marriage, and a little more than a month before Suzanne forgave Brian and took him back, a Saturday morning came slowly into being in soft shades of pinkish blue. As the sun rose over the river and filtered through the kitchen window of Leona Quick's twelfth-floor apartment, it touched its light on the garish colour scheme of a Smeg stand mixer.

Since her birthday, she had seen Brian only once. He'd invited her for lunch at a restaurant in a small Japanese restaurant in a gentrifying suburb that must have seemed to him a safe distance from Alexandria Park. In the course of their conversation, which was only a little stilted, he'd been both appropriately sorry for playing with her emotions, and gratifyingly complimentary about how much he'd loved her, how much she'd meant to him, back in their youth. They had agreed, over sashimi and sake, that it had been a mistake for them to revisit the past. But they had not, at any point, discussed the fate of the misdelivered gift.

She addressed the Smeg. 'So, what am I supposed to do with you? Hm?'

But the stand mixer only sat there mutely, looking like a piece of carnival equipment fallen silent after the fair. The appliance bothered Leona in some vague and unspecified way that had nothing to do with Brian, or his wife. Rather, it was to do with its brightness, its cheerfulness, its promise.

The previous night, triggered by its incongruous presence in her kitchen, she had found herself standing on a stepladder in her bedroom, pulling down from the top of her cupboard a dust-laden hat box. She had spilled its contents onto the bed. There were family birth and marriage certificates, and the ribbon-wrapped packets of letters exchanged by her parents in their youth – none of which she had the least idea what to do with. There was nobody to pass them on to, and yet it didn't seem right to throw them away or destroy them.

The same could be said of the letters she'd kept from her earliest days with James. Most of these dated from their engagement, when she had gone overseas without him as some sort of stupid emotional challenge to test out the truth and depth of her feelings for him. It had worked, she supposed. She'd missed him terribly, realised she loved him passionately. But in hindsight all she'd done was deny them six months of marriage. After James died, she'd have given anything to be able to gouge a hole in the fabric of time and, through it, drag back that stretch of lost, precious days.

Amid the letters and the certificates was the thing she was looking for. A scrapbook, covered in shiny red paper, given to her by her mother when Leona had first left home. It was filled with recipes, some for Leona's favourite dishes, and others that her mother had considered indispensable in the repertoire of an elegant homemaker. At the time, Leona had thanked her mother with exaggerated politeness, even though she'd been thinking, *Just who the hell do you think I am?*

But now, leafing through the book while sitting on the edge of her bed, having reached the age her mother was at the time of her death – sixty-five – Leona hungered for the comfort of her mother's picnic pie, and for the flavour of proper tomato soup, made with real tomatoes from the garden, for the afternoon tea-time treat of her mother's passionfruit sponge cake. But most of all, she longed for the woman who had written out, in blue biro, every ingredient, every method.

Leona had brought the scrapbook out into the kitchen without any sense of clear intent and left it lying next to the stand mixer. She was both pleased and discomfited by the perfect match between the book's red covering and the base colour of the machine.

Now she stood, considering. What ought she do with the mixer? Have it delivered to Brian's wife? In a sense it was Suzanne's, after all. But no. There was no point fomenting drama. Naturally, she had picked up a few threads of gossip. A couple of people had been bold enough to ask direct questions, but of course, she had deflected, diminished, denied. If the situation were a sleeping dog, it was twitching in pursuit of a dream-rabbit. And it was better left to lie. Every now and then she missed Brian – their coffee dates, their weekends away. Especially, she missed trouncing him at online Scrabble, but his absence from her life had left room for other things to develop. She'd never imagined herself on the arm of a man who wore elbow patches, but it was coming to pass that Cameron's wit and insight easily compensated for his taste in jumpers and jackets.

She supposed she could take the mixer to a charity shop. If the right person found it, it would make a great story for them – the time they found a brand-new Smeg stand mixer just sitting there on the shelf at Vinnies. Probably that was what she should do. That would be the right thing under the circumstances. But Leona was surprised to discover that it was not what she wanted.

And so, Leona set off shopping. Unlike many people's pantries, Leona's did not habitually contain things like caster sugar, cornflour and cream of tartar. Neither did her equipment drawer house anything that resembled a nine-inch sandwich tin, let alone a matching pair of the same. When she returned with all the necessaries, she put Delius on the stereo – somehow, he seemed right for a sponge cake – and began.

She had to Google a few things, such as what actual measurement corresponded to her mother's notion of a 'dessertspoon', and how exactly one made passionfruit icing. At last, it was done: baked, cooled, iced and transferred to a pretty plate. The good thing about her mother's scrapbook was that it had no pictures to demand compliance or comparison. But to Leona's unexpected pride, the cake she had produced didn't look so very different from the ones she could remember being set out on her mother's table, covered with its fussy Battenburg lace cloth.

Carrying the cake on its pretty plate, and her mother's china-handled knife, she rode the elevator down to the tenth floor and rang Cameron's doorbell.

'I made a cake,' Leona announced, aware that she was probably not adequately concealing how proud she felt of this achievement.

'You did,' Cameron confirmed, and inspected the icing. 'Passionfruit, no less.'

'My mother's recipe. I thought we could . . . have a piece together.'

'Then I shall make the tea.'

Leona followed Cameron through to the kitchen, where soft, classical music was playing.

'I take it this was made with that rather surprising gift?'

'Correct.'

Cameron considered, a wry smile on his face. 'The case of the mixed-up mixer. I'm sure there's a marvellous pun in there somewhere. Doubtless I'll think of it later.'

He poured the tea and produced two small plates, as well as two forks that Leona's mother would have considered vastly too large to use as cake-eating implements. Then Leona cut the cake and slid two modest-sized pieces onto the plates.

'*Bon appetit,*' Leona said.

'*Mahlzeit!*' Cameron agreed.

Leona carved into her slice of cake and lifted a forkful to her mouth. Eyes closed, she let her tastebuds take up the tang of the passionfruit icing. The cake itself, light and airy, gently collapsed on her tongue. It tasted – sadly, sweetly, wistfully, but conclusively – of once upon a time.

Suzanne and Brian's Anniversary Luncheon Menu

Starters

Toffee Truss Tomatoes on Basil Leaf (Valli Little)

Served with Duperrey Brut Rosé

&

Oysters

Served with a chilled, fruit-forward Junmai Ginjo sake

Main

Stuffed Baked Quail

Stuffing of chicken mince, herbs, almond meal, pine nuts and butter accompanied by pomegranate jus or Sparkling Shiraz Jelly (Maggie Beer), charred young broad beans, honey-roasted carrots and kipfler potatoes

Served with: Frogmore Creek Pinot Noir for the red drinkers, or Jean-Marc Brocard Chablis Grand Cru Valmur for those who prefer white

Dessert

Classic French Croquembouche (The Spruce Eats)

Served with: De Bortoli Noble One

To keep drinking through the afternoon

Fat Bastard Chardonnay

And one last thing

Homemade panforte (Kate Spina)

Leona's Passionfruit Sponge
(with thanks to Ruth Brown, 1920–2019)

Ingredients
⅔ cup caster sugar
4 eggs
4 dessertspoons cornflour
2 tablespoons custard powder
1 teaspoon cream of tartar
½ teaspoon bicarbonate of soda

Method
Beat egg whites until stiff. Add sugar slowly, then egg yolks gradually. Add sifted dry ingredients. Bake in two 9" sandwich tins at 375° Fahrenheit (190° Celsius) for 30–40 minutes. Top with passionfruit icing.

Acknowledgements

The original Fairchild & Sons is based on a real building, which can be found at 121 Harrington Street in Hobart, Tasmania.

Marnie's understanding of tarot cards is loosely based on that of Brigit Esselmont of Biddy Tarot (www.biddytarot.com).

My love and thanks go to:

- 🎁 Everyone who told me their gift stories – the good, bad and ugly.
- 🎁 Lou-Lou Angel, kitchen goddess and all-round nurturer, who knew exactly what Suzanne would serve for her anniversary luncheon.
- 🎁 Freda Fairbairn, favourite reader and co-processor of all matters remarkable and/or perplexing.
- 🎁 Lee Matthews, who probably didn't imagine he would end up advising on the financial affairs of imaginary people.

- 🎁 Walter Beery, whose loving pedantry ticks away in the background like a metronome.
- 🎁 The crew on the home front – Jack McWaters, Alaska Fox, Dash Hawkins, Tiki Brown, the canines, the felines – whose adventures are many things, but never boring.
- 🎁 The crew on the publishing front – Gaby Naher, Dan Lazar, Beverley Cousins, Hilary Teeman – whose professionalism and love for story make everything better than it might otherwise be.
- 🎁 And, most especially, Marie Bonnily, queen of table settings, patron saint of napkins that match the candles, world-class ironer of complicated dresses and Battenburg lace tablecloths, gift-wrapper extraordinaire and the undisputed queen of giving. Love you, Mum.

Book Club Questions

1. If you discovered that your partner had outsourced the selection and purchase of gifts to a gift-buyer like Marnie Fairchild, how would you feel? Would you feel that the gifts were less special because they were chosen by someone other than your partner?
2. Perhaps you know the work of Gary Chapman, who put forward the idea – in his book *The Five Love Languages* – that different people have distinct ways they most like to express and receive love: words of affirmation, quality time, physical touch, acts of service and . . . gifts. What do you think are the 'love languages' of the main characters in *With Love from Wish & Co*? Which characters are the most, and least, likely to show their love in the language of gifts?
3. What role does gift-giving play in your family? Does your family go all-out with gifts, or not so much? Is there pressure around gift-giving in your family?
4. What's the best gift you've ever been given? What made it good? What's the worst gift you've ever received? What made it less than great?
5. A gift we see Marnie give, in *With Love from Wish & Co*, is the baby quilt for her pregnant best friend, Saski. What makes it such a special gift?
6. The epigraph of *With Love from Wish & Co* is a quotation from Argentinian poet Antonio Porchia: 'I know what I have given you. I do not know what you have received.' How do

you think it relates to the stories of Marnie and Luke, and Suzanne and Brian?

7. Gift giving and receiving is often part of the building of a new relationship. How do gifts show up in the developing father–daughter relationship between Luke and Ivy?

8. In *With Love from Wish & Co*, Brian uses gifts to apologise, and seek restoration of his relationship with Suzanne. What do you think about gifts as apologies? Are they a good idea, or does that depend?

9. Is Marnie's bespoke gift-buying service an ethical business? Should she agree to buy gifts for the mistresses of men, like Brian, who cheat?

10. What do you think Brian has learned about gift-giving, and about relationships, by the closing pages of the novel?

11. In an article about the sociology of gift-giving, Jean-Claude Kaufmann writes that the 'beautiful gift' has three key features: it is both beautiful and sophisticated and 'its revelation aims to stun and surprise'; it reflects the 'secret desires' of the receiver; and it creates a magical moment that draws one away from the daily grind. Do any of the gifts in *With Love from Wish & Co* meet these criteria?

'The funny, clever, big-hearted love story of the year'
Heather Rose

Star-crossed

Why rely on fate, when you can rewrite the stars?

MINNIE DARKE

STAR-CROSSED

A young journalist tampers with her magazine's horoscopes to win her friend's heart – and sets in motion an unpredictable and often hilarious ripple effect . . .

When Justine Carmichael (Sagittarius, aspiring journalist and sceptic) bumps into her old friend Nick Jordan (Aquarius, struggling actor and true believer) it could be by chance. Or perhaps it's written in the stars.

Justine works at the *Alexandria Park Star* – and Nick, she now learns, relies on the magazine's astrology column to guide him in life.

Looking for a way to get Nick's attention, Justine has the idea of making a few small alterations to 'Aquarius' before it goes to print.

It's only a horoscope, after all. What harm could changing it do?

Charting the many unforeseen ripple effects of Justine's astrological meddling – both for herself and for others – *Star-crossed* is the funny, super-smart, feel-good novel of the year!

'The funny, clever, big-hearted love story of the year. Brilliant!' Heather Rose, bestselling author of *The Museum of Modern Love*

'This delightful debut will leave you with a warm glow . . . In every way a delight, *Star-crossed* was so much fun this reviewer fell head over heels for it. If you loved David Nicholls' *One Day*, go out and buy this now.' *Herald Sun*

AVAILABLE NOW

The Lost Love Song

MINNIE DARKE

Bestselling author of Star Crossed

'If you are looking for a charming read, then Darke has written a beauty . . . Expect laughter and tears.' Herald Sun

THE LOST LOVE SONG

For every love lost there is another to be found . . .

In Australia, Arie Johnson waits impatiently for classical pianist Diana Clare to return from a world tour, hopeful that after seven years together she'll *finally* agree to marry him.

On her travels, Diana composes a song for Arie. It's the perfect way to express her love, knowing they'll spend their lives together . . . *Won't they?*

Then late one night, her love song is overheard, and begins its own journey across the world.

In Scotland, Evie Greenlees is drifting. It's been years since she left Australia with a backpack, a one-way ticket and a dream of becoming a poet. Now she spends her days making coffee and her nights serving beer. And she's not even sure whether the guy she lives with is really her boyfriend or just a flatmate.

One day she hears an exquisite love song. One that will connect her to a man with a broken heart . . .

'Lively and charming.' *Sydney Morning Herald*
Pick of the Week

'If you are looking for a charming read, then Darke has written a beauty . . . Expect laughter and tears in equal measure.' *Herald Sun*

AVAILABLE NOW

Discover a new favourite

Visit **penguin.com.au/readmore**